What reviewers are saying about
THE DOWRY BRIDE

"Bantwal tells an engaging story about Indian culture. . . . The mother-in-law character is particularly well-drawn."
—*Romantic Times*

"*The Dowry Bride* is Shobhan Bantwal's first novel, and it's an incredible beginning. . . . Both the brighter and darker sides of India leap off the pages of this excellent, beautifully composed story. For a very exciting, enlightening, and entertaining way to start your autumn reading, do not miss *The Dowry Bride*. It's a real page turner!" —*RomanceReviewsToday.com*

"*The Dowry Bride* is an insightful look at India's culture. . . . The story line is incredible . . . a powerful discerning look at relationships . . . a fabulous look at the importance of a dowry in India in spite of laws protecting the rights (and apparently the life) of a bride." —Harriet Klausner (Amazon's #1 Reviewer)

"It's a beautifully written book. . . . *The Dowry Bride* will make you cry, laugh, frown and most of all think. . . . Bantwal takes a brave look at an old topic and delivers a piece of work that may just make an impact. Wonderful, Vivid, and Worth Reading."
—*BookIdeas.com*

"*The Dowry Bride* is an amazing story of modern India . . . kept me up late, hoping for the best for Megha and the friend who hides her. . . . I nominate *The Dowry Bride* as a Book Sense Pick."
—The Kaleidoscope—Our Focus is You Bookstore

"*The Dowry Bride* is an eye opener to the challenges many Indian women face in a culture few foreigners comprehend."
—*ArmchairInterviews.com*

"Shobhan Bantwal has written a passionate, suspense-filled story of one woman and her fight to survive another's evil greed and jealousy. *The Dowry Bride* is a fascinating look into an exotic culture and a story that I recommended to everyone."
—*RomanceJunkies.com*

"This is one story that is a great read for any time of the year and one that should be read and shared. I hope Ms. Bantwal's work brings hope to women everywhere."
—*CoffeeTimeRomance.com*

Also by Shobhan Bantwal

THE DOWRY BRIDE

Published by Kensington Publishing Corporation

The Forbidden Daughter

SHOBHAN BANTWAL

KENSINGTON BOOKS
http://www.kensingtonbooks.com

KENSINGTON BOOKS are published by

Kensington Publishing Corp.
850 Third Avenue
New York, NY 10022

ISBN-13: 978-0-7582-2030-1
ISBN-10: 0-7582-2030-8

First Kensington Trade Paperback Printing: September 2008
10 9 8 7 6 5 4 3 2

Printed in the United States of America

This one is dedicated to my little granddaughter,
Karina Uma—my fountain of joy and inspiration.

Acknowledgments

As always, I offer my initial prayer of thanks to Lord Ganesh, the remover of obstacles.

My heartfelt appreciation goes to my generous, warm and supportive editor, Audrey LaFehr, who has placed her faith in me once more. You are the best! The friendly and efficient editorial, production, public relations, and marketing folks at Kensington Publishing richly deserve my gratitude and praise for a job well done. I look forward to working with you on my future projects.

To my agents, Stephanie Lehmann and Elaine Koster, a huge thank-you for your invaluable help and guidance.

I am greatly indebted to my critique partners, Teri Bozowski and Carol Aloisi. They are gentle in their criticism but right on target. They cheer me on at every step.

The Writers' Exchange at Barnes & Noble in Princeton, New Jersey, and the Writers' Group at the Plainsboro Public Library deserve my thanks for their insightful comments and suggestions. I offer a grateful hug to my many other friends, who are my cheerleading group.

To my daughter, Maya, and son-in-law, Sameet, I owe more than I can ever repay. I also want to thank my talented sister and fellow writer, Nirmala, an infinite source of support and encouragement. She inspired me to step into the exciting world of creative writing.

And last but not least, to the love of my life, my partner, best friend, and husband, Prakash: I am deeply grateful to have you beside me, loving me unconditionally, and taking care of the business end, so I can write to my heart's content. We're in this together, my dearest. I couldn't have done it without you.

Prologue

Oh, Lord, I beg of you.
I fall at your feet time and again.
In my next incarnation, don't give me a daughter;
Give me hell instead . . .

—Folk song from the State of Uttar Pradesh, India

July 2006

"Your child will come at the harvest full moon," the old
man said.

Jolted out of her dark, melancholic thoughts, Isha Tilak looked
up and stared in astonishment at the man who had uttered the
startling words. He was obviously addressing her, because there
was no one else in the immediate vicinity.

His strange remark captured her attention, thrusting aside
her private musings.

"It is called *Kojagari Purnima*. It is the night when Lakshmi,
the goddess of wealth and abundance, descends from her heav-
enly abode to bless her devotees," he added, stroking his luxuriant salt-and-pepper beard that more than compensated for the
total absence of hair on his large, misshapen head.

He was supposedly a *sadhu*—a sage or holy man. He was certainly dressed for the part in his faded saffron robe—typical
garb for Hindu holy men. The garment was darned in various
places, a haphazard job that showed exactly where the holes

had been. His teeth had the yellow-brown hue that told the world they hadn't felt the bristles of a toothbrush in a long while. Perhaps never. His oral hygiene probably didn't extend beyond the chewing of a *neem* stick, a twig from the bitter *neem* tree used by poor folks to clean their teeth.

His wide lips looked dry and chapped, like the parched, sun-baked dunes of the northwestern deserts of India. Then she noticed his dark, deep-set eyes. There was an intriguing quality about them, a mystical luminescence that compelled a person to meet them and hold their gaze.

He had never uttered a word to her before, never acknowledged her presence. She came to this particular temple often, the small shrine built for the elephant-headed god, Ganesh. He was a highly revered god in the Hindu religion, one whose blessings were sought before embarking on any venture or ceremony, large or small. No *pooja*—ritualistic worship—could begin without first invoking the Great Ganesh, because He was the remover of obstacles.

And Isha had obstacles, serious ones—more than she could count on her slender fingers.

No one seemed to know anything about the *sadhu*. He was an enigma. All he did was sit cross-legged on a threadbare blanket under the ancient, atrophying mango tree that produced no fruit. His eyes were shut in silent meditation. Or perhaps he dozed from the boredom of doing nothing. His dented steel bowl contained a handful of coins and some fruit that people gave in charity, probably his only source of income and food.

He'd been sitting in the same spot for years—right outside the walled temple compound. On rainy days, like today, he had an oversized umbrella mounted on a pole to protect him. Isha couldn't even remember when he'd appeared on the scene. It seemed like he'd been there forever. He ordinarily spoke to no one, and no one disturbed him. The hundreds of devotees who came to pray at the temple each week accepted him as a permanent fixture, like the centuries-old shrine itself and the hill atop which it sat.

This was Palgaum, a small rural town in southwestern India, where *sadhus* were respected, and nobody questioned their presence, especially in the environs of a house of worship. And even the most impoverished worshippers thought nothing of giving a coin to a holy man.

She had never heard his voice before. It was muffled and raspy, an alien sound emerging from a voice box that was hardly ever used.

Perhaps because she continued to wear a baffled look, he smiled. The simple motion transformed and softened his austere face, creating deeper furrows in his gaunt cheeks. "Yours will be a female child who will bring light and abundance to the people around her."

She shook herself out of her stunned silence. It took her a moment to comprehend his words. Then natural curiosity took over, prompting her to goad him, test him. "How do you know my child will be a girl?"

He ignored her question. Instead he said, "Your daughter comes as a gift from Lakshmi, so she will enjoy prosperity and many comforts in her life, and, being generous, she will share them with others."

"But my in-laws think she's a curse," Isha informed him, the bitterness in her voice hard to conceal and the despondency in her tear-swollen eyes a testimony to her despair. "In fact, they have forbidden me to have this child."

"I know," he said, with a thoughtful nod. "I am also aware that there is something which some evil doctors use to eliminate female children before they are born. It is one of the many scourges of *kaliyug*—modern society."

She was amazed at what this man knew, and how much he knew. But how could he? Did he read about such topics or was it intuitive knowledge? "They call it selective abortion," she told him. "That's the medical procedure my in-laws wanted me to have."

The man barked out a laugh—a harsh, braying sound. Isha wondered if he could be a lunatic and whether it was safe for her to be conversing with him.

"What do they know?" he snapped. "They are ignorant people, steeped in greed and worldly desires. But it is not their fault. They have yet to go through the many karmic cycles of life and death before they evolve into more rational beings."

Perplexed even further, she frowned at him. "You know my in-laws?"

He shook his head. "I can see them in my mind, and your recently dead husband, too."

Isha drew in a shocked breath. He even knew she'd lost her husband! How did he know so much about her? Was he really a *sadhu* or a spy of some kind? But why would he spy on her—a nobody, a recent widow with her life in shambles? Who was this peculiar man? And why was he talking to her all of a sudden when he'd never bothered before? He was beginning to make her uneasy.

She threw a fleeting glance around to make sure there were other people nearby and sighed with relief when she noticed several men and women inside the temple within hearing distance.

Perhaps reading her mind, he shook his head. "I do not mean harm. I am a prophet. I can see with my inner eye." He pointed to his forehead, smeared with *vibhuti* or holy ashes. "I have watched you for a long time. You are a woman overcome by grief and you come here to seek solace for yourself and your unborn child, do you not?"

Despite the folds of her bulky sari, Isha's large and distended belly told its own tale. She always sat in a sheltered but remote area of the courtyard, close to the mango tree, shedding silent tears. So he must have observed her. No surprise there. But the rest of what he was saying was astounding. Those were intimate details of her private life very few people knew about.

"Your first child is blessed by Saraswati, the goddess of knowledge and intelligence. She is a clever girl with a talent for healing."

"You mean she'll grow up to be a doctor?" Isha was reeling from the fact that he even knew she had another daughter.

"She will heal what is broken."

"What does that mean?"

Again he ignored her question. "Your late parents' good deeds and your own have earned you sufficient *punya*." Blessings.

"Punya!" She dried her moist eyes with a handkerchief and suppressed the wry laughter rising in her throat. "Losing a husband at such a young age and having to raise two children that nobody but me wants, are considered blessings? If you ask me they're a *shaap*." A curse.

He raised his gnarled hands, with their blackened and overgrown fingernails curving inward, in a dismissive gesture. "Life in itself is a blessing. Your mother, father, and husband were your past blessings; your forbidden daughters are blessings for your present and future."

"Then why am I suffering so?"

"Ah, everything in life has to be earned. And that takes time and patience. In time your children will bring you the comfort and peace you desire and pray for."

"But children are small, helpless. How much can they do?"

He pointed to the stone idol of Lord Ganesh sitting high on his throne within the inner sanctum of the temple, his trunk imperiously curved toward his left. "He works in mysterious ways. Have faith in Him. What He bids no mortal can forbid." He chortled, sounding thoroughly amused. "Not even your inlaws."

"If you know so much, then tell me more about my daughters' futures. Will they have happy lives?" she asked, now entirely mesmerized by the old man. In spite of her misgivings, she was drawn to his words. She wanted him to continue talking.

There were so many things she needed to ask him. Had her beloved husband been intentionally killed in cold blood? If so, why? And by whom? Would it be wise for her to take her destiny in her own hands, take Priya, and walk away from her in-laws' home?

The thought of leaving had crossed her mind a few times in recent days. Every day with her in-laws was more stifling than the previous one. But could she afford to leave? Would she be hurting her precious daughter by resorting to such rash measures and depriving her and the new baby of their rightful legacy?

She desperately wanted some answers. But instead of responding to her request, the old man slipped back into his meditation mode, cutting her off as abruptly as he'd engaged her in conversation. It was as if she'd imagined the whole dialogue with him. When she respectfully pleaded, "Sir, please . . . please tell me more. I need to know," there was no indication that he'd even heard her. He was back in his own silent world.

Had she been hallucinating? Along with everything else, was she losing her mind, too?

She struggled to her feet, joined her hands in one last genuflection to Ganesh and put on her *chappals*—her slip-on footwear. It was just beginning to get dark outside, and flocks of birds were returning to their sodden homes, their wings resembling raised eyebrows.

The first of Palgaum's notorious mosquitoes were buzzing around her, reminding her it was time to leave. There was a noticeable chill in the air, too. She wrapped the loose end of her sari, the *pallu*, around her shoulders and unfurled her umbrella.

Before long the thick, gray fog that swept in from the river each night would begin winding its way toward the temple to join the rain, making it hard to see beyond two meters. In her condition she couldn't afford to get lost in that damp cloud of nothingness.

Getting back on the road, she began the long walk home—a place she'd started to detest. It didn't feel like home anymore—not since her husband's death. It was a huge house with an equally large and boastful garden and an impressive retinue of servants—a showcase to suit her in-laws' inflated egos. It was an ostentatious shell without a soul.

All the way there she mulled over the *sadhu*'s words. He couldn't be serious, now, could he? All that wild talk didn't make any sense . . . and yet, on some level, it made plenty of sense. In her present state of mind, she couldn't decide which.

Oh well, the monsoon season was in its concluding phase and

Kojagari Purnima was several months away. She'd know then if there was any truth to the *sadhu*'s bizarre predictions. Like he'd said, Ganesh worked in mysterious ways. He certainly took His own time about it too, not to mention the fact that He had an odd sense of humor.

She had come to learn that the hard way.

Chapter 1

April 2006

Today was the day! Today Isha would most likely have an answer to that single question she'd been obsessing about for weeks—ever since she'd found out she was pregnant: Was it a boy, or . . . God forbid . . . a girl?

Nonetheless, she wasn't sure if she *wanted* to know. Even if she did, would her doctor be willing to reveal the fact, since it was illegal to discuss the sex of an unborn child with its parents? For Isha it was a case of mixed emotions and desires. There was a popular Americanism that described her feelings perfectly—*damned if you do and damned if you don't.*

Nervous anticipation made her stumble a little as she stepped out of the car to walk toward her obstetrician's comfortable and well-appointed medical office.

Nikhil, her husband, quickly grabbed her arm to steady her. "Are you all right, Ish?" he asked with a slight frown. He was the only person in the world who called her Ish.

She nodded. "Just a bit tense, that's all," she replied and lifted the hem of her cream chiffon sari a bit, so she wouldn't trip over the long, trailing pleats while climbing the single concrete step leading up to the front door.

"You're not dizzy or anything?" Nikhil's deepening frown and gently solicitous voice told her he was worried—more so than usual.

"No. I'm feeling fine," she assured him. No point in scaring him by saying she had huge butterflies, the size of bats, flitting around in her tummy. She was jittery enough for both of them.

She stole a brief sidelong glance at Nikhil. Dressed in elegant gray slacks and a blue designer shirt, he was the picture of polished good looks combined with affluence. But he wasn't his usual confident self today. He seemed edgy—almost as much as she.

He kept a protective hand curled around her arm. "Good. Let's keep it that way."

The black and white sign outside the single-story brick building was both prominent and impressive. KARNIK MATERNITY CLINIC— a proud testimonial to the doctor's professional success. Beneath it were his name and credentials: *Dr. V. V. Karnik—Obstetrics & Gynecology Specialist.*

Although male ob-gyns were still rare in small towns, this particular doctor had an outstanding reputation; consequently, he had acquired a large and exclusive clientele.

Isha was at the clinic to get an ultrasound test done—one of the most brilliant inventions in the medical field since the discovery of antibiotics. It could reveal whether the baby was healthy or not, and the most interesting thing was that one could see the fetus as a three-dimensional image on a computer screen. How fantastic was that!

Although she wasn't sure if she wanted to find out the sex, she still couldn't wait to see her unborn child. It would be thrilling to have a chance to be introduced to the tiny person growing inside her.

"Nervous?" asked Nikhil, after they'd announced themselves to the receptionist and settled down on the blue-and-gray upholstered sofa in the waiting room.

"Very." She searched his face. "Are you?"

He smiled at her, his hazel eyes warming up. "A little, I guess."

"A *little?*" she asked with a wry chuckle. She knew her husband well. He often covered up his negative feelings with that attractive smile. He rarely fooled her, though. And he hadn't slept well the previous night. "I think *you* are more anxious than I am."

He took her hand and rubbed his thumb over the wrist, the laughter fading from his eyes. "Everything's going to be okay. You'll see."

She knew he was trying to reassure himself while doing the same for her. They were both pulsing with tension. There was a lot at stake here.

Twenty minutes later, it bubbled up like a fountain, warm and effervescent—the emotion that could be experienced only by a mother-to-be. Her baby! With damp palms and a racing heart, Isha observed the fuzzy movements on the monitor. The word *amazing* hardly described it. It was like watching a fantasy show on television.

That funny little glob was the living, moving baby in her womb. But even at this early stage of pregnancy, the little arms and legs were identifiable. With its oversized bald head and a protruding forehead it resembled some alien creature in a science fiction movie.

But the elation quickly dampened when other thoughts began to crowd her brain. Oh no! What if . . . ? She said a quick, silent prayer. *God, please let it be a boy. Please! If I don't have a son this time, I'm finished.*

Her in-laws had made such a ruckus about her giving birth to a girl the first time. Her mother-in-law, supposedly an enlightened woman, with a college degree and an interest in music, world affairs and literature, had wrinkled her brow when she had first learned Isha had given birth to a girl. *"Arré Deva, moolgee!"* Oh God, a girl!

Dr. Karnik allowed both Nikhil and Isha to gaze at the image on the screen for several more seconds. Isha looked for the small but significant part of the baby's anatomy that would establish its gender. So far there was no indication of it on the screen. Was it something that didn't appear until the fetus grew a little bigger? She studied the image more closely. What she desperately hoped to see wasn't there.

The doctor looked at her and Nikhil by turns. "So, do you want to know the child's sex?"

Isha closed her eyes for an instant. Did she really want to know?

But then she heard Nikhil say, "Um . . . yes." He sounded hesitant.

"Are you sure?" The doctor gave him a pointed look.

Nikhil glanced at Isha and she nodded, albeit reluctantly. Was the doctor serious, or was this his idea of injecting a little levity into a grave situation? But he wasn't smiling. And it was common knowledge that some doctors did manage to reveal the sex of the fetus discreetly, despite what the laws dictated, perhaps to accommodate the parents' natural curiosity.

They exchanged brief glances. It was an unspoken agreement that the three of them would keep this confidential.

Deep down, she already knew the answer. The tiny image on the screen was plain enough.

"It's a girl."

Silence fell over the examination room as Isha and Nikhil tried to digest the doctor's casual announcement. Nikhil stood motionless, his gaze fixed on some unknown spot on the wall.

Another girl! That was all that went through Isha's mind over and over again, although she'd known it in her gut. Official confirmation just made it harder.

Assuming their silence indicated disappointment, Dr. Karnik said, "It is not the end of the world, you know."

Isha rolled her eyes. "Maybe not to you, doctor. My in-laws will be devastated."

Dr. Karnik shrugged. "So . . . we can fix that."

"Excuse me!" Isha stared at the doctor. Had he really meant to say what she thought he'd meant? Or had she misunderstood him? She looked toward her husband, wondering if he had read the same message. All she saw was a puzzled look on Nikhil's face. "What does that mean, doctor?"

"We can easily perform a clinical abortion," the doctor replied. "You're only in the beginning of your second trimester, and it is a fairly simple procedure."

"Fairly simple!" Isha felt like she'd been punched in the stomach.

"Simple, safe, and fast, with today's techniques," assured the doctor.

"No!" Glancing at the screen again, she saw the fetus move. The baby! "That's not an option."

Dr. Karnik eyed her calmly. "It's up to you, of course." He had thinning gray hair and steel-rimmed glasses. His thin mustache was all gray. His shoulders were beginning to droop. Dressed in mousy brown pants and a long white lab coat, he looked like a harmless old grandfather. Isha wondered how a gentleman could say such hideous things with such nonchalance.

Nikhil spoke for the first time, his voice sounding uncharacteristically shaky. "She's right, doctor. As long as the child is healthy, we won't discuss anything like . . . abortion." Even the word seemed to be stuck in his throat. In fact, there was that familiar spark of anger in his eyes. He was clearly upset by the doctor's outrageous suggestion.

Isha sent her husband a grateful look. Thank goodness he was in total agreement with her. But along with the annoyance she could also see the disappointment in his face. He was the Tilaks' only son, and his parents were looking forward to two or more grandsons to carry on their name and inherit the prosperous family business of selling tires.

Instead Nikhil and Isha already had one daughter, and now they were going to have another. In its own way it was a nightmare.

Later, as they left the doctor's office and climbed into the car, Nikhil turned to her. "Some nerve that idiot had, suggesting an abortion!" His eyes continued to gleam with suppressed anger.

Isha's sense of shock was still lingering, too. "We often hear about female infanticide and feticide taking place in big cities, but I never dreamt that our own gentle doctor in Palgaum would suggest it so easily." She shook her head. "I can't believe how coolly he said it could be *fixed!*"

"Someone ought to report that man to the authorities," said

Nikhil through clenched teeth. "Doesn't that old fool know that there is a law against selective abortion? He could end up in prison."

"I'm sure he's well aware of the law, but how many people in this country really and truly follow the law? Practically everyone we know does something illegal on a daily basis. *You* do it yourself when you grease the palms of the government people to get your import permits and licenses, don't you?" She narrowed her eyes on him. "What about all the money you hide from the income tax people?"

A guilty flush suffused his face. "But killing an unborn baby is not on a par with black marketeering or bribing a government officer. Feticide is tantamount to murder!" Nikhil's jaw seemed to work furiously as he drove them home, and Isha knew it was best not to feed his sense of outrage. He had a short fuse and a very righteous attitude about certain things, and he tended to react accordingly.

After that outburst they drove home mostly in silence. Isha looked out the window, wondering how they'd break the news to Srikant and Vidula Tilak—her father-in-law and mother-in-law.

As it was, their daughter, five-year-old Priya, got second-class treatment compared to Isha's sister-in-law Sheila Sathe's sons. Sheila was beautiful and she was married to a wealthy man. The proverbial icing on her cake was the fact that she had produced two beautiful boys.

And in the Tilaks' eyes, the boys could do no wrong. They received lots of attention while Priya got almost none. Ayee and Baba, as the grandchildren called Isha's in-laws, although not overtly abusive to Priya, never showed her any affection. She was kept at a distance and often subjected to stern discipline. Priya was now old enough to notice their behavior and had started to complain that the boys got so much while she got so little.

Isha and Nikhil tried to make it up to their little girl as much as they could, but since they lived in the same house as the elder Tilaks, and Priya saw her grand parents everyday, it was hard to explain to a child that her gender had everything to do with the way they treated her.

To offset the neglect, Isha often found herself spoiling her child. And that led to a lot of friction with her in-laws, too. They thought she bought Priya too many toys and clothes, and that she never corrected Priya's behavior whenever she acted up. Occasionally Isha would try to explain to them that Priya acted up only when she noticed Sheila's boys getting extra attention.

Ayee and Baba always brushed it off as Isha's misguided perception.

Nikhil took his hand off the steering wheel for an instant to take Isha's hand. "Don't make yourself sick. It's not a big deal." It seemed like his rage had diminished.

Tears pooled in her eyes. "It *will* be a big deal when Ayee and Baba find out."

"We'll explain to them nicely. They're not unreasonable. These things happen. Maybe we'll try for a boy next time."

"There won't be a next time. Who in their right mind has more than two children in this day and age? You really think India's exploding population can sustain one more child?"

"Honestly, when you think about it, what difference does it make whether one has a boy or a girl?" said Nikhil, obviously trying to rationalize a difficult situation. "They all get educated the same way and they follow similar careers. To me it makes no difference."

"*I'm* not the one that needs convincing, Nikhil." She tossed him a look of mild disdain. "Go explain that to *your* parents! Haven't you noticed how they treat Sheila's kids and Priya differently? While Sheila's boys' birthdays are such a big, fussy affair with a dozen gifts, they forgot all about Priya's birthday last week. You and I had to go out and buy a cake and presents and lie to her that some of them were from Ayee and Baba."

Nikhil took a long, tired breath. He had no response to his wife's remarks. Isha knew he was fully cognizant of his parents' petty biases. But he was a good Hindu son, one who'd never acknowledge his parents' shortcomings. Those were never to be discussed openly.

Besides, Nikhil and she had no choice but to live with his folks. It was the old-fashioned Indian way. The son, especially an *only* son, lived with the parents, obeyed them, humored them, tolerated their foibles, and took care of them.

Isha dried her tears, leaned back and closed her eyes. She needed to prepare herself before informing her in-laws that there would be another female baby in the house. God, they'd be tearing their hair out. Or, maybe they'd toss Isha and Priya out and find another wife for their precious son. She wouldn't be surprised if a thought like that crossed their minds every now and then.

Well, thank goodness at least Nikhil's sister, Sheila, was a good woman. Despite her looks and money and all the coddling, Sheila treated Isha with respect and affection. Isha couldn't have asked for a nicer sister-in-law. In fact, Sheila often pointed out to her parents that they should treat Priya the same way they treated her sons. But her advice didn't make an iota of difference to their way of thinking or behavior.

Isha opened her eyes when the car slowed down and made the sharp turn into their driveway. Nikhil brought the car to a stop under the carport outside their house and turned to her. "Feel a little better now?"

She shook her head. "Worse. We have to go in there and tell them the news."

He cupped her cheek in his hand, his expression tender and sympathetic. "I'll do the telling, Ish. You just sit down and relax. You need to rest after the sleepless night you've had."

She tried to summon a smile but didn't quite succeed. He could be so kind sometimes, and he was so good-looking he still made her heart skip a beat. She'd been instantly attracted to him the day he'd come to her parents' home for the bride-viewing. One look at those sparkling gray-green eyes, the strong jaw and nose, the tall, proud carriage, and she'd made up her mind that this was the man she wanted to marry. Fortunately he'd felt the same way about her.

She'd fallen in love the first day and fallen deeper over the years as she'd come to recognize his many sterling qualities: loyalty, sense of humor, his capacity for hard work, and mostly his love and devotion to her and Priya—and now his commitment to their unborn child.

She loved Nikhil more than anyone else in the world. But even that wasn't going to be enough to provide a buffer between his parents and her.

But such was her fate. She had been destined to marry Nikhil Tilak, a good man with not-so-good parents. As his wife, Isha had no choice but to put up with his family. In their culture, marriage was a package deal.

Opening the car door, she stepped out. "All right, then. You tell them and I'll sit there like the good little wife and pretend to be happy."

Despite her bitter sarcasm, Nikhil smiled. "Good decision."

Chapter 2

June 2006

Isha listened to the relentless rain beating down on the roof as she coaxed Priya to finish her dinner. The monsoons were in full swing. Late evenings seemed drearier than the rest of the day for some reason, perhaps because it rained even harder, or because she dreaded dinnertime. It almost always followed the same pattern: the meal started with stilted conversation, then deteriorated into emotional arguments, and finally sank into sullen silence.

It was nearly two months since Nikhil and she had informed Ayee and Baba about the baby's gender. As expected, their reaction had been shocked silence followed by disappointed sighs.

Then one evening, they had nonchalantly introduced the subject of abortion. From that point on, it became almost the sole topic of discussion, and also a bone of contention. The relationship between the younger and elder Tilaks had begun to fracture immediately. With each passing day it became more strained, more resentful, even turbulent at times. The bitterness and animosity seemed to accelerate at about the same rate the baby grew in her womb and kicked with more intensity.

"I wonder why Nikhil is not home yet," said Isha's mother-in-law, interrupting Isha's gloomy thoughts. Ayee had made the remark for the second time in ten minutes, frowning at the wall clock in the dining room.

Baba was in the drawing room, watching television. They were all waiting for Nikhil to return home from work.

"He's probably taking care of a last minute customer, Ayee," Isha explained to ease Ayee's obvious agitation—although she'd been wondering about the same thing herself. Nikhil knew his parents' tendency to worry excessively about him, so he indulged them by keeping them informed of his whereabouts as much as he could.

So where was he at the moment? Why hadn't he called?

"Priya, it's getting late." Isha threw her daughter a no-more-arguments frown. "Now finish what's on your plate!" A fussy eater, Priya usually toyed with her food and wasted a lot of what was served, so she needed to be prodded into eating.

Priya shook her head, making her pigtails bounce. "I'm not hungry." Her large hazel eyes had that familiar stubbornness about them.

That particular expression was so much like Nikhil's when he got mulish about something that it made Isha smile inwardly. Like father, like daughter! But they were such beautiful, expressive eyes. She was glad her child had inherited them from her father, because her own light brown eyes weren't all that spectacular.

"If you don't eat, you don't get a bedtime story," Isha warned her. The enticement of a bedtime story was rather trite, but it almost always worked with Priya.

The little girl reluctantly shoveled the last of the rice and lentils into her mouth, then slid off the chair and skipped out of the dining room. Isha motioned to the maid hovering nearby to remove the empty plate and rose to her feet.

The clock read 8:56 PM. Ayee was sighing audibly. There was still no sign of Nikhil. Isha threw another anxious glance outside the window. No headlights coming up the driveway. The phone remained silent. The first real frisson of apprehension tiptoed through her mind.

Where was her husband?

Nikhil usually left his office around 8:00 PM and came home well before 8:30 every evening. Now Baba was getting impatient and pacing the floor, so Isha called the shop to find out what was keeping Nikhil, but there was no reply. The voice mail came on and she left a message asking Nikhil to call home right away.

But he didn't call back; and several minutes after the clock struck nine, and there was still no sign of Nikhil and no call, either, Isha and her mother-in-law exchanged worried looks.

Ayee's frown became deeper. "Why is he not home yet?" she repeated, echoing Isha's thoughts. "He always informs us if he is going to be late, no?"

Dinner was getting cold, so Isha encouraged the elders to eat. Besides, they were rigid in their eating schedules.

A little later Isha read Priya her promised story and got her settled in bed, then decided to wait up for Nikhil in the drawing room along with her in-laws. She kept trying both the office land-line as well as Nikhil's mobile phone every few minutes, but both came up with voice-mail each time.

At 9:49 PM, Baba, dressed in white pajamas and a loose muslin shirt, was pacing the drawing room floor more furiously than before, his jaw clenched tight. For a sixty-two-year-old he was in excellent shape, trim-bodied, smooth-complexioned, and in full control of his faculties. Despite his shock of silver hair, he looked ten years younger than he was. Technically he had handed over the business to Nikhil and retired, but he was very much involved in its overall operation.

He finally stopped pacing and turned to Isha. "This is going on too long. Call Patil, the Superintendent of Police. Maybe there was an accident or something."

So Isha called Mr. Patil's home number and explained the situation. The superintendent was a family acquaintance, and he immediately offered to send out a couple of men to discreetly find out if there was any sort of trouble at Nikhil's office.

Ayee looked even more distressed than Baba. Her hair was done in a braid in preparation for bed, and she had on a soft cotton kaftan. At fifty-eight, unlike her young-looking husband, she certainly looked her age, perhaps because she frowned so much and had wrinkles in her brow.

But she had the gorgeous hazel eyes, high cheek bones, and chiseled features that her son, her daughter, and all her grandchildren had inherited. She must have been a lovely woman in her youth. Baba and she still made a handsome couple.

Isha and her in-laws waited a long time, willing the phone to ring. The tension in the room was oppressive, especially when Baba kept switching the television on and off every few minutes and murmuring under his breath. But it wasn't Isha's place to tell him to cut it out, stop pacing, and sit down for heaven's sake. He was driving her crazy with his slippers going clop-clop on the marble-tiled floor.

It was nearly an hour later that Mr. Patil himself came to their door, looking uncomfortable as he stood under his dripping umbrella and shuffled his large feet. He was a tall, stiff man with a somber face, and a heavy mustache that was just turning gray. Maybe it was his profession that made him so glum.

The moment Isha opened the door to him, her heart sank. Instinctively she knew he was the bearer of bad news. Why else would he come all the way out here in person? She had no idea what the details were, but somewhere in her gut she knew something horrible had happened to Nikhil. The negative vibes she'd been feeling since the clock had struck nine had been rising with every passing minute.

And now, looking at Mr. Patil's face, she knew her instincts had been right. Nonetheless she joined her trembling palms in the expected greeting. "*Namaste*, Patil-*saheb*. Please come in."

He stepped inside with some hesitation and discarded his wet *chappals* and umbrella near the door. "*Namaste*, Mrs. Tilak." He greeted the elder Tilaks in the same manner.

Both Ayee and Baba immediately bombarded him with questions. "*Did you find out anything? Was there an accident? Is there any news of our son?*"

Patil remained silent. Baba shot him a blistering look. "Have your men been sent to check on Nikhil or not?"

Patil chewed on his lower lip for an instant. "Yes, sir."

Isha looked up at Patil, the tightening in her chest reaching the point of strangulation. "And?"

He stroked his luxuriant mustache and blinked a couple of times. It took a moment for him to look her in the eye. "The news is bad."

Baba's face contorted into a ferocious scowl. "What kind of news?"

"I'm coming to that, Tilak-saheb," said Patil, patting the air with both hands. "My constables went to your shop. The lights were off. They assumed the store was closed. But when they tried the door, it opened, so they went in and turned on the lights. It looked like—"

"Like what?" interrupted Baba.

"—there might have been a robbery."

Feeling weak and nauseated from not having eaten for several hours, Isha moved to the nearest chair and sank into it. "Robbery?" *It's not serious . . . calm down.* She took a deep, calming breath. *A few stolen tires . . . can't be the end of the world.*

Patil gestured to her in-laws to sit down on the sofa. "When they rang me, I went out there to look for myself. It looked like all the staff had left and Nikhil was closing up the shop and someone came inside and tried to rob the store. He must have tried to fight them off."

"What about Nikhil?" Isha demanded. All she wanted to know was how her husband was.

"They . . . they stabbed him."

The breath left Isha's lungs in that instant. "Is he badly hurt?" she managed to whisper.

"He was stabbed to death." Patil shut his eyes tight for a moment, the anguish clear on his face. "There are multiple wounds . . . a lot of blood." He fell silent before adding, "He probably tried to wrestle with them and things became violent."

"But Nikhil's a strong man . . . and very capable. He won't lose a fight." She quashed the tide of ice-cold panic flooding her. She couldn't lose hope. "He can't." He used to be an athlete.

"But, madam, this is . . . ." Patil made a helpless gesture with his hands.

"Did you check thoroughly to see if it was Nikhil or someone else? It could be one of the men who work for Nikhil."

Patil shook his head. "It was Nikhil. I am one hundred percent sure. I know . . . knew Nikhil quite well."

"But did anyone check his pulse?" Baba demanded.

"Yes, sir," replied Patil, his voice brimming with regret.

"How can you be so sure?" Ayee demanded.

Patil took a deep, audible breath. "I'm sorry, Tilak-bayi. I wish I could say I wasn't sure, but I cannot."

The small bubble of hope Isha had been desperately clutching at popped.

All at once her mind went blank. The red upholstery on the furniture, the reds in the hand-woven area rug and in the curtains seemed to turn gray. Everything around her changed to the same shade of ash.

The tightness in her chest started right in the center and then radiated outward, slowly exerting a choke hold on her lungs, but the expected sobs and drenching tears never came. She could only stare dry-eyed at the grave man sitting across the room from her.

He was the one who had told her she was now a *widow*. The dreaded *W* word.

All she could remember later was the silence that descended over the room that night. She had no idea what her in-laws were doing at the time, but she had remained motionless and speechless. Even if she had tried to say or do something, there probably wouldn't have been a sound emerging from her throat or a muscle that would have cooperated.

All her systems had shut down, as if they were operated by a single kill switch.

Chapter 3

July 2006

Dr. Vivek Karnik wiped the sweat off his brow with a handkerchief and stood by the window of his study, watching the man drive away. He hoped he'd never have to see that man again. He was loathsome and yet Karnik had to put up with the bastard and with his cool arrogance.

He saw the vehicle's taillights disappear around the corner and wished for the hundredth time that he had never become embroiled in this complicated web of lies, deceit, and illegal activities.

What in heaven's name had possessed him to start doing something unlawful in the first place? Why had he even needed to do it? A bright, educated man nearing retirement, and with enough savings to do it in comfort, had no business ruining his life's work—and his reputation.

But greed was an integral part of human nature and he had succumbed to it.

He turned away from the window, sat in his desk chair with a weary sigh, and stared at the computer. The weariness went bone-deep. It had been a long day at work. He had delivered two babies, one of them by Caesarean, performed one hysterectomy, two tubal ligations, and seen several pregnant and menopausal women. He'd done all those things routinely before, practically every day of his professional life, but he'd never disliked his work.

He had made a substantial income by performing abortions. The ultrasound was a modern-day miracle for a lot of young couples on the way to becoming parents. But like many other technological marvels, it had its dark side. It wasn't really his fault, though. He hadn't deliberately set out to do something that went against his conscience. The idea had been planted in his head by someone else, and the seed had slowly sprouted and grown over a period of time.

A few years ago, one of his patients had casually mentioned that many Indian doctors had been using the machine to detect female fetuses, and if a patient wanted their fetus aborted, the doctors did it—for a fee, of course. Apparently abortions were a very lucrative side business for any ob-gyn in a society obsessed with male children.

That simple remark had started Karnik thinking, but not seriously. A few months later, the husband of one of his patients had asked him in confidence if he would be willing to perform an abortion because he and his wife were tired of producing girls. They already had three, and they were desperate for a boy.

Karnik had shaken his head at the man. "It's illegal in this country, you know."

The young man had laughed. "So is bribery, dowry, tax evasion, and black marketeering, Doctor-*saheb*. Does that stop anyone?" He'd given Karnik a meaningful look. "My wife and I are thinking about maybe going to . . . um . . . a Mumbai doctor and getting it done. If you can do it here . . . then we'll pay you the same amount we'd pay the other doctor."

"Mumbai, huh?"

"We have a list of doctors in Mumbai who do this . . . so perhaps . . ."

The young man had left it hanging, letting Karnik ponder it. Karnik had refused—but later wondered if it was a mistake.

After that he'd had a few more secret inquiries from patients. What was the harm in it? he'd asked himself. When one analyzed the matter in strictly scientific terms, a fetus was only a tiny bunch of cells. And if getting rid of a female fetus gave so many couples and their families so much satisfaction, why couldn't *he* be the one to give it to them? Besides, with the available techniques, the procedure was simple, efficient, and very safe if performed within the first few weeks of pregnancy.

Karnik had rationalized it by telling himself that he was only the facilitator and not the instigator.

If he didn't maintain official records, who would know? The patients and their families needed anonymity and so did he. Discretion wouldn't be a problem. So, after some initial trepidation, he had performed one abortion, then two . . . then three . . . and soon it became routine. The fear and anxiety were long gone. He began performing them regularly.

However, in all honesty, he didn't need to perform abortions. It wasn't as if he didn't make enough money from his regular practice. In fact, he had so many patients, most of them wealthy, he could barely schedule them in.

But patients who wanted abortions were a different breed. They were desperate, willing to pay any amount. He could name his price and they paid it. For them, money wasn't the issue, not producing a son was. So the abortion business had become a large part of his practice—much more lucrative than the other, legitimate portion.

And he'd never had a problem. Until now. His mistake hadn't been in getting into the selective abortion game—it had been mentioning the possibility to that headstrong, egotistical Nikhil Tilak. So, Tilak and his wife didn't want an abortion. Fine, but the man hadn't stopped at saying no. He had stunned Karnik by threatening to start an official investigation.

That was when Karnik, out of sheer desperation, had hired someone reliable to send a few discreet threats to Tilak. He'd hoped to put a little fear into him and stop him in his tracks . . . because he was a young man with a wife and children to support. And a reputation to uphold.

But had the stupid Tilak backed off? No! He'd become

bolder still and reported the threats to the superintendent's office. When the police had demanded solid proof from Tilak to back up his abortion allegations, he had paid some hoodlum to break into Karnik's house one night, when he and his wife were at a dinner party, to steal private records from his computer.

Like an idiot, Karnik had never put in a password or any kind of protection on his computer. After all, this was Palgaum, where few people knew how to use computers. He had never imagined anyone breaking into his house and stealing data from his machine.

Thieves in Palgaum were typically starving and illiterate. They came looking for cash, jewelry and electronics like TVs and cameras that could be hawked in a minute. They would steal a computer for its resale value but never pilfer data from it. However, this time they had.

And Nikhil Tilak was the one who had managed to do it—there was no doubt in Karnik's mind that Tilak was behind the theft. So, Karnik felt he had no choice but to defend himself by ordering his own man to stop Tilak immediately from going any further.

Thank God he had succeeded! Karnik's hired *goonda* had managed to make it look like a robbery before Tilak had a chance to take any kind of evidence to the police.

The hired man had guaranteed Karnik that no proof had reached the superintendent's office—and nothing would.

But the doctor was still uneasy. His man hadn't found anything in Tilak's office. So where was the stolen data? Had Tilak given it to someone else for safekeeping? Had he made copies and distributed them to various people? If yes, who were they? There were too many unanswered questions.

But Karnik had justified his decision to himself as righteous payback. He was only paying someone to steal what was originally stolen from him.

However, the stupid *goonda* he'd hired had killed Tilak in the process. Murder had not been part of the plan. Catching Tilak off guard when he was alone in his store, then forcing him to turn over the data by using a little intimidation—that's what Karnik had instructed his man to do. Killing was never mentioned.

The hired moron had taken it upon himself to stab Tilak to death. He claimed it was self-defense because the strong and athletic Tilak hadn't capitulated as expected. Instead he had allegedly attacked him viciously with both fists. Consequently the confrontation had turned serious and bloody.

When a rich, influential, and charismatic man like Tilak became the victim of a brutal killing, the media turned into a greedy flock of vultures. All of a sudden, every newspaper, and every radio and television station in the country had done a dramatic piece on the killing, leaving Karnik even more anxious.

Fortunately his own name had never been mentioned in the media. Everything had been hushed up, with very little damage done.

Now, a month later, the furor was finally dying down. The hired killer, who had just driven away from his house, had come to inform him that the investigation was also beginning to wane. The superintendent was getting frustrated with the dead-end case and was talking about closing it, calling it a robbery gone awry. The police still had no clue as to who had committed the murder.

Karnik's prayers had been answered.

Meanwhile, he had paid several hundred thousand rupees of his hard-earned cash to the killer. He could only hope the man didn't plan to blackmail him at a later date. He was a sly one, that fellow—and greedy. He was capable of extortion, too. If he could kill so casually, blackmail would come just as easily. If that happened, Karnik was doomed.

At this point, he had no faith in anyone. If he himself could go from being a decent, family-oriented man of medicine to someone who blatantly broke the laws of the country as well as those of God, then why couldn't someone else?

Both his children, the son and daughter, were good people, both honest doctors and well settled. His wife was a pious woman. He and his family were respected in this town. At the tail end of his career he had managed to jeopardize the esteem he'd earned over a lifetime.

Stupid, stupid! But it was too late to turn back.

Shutting off the computer, he rose to his feet and stretched. He had deleted all the records from his computer, then made sure they were purged from the electronic trash bin. Hopefully there was no trace of his abortions left anywhere.

Fortunately he had always performed the clinical procedure alone, each and every time, with no nursing staff or any of his servants present. It had been done privately in his office, after hours and on Sundays. Even his wife had no idea about it. No one except the patient and her husband knew what was happening, and they had more to lose than he by making the information public.

Shutting off the lights, he shuffled off to eat his supper. As he started to sit in his usual chair at the head of the dining table, his wife, Neela, looked at him with a slight frown. "Who was that man you were meeting so late?"

"He is . . . the repairman who came to fix my computer." He hated lying to his wife, especially when she was so trusting of him.

While he waited for the cook to serve their dinner, Karnik sensed Neela's discerning eyes studying him. How much had she guessed?

He made a silent resolution. He would perform no more abortions. Never again.

Chapter 4

The early morning gloom was so thick Isha could almost feel it around her shoulders, like a mantle, too heavy to be removed and tossed aside. The Tilak household was still in deep mourning. It was five weeks since Nikhil's death. And yet it felt like it had happened yesterday.

To add to her anguish, the more she analyzed Nikhil's bizarre death, the more she was convinced he had been murdered for a reason. She didn't know for sure what it was or who was behind it. However, after some speculation, she had drawn a few conclusions. Nothing concrete, though—just some theories based on a gut feeling.

Nikhil had been a friendly individual, well liked and respected by most . . . unless, one of his employees had a grudge against him? Or it could be a competitor. But if that were the case, Nikhil would have mentioned something to her. Every night, as they lay in bed together, they used to share the day's experiences with each other. He used to talk to her about the business, tell her details of his day at work.

Shaking off the grim thoughts temporarily, Isha tried to focus on what she was doing: urging Priya to eat her breakfast. Nikhil used to apply some fatherly discipline to make sure the finicky Priya ate.

Ayee emerged from the *devghar*—altar room—after finishing her *pooja*. Her elaborate worship. The night she'd received the shattering news about Nikhil, she'd promptly fainted. The doctor had been summoned and she'd recovered from the fainting spell, but afterward she was never the same. She'd suffered an emotional breakdown and taken to her bed for more than three weeks. She had lost some weight from the trauma, too. And what little humor she had possessed before the episode was gone.

Now, although she was gradually beginning to ease back into her social pattern and dress elegantly like she used to, she walked around in a surly mood, with a perpetual line between her eyebrows.

Ayee wore a turquoise print cotton sari this morning. Her hair was neatly coiled into her usual bun. There was plenty of gray in her hair, much more than most women her age. But she covered it with hair color. With the sudden weight loss, her face looked drawn, her blouse hung loose in the sleeves and waistline, and the excess skin jiggled around her upper arms whenever she moved them.

As Ayee entered the dining room, Isha could smell the lavender-scented talcum powder the older woman liked to wear.

Seeing Priya in Isha's lap, sniffling, with her face buried in her mother's shoulder, Ayee frowned. "Why is she crying again?"

"The usual morning blues," replied Isha, hoping Priya would cease the fussing and get on with her breakfast. Ayee seemed particularly cantankerous this morning. It didn't bode well.

"Such a crybaby." Ayee shook her head. "Every morning and night it is the same story. She does nothing but cry."

"She's crying for Nikhil, Ayee. She misses him." He was the one who dropped her off at school before he went to work. Poor Priya couldn't understand why her father wasn't around anymore. The palpable misery around her didn't help matters, either.

"She's not the only one. We all miss him," Ayee said, her lower lip trembling, the tears already glistening in her eyes.

Isha nodded, keeping her own emotions tightly reined in. If she broke down, Priya's sniveling would only get worse. Nikhil's presence was still very much there. Everywhere. It would always remain with them.

Ayee blinked and looked at the wall clock. "Priya has to go to school soon, no? Why is she wasting time?"

"I'm trying to get her to eat her breakfast so I can get her ready for school," Isha assured her mother-in-law. Couldn't the woman see that Priya was only five years old and needed a little extra comforting at the moment? Had she forgotten that the child was usually very sunny by nature? Labeling her a crybaby was so unfair!

"What she needs is strictness, not more coddling." Ayee threw an exasperated look at Priya's pajama-clad back.

With a resigned sigh Isha said, "Time to finish your breakfast, sweetie. I bet all your friends are dressed and ready for school. You don't want to be late, do you?"

A sob erupted from Priya. "I don't . . . want . . . to go . . . to school." She refused to remove her face from Isha's shoulder. "I want Papa."

Stifling her own desire to burst into tears, Isha patted Priya's head. "I told you Papa is in heaven. *Dev-bappa* needs him more than we do," she whispered in her ear, using the child's term for God, or Holy Father. "But I'll take you to school. Maybe we can go for ice cream after school."

Instead of making things better, Isha realized she'd made them worse. Priya threw a full-blown tantrum, her ears turning red. "I don't want ice cream! I want my Papa!"

Ayee accepted the cup of tea poured for her by one of the servants and let out a long-suffering sigh. After taking a sip she gazed out the window at the interminable rain, making her aggravation very clear to Isha. Her mother-in-law had her own passive-aggressive ways of making her feelings known.

Realizing that sternness was the only way to deal with the child, Isha held her by the shoulders and forced her to make eye contact. "Priya, I told you Papa can't be here. I want you to finish your egg and toast and then change into your uniform. I want this crying to stop! Now!"

Priya's full mouth started to quiver and large tear drops started to tumble down her cheeks once again, breaking Isha's heart. "I don't . . . want . . . breakfast."

Tears gathered in Isha's eyes, too, which she hastily dabbed with a handkerchief. Was this bone-deep grief ever going to go away? She wanted to gather her little girl close to her heart and cry with her. Maybe they could help wash away each other's misery. But there were practical matters to consider, for example, her father-in-law.

As if on cue, his heavy footsteps sounded nearby. From the corner of her eye she saw him stride in, dressed in charcoal pants and a tan shirt. His thick silver hair, slick with hair dressing, was combed back from his wide forehead.

He pulled out the chair at the head of the table and accepted the steaming cup of tea one of the servants brought to him. He liked it superhot and sweetened with precisely one teaspoon of sugar. Then he reached for the customary newspaper Ayee left for him in the exact same spot each morning—at his right elbow.

When he heard Priya's sobs, he adjusted his glasses and glared at her over the rim. "Why are you crying, Priya?"

The little girl continued to sniffle and ignored her grandfather.

"I asked you why you are crying." His voice rose a bit, planting the first germ of fear in Isha's mind. Baba's temper was quick to flare, and it was notorious. Since Nikhil's death, Baba had been forced to come out of semiretirement and take over the running of the business. Between the loss of his only son and the responsibility of the store, Baba's temper fits had escalated in frequency and intensity.

When Priya continued to ignore him, his gaze settled on Isha. "What is her problem? Should she not be ready for school by now?"

Before Isha could answer him, Ayee chimed in. "Every day it is the same thing. Priya does nothing but cry. You don't see Milind and Arvind crying like that. Girls are always fusspots. Soon there will be another girl to add to our headaches."

"Priya's only a child, Ayee," argued Isha. "And she misses her Papa." But she knew her attempts at defending Priya were weak at best.

Ayee rolled her beautiful eyes and gave another dramatic

sigh. "If you had not insisted on ignoring our request to have an abortion, Nikhil would still be here. I was telling you for weeks that the unborn child is showing all the signs of bad luck."

Her own temper stirring, Isha looked up at her mother-in-law. "Nikhil and I never thought of our child and your grandchild as a bad omen. A child is a blessing, Ayee, never a curse."

Ayee put down her cup with a flourish. "The astrologer warned me that the child was conceived on a bad day. But who is going to listen to me in this house? The baby is not even here yet, and already she has caused such tragedy for us. What will she do after she is born?"

"Ayee, please . . . Let's not blame an unborn child for what fate decreed. Nikhil would be very upset if he could hear that." Isha cast an uneasy glance at Baba. He was reading the news headlines and nibbling on his buttered toast. "As you know, Nikhil was against abortion. In fact, he was very upset when he found out that Dr. Karnik performs gender-based abortions in the first place."

Baba slapped his newspaper on the table. The teacups on the table rattled. "Dr. Karnik is a good man and a good doctor! He only does what is right for certain people."

As rebellion began to stir in her gut, Isha couldn't help retorting, "But deliberately aborting fetuses just because they're female is wrong. Morally and legally wrong!"

Baba's imperious eyebrows shot up. "What is wrong in letting people decide if they want a girl or boy, huh?"

"What's next? Genetically engineered, identical, perfect little boys populating the entire world?" she rejoined, her voice dripping with bitter cynicism. "Where are they going to find perfect little girls to keep them happy?"

Baba ignored her caustic comment. "Has China not made it possible for people to have only one child, and if they want a boy, they can have a boy?"

"And look what's happened in China, Baba. They have such a shortage of girls that men are forced to marry their cousins. Many of their men are either doomed to remain single or resort to some dreadful measures to acquire a wife."

"India has not come to that point, and never will," said Ayee, joining in the argument. "We have more girls than we know what to do with. Look at our own family—already one girl and another on the way. What sins did we commit in our previous lives that we are punished with girls?"

"Girls these days achieve just as much as boys, if not more," argued Isha. "They're assets, not burdens." She was sorely tempted to say something like, *Ayee, what are you if not a female? Have you looked at yourself in the mirror lately? And didn't you give birth to a girl many years ago? I suppose that makes you worthless, too, just like me?*

But she curbed her tongue, because talking back to one's in-laws was certainly not allowed in her family. Also, realizing that Priya had stopped fussing and was curiously observing the adults arguing, Isha took the opportunity to push the toast in front of her. "Eat." Besides, she didn't want an impressionable five-year-old to be exposed to her in-laws' contemptuous and outdated views about girls.

"Just because they get educated and hold jobs doesn't mean they are not a burden to their families," growled Baba, clearly in a fighting mood and itching to prolong the dispute. "In the end, after all that money parents spend on girls, they have to get married, and then their earnings go towards the husband and his family."

Isha didn't want to continue the pointless debate. She had things to do, like getting her child to school. "I don't agree with that philosophy, Baba. You and Ayee can believe what you want."

"What!" Baba rose from his chair, the veins in his neck visibly bulging, the color rising in his face. "How *dare* you talk to me like that! Just because your husband is no longer here, you think you can say whatever your long tongue wants to say?"

Regretting her outburst, Isha swallowed hard. "I'm sorry, Baba. It must be the strain of the last few weeks." Perhaps sensing her mother's fear, Priya burst into noisy tears once again.

Isha realized that with her desire to argue she had inadvertently made a bad situation worse. Why hadn't she just shut up and let the old folks hang on to their arcane beliefs? "Priya, if you don't want to eat, fine. Let's go upstairs and get dressed." She put Priya on her feet and rose from her chair.

"I don't want to go to school." Priya rubbed her swollen eyes with her knuckles.

"You *will* go to school!" growled Baba.

"I *won't!*" Priya retorted. Unfortunately she'd picked the worst day to be bratty.

"I will *not* tolerate disobedience and disrespect to elders in my house." Already incensed with Isha, Baba pushed his chair back with a screech and came around the table toward them. Before Isha could do or say anything, he grabbed Priya by the arm and whacked her bottom.

Shocked by the unexpected assault, the child let out a high-pitched scream. And for that she got whacked a couple more times, and harder, too.

Isha stared in disbelief. Priya had been reprimanded, punished in other ways, and yelled at, but never dealt with physically. A moment later, regaining her equilibrium, Isha stepped forward, her breath coming out in gasps. "Baba, stop it! Please!"

When he stopped and let go of Priya, the child ran into her arms, the sobbing now literally choking the breath out of her. Her skin felt hot to the touch and looked red. And Priya's tiny buttocks were probably even redder from the thorough beating they'd taken through the thin fabric of her pajamas.

Rage began to fire up inside her. How dare he! How dare the old man strike a helpless child!

The cook and her helper had both come out of the kitchen, their eyes wide with curiosity and fear. Sundari, Priya's elderly nursemaid, stood in a corner, looking petrified.

All Isha could do was hold Priya close and soothe her for a minute, all the while trying to keep her own mounting wrath in check. "Shh, baby . . . shh." Then she turned to her father-in-law, who still looked livid. "I can't believe you struck a child for something as minor as refusing to go to school."

"Missing school is *not* a minor matter!"

"Is this the way you dealt with Nikhil and Sheila if they did the same thing in their childhood?" Shaking with fury, Isha turned her gaze on her mother-in-law, who seemed to be taking it all in as if she were watching a scene in a movie. "How can you sit there and let Baba beat up your granddaughter? This is your son's child, can't you see?"

"She seems to need more discipline than any other child I know," said Ayee, looking nonchalant as she chewed on the last of her breakfast. "God knows you and Nikhil never tried to teach her to be a good girl. Someone has to."

The bitter truth struck Isha in that instant. These people despised her and her child. Now that Nikhil was gone, they resented them even more, especially because in their warped minds they were convinced that Isha's unborn daughter was responsible for Nikhil's death. They were hurting from losing their beloved son and needed someone to blame for their pain. Isha and the innocent babe in her womb were convenient scapegoats and therefore by association Priya was also to blame.

Why hadn't Isha seen that earlier? Maybe losing Nikhil had made her deaf and blind to everything else around her.

But now her eyes were wide open to the truth.

The elder Tilaks were misguided individuals and she and Priya had no place in their home. Things were never going to get better for them, either. Matter of fact, they were only going to get worse. How long was she going to sit around and watch her daughter getting abused?

If Priya was subjected to this, how much was the new baby going to suffer, the one they'd labeled a bad omen and a curse? They probably wouldn't hesitate to kill her in their smug, self-righteous way and justify it in some fashion.

No wonder they condoned Karnik's decadent practices.

The urgent and potent need she felt to get out of that house didn't really surprise Isha. It had been building up gradually over a period of several weeks.

Right after being told about the results of the sonogram, Ayee had started sharing little tidbits of gossip. "Did you know Mrs. Datar's daughter had an abortion? Good thing, too, since it would have been a third girl."

When Nikhil and Isha had reacted with outrage, Baba had merely added his chauvinistic opinion. "When modern technology has made it possible to pick and choose the sex of one's progeny, is it not stupidity to ignore it?"

"It is stupidity to interfere with nature, Baba," Nikhil had countered. "You and Ayee are religious, God-fearing Brahmins. How can you even think such things when you have a fancy *pooja* room and you pray twice a day and celebrate all the religious festivals with such devotion? In fact, I'm tempted to report that idiot Dr. Karnik to the police."

His father had sternly warned Nikhil against any such action. "Don't get involved in Dr. Karnik's affairs. He is a good person and a loyal customer, and he is only doing what his patients ask him to do."

"Even if it is highly illegal?" Nikhil had looked at his father in total disbelief. "Baba, do you know there is a law against even *revealing* the sex of an unborn child? Do you have *any* idea how many female children in this country are cruelly destroyed either as fetuses or newborns?"

"Bogus statistics cooked up by feminist groups!" was Baba's disdainful response. "What Karnik does with his medical practice is none of our business. You stay out of it, you hear?" It was a clear warning.

Nikhil had never again mentioned reporting against Karnik, and of course Isha had immediately switched doctors after that disturbing ultrasound appointment. But every day after that point the debate over abortion had insinuated itself into the conversation in the Tilak home, until it had come to a head when Ayee and Baba had come right out and ordered Nikhil and Isha to schedule an abortion.

"We *forbid* you to have the child," Baba had said to them. "What is the point in having another girl? We need a *boy* to carry on the family tradition."

For once Nikhil had put on his most intimidating expression

and stared his father down, making Isha's heart swell with pride. "You have no right to forbid a child from coming into this world," he'd countered. "Neither you nor Dr. Karnik can play God. So I would appreciate your not bringing up this topic again. From now on, the word abortion is *not* to be mentioned in my presence or Isha's, or Priya's, for that matter."

He had thrown his mother a blistering glance, silently warning her to keep her mouth shut, too.

Amazingly the "A" word had never been brought up again, at least while Nikhil was alive.

So now, as Isha's heart was breaking over how her father-in-law had punished her grieving child, she knew the time had come to go off on her own. God alone knew where she would go or how she'd survive. She had no real skills, no more than a bachelor's degree, and one and a half children to protect, but she couldn't live in this sorry excuse for a home a minute longer.

She waited till Priya's sobbing subsided, then turned to her in-laws. "I think you're clearly trying to tell me to get out and take my child with me, aren't you?"

Ayee remained silent and pretended to look out the window. The servants had retreated from the room but stood just inside the kitchen door, riveted by the unfolding drama. They were probably making plans on how best to spread the juicy gossip. They lived for such moments.

Baba took a sharp breath, his color still high. "With Nikhil gone, I personally don't care what you and your daughter do."

"Is this how much you care for your son's memory and his child—your granddaughter, your flesh and blood?" Isha shot back bitterly. "According to you, she and the unborn child have no right to exist. Well, let me tell you this much: you can sleep in peace tonight because I'm taking Priya and leaving you right now."

"Where do you think you're going, huh?" Baba snorted and went back to his chair. "You have no family; you have nothing."

"I'll go to my cousin's home in Mumbai if necessary. Anywhere is better than being here, where girls are considered no more than insects to be exterminated." She grabbed Priya's hand

and dragged her upstairs. Sundari followed them, wiping away the tears that rolled down her wizened cheeks. She was a sweet and dedicated woman who was much more than a servant.

Within a short time, Isha managed to pack three large suitcases with Sundari's help, all the while aware of Priya staring in grim silence. The child was clearly traumatized and confused by everything that was happening.

But what could Isha say to her daughter? Priya was too young to understand what was going on around her, so Isha let her sit on the bed, clutching her favorite doll close to her chest. Her tear-swollen eyes looked at Isha as if she wanted to ask a hundred questions but didn't quite know how.

"Isha-*bayi*, please don't leave," pleaded Sundari for the umpteenth time. "Where you will go with Priya-baby and your belly filled with one more?"

"I can't stay here any longer, Sundari. Didn't you see how Baba beat up Priya? Do you think he'll spare my other child if she cries? Every time they cry, they will remind Baba and Ayee of their dead son."

"Why not go to Sheila-*bayi*'s house, then? It will be a good home for Priya-baby, no? I will come with you," said Sundari, a simple woman who probably couldn't comprehend Isha's logic.

Isha patted Sundari's brown, work-worn hand. "It's kind of you to offer, but your place is here. You have worked for Ayee and Baba almost all your life. I'm the outsider and I need to go."

"But where will you stay, and what will you eat? What will Priya-baby eat?"

Isha sighed with regret at seeing the old woman looking so brokenhearted. She was so caring, so kind. "Please, Sundari, try to understand. I'm not going to harm Priya. I'll make sure she has enough to eat."

As Isha went about packing things, taking only a few essentials for herself, including some pictures of Nikhil, but plenty of Priya's belongings, she tried to beat her brain to think of where she could go. She had no family, as Baba had gleefully reminded her. All her close friends were couples that belonged to the elite Palgaum crowd and they were friendly with the elder Tilaks, as well.

Sheila was sympathetic and affectionate, but she was still a Tilak, and Isha would never put Sheila in the position of being forced to choose between her parents and her sister-in-law and niece. That would be grossly unfair.

In the end, the convent came to mind as a possible safe haven, at least as a provisional shelter until she handed the insurance claim to their agent. She hadn't submitted it yet because she hadn't seen the need for money. Now she had no choice but to cash in the policy.

She had heard somewhere that the nuns who ran the parochial school that she'd attended in her childhood occasionally gave shelter to needy women on a temporary basis. Besides, how long could the insurance settlement take—four weeks, maybe six? She would use the money to buy a place of her own and then see if she could find herself a job.

In fact, quite recently Nikhil had talked about investing in some real estate, perhaps buying one or two flats in that shiny new high-rise building that was in their neighborhood. She could follow up on that idea and buy two flats, since the insurance money would likely be enough to buy two. Living in one and renting the other as a source of income sounded like a viable idea.

She convinced herself she could do it. She didn't need the Tilaks and their jaundiced philosophy. She could make it on her own. And she would.

There were two thousand rupees and change—something Nikhil and she kept in their room at all times for small, unexpected expenses—in her *almirah*, or armoire. She shoved the money into her handbag. There was plenty more cash in Baba's safe, several hundred thousand rupees that were earmarked for emergencies, but she wasn't going to beg for that. Baba wouldn't have given her a *paisa* of it anyway.

Picking up the phone, Isha called for a taxi. A few minutes later Sundari and she dragged the suitcases out the bedroom door and onto the landing. Still sniffling, Priya reluctantly put on her uniform, a blue pinafore and white blouse, then slipped into her red raincoat. "Why did you put my things in a suitcase?" she finally asked.

"Because we're going away," Isha replied.

"Why?"

"We can't stay here anymore. We're not welcome here."

Priya seemed to give it some thought. "Are Papa and Sundari going with us?"

With a tired sigh Isha tried her best to explain once again that Papa was *never* going with them anywhere. Ever. Sundari couldn't go with them for other reasons.

"Where are we going?" Priya asked, hugging her doll closer.

"At the moment, I don't know. Maybe to the convent."

"I don't like the convent." Priya's mouth settled into a thin, stubborn line.

Isha sat next to Priya on the bed and gently cupped the small face in both her hands. It broke her heart to tear her child away from the only home she'd known. "I'm sorry, pumpkin. It's not my favorite place, either. But we may have to stay there for a few days. Just trust me, okay?" She placed a soft kiss on the flushed forehead. "Everything will be okay soon, I promise."

There was no response from Priya, but her silence was enough acquiescence.

When Sundari and Isha hauled the suitcases downstairs, they found that Baba had already left for work. Ayee was reading the paper. Isha stood before her. "Looks like you got your wish, Ayee. Someday, I hope you'll realize that with Priya and your other grandchild gone, you will have lost all links to your only son. For Nikhil's sake I hope you don't suffer too much grief when that happens."

"I have already suffered more than my share of grief. There is no more left." Ayee gave Isha and Priya a disinterested look and went back to her newspaper. She clearly didn't believe a word Isha had said. Priya and Isha could have been leaving on a shopping spree for all the interest Ayee showed in their departure.

Sundari put her palms together before Ayee in a desperate plea. "Ayee-saheb, please stop them from going—at least for the sake of peace for Nikhil-saheb's soul."

"Where can they go?" asked Ayee. "By this evening they will be back."

Perhaps realizing finally that she wasn't going to get any help from her employer, Sundari stood by the door, the anguish on her face squeezing at Isha's heart. In her faded cotton sari and her gray hair in a loose bun at the nape of her neck, she was the very image of a doting grandmother. If only Isha had a definite place to go to, she'd have taken Sundari with her.

And she wished she could take her own car, too. The temptation to climb into the driver's seat of the silver Maruti Esteem Nikhil had bought for her recently tugged at her, but she suppressed it. She didn't want anything of value from the Tilaks. Besides, how was she going to afford the petrol and the car's upkeep?

By the time the taxi arrived, Priya was more or less back to normal. Sundari offered both of them hugs and tearful words of advice to Priya. "Be a good girl and eat the food on your plate, baby. Don't give Mummy any trouble. And say your prayers every night."

Priya readily got into the seat next to Isha. She probably still harbored the hope that the two of them were going on a trip somewhere, and that Papa was magically going to appear.

Their first stop was the bank, where Isha went to the safety deposit box and retrieved the insurance policy that Nikhil had secreted away so his parents wouldn't find out about it. They'd never have understood the need for a man taking out a policy and naming his young wife as the sole beneficiary.

And now Nikhil's forethought had come in handy. Did he have a premonition that his end was near? Was that why he'd taken out such a large policy, and so recently? Something must have compelled him to do it. More and more she was convinced of that, considering how he'd made haste to contact the agent secretly and put the plan in motion.

He'd told only Isha about the policy, warning her never to mention it to his parents. When asked about the need for such secrecy, he'd simply said, "It's for you and the children. What if something happens to me?"

"Nothing's going to happen to you," she'd chided him, trying to suppress the chill creeping up her spine. Such macabre thinking was simply tempting fate.

"Life is unpredictable, Isha," he'd said on a quiet note.

At the time it had sounded like a strange conversation, but now it didn't seem that weird.

Besides the policy, there was another large envelope crammed with papers in the safe deposit box, mainly their passports, marriage certificate, Priya's birth certificate, and other things that she had no time to inspect. She also emptied out all the extra jewelry she'd stored there. It was substantial, thank goodness. Her parents had given her a lot of gold and diamonds over the years.

The conventional rationale behind giving a daughter jewels was this very scenario: if something happened to her husband and she needed instant cash, they would come in handy. Wasn't it ironic that that piece of ancient wisdom had come into play for her?

She'd always thought of it as some antiquated custom that was too obsolete for these modern times. But then again, she'd never pictured herself a widow at such a young age, either.

She informed the bank's manager that she had no more need for the safe deposit box, and that he could cancel the account. After signing the necessary forms, Isha asked the taxi driver to take her to Anvekar Jewelers in the heart of town.

At the jewelers', she took out three elaborate sets of gemstone jewelry, expensive but with the least sentimental value attached, and asked old Mr. Anvekar to give her a fair price for them. The old man was someone she and her mother had dealt with for many years. He gave her a puzzled look before bringing out his scale and jewelers loupe to examine the pieces.

"Are you sure you want to sell these sets, Isha? They are top quality and will be good for your daughter when she grows up," he said, casting a glance at Priya.

Isha took a deep, regretful breath and nodded. "I'm sure."

When he handed her the cash, the old man looked sympathetic, perhaps recognizing her desperate need.

Isha put the wad of cash in her handbag and walked out with

Priya. She knew Mr. Anvekar's speculative eyes followed her all the way to the taxi. That was another thing that would seem strange to him: a wealthy woman like her traveling in a dusty taxi when her family owned multiple cars and had a chauffeur.

The old jeweler would be sure to call his wife right away and share his news. Soon half the town would know Isha had sold some of her choice jewelry. And they would draw their own conclusions.

She ordered the taxi driver to take them to St. Mary's Convent and pulled Priya close.

A new chapter in both Priya's life and hers was about to begin.

Chapter 5

October 2006

The extreme discomfort in Isha's belly made her wince. With mounting anxiety she'd been waiting for this signal for a while. She was overdue by a full week. But now that she was nearly there, it caused her heart to flutter.

Excitement combined with dread had been nipping at her since she'd awakened at dawn that morning. And throughout the day, while she had read aloud to the children at the orphanage, sung nursery rhymes with them, and tended to their needs, the pain had put in an appearance every now and then, reminding her of the imminent arrival.

There had been small signs in the past couple of days—minor indications that could have fooled a neophyte, but not her. The nagging ache in her lower back and the intense pressure on her internal organs were gradually escalating. Isha had been through this once before, and knew what to expect.

Millions of women experienced similar trauma all over the universe, and yet there was stark fear in her heart at her impending ordeal, mostly because she was in it alone.

She didn't know what her future held. When the next contraction came, she had no more time to ruminate. The sheer agony of it forced her to focus on one thing and one thing only: the baby inside her womb conveying a clear signal that it was ready to face the world.

Taking short breaths, she massaged her swollen belly till the contraction subsided. This one was stronger and more painful than the last, the one that had racked her body less than three minutes ago.

Concentrating on the framed picture of Ganesh, she prayed for His help. Of course, most of her prayers in the recent past had gone unanswered, but that didn't mean He hadn't heard her, nor did it mean she was going to give up her staunch Hindu faith.

Next to Ganesh was a crucifix, reminding her that this was a convent. It was the only convent in Palgaum. Now it was her home. Thank goodness, when Isha had asked for help, the nuns, although hesitant at first, had been kind enough to let her stay there with Priya and earn her keep by working as a teacher's aide in their orphanage.

At the moment, Priya was sitting on an oblong *chatai*—a reed mat—placed on the gray flagstone floor, with a notebook open in front of her. Oblivious to her mother's distress, she sat with her legs crossed, engrossed in her task. She carefully wrote words in her notebook as she hummed a tune. She was doing her homework—learning to write in running-hand, or *cursive,* as the Americans called it.

Isha gazed fondly at the little head bent over her work. The curly brown hair was pulled back in the usual tight pigtails, secured with white ribbons. Her pink jeans were faded at the knees. The white T-shirt was getting a little too short. Soon Priya would need new clothes and shoes. At the moment, Isha had no idea how she was going to pay for those.

Priya had been her only solace in the past few months. Without her, Isha would have been almost suicidally depressed. But children had a way of keeping adults on an even keel. Priya had done her part in maintaining Isha's equilibrium when she had sunk to her nadir. The child had miraculously overcome her own grief in a hurry and then managed to pull Isha out of the murky depths by the sheer sweetness of her disposition.

The child lived up to her name—*beloved* in Sanskrit.

Priya looked up at her with a triumphant expression. "Mummy, look! My *B* words are just like Sister Alice's." She held her notebook under Isha's nose and pointed to the words. "See?"

Feigning surprise, Isha widened her eyes. "You're right! Your handwriting is getting better and better, pumpkin." Isha was delighted with Priya's progress. Her little girl was learning exceptionally fast since she'd entered first standard, much faster than her classmates. That was what her report cards indicated.

An angelic smile transformed Priya's oval face into a vision of dimples, starry eyes, and even white teeth, except for the one missing lower tooth that had fallen out only days ago. "That's what Sister Alice told me, too."

Isha's maternal heart warmed with pride. "That's wonderful!"

In the next second, Isha had a strong contraction, making her wince. "Oh God—"

Priya's smile vanished. "Mummy, are you sick?"

"I'm . . . in pain . . . dear," Isha managed to gasp.

The homework entirely forgotten, Priya stared at Isha with wide eyes. "Is the baby coming?" She'd been told a little bit about the pain associated with labor and childbirth, so she wouldn't panic when it happened.

"Yes." Isha shifted in the chair to try to ease the agony. It was time to summon Mother Regina and Mother Dora. Mother Regina was the elderly Italian nun who was also the principal of the school and chief administrator of the convent. Mother Dora was the Indian nurse-midwife who took care of the everyday medical needs of the convent's residents.

Isha had been putting off calling the two nuns for the last hour or more. *Let the contractions get a little stronger before I ask for help,* she'd convinced herself. Seeking assistance was still alien to her, despite the fact that she'd been forced to do it time and again lately, much of it from strangers, no less.

"Is it hurting a lot?" Priya stood up and bit her lower lip, telling Isha that her little girl's nerves were tightening. She was a compassionate child.

"Yes," replied Isha, now having ridden the wave of pain. "But I'm not sick, so don't be scared. It always hurts a little when a baby's coming. As soon as it comes out, the pain goes away."

"Why does a baby hurt?" Priya put a hesitant hand on Isha's belly.

Isha smiled and smoothed her daughter's stray curls away from her face. "It's the way God meant it to be. Sometimes good things come with a little pain attached. Remember what your PE teacher, Miss Maria, always repeats in your physical education class? 'No pain, no gain.'"

"But in PE we don't have babies."

Despite her discomfort, Isha couldn't help laughing at the innocent remark. "Thank goodness for that." Only a child could think in such quaintly logical terms.

"Do you want me to call Mother Regina?" Priya asked.

"Yes." With some difficulty Isha rose from the heavy armchair the nuns had generously moved into her room so she could relax in it when her feet swelled up and her back hurt. "I'm going to the bathroom now. Go tell Mother Regina that the baby's coming."

"Okay." Seemingly relieved at being able to do something constructive for her mother, Priya ran out of the room. Isha watched her race down the long corridor, her skinny legs moving at lightning speed, her pigtails waving like a moth's wings.

With slow, careful steps Isha went halfway down that same hallway to the row of toilets. Her bladder had been working overtime in the past several months, as expected, but the past week had been worse than ever. That was when she'd known her uterus had descended in preparation for birth. The nervous jitters had been increasing since then.

How in heaven's name was she going to raise two children on her own? She was already a burden on the nuns. They were feeding two mouths at the moment. Soon there'd be three.

Moments later, as she came out of the bathroom, she felt another one of those killer contractions coming on, and she stopped in the corridor. Leaning against the wall, she started taking quick, shallow breaths. She heard Priya and Mother Regina coming up behind her.

Mother Regina caught her by the shoulders. "Come, my dear. Let me help you back to your room."

A buxom woman who easily weighed about a hundred kilos, well over two hundred pounds, Mother Regina let Isha lean on her and trudge back to the room. Priya walked beside them with a pinched look. With her pregnant belly protruding from her slim frame, Isha's gait was more like a waddle—a walking penguin.

She went to her cot and lay down. "Thank you, Mother," she managed to murmur.

Mother Regina slipped a large sheet of rubber padding underneath Isha's loose kaftan and adjusted it in preparation for the coming event. Then she studied Isha for a second, her bright blue eyes narrowed in thought. "How far apart are the contractions?"

"About a minute and a half."

"Then you're ready. I will get Mother Dora," she said. "Is there anything you need while I fetch her?"

Isha glanced at her daughter. "Could you please make sure Priya is kept occupied while the baby comes?"

"Certainly." Mother Regina took Priya's hand. "Come on, Priya, let us go tell Mother Dora that your baby sister is about to come."

Priya shook her head. "I want to stay with Mummy. I want to see my baby." She had taken to calling the unborn child "my baby" ever since Isha had explained to her that the two of them were in this together, and that the baby was going to need both of them.

"You can see your baby when she comes, dear. Until then your Mummy needs Mother Dora to take care of her."

"Can I stay, please . . . ?" Priya tugged on Mother Regina's hand.

Mother Regina wasn't known for her patience. Isha knew that from experience. She had a few scars on her knuckles from her own student days at St. Mary's, inflicted by the sharp edge of Mother Regina's infamous ruler. So she wasn't surprised when Mother Regina's face hardened. "No! Pick up your home-work and let us go do it with the other children."

It broke Isha's heart to see Priya's lower lip tremble and the tears gather in her eyes. But what could she do under the cir-cumstances other than let Mother Regina take the child away and keep her in a secure place?

Despite the nun's forbidding and sometimes cruel ways of disciplining children, Isha knew her child would be safe with the older woman. As the next wave of pain started to crest, Isha watched Priya quietly pick up her book and pencil and follow Mother Regina out the door.

Priya turned around one last time to look at her, the tears now rolling down her cheeks. Isha managed to send her an en-couraging smile. "Go, sweetie. I'll be okay."

A few minutes later, Mother Dora appeared with a bucket of hot water, a steel tray with some formidable-looking surgical in-struments (to be used if needed until an obstetrician could ar-rive), and some towels and sheets.

She looked frail in her heavy white cotton habit. The starched white cap with its black border seemed to overwhelm her tiny cocoa-brown face. "Don't look so worried, my dear. We'll take care of this," she assured Isha.

"I'm trying . . . but babies can sometimes be born with prob-lems, right?" There was no incubator or resuscitation equip-ment if the baby needed them. How could she not worry? The next contraction was so painful that Isha groaned. She couldn't wait for her ordeal to be over.

Mother Dora wiped the sweat gathering on Isha's brow with a towel. "We may be able to ease your worries about the baby. The orphans are scheduled for their inoculations tomorrow, and the pediatrician will be here to do that."

"He comes *here* to vaccinate them?" Isha's eyes went wide.

"Oh, yes." Mother Dora looked amused. "I know it's hard to imagine a man in a convent, but it's necessary, and the doctor is very kind and reliable." She glanced at Isha. "Maybe Mother Regina can request him to take a look at your new baby."

"That would be nice. Would you mind mentioning it to Mother Regina?"

"Not at all, my dear."

Isha took a deep, relieved breath. "Thank you." The bedside clock read 8:34 PM. She hoped the baby would come quickly.

"Let's pray that all goes well." Mother Dora adjusted her glasses, joined her hands before the crucifix on the wall and recited the Lord's Prayer. "Our Father, who art in heaven . . . Amen." Then she made a sign of the cross and turned her attention to Isha.

Isha closed her eyes in an effort to brace herself for the next contraction. This one was so powerful that she felt it bearing down on her belly like a mega-ton truck. As the torture peaked, then slowly began to recede, she said one last prayer before concentrating on bringing her second child into the world.

Just before the excruciating pain gripped her one more time, her gaze went to the window and the moon outside. She'd been observing that moon rising in the night sky for a while, a cool and perfect yellow circle. There was a mystical quality about it.

That's when she recalled something in total amazement, something she'd tucked away in a remote corner of her brain and hadn't paid much attention to—the holy man's prediction that her baby would be born on an auspicious night. How could she have forgotten his prophetic words?

Tonight was *Kojagari Purnima!*

As her pregnancy had progressed and her life had become more complicated, Isha had discounted his prediction as hocus-pocus, a crazy old man's ramblings. But now it seemed he was right on target—at least about the baby's birthday. Could it be why the baby was late by a week? Was she waiting for this particular night to come into the world?

So, the *sadhu* could be a genuine oracle! Could he be right about the other things, too?

Baby Diya Tilak came into the world at exactly 9:02 PM. Other than the high-pitched wail typical of a newborn upon its arrival, she seemed rather quiet. She was thin. Since there was no scale to tell Isha how much the infant weighed, she could only guess. Three kilos or so, perhaps? About six and a half pounds. But then Isha was a petite woman, and since Priya had been a small baby, she had expected this one would be, too.

Nonetheless, the little one was perfect and Mother Dora had pronounced her healthy. All her fingers and toes were well formed and she had soft brown hair with lighter streaks, just like Priya's had looked at birth.

Isha gazed on the wrinkled pink bundle wrapped in a once-white sheet lying beside her, and breathed in her scent, the distinctive smell of a newborn. No matter how many times a mother did this, it still felt like a miracle each time, she thought, wiping away the tears. The tears just wouldn't stop flowing for some reason.

She knew all about postpartum depression. She'd been through it after Priya's birth. But this time the melancholy was of a different sort. She longed to have Nikhil beside her. Of course, if he were alive, she would have been giving birth in a comfortable private hospital with her doctor and nurses attending on her.

Nevertheless, in spite of the limited resources, Mother Dora had successfully brought her baby into the world, and Isha was very grateful.

The baby's name, Diya, meant "light." Maybe it was sheer coincidence, but once again the *sadhu*'s words came back to Isha. Diya probably was a child born to bring light into her life. The past few months had been discolored by the grim shades of death and destruction and loss of home. But now, in looking at the sleeping infant, it was like discovering the first green shoot poking its head out of the ground after a long, hard winter, heralding the promise of spring—a reaffirmation of life.

Nikhil was no longer there to share in the joy of Diya's birth, but the child was still a product of their love. In all the darkness surrounding her, Isha was determined to introduce some brightness. Diya and Priya would hopefully bring that.

The new baby looked so much like Nikhil, it was heartrending. She had his hazel eyes, just like her big sister. Light-colored eyes like gray, hazel, light brown and even blue, combined with fair skin tones, were typical characteristics of the caste Isha and Nikhil belonged to—the *Koknastha* Brahmin community. They were a legacy of the early European settlers, whose blood had mixed with that of the local Indians centuries ago.

It was now past eleven o'clock. Mother Dora was long gone. Priya, after she'd had a chance to make sure her mummy was okay, had kissed the baby's cheek, looking thrilled about being the big sister. Now Priya was fast asleep on her bedroll on the floor, enjoying the kind of blissful sleep only children can lose themselves in. Forgotten were the earlier tears and Mother Regina's reprimand. The arrival of a new baby and hence a new doll to play with had meant putting aside everything else for one night.

The birth of a healthy child should have been a joyous occasion. Instead, Isha was here, in a gloomy convent—a cold building with ten-foot-high stone walls surrounding the compound, and with no more than a midwife to help her in delivering the baby. But as a young, nearly penniless widow and mother of two small children, who had nowhere else to go, this was better than being out on the streets.

At least here she had a place to sleep, eat, and keep her girls safe and dry. For now this was home.

Chapter 6

Harish Salvi plopped into his office chair. This was his much-needed five-minute afternoon break, when Rama, his Man Friday, made him a cup of tea. Harish took a sip of the now-tepid brew. Peeling off his glasses, he closed his tired eyes for a blessed moment. *Phew,* what a day!

The latest strain of the flu virus had turned out to be more invasive than anyone had anticipated. He'd seen more children with the flu and its secondary complications in the past week than he had in the past three years put together. Ear and throat infections, sinusitis, bronchitis, pneumonia—he'd treated them all.

Gulping down the rest of the tea, he put aside the cup and looked at his wristwatch. Nearly five o'clock and he still had three more patients to see. After that he had to go to St. Mary's Convent to inoculate the orphans. He hoped those kids hadn't caught the flu bug, too. Now *that* would be a disaster, since they lived together in such cramped quarters with minimal hygiene.

When Harish had started his pediatric practice in Palgaum a few years ago, he'd never imagined his life would get this hectic. But here he was, often working six days a week, and on some days, up to twelve hours or more.

Of course, he was earning a considerable income, much more than he had anticipated. After growing up in a lower-middle-class household, one of the reasons he'd pursued medicine was to be able to have a better life. Living in a tiny, badly ventilated,

two-room rented home in the heart of town along with a sib-
ling, and watching his father struggling to raise the two of them
on a schoolteacher's salary, had taught Harish the value of striv-
ing for more. But money was not his sole incentive for going
into private practice.

Fortunately he was brighter and more motivated than most
of his contemporaries. He had qualified for a scholarship at the
local science college and then again at a medical college, en-
abling him to become a pediatrician.

The only problem with all this work was that he didn't have
much time for a personal life. He was thirty years old, and his
old-fashioned parents wanted to see him married, but he had yet
to make time to meet a girl from amongst the several his mother
had chosen after having matched his horoscope with theirs.

The intercom on his desk buzzed, rousing Harish from his
thoughts.

"Doctor-saheb, patient number nineteen is waiting," announced Saroj, his nurse-receptionist. She had a loud, gruff
voice that belied her petite size. In spite of using the respectful
handle of *saheb*—sir—she was more like his mother. With two
grown sons and three grandchildren, she considered herself old
enough to boss Harish around. In deference to her age, everyone
called her Saroj-bayi, including Harish.

But Saroj-bayi's authoritarian attitude had its advantages. It
helped in keeping his more rambunctious young patients in line.
All she had to do was toss them a certain look over the rims of
her glasses, and the little hooligans went back to their seats and
hung their heads.

The door opened and Saroj-bayi stuck her head inside for a
moment. "Just wanted to warn you that your next patient is the
Motwani boy," she informed him in a conspiratorial whisper.
"He has a nasty cough. My guess is bronchitis, and his mother
is very agitated."

"Oh no!" Harish groaned. The Motwani boy was a spoiled
brat. He was the Motwanis's only son and he'd been born after
three daughters. As usual, Mrs. Motwani would expect Harish

to find an instant cure for her son's ailment. If only it were that simple!

Putting his glasses back on, he rose from his chair. "Send them in." He opened the connecting door to the examination room and went in.

It was well after six o'clock by the time the last patient left. "Time to go to the orphanage, Doctor-saheb," Saroj-bayi reminded him.

"Thanks." He didn't need reminding, but she delighted in keeping a strict eye on his schedule. "Could you please help me pack the supplies?"

"Of course." Saroj was quick and efficient in her ways. In spite of all the hours she'd worked in the office, her starched white sari still looked crisp and wrinkle-free. Her mostly gray hair was neatly twisted into a bun at her nape. For her age, she was amazingly fit and trim.

Within minutes she had a cardboard box filled with vaccines and other items ready to go. "You should start thinking about charging those nuns for your services, you know," she said blandly. It wasn't the first time she'd expressed her opinion on the subject.

"That's out of the question." Harish took off his lab coat and put it on a hanger. "These are orphans we're treating. The nuns are barely able to feed them, let alone pay for medical care."

Saroj-bayi rolled her eyes. "I know that, but if you keep giving free treatment, how are you going to provide for a wife and children?"

He couldn't help smiling. He knew his mother and Saroj conspired behind his back about ways to nudge him toward marriage. "Why worry when I don't have a wife and children?"

"Then it is about time you got yourself a wife," she sniffed. "That poor mother of yours is longing to see you settled. Right now she has half a dozen nice girls lined up for you."

He patted her shoulder. "One of these days I'll see what I can do to make Mamma and you happy."

"If you keep putting it off, all the good girls will be taken and you will be stuck with some ugly old maid with dentures and a balding head."

With an amused laugh he slung his medical bag over his shoulder and grabbed the box. "Thanks for helping me. I'll see you tomorrow."

He put his gear in the trunk of his compact four-year-old Ford, got behind the wheel, and headed out to the convent. It was a trip he made every three months. This was something he looked forward to, even though he didn't get paid for it. It was his modest contribution to the community. He was blessed, and as a good but not devout Hindu, this was the only way he could give something in charity.

When he got to the locked steel gates of the convent, he stopped, pulled out his mobile phone, and called Mother Regina's number so someone could let him in. Returning the phone to his pocket, he smiled to himself. The nuns took their job of protecting the girls under their guardianship very seriously indeed.

However, neither stone walls nor steel gates could prevent the really tenacious and enterprising ones from sneaking in or out. The previous year's bizarre episode was a prime example. In spite of the keen-eyed nuns watching over their wards day and night, one of their teenagers had still managed to become pregnant.

The baby's father was a boy from St. John's School for Boys, located across the street from the convent. It was run by Catholic priests. St. John's was Harish's alma mater.

Nobody could figure out how those two teenagers had managed to meet, let alone have sex. It was still a mystery, but a testimony to human ingenuity.

Eventually, the boy and girl had been expelled from school and each sent home to their parents. And that's where it ended. The nuns never talked about it afterward. Anything that sinful wasn't meant to be discussed in the hallowed atmosphere of a convent.

A minute later, a novice came to open the gates for him. Harish drove his car around to the back of the cluster of buildings. That's where the old stone boardinghouse and the orphanage were located. The more modern brick buildings facing the street were reserved for classrooms, where day-students as well as boarders studied together.

The same novice who had opened the gates appeared from somewhere. "Good evening, Dr. Salvi. I'm Sister Rose," she said. "I'll be helping you with the children this evening. I can carry some of your supplies if you'd like."

"Thank you, Sister Rose. Appreciate the help," he said and handed her his bag. He hadn't seen her before. Like the other novices, she was very young and didn't wear a cap. They were also referred to as Sister. He had learned that the white cap with black border was something that came after they took their final vows and shaved their heads. That's when they dropped the title of Sister and took on the venerable title of Mother. Until then, they usually braided their hair and twisted it in the back in a severe knot.

He picked up the box from the trunk and followed her brisk steps into the building. She looked like a teenager—fresh-faced and innocent—too young to give up everything the world had to offer and embrace this austere lifestyle. Was she an orphan, too? Had she chosen this type of existence for herself, or was it the only option for a homeless child raised in a convent?

The next two hours were spent in vaccinating the children against a variety of childhood ailments. He needed extra help from one other nun besides Sister Rose to hold the children and comfort them while he performed his work.

As always, there were lots of tears. It came with the territory, so he always brought a large bag of lollipops. A brightly colored lollipop went a long way in putting an end to the fussing, and it worked effectively. And for these poor children, a lollipop was a luxury—pure delight on a stick.

The pathetic faces of the children never failed to touch him. Many of them had been abandoned on the convent's doorstep.

There were both boys and girls. The boys stayed at the convent until they turned five and then they got moved to some orphanage in another town that took in only boys.

No matter what their gender, they all seemed to be starved for affection. The more outgoing ones clung to his legs and often refused to let go. He gave them a hug and a lollipop. The nuns had to pry them away from him.

Harish didn't consider himself an emotional man, but at times he had to suppress tears when that happened. The little tykes nearly broke his heart.

They were all very thin and suffered from malnutrition in various degrees. The nuns did what they could, but there was only so much they could provide with their severely limited budget and staff.

He admired the nuns' efforts and tried to help out in whatever way he could. He gave them free samples of vitamins, baby food, over-the-counter medications, and first-aid supplies. He often wished he could do more, but there were restrictions on his time and money, too.

Exhausted and hungry, he finally put away his supplies, pulled off the rubber gloves and tossed them in the rubbish bin.

He saw Mother Regina coming his way, a smile warming her wrinkled face. Her ample hips seemed to bounce as she hurried. He had no idea how old she was. He suspected she was at least eighty. But she was a bundle of energy, and despite her enormous proportions, always moved nimbly. He had never seen her sitting down.

"Thank you so much for everything, Dr. Salvi," she said to him. "God bless you. You are our messenger from Jesus."

Harish smiled. "I do what I can, Mother."

"But it takes a generous heart to do what you do, sir. You are a good man." She was Italian by birth, and despite her very proper English, the slightly soft accent persisted. "So, tell me, Doctor, how are our children doing?"

"As well as can be expected. And I'm relieved that the flu hasn't spread here. It's been a difficult epidemic this year."

"Well then, we shall pray that it never comes here." She did a quick sign of the cross. "If it is not too much trouble, may I ask another favor of you?"

"Certainly." Harish's eyes went to his wristwatch. It was nearly nine o'clock. What could Mother Regina want at this hour?

"A baby was born here last night and I was wondering if you might spare some time to check out the little one."

His brows climbed in surprise. "A baby born *here?* You didn't have another . . . um . . ." A second unwanted pregnancy in less than a year was a bit much for a convent.

Mother Regina's blue eyes went wide behind her bifocals. "Oh no! Nothing of *that* sort! The mother is a young widow. This is a very unusual and tragic case. She recently lost her husband, and because of serious problems in her in-laws' home, she was forced to leave them. She no longer has family of her own, you see."

"How did she end up here?"

"She's one of our former students, and being a mother of one child and about to have another, we could not turn her away when she asked for help."

Harish nodded. "I understand."

She looked at him with that questioning tilt of her head. "You will see this child, then?"

"Of course." How could he say no to such a simple request? He picked up his bag and motioned to her to lead the way. His stomach rumbled, reminding him how hungry he was.

As he followed her through the heavy steel door he realized he was stepping into normally forbidden territory. He had never seen this part of the boardinghouse. No men were allowed here. In fact, they were barred from most of the areas except the offices, classrooms, and the orphanage—and that only when strictly necessary.

Needless to say, he was curious, so he looked around as he followed the aging nun down a long corridor with rooms situated on either side. All the doors were shut, which meant the boarders were either studying or sleeping at this hour.

The nuns probably didn't tolerate breaking of any house

rules regarding lights out or anything else that was part of their rigid lifestyle. He knew for a fact that the girls were expected to wake up very early and attend mass at the on-site chapel before they ate breakfast.

The passage was dimly lit. The nun's sturdy black shoes and his own sounded loud on the gray flagstone floor. There was a faint acidic smell of stale urine combined with disinfectant in the air—an indication of toilets somewhere nearby.

At the end of the corridor, Mother Regina knocked on a closed door. "Isha."

He heard a muffled reply. "Mother Regina?"

"Yes, dear. I have the doctor with me. He's here to examine the baby."

"One second, Mother," said the soft, feminine voice. They waited until she called, "Please come in."

They walked into the small room. The woman said, "Praised be Jesus and Mary, Mother," in the standard way to greet a nun in this particular convent.

"Forever," said Mother Regina, using the usual response to the greeting.

It took Harish a second to adjust to the dim light coming from the single low-wattage lightbulb dangling from the ceiling. He looked around the quarters.

A narrow cot, covered with a faded green bedspread, hugged the wall on one side and an ancient nightstand stood next to it. It had a jug of water, a tumbler, and a short stack of children's books.

On the floor next to the bed was a bedroll with a child sprawled over it. He could see a small head with curly brown hair resting on a pillow. A little pink ear and cheek were visible, but the rest of the face was buried in there somewhere. The tiny body was covered with a sheet. The child appeared to be asleep.

Three large, bulging suitcases were stacked against the far wall. There was no wardrobe, or dresser, so the residents obviously lived out of their suitcases. The room was small and cramped, especially for three individuals, one of them being an infant that needed a lot of paraphernalia.

After a quick sweep of the room, his gaze latched on to the tableau in the chair by the window. A woman sat in it with a small bundle swaddled in white in her arms. It looked like she might have been nursing the baby. She had a small towel over her shoulder, covering one side of her chest. She wore a simple yellow kaftan.

When he studied her face more closely, he nearly gasped. "Isha Ketkar!"

She looked up, and her eyes went wide. She seemed equally astounded to see him.

Chapter 7

It took Isha a few seconds to recover from the surprise. She couldn't remember his name. Mother Dora hadn't mentioned it yesterday, either. This was going to be embarrassing since he had addressed her by her name—her maiden name of Ketkar.

She had recognized that face at once. It hadn't changed much over the years. This was a man she'd often seen in college. He was a year senior to her, if her memory served her correctly. She managed to smile. "It's Isha Tilak now."

"Oh . . . of course. I'm sorry, Isha Tilak." He looked a little flustered. "What a surprise to see you here."

"I'm sure it is a surprise. It has been many years." Who wouldn't be surprised to see someone like her, a Brahmin woman, residing in a convent, and giving birth to a baby there to boot? It was humiliating to come across someone she'd known in her younger days, when she'd had her looks, youth, and the promise of a bright future.

Mother Regina looked at her with a puzzled frown. "You know Dr. Salvi?"

Salvi! It came back to Isha in a flash. His name was Harish Salvi. Saved by Mother Regina! So the quiet, studious boy with the owlish glasses had gone on to become a doctor. Not surprising at all. He was so withdrawn compared to most of the other boys in college, one hardly noticed him.

She couldn't remember ever talking to him. The only thing she could recall clearly about him was his scholastic record. His name was synonymous with all the top academic honors in those days. At the annual college award ceremony, he was called to the podium again and again amidst thunderous applause to receive his shiny silver trophies and certificates.

"Dr. Salvi and I were contemporaries in college," she explained to Mother Regina.

Dr. Salvi busied himself with his medical bag and pulled out his paraphernalia: stethoscope, reflex hammer, tongue depressor, otoscope, pen, and writing pad. "I was a year senior to Mrs. Tilak, but you know how it is in a small town—everyone knows everyone else."

"I see." Mother Regina seemed satisfied with the explanation. "Why don't you put the baby on the bed, Isha, so the doctor can examine her?"

Isha tried to get up from the depths of the sagging chair, but the pain that shot through her with the abrupt movement was so sharp that she flinched and blew out a shallow breath. Her perineal tear was still painful and it hurt to move. Mother Regina would never understand such things. Only a woman who'd gone through childbirth would know.

But the doctor immediately stepped around the slumbering Priya and came forward, holding out his arms. "Here, let me take the child. You can stay right there." He gently lifted the baby and placed her on the cot.

With infinite care he pulled off the sheet until she lay with nothing on except a cotton nappy, which looked gray with age and years of washing with cheap soap. Mother Dora had produced a supply of those nappies from somewhere.

Exposed to the cooler air and deprived of her cozy cocoon, the baby started to thrash around and fuss. The little wrinkled face scrunched into a tight, red ball of indignation. Isha's immediate instinct was to go to her, but she knew this wasn't the time for it.

The baby needed to be examined by a qualified doctor, and she was glad Mother Regina had very thoughtfully arranged for Dr. Salvi to come all the way up here to do it. Knowing how strict the nuns were about men coming into this area, Isha realized the aging nun had broken a few sacred rules to do her a favor.

Isha watched as Dr. Salvi carefully examined the baby. He was gentle and thorough as he scrutinized every inch, from fuzzy head to tiny toes. He took his time about it and made notes on his notepad. All the while, Mother Regina studied him, too.

While he went about his task, Isha had time to notice other details about him. He was dressed in neat khaki pants and a tan-and-white-checked shirt. His brown leather shoes had a polished gleam. His clothes, although not fashionable, were of superior quality. The scholarly look, with short cropped hair and rather thick glasses, was still the same, but now he looked more mature, comfortable in his skin. Very professional.

He had the calm, dependable look and demeanor of a medical practitioner.

Isha would have liked a few private moments with the doctor to ask him questions and get a few recommendations on the baby's care, but with Mother Regina hovering over them, it was impossible. Besides, there was no way the old woman would leave a young man and woman alone, no matter how professional the relationship.

Meanwhile, piqued about being prodded, turned over, and having a cold stethoscope placed on her chest, the baby let out a gusty wail.

"Good lungs," pronounced the doctor with a pleased smile.

Disturbed by the baby's cries, Priya woke up. She sat up and looked around, seemingly disoriented. "Mummy!"

"I'm right here, sweetie," Isha answered, hoping the crying baby hadn't disturbed the other girls in their rooms. If this happened every night, the nuns were likely to toss her and her children out.

Fortunately the orphanage was housed in an adjoining building, so the really small children weren't nearby. The nuns had given Isha a room of her own in the older girls' boardinghouse, where she could keep her girls. Priya and she could eat in the dining room in return for the work she did at the orphanage. They couldn't afford to pay any wages to Isha, so room and board were her main forms of reimbursement, plus Priya could attend school for free.

Seeing a stranger and Mother Regina, Priya sprang to her feet and snuggled close to her mother. "Who is that?" she asked, glaring at Dr. Salvi.

"Shh, it's bad manners to speak that way," scolded Isha, hoping Mother Regina wouldn't chastise the child for her behavior. "This is Dr. Salvi. He has kindly offered to examine your baby sister. Please say *namaste* to him."

Instead of greeting him, Priya continued to stare at him. Then her gaze went to Mother Regina. "Why is he touching our baby?"

"Sorry, doctor, she has become very possessive about the baby," explained Isha, hoping he wasn't offended by Priya's surliness.

"Perfectly normal at her age," said the doctor, taking it in stride. Then he turned to Priya. "I need to touch your sister so I can make sure she's healthy."

Priya's eyes were still round and ripe with suspicion.

He didn't seem to be bothered by her guarded gaze. "What's your name?" he asked her.

"Priya Tilak," the child answered after a long pause.

"That's a very nice name," he said. "Do you have one for your baby sister yet?"

A little less leery of him now, Priya nodded. "Diya."

"Priya and Diya!" He raised a brow at Priya, pretending surprise. "How did you manage to find an equally pretty name? And one that rhymes with yours? You must be very clever."

That melted Priya's frosty attitude in an instant, and even elicited a pleased smile. "Mummy chose the name, not me."

"Then your Mummy must be clever, too." He glanced at Isha with a hint of conspiracy in his dark eyes.

Isha returned the look. It was he that was clever. With very little effort he'd managed to break through Priya's reserve. The discovery came as one more surprise. When had this quiet and serious man become so friendly and witty? Was he always like that, even in his youth?

Entirely comfortable now with the doctor, Priya slowly

shifted from her mother's side to stand beside him. Natural curiosity about what he was doing to the baby was another possible reason. Pointing to the dark stub sticking out of the baby's navel, she wrinkled her nose. *"Eew!* What is *that?"*

"That's her navel, her belly button," replied Dr. Salvi, the picture of patience. "In a few days this will fall off and her belly button will look just like yours."

"Oh." Priya looked at the baby with awe. "Why is she so red?"

Mother Regina sighed. "Regular little chatterbox, isn't she? So full of questions. In the classroom, her teachers often have to tell Priya to hush up."

Dr. Salvi shook his head. "That's okay, Mother. Children need to be curious. Their brains are able to develop and grow in a healthy manner only through inquisitiveness and experimentation."

Isha realized that in his own way the good doctor had put the old nun in her place. Good for him, she thought with an inward smile. The nuns were way too obsessed with discipline. They often managed to suppress and gradually kill a child's natural curiosity and spirit. That's probably why some of those orphans seemed so listless and slow to learn. She'd often wondered why such a large and diverse group of children showed similar mental and emotional characteristics.

Over the next few minutes, the doctor answered Priya's long list of questions in terms easy enough for a child to understand. He had a well-modulated voice that was both soothing and commanding at the same time.

Isha found herself immensely interested in the way he explained things. She realized she was learning a few fascinating facts about babies along with her daughter. Mother Regina, too, was paying serious attention to him. If he weren't a doctor, he probably would have made an excellent teacher.

Priya seemed impressed at having an adult treat her like a grownup. Meanwhile, the baby, perhaps because her nappy and chemise were now back in place, had gone from bawling to soft whimpering.

Dr. Salvi, having completed his exam, swaddled the baby once again. That quieted her down to the point of drowsiness.

Her translucent eyelids were beginning to close. He returned her to Isha's arms. "She's a healthy baby."

"Everything is normal?" Isha looked at him, trying to keep the anxiety to herself.

"Yes. Nothing to worry about." He inclined his head toward Priya. "Who's Priya's pediatrician?"

"Dr. Bajaj."

"I'm assuming Priya has been inoculated on a regular schedule by Dr. Bajaj?"

"Yes, always. Nikhil . . . uh . . . my late husband and I made sure Priya had regular checkups. She had her boosters five months ago."

He nodded. "That's good. We only need to concern ourselves with Diya at this time, then. If you're planning to nurse her, she won't need any other kind of nutrition right now. But if you feel she's not getting enough, you might want to consider supplementing with a good formula."

"Oh." Isha wondered how she was going to get baby formula. With all the things going on in her life, she hadn't even thought about such things. Formula cost a lot of money and she needed to save what little she had for emergencies.

The doctor must have noticed her anxious expression. "I have plenty of samples in my office. I can drop them off with Mother Regina tomorrow." He turned to the nun. "Is that okay, Mother?"

"Of course," said Mother Regina. "It is very kind of you, Dr. Salvi. We are very grateful."

Isha seconded the sentiment. "Yes, Doctor. Thank you so much for coming all this way to do me a favor. I really appreciate it."

"Please, don't even mention it," he said with a shake of his head. He turned to address Priya once again. "Priya, are you going to help your mummy take care of your sister?"

Priya gave him a solemn nod. "I get to hold her bottle."

"Then you're in charge of the bottle. And you have to be careful with Diya because she's a tiny baby and very delicate."

"Okay." Priya looked thrilled at being treated like a responsible adult.

He pulled a business card out of his pocket and scribbled something on the back of it before handing it to Isha. "If you have any questions, please contact me. Diya's going to need her first immunization against tuberculosis right away. I'll stop by later in the week and give it to her. At six weeks she'll need to get the first doses of DPT and OPV."

Both Isha and Mother Regina were knowledgeable about the acronyms and he seemed to assume they were. She looked at the card, then back at him. "Thank you very much." She knew she'd never be able to repay such kindness on the part of a stranger, or near-stranger. She watched him repack his bag and follow Mother Regina out.

As soon as Mother Regina closed the door behind them, Isha looked at the back of the card where he had scribbled something. It took her a moment to decipher the writing: *"Call me if you have questions or need help."* His mobile number was indicated next to it. Puzzled, she read the message once again. Why had he given her his mobile number?

He obviously didn't want Mother Regina to see the note. It was very generous of him to want to help, but Isha didn't think she would take him up on his offer. She needed help for sure, but what was she going to say to a stranger? How could she tell him about her circumstances?

Dr. Salvi probably had a wife and children of his own. He'd never understand what he'd consider Isha's irrational decision to put her children's lives in jeopardy by walking out on her in-laws and the comforts they provided.

But she couldn't live like this forever, either. Maybe if she did reach out to Harish Salvi, he could help her find a job or something. As a local doctor, he must have a few connections. But with two small children depending on her and with no more than a bachelor's degree to her name, what was she qualified to do? Besides, half the town knew her as Nikhil Tilak's widow and the daughter-in-law of Srikant and Vidula Tilak. What would be their reaction if she applied for a job?

She was in a tight spot. Would she ever find her way out of it?

Asking Priya to watch the sleeping baby for a few minutes,

she took the opportunity to use the bathroom and wash all the dirty nappies that had been accumulating all day. Every little chore was such an effort. She just wanted to lie down and rest. But there was no question of rest. She had promised the nuns she'd resume work within four weeks.

Later, after she had hung the nappies out to dry on the clothesline outside the bathrooms, it took her a while to get Priya to go back to sleep and to get herself and the baby settled. Diya woke up nearly every hour, hungry and wet.

For the hundredth time Isha wished for the marvelous help she'd had when Priya was born. Back then, she'd gone to her mother's house to have the baby in the conservative Indian tradition. Women went to their parents' home to have their babies, and in the process were pampered by their mothers.

Since her mother had also lived in Palgaum, Nikhil was there beside Isha in the delivery room, and then came to visit her and the baby every day, until he could take them both back to their own home. Isha hadn't had to lift a finger back then.

Sundari had been there exclusively to tend to her and the baby. She'd given both Isha and the infant Priya an oil massage every day, followed by a hot, leisurely bath.

It was heaven in those days. Both Sundari and Isha's mother had made sure Isha drank milk and ate nutritious foods to keep up her strength and generate plenty of breast milk for the newborn.

But her widowed mother had passed away three years ago, after losing her fight with breast cancer. Then, last summer, Nikhil had become a murder victim, and now Isha had no one to rely on but herself to raise her two children.

Fresh and nutritious food was only a dream. She was lucky if she could have a slice of bread and a boiled potato or carrot in the convent's meager dining hall. They served tiny portions of pork and beef, which she and Priya had never tasted, because it went against their Brahmin faith. Poor Priya literally gagged on the bland, uniformly gray food.

How could her idyllic life have taken such a sharp turn in such a short time?

* * *

As Harish reloaded his things into the car, he felt a strange kind of uneasiness. It had set in the minute he'd walked into that small, airless room in the boardinghouse. Now, nearly thirty minutes later, the feeling was still with him.

There was something odd about that scene, as if it didn't belong there, like seeing an exotic animal outside its natural habitat. It just didn't add up.

Isha Ketkar, or rather Isha Tilak, was the last person on earth he'd imagined he'd run into at a convent—as a resident, that is. When Mother Regina had mentioned a recent widow who'd come to seek asylum, he'd never expected someone like Isha.

What exactly had reduced her to this degree of destitution? She had to be desperate to beg the nuns to take her in. How heartbreaking was it to become a widow at such a young age and, moreover, to have been pregnant when it happened?

A minute later, he drove out of the convent compound and saw Sister Rose in the rearview mirror, shutting the gates behind him and slapping the iron padlock on them.

Despite the convent's location in the center of town, it might as well have been in a godforsaken desert. Once that lock was in place, the outside world probably ceased to exist for those living inside.

His thoughts remained centered on Isha as he maneuvered the car along the narrow, pedestrian- and bicycle-clogged streets. Recalling the rough, worn sheet her beautiful newborn baby was wrapped in, he sighed. An infant from a family like hers should have been dressed in spotless clothes and swaddled in a soft blanket. The older child, Priya, who seemed so bright and pretty and inquisitive, should have been sleeping on a proper bed and not a hard floor.

How was Isha going to manage the care of the children? Did she have any money at all or had she fled her in-laws' home with nothing? Had they abused her in some way? Was that why she had left them, or had they cast her out with no mercy? What kind of people were they?

In the next instant something triggered in his brain. The truth dawned on him. There were very few Tilaks in town. Her in-laws were probably the most prominent ones—owners of the largest tire distributorship in the state. They were wealthy folks and well-known in the area. And she'd said her husband's name was Nikhil.

As Harish slowly started to put together the missing pieces of the puzzle, he recalled the media frenzy some months ago surrounding Nikhil Tilak's puzzling and brutal murder. So, Isha had been married to the late Nikhil—a handsome, wealthy, charismatic businessman—every girl's dream husband. Why hadn't Harish made the connection immediately? Nikhil was just the sort of man he had imagined a girl like Isha would end up with.

Nikhil had been about three years senior to Harish in college, but Harish remembered how the girls had tripped over each other in trying to capture Nikhil's attention. He used to be the college tennis champion. He had a mediocre academic record, but he hadn't needed brilliant marks or advanced degrees since he had a thriving business handed to him on a platter.

Harish even recalled his own family talking about Nikhil's shocking homicide and shaking their heads in bewilderment.

"A brutal murder in a town like Palgaum!" his father had exclaimed. "Very strange. Someone must have had a reason to do it, because those Tilaks are involved in all that black-marketeering business."

His father was old-school and disdained illegal business practices. But he could be right. Powerful and wealthy people made enemies.

"Such a tragedy, no?" his mother had clucked. "Imagine what the man's parents are suffering. And that poor girl who was married to him is now a widow. She is so young, too."

As far as Harish knew, Nikhil's killer was still at large. The whole episode was a mystery.

Harish hadn't known then that Nikhil's widow was Isha Ketkar. After he'd left for medical school, Harish had not stayed in touch with Palgaum and most of his classmates, let alone kept up with who was married to whom. Nor did he read the local newspapers much. He watched some national news on TV every night and read the headlines *in The Times of India* each morning.

Besides, the papers had focused mainly on the bizarre killing and the ensuing investigation, with the names of the grieving family members rarely mentioned. Perhaps the Tilaks had requested the local media to keep their names out of the limelight so they could deal with their sorrow in private.

But now that he'd more or less solved the puzzle, Harish knew exactly who Isha was. Nonetheless, how had the Tilaks' widowed daughter-in-law ended up in such dire straits? That he couldn't understand.

Suddenly he realized he wasn't hungry anymore. Seeing the little girl, Priya, who was probably getting much less than the basic minimum nutrition, he no longer felt like eating.

Pulling out his mobile phone, he called his mother. "Mamma, I'm running very late and I'm not hungry. Please don't wait up for me." Although Harish had his own house, he generally ate his meals at his older, married brother's home, which also happened to be where his parents lived.

"But you can't miss a meal, Harish," his mother chided. "It is bad for you. You work so hard; you need to eat."

"I won't starve. I'll stop at a restaurant or something," he assured his mother.

"But restaurant food is not even hygienic, let alone healthy." His mother sounded disappointed at not being able to feed him her home-cooked meal.

"One restaurant meal won't kill me, Mamma. It's late. Go to bed and stop worrying about me." He didn't want to hurt her feelings, so he added, "I'll come over for breakfast tomorrow."

"Okay, then." That seemed to appease her. "I'm making *poori* and *bhaaji*," she added, perhaps hoping to entice him with the puffy fried bread and its traditional accompaniment: a spicy sautéed potato-and-onion dish seasoned with mustard and cumin seeds. He was spoiled in that respect. And it made him feel even guiltier when he thought about the sad, neglected faces of the kids at the orphanage.

Finally he decided to forego the restaurant as well. Parking his car in the portico of his modest house, he let himself in. It was a small, single-story bungalow with two bedrooms, an old-fashioned bathroom, a drawing room, a dining area, and a kitchen.

He had purchased it only months ago from an elderly couple. The neighborhood was desirable because of its prime location. Maybe someday he could get a big, rambling custom-built home like some of the other successful doctors in town. But for now, he was young and single, and this was plenty for his needs.

Inside his kitchen, he helped himself to a glass of milk and a banana. He didn't really taste any of it because his thoughts were occupied by Isha Tilak and her children. The woman had gone through labor only a day ago and she looked exhausted. She badly needed some rest.

He hoped she had a mobile phone at least and would make an effort to call him. He'd made it clear that he was willing to help her in any way he could. Under Mother Regina's watchful eye, the only way he could convey his offer to Isha was by way of that cryptic message he'd scribbled on the back of his calling card. Had she even thought of reading it?

In any case, he needed to make a list of some of the things he could give her. Picking up a notepad, he stood at the kitchen counter and started on it while he sipped the milk. Naturally, any medical care that the children needed, including inoculations, he could give her at no cost.

His list grew as he thought of more and more items: formula, first-aid supplies, baby soap and shampoo, nappies, talcum powder . . . What he didn't already have in his clinic, he could buy.

He decided he'd drop off all the items at the convent for her before he started work the following morning. When he slipped into bed sometime later and tried to sleep, he wondered why he was so deeply affected by the plight of one woman and her children. There were millions like them in the world, and yet he was fixated on Isha Tilak and her children.

Somewhere deep down, he knew the answer. Back in his college days, he'd had a crush on her, just like a lot of other boys had. She'd hardly even bothered to look at him. But then, no-body did, since he was a typical nerd who kept his bespectacled eyes glued to his books and on his dream of becoming a doctor.

Besides, Isha and he came from entirely different castes and circumstances. She was an upper-caste Brahmin girl from a well-to-do family while he was a poor non-Brahmin. Their parallel worlds were not meant to intersect at any time. In spite of all the modernization India had undergone, the caste system still ruled social interaction to a large extent.

With her smooth skin, attractive honey-colored eyes, and curly brown hair, Isha Ketkar could hold her own in any crowd. He had admired the petite, elegant girl with the sunny smile from afar, like one would gaze at something in an exclusive shop window or museum, wanting to touch it, wishing to take it home, but knowing all along that it was impossible.

After he'd gone off to medical college, she'd faded away, along with all his boyish interests. He had assumed that like all respectable girls, she had married, and had a happy home and a family. His life as a medical student had become too busy to think about girls or anything else. He had kept his focus strictly on his career goals.

And he'd achieved them. He was content.

However, tonight that sense of contentment was curiously absent. He had laid eyes once again on the fantasy girl of his student days. She was still as appealing as she was then, only a little more mature. And, oh, yes, she'd been married to a man her parents had picked for her with great care, and she had the projected two children. But other than those two things, she didn't seem to have that dream life he had envisioned for her. In-stead she was a widow. And she didn't appear to have what most wealthy widows had—enough money to live well.

So why was he getting upset over Isha Tilak's unfortunate fate? He couldn't find a logical answer. All he knew was that he felt compelled to do something for her—anything that would make her life easier. So he'd start helping her first thing in the morning.

Now that the monumental decision was made, maybe he could get some sleep.

Chapter 8

The boardinghouse was quiet at the moment, except for the shuffling footsteps of the elderly maid, Clara, who cleaned the bathrooms and floors every other day. It was nearly eleven in the morning and Priya was at school.

The boarders, young, active girls between the ages of nine and seventeen, made a racket each morning and noon as they rushed up and down the corridor, used the bathrooms, and gossiped and giggled before heading for breakfast or lunch, and then to the building next door that housed their classrooms. The dinner hour at sundown was the same way—noisy and boisterous—despite the nuns' censorious frowns and frequent reprimands.

Thank goodness for the stringent lights-out rules, which meant they went to bed early. It gave Isha some quiet time before she settled in for the night.

She watched her infant as she nursed hungrily. Finally, after a day and a half of suffering hunger pangs, the poor angel was getting some nutrition. Isha's milk had finally come in, and it was a relief. The child would have to survive on mother's milk for God knew how long. Eight to ten months was usually the maximum a baby could be nursed. After that, what was Isha going to feed her?

Just as she had finished nursing and had laid the baby against her shoulder to burp her, there was a knock on the door. Who could it be? Nobody ever came to visit her. "Come in," she called. "It's unlocked."

The door opened and two novices carried in a large cardboard box. Isha raised a brow at the two fresh-faced young women in their stiff white habits. "What is it?"

"We don't know. Mother Regina asked us to deliver it to you."

"Is she sure it's for me?"

They both nodded. "She said it's for the baby."

More puzzled than ever, Isha thanked them and they went on their way. Putting the snoozing baby down on the cot, she sat on the floor beside the box and ripped open the plastic tape holding the flaps together. She couldn't wait to see what it was. Who could have sent anything for Diya? Nobody even knew of her birth other than the nuns.

For a moment she wondered if her in-laws had experienced a change of heart. In the next instant she dismissed it as wishful thinking. Those people had no heart.

Discovering a folded sheet of paper inside the box, she began to read. There was something familiar about the handwriting. It took her a second to recognize it. Dr. Salvi! Again it took some time to decipher the scribbled words, but she managed to read it all the way through.

> *Dear Mrs. Tilak,*
>
> *Enclosed is the powder formula I promised for Baby Diya, and a few other items I felt you will need at this time. I added some chocolates and books for Priya and you. Please consider them a humble gift.*
>
> *Once again, please ring me if you need any help.*
>
> *—Harish Salvi*

After reading the letter once again, Isha put it aside and stared at the box for a long time before taking inventory of its contents. Incredible! These were gifts from someone she barely knew. She started lifting out each item, marveling at the thoughtfulness of the sender.

In addition to most everything an infant could need, from

nappies and pacifiers to baby lotion, there were two children's books and three bars of chocolate for Priya. And as if that weren't enough, he had two paperback novels for Isha.

He had thought of everything and everyone. Oh God!

She buried her face in her hands and burst into tears. Such kindness from a man she'd technically met yesterday. What was she going to say to him? Of course she couldn't accept such a generous gift. And yet, would she hurt his feelings if she returned it? Besides, most of the items she badly needed.

Had he asked his wife to help him with this package, or had he taken it upon himself to do it alone? But then again, the types of things in the box seemed to show a woman's touch, especially the paperbacks for her and the chocolate for Priya.

Whoever was responsible for the gift box was very caring and gracious. And the thought made her weep some more.

After a lot of deliberation, she decided she'd offer to pay for it. She wished the insurance money had come through. Didn't those lazy, callous people realize how desperate she was for that cash? Had they no idea how difficult it was for a widow with two children to make ends meet? The bureaucratic red tape in India was tangled beyond imagination.

All these years, with her sheltered way of life, she'd never had to deal with any of it directly. But now she knew exactly why Nikhil used to get so frustrated at times with the business of selling tires. She also realized why he had to go against his principles and bribe several people just to be able to get some simple things done. It was a matter of survival.

From deep inside her suitcase she pulled out the mobile phone Nikhil had bought for her a while ago—for use in an emergency. She'd kept it hidden from the nuns. They didn't approve of such expensive, modern gadgets. It went against their puritanical code of living.

But the mobile was the one thing she intended to keep. Fortunately, in spite of her lack of enthusiasm about owning a mobile phone, Nikhil had insisted on buying her an advanced model along with a comprehensive, unlimited-calls service plan for an entire year in advance. "Just keep it in your purse. You never know when you're going to need it," he'd advised her.

She gazed at the phone for a moment. Was this, too, something Nikhil had anticipated as her future need? She'd hardly ever used the phone, but now it was her lifeline to the world outside the convent walls.

With some hesitation she dialed the number indicated on Dr. Salvi's card. He was a busy man, so she was probably interrupting his work, but she *had* to talk to him. The phone rang several times before his voice mail came on. She left a brief message requesting him to call her back.

Noticing the phone's battery was low, she retrieved the cord from the suitcase and plugged it into the only electric outlet in the room, and then covered the phone with a sheet. If Mother Dora or someone else came by, she didn't want to be caught with it. Since the walls were thin and the girls around her were naturally curious, she shut off the ringer and set it on vibrate mode.

Half an hour later, an odd buzzing sound startled her. It took her a second to realize it was her phone vibrating and not an insect hovering around the baby. She picked it up quickly, before it could go to voice mail. "Hello."

"Mrs. Tilak?"

"Yes."

"Harish Salvi here."

"Oh . . . thanks for ringing back." Now that he was on the phone, she didn't know what to say. Earlier, she'd had it all planned, what she would say, and how she'd say it, but now she felt awkward and tongue-tied. "I . . . um . . . I wanted to thank you for your generosity. I got the package this morning."

"I hope you can use most of the things. As a pediatrician I know exactly what Diya needs, but with Priya and you, I wasn't very sure."

"It's still very kind of you. You even sent *me* some books."

"It's nothing." He laughed. "Although, I don't know if you're fond of reading and whether you like that type of fiction."

She couldn't help smiling. "I love reading, and the novels are perfect for my tastes. How did you know what to buy?"

"I asked my sister-in-law, my older brother's wife. She reads quite a bit."

"Then I suppose she and I have similar tastes in books." A long and awkward silence ensued. She had to put an end to it. "The . . . uh . . . reason I rang was to say I'd like to pay you for the things you brought over this morning."

"What!" He sounded shocked. "They're a gift. Didn't I say that in my note? Or was it my horrible handwriting you couldn't read?"

"No, I read every word, but . . . but you hardly know us, Dr. Salvi. I can't accept all this from a virtual stranger."

"We're not strangers. We knew each other in college, didn't we?" he said in a flat voice.

"We didn't *know* each other, Doctor. We attended the same college, but we never exchanged a word."

"Does it really matter? We know *of* each other and I wanted to make your life a little easier, that's all." He was quiet for a second. "No strings attached, Mrs. Tilak—none whatsoever."

Oh, no! He'd completely misunderstood her. "Dr. Salvi, I'm sorry if I didn't make myself clear. I only meant to say your generosity is overwhelming and I feel burdened to accept something this expensive from someone I barely know. I realize there's no hidden agenda here. You're just being kind."

His drawn-out breath was audible, even over the static of the mobile phone. "I'm glad you don't think I have an ulterior motive. Most of the baby items are samples from my clinic, so I didn't purchase them. The rest were very affordable, so please don't worry about it."

"You're sure?"

"I'm positive. So let's forget about it." After a brief hesitation, he asked, "How's the baby doing? Any concerns?" He was clearly relieved to move on to a safer subject.

"She's been waking up practically every hour. She nurses for a minute or two and dozes off, but wakes up again." She chuckled. "Nothing unusual for a two-day old infant, I suppose."

"Why don't you let her fuss a little and see if she'll wait for about two hours?"

"I'm afraid to let her cry. There are dozens of young students in the building and a screaming baby is not going to be popular."

"Then between feedings try using that pacifier I sent you. Stretch the gap between meals to a minimum of two hours. She'll gradually adjust to eating more each time."

She turned that over in her mind. Priya had been a different kind of baby, but then, Isha had had Sundari to help her. "Since you're the expert, I'll try it."

"Good. I'll stop by in a couple of days to give her the TB vaccine."

That was an offer Isha couldn't refuse. She knew tuberculosis was a serious threat to the baby and the vaccine was a must. "Thank you so much, Doctor, for everything."

"Don't mention it."

"Did I interrupt your busy schedule?"

"No. This is my morning tea break," he said. "Rama, my assistant, makes the most dreadful tea, but I drink it anyway. He's convinced that I love his tea." His voice was filled with mocking amusement.

"I'm sure Rama means well."

"He does," he admitted with a chuckle. "I better go. Sarojbayi, my nurse, is trying to remind me I have patients waiting."

Isha thanked him again and ended the call. A smile tugged at her mouth. Now *that* was a very interesting conversation—and refreshing. It had been a while since she'd conversed with an intelligent adult who wasn't a nun.

Chapter 9

Dinner at the Salvi home was something Harish looked forward to every evening. It was an excellent way to relax after working with sick and weepy children all day. He looked fondly at his family seated around the table.

His father, Dinanath Salvi, now retired from teaching high school mathematics and physics, was still very much into reading and discussing politics, his favorite pastimes. He loved a good debate with his family at the table. But he had retained the stern schoolteacher stance and rarely tolerated any opinions that didn't agree with his. He still continued to dress like a teacher, too, in black pants and white or cream shirts.

His mother, Shalini, was a plump, homely woman who chose not to argue with her husband on most topics. If she didn't happen to like his views, she merely shook her head and rolled her eyes—always behind his back, never to his face. A good Hindu wife wasn't supposed to disagree with her husband, at least not overtly.

Harish's older brother, Satish, a chartered accountant with a prosperous financial consulting business, was a gregarious individual who liked to tell the family witty stories about his vast number of clients. Satish's wife, Prachi, was an ob-gyn, with a flourishing practice of her own and her own repertoire of anecdotes.

Satish and Prachi had a four-year-old daughter, Reshma, an adorable girl with her father's sense of adventure and her mother's lively, dark eyes and capacity for laughter. Being the only child in the family, she was the center of attention in the Salvi clan. She had been fed by her doting grandmother earlier and was asleep in her room at the moment.

With three professionals who worked odd hours, dinner was usually at a late hour. But there was always plenty of interesting conversation at the table.

"So, what's going on with your tiny tots lately, Harish?" his brother asked him. "You haven't told us a single interesting story this month."

Harish shook his head. "That's because there's nothing to tell. Most of my patients are too sick with the flu these days." He gave his brother a wry smile. "You're the one with the funny stories."

As compared to Satish's tales of stingy old foxes, who tried every dirty trick to avoid paying taxes and were amassing a fortune, Harish's anecdotes about naughty and snotty kids seemed too tame.

Prachi's hilarious accounts of how some woman gave birth while taking a bath or how one patient's husband insisted on singing at the top of his lungs in the delivery room because he wanted his child to appreciate good music and recognize his father's voice, were so amusing, they had everyone in stitches.

Anyway, Harish, the more serious of the two brothers, preferred to be entertained rather than play the entertainer.

Tonight, they were eating their mother's *Kolhapuri* Chicken Curry, *dal*—seasoned split lentils—cauliflower and peas cooked in a coconut gravy, cucumber salad, and *chapatis*—thinly rolled whole wheat bread. Harish helped himself to more of the chicken. "Mamma, this is superb," he told his mother.

His mother's round face lit up. "I will give you the leftover curry with some *chapatis* and rice for tomorrow's lunch."

"I don't have time to eat an elaborate lunch. I rarely have time to eat at all," he told her.

His father frowned at him across the table. "*Arré*, what kind of nonsense is it to skip lunch? If you don't eat properly, then how can you advise your patients about proper nutrition?"

"Dada, my patients are young, growing children who need

good nutrition," Harish reminded his father. "I'm a grown man and can afford to miss a meal or two."

"No missing-bissing of meals, understand?" chimed in Mamma. "I will not hear of it!" His mother could be just as rigid as his father when it came to nutrition and health matters. "Have Rama heat up the chicken in that costly microwave oven you bought for your office."

"But, Mamma . . ." He shrugged and gave up. When his mother decided to fill him up with food, there was no arguing with her. Besides, her chicken curry was the best.

She gave him one of her hopeful looks, her soft brown eyes turning softer. "You know something, Harish? I got a letter from an eligible girl's father today. He says your horoscope and hers are matching nicely." She gave Harish a second for that little tidbit to sink in. "Nice girl she is, good-looking and clever also. She is a children's doctor, just like you."

Harish shifted in his chair. *Here we go again,* he thought wearily, *talking about eligible girls and marriage.* He put a hand on his mother's to soften the impact of what he was about to say. "Mamma, how many times have I told you I'm too busy to get married?"

This time Satish jumped in, looking so much like their father when his expression turned serious that Harish was amazed at the resemblance. They had the same sharply angled jaw and the hooked nose that reminded Harish of a hawk's beak. They both had the schoolmaster look.

But their personalities couldn't be more different. Dada didn't have a single humorous or adventurous bone in his body, while Satish had an abundance of both. Which ancestor had passed those on to him? It was still a puzzle.

"If this girl is a pediatrician, then she's the best solution to your problem of overwork," said Satish. "She and you can share the practice." He threw Harish a grin. "Perfect arrangement, if you ask me."

Unfortunately for Harish, his sister-in-law, too, nodded enthusiastically. "All the girls so far were not pediatricians, but this one is. Satish is right. What could be more perfect?"

Having finished his meal, Harish rose from his chair. "I'll think about it." Usually that appeased them for a while. Seeing their dubious expressions, he added, "Seriously."

That was all the encouragement his mother needed. "Very smart she is, just like Prachi, no? My sister says she knows the family and the girl is very beautiful—"

"In that case," Harish interrupted her, "she may be far too good-looking for me. Why would she want to settle for someone as plain and boring as me?"

Satish chuckled and leaned back in his chair, looking smug. "That's the lamest excuse I've heard. Prachi married me in spite of my looks, didn't she?"

"But you're a handsome specimen compared to me," argued Harish, despite knowing that in their culture a man's looks didn't matter one bit as long as he had a healthy income and a good, solid family background. Only girls were assessed by their appearance. How unfair was that?

"Who says you are not good-looking?" His father pounded a fist on the table, his trademark gesture for demanding attention. Sometimes he seemed to forget that he was no longer a stick-wielding schoolmaster. "You have good stature and you are a brilliant doctor. Any girl should be honored to marry you."

Harish laughed. "I'm your son, Dada. Even if I were a bald-headed midget with no teeth, you and Mamma would think I was good-looking."

Prachi snickered at Harish's droll comment but quickly suppressed the laughter as her eyes traveled to her father-in-law's bushy eyebrows knitted in a piqued V. She managed to clear her throat and supported his opinion instead. "Dada's right. Any girl would snatch you up in a minute, Harish."

Harish angled an amused look at her. "Is that a fact? Would *you* have agreed to marry me?"

"Well . . . I suppose." She cleared her throat again. "But . . . I liked your brother better. That doesn't mean I wouldn't have considered you, of course," she said with a wicked smile. She had an impish sense of humor.

"Excuse me! What's this I hear?" Satish stared at his wife, feigning dismay.

"You heard me, my dear," she replied coyly. "I preferred you."

It was Shalini who put an end to the gentle ribbing, which she probably construed as flirting between her daughter-in-law and her younger son. "*Chhee-chhee,* what kind of silly talk is this— a married woman considering another man?" She tossed a disapproving glance at Prachi and started to clear the table. "In our society, once a woman marries, then she should be *pati-vrata.*" Completely faithful and devoted to her husband. "She should not even be thinking about other men, let alone talk this way."

Harish put a playful arm around his mother's shoulder. "Oh, come on, don't tell me you've never looked at another man since you married Dada."

"Of course not!" A slap on the hand was what Harish earned for his brazen comments. "I married your father thirty-six years ago and I have not cast an eye on another man since then."

"What about before you married him?"

Shalini sniffed in disdain and started stacking the *thalis*—the large stainless steel plates used as everyday dishes. "Respectable Maharashtrian girls don't make flirty eyes at men."

Harish noticed the veiled amusement in Prachi's dark, sparkling eyes. He suspected that later, after the elders went to bed, Satish, Prachi, and he would likely get a good laugh out of this topic. They often roared with laughter at Dada and Shalini's antiquated notions.

Satish stood up and pushed in his chair. "But, Mamma, what about all those romance novels and women's magazines in your room? The magazines have articles like 'Ten Ways to Heat Up Your Sex Life' and 'Making Love in the Most Unlikely Places.' "

"That kind of nonsense I do not read!" Shalini snapped. "I only look at recipes and good spiritual articles and stories." She took her stack of dishes and swept out of the room.

Satish and Harish burst into laughter. Under pressure to be the well-behaved daughter-in-law, Prachi barely allowed her lips to twitch.

"Stop making *tingal* of your mother!" The sharp reprimand from their father brought the hilarity to an abrupt stop. *Tingal* was a slangy Marathi word for mockery.

The three of them watched the older man rise from his chair and stride toward the drawing room. They knew he would settle down to watching some TV and then head for bed. The minute they knew he was out of earshot, they all started to snicker once again.

"*Tsk-tsk*. So many years since he retired and he still thinks he's a teacher and we're his pupils," murmured Satish.

Harish shook his head. "After coming to live with you two hell-raisers, I'm surprised he hasn't changed."

Just then his mother came out of the kitchen and handed him a plastic bag. It had containers filled with the leftovers she'd promised him. "Now don't forget to take it to the office tomorrow."

"Yes, Mamma."

"And tell Rama to heat it for several minutes. Nonvegetarian food needs to be reheated thoroughly."

"Yes, Mamma."

"Refrigerate the bag immediately after you reach home." Shalini headed back to the kitchen.

"Yes, Mamma."

Satish snickered. "You're such a bull-shitter, Harish Salvi. You have no intention of eating that chicken for lunch, do you?"

Harish smiled. "You're right, but I promise it won't be wasted."

"That's enough for tonight, Priya," said Isha, inserting a bookmark in the colorfully illustrated storybook and setting it aside.

"More please, Mummy." Sitting on the floor at her feet in mauve- and white-gingham pajamas, Priya looked tired and more than a little sleepy. But she loved a good story.

"Uh-uh, it's past your bedtime." Isha glanced at the baby sleeping peacefully on the cot. "I need my rest, too. In about an hour your sister is going to wake up hungry."

Priya lay down on the bedroll with a resigned sigh. "Will you read some more tomorrow?"

Isha shut off the light and settled next to the infant. "I promise." Within two minutes Priya was fast asleep. Isha could clearly hear her daughter's soft, even breathing.

Despite the need to sleep, Isha remained awake a while longer, pondering the immediate future. When was the money going to be released by the insurance company? She had filed the papers months ago and she desperately needed the funds to get on with her life. And her plan.

God only knew if her plan had any merit, but it was the only viable one she could think of under the circumstances. Just before she fell asleep she made a resolution to ring the insurance man once again, that useless, good-for-nothing excuse for an agent. This time she was going to give him a piece of her mind, too. She was thoroughly tired of waiting.

Chapter 10

"Are you sure it was my sister-in-law you saw and not someone who looks like her?" Sheila Sathe frowned at her friend Anita Yalgi, wondering if what she'd just heard was a figment of Anita's imagination.

"Of course I'm sure," Anita assured her. "I know Isha well enough. There's no way I could mistake someone else for her." Anita was an attractive woman with sharp features and a wide smile. At the moment, she was wearing a cool white sari with a pastel print and matching pearl accessories—perfect for a warm, leisurely morning.

They were sitting on wicker chairs on the shady verandah behind the spacious house the Yalgis had owned for two generations. It was a peaceful haven with a canopy of bougainvillea creepers heavy with fat pink and white flowers.

Sheila watched her friend pour tea from the elegant porcelain teapot the servant had just delivered.

Accepting her cup from Anita, Sheila took her first scalding sip. Her hands shook and the cup rattled. But the tea was soothing, just the thing to calm the sudden churning that had started in her stomach at hearing Anita's disturbing news.

How could Isha, her estranged sister-in-law, still be in town? Apparently when she had packed up her things and said her terse good-byes to Sheila's parents, she had mentioned something about going to her cousin's home in Mumbai. Sheila had tracked down every cousin she could think of. But no one had heard from Isha. She had left no forwarding address and had never bothered to write or call. It was as if Isha and Priya had disappeared into thin air.

So why was Isha still here in Palgaum? Had something happened to prevent her from traveling to Mumbai? Was she okay? Was little Priya sick or something?

Anita gave her an anxious look. "Are you all right? You look stunned. I hope I didn't upset you."

Sheila put down her cup on the teapoy before her trembling hands dropped it. "I'm just a little surprised." Anita had been Sheila's best friend ever since college. Fortunately they had both married wealthy local men, and hence they could still see each other regularly.

They went to the ladies' club together to play mahjong and badminton, they shopped together at the trendy stores in town, and at least twice a month the two women got together to have tea at each other's homes and share gossip. They preferred to call it news.

But to hear about Isha was upsetting. She had been on Sheila's mind for the past three months. Sheila had discreetly tried to find out where Isha could have gone but without success. Unfortunately, Sheila had never bothered to find out the number for Isha's mobile phone. They'd never had reason to call each other on their mobiles. In fact, they practically never called. Their homes were so close, they'd seen each other nearly every day. She didn't even know if Isha still had the mobile service.

Isha's silence was hurtful, because although there was friction between Isha and the elders, the two of them had always had a cordial relationship. More than sisters-in-law, they were friends. And now there was this news. Why hadn't Isha asked for help? Why had she taken off on her own with a small child in tow?

"So what exactly is going on with your sister-in-law?" asked Anita. "I know she was depressed after your brother passed away." She shook her head. "What a tragedy, losing her husband at such a young age and in such a brutal manner, especially when she's expecting her second child." She leaned forward and touched Sheila's hand. "And you, poor thing, you're still grieving."

Sheila blinked back the threatening tears. Her younger brother had been her constant companion in childhood. Nikhil and she were close in age and he had always looked out for her. She still couldn't believe he was gone—murdered in cold blood. She continued to have nightmares about that.

The whole robbery-murder case was very bizarre. If it was indeed a robbery gone bad, then why were Niku's expensive gold watch and diamond ring still on his body? Thieves generally took everything they could get their hands on, especially jewelry.

Sheila was convinced her brother had been murdered for some other reason. But what? Niku was a decent man who had worked hard to nurture the business started by their father. Who would want to kill him? The police didn't seem to have a clue, or at least that's what they claimed. She had a feeling they were hiding something.

Months after his death, they were still looking for the killer. Poor Isha was heartbroken, and so were Sheila's parents. Her mother had taken to her bed for a long time. Ayee was only now beginning to recover. "I can't imagine what poor Isha went through and is now suffering," she said to Anita. "I wish I could have stopped her from leaving."

"What do you mean? Leaving for where?"

"She packed her bags and left my parents' home a few weeks after Niku's death."

Anita's eyes went round with shock. "Left as in . . . permanently?"

"She couldn't handle living with Ayee and Baba anymore. They're not easy to live with."

"But where did she go? I know her father died in an auto accident some years ago, and her mother died of cancer recently. She doesn't have anyone else, *nah?*"

"She apparently said she was going to Mumbai to stay with her cousin for a while, until the baby arrives. I managed to contact the two cousins I know of, but neither of them has seen her or heard from her. By now she's very close to her due date." Sheila sighed in utter misery. "Who knows, her daughter may have been born already."

"How do you know it's a daughter?"

"She had an ultrasound done." Sheila picked up her cup and took another sip of tea. "My parents gave her hell about it. I feel terrible about that."

"I'm completely confused. You're talking in riddles."

"I haven't told anyone about this, so I want you to promise not to say anything to anyone."

"What could be so bad that you'd hide it from *me*, Sheila? We tell each other everything. We always have."

"My parents were pressuring Isha to have the baby . . . aborted."

"Why?"

"Because it was a girl."

Anita's mouth fell open. "Really! I hear about female feticide often enough . . . but *your* parents? I thought they were such modern, liberal people."

"On the surface, yes, but deep down they're very conservative. Besides the religious and philosophical reasons, since Nikhil was their only son, they wanted a grandson to carry on the Tilak name."

"Hmm."

"So when they found out Isha was going to have a second girl, they more or less ordered her to go for an abortion."

"And what did Nikhil have to say about that?"

"He was against abortion, just as much as Isha was. That's what caused a lot of friction between my parents and Nikhil and Isha. And then on top of all that, Nikhil died suddenly and Isha had to face my parents on her own. I think that's what forced her to leave."

"That poor woman." Anita seemed to turn something over in her mind for a minute. "She's obviously still in Palgaum. At least we know she was at St. Mary's—last week, anyway."

"She may still be in town. I'm going to find out."

"How?"

"Maybe the nuns have an address for her or something." Sheila sprang to her feet and picked up her purse. "Did Isha see you?"

"I doubt it. I was driving by the back of the school after

dropping my Reena off to class when I saw Isha walking past one of the buildings. I know it was she because I saw the big pregnant belly. It was definitely Isha."

"Why didn't you tell me this right after you saw her?"

Anita shrugged. "It didn't seem important. You never told me she had left home. All these months I thought she was with your parents."

"Your servants didn't bring the gossip to you?"

Anita shrugged again, signaling the answer was no.

"It wasn't something we told anyone," admitted Sheila. "Imagine the scandal when people discover Isha left her in-laws and took off with her daughter soon after her husband passed away. And the reason for her leaving would be even more scandalous."

"Since I didn't know of her disappearance I thought she was at St. Mary's to bring Priya to school. It seemed perfectly normal."

Sheila realized how it must look to her friend. "I'm sorry. I know it's difficult to understand. I don't understand any of this myself. It's like a bad dream. My parents pretend like they never had a daughter-in-law or a granddaughter. They mourn for Nikhil, and Ayee still cries over his loss, but Isha and Priya don't seem to exist in their world."

"That's terrible!" Anita looked contrite. "Maybe I should have stopped and talked to Isha, *nah?* I was tempted to, but I hadn't seen her since Nikhil's passing and you know how awkward it is to carry on a conversation under the circumstances." She made a helpless gesture with her hand. "What can one say to a woman whose husband was found brutally murdered?"

"I know." The guilt settled around Sheila. Some of it was her own fault, that Isha had been forced to make the decision to leave her parents' house.

If she was any kind of sister-in-law, she should have lent some support to Isha when her parents had, time and again, said nasty things about Isha and the unborn baby's ill-fated astrological auras casting a karmic shadow on the Tilaks' lives. And each time, Isha had tried to defend her actions on her own. Without Nikhil's support, the poor woman had borne the brunt of Ayee and Baba's foolish beliefs all alone.

Sheila had been afraid of her parents' wrath, especially her father's. Nikhil had always been the stronger of the siblings, and he had managed to stand up to them whenever the need arose, like when he'd told them to back off when they kept pushing for abortion. But Sheila was the weak one, the subservient girl raised in a strict Brahmin environment. All along she'd been obedient and let her parents make all the decisions for her.

So when it had come to defending Isha, Sheila had done nothing. She'd stood by helplessly, secretly hoping that things would settle once the baby was born. But now she wondered if she should have offered Isha her support. After all, Isha was her brother's wife and the mother of his child. Priya was Sheila's niece and she loved her like she did her own kids.

The thought of Priya made her wince. Ayee and Baba had never treated their granddaughter with affection. No wonder Isha had decided to get away from that cold and loveless house. After Niku's death, it had turned downright grim.

Was it too late to make amends? Maybe not. She could at least help Isha financially. Sheila wasn't sure if Isha had any cash on her. In spite of her gentle disposition, her sister-in-law was a proud woman and had probably left home with nothing. Perhaps that's why she was still in town, because she couldn't afford to buy tickets to Mumbai. Oh God, what a terrible thing for a woman who'd lacked nothing until a few months ago.

Sheila looked at Anita. "I think I'm going to go to St. Mary's right now and see if Mother Regina knows Isha's address."

"What if Mother Regina doesn't know?" Anita asked. "Or what if she knows but won't tell? Isha could be in hiding."

"Maybe, since she hasn't made any effort to contact us all these months." Sheila was doubtful about being able to press Mother Regina into divulging anything. She had attended St. Mary's and knew the elderly nun well. Too well. The old bat was stubborn and difficult. But she was fair, and Sheila was determined to try her best to persuade the old woman.

"How are you going to explain your visit to her?" asked Anita. When Sheila remained silent, she patted her arm. "Do you want me to go with you?"

Shaking her head, Sheila started moving toward the walkway that wound around the side of the house and to the front portico. "This is something I have to do on my own. It may be too little too late, but maybe I can help Isha in some small way."

"At least give me a ring later and tell me what happened, all right?"

"Okay. And remember, don't say one word about this to anyone."

"I won't."

Sheila slid behind the wheel of her car. Good thing she'd driven herself and not arrived in the chauffeured car. She had to do this stealthily. Now that she had a way to perhaps track down Isha, she was going to try and make it up to her.

She sat in the car for a minute or two, deliberating. How would Baba and Ayee react if they found out what she'd just discovered? Could it be possible they already knew about Isha? But then, they would have said something if they had.

Even now, as she sat with her fingers drumming the steering wheel, she wondered if seeking out Isha would mean alienating Ayee and Baba. They could end up severing all ties with her if they found her doing something they viewed as disloyalty to them. That would mean her own sons would be cut off from their grandparents, too. Was all that worth risking?

After a moment of contemplation she realized her answer was a resounding *yes*.

Reaching out to one's family was the right thing to do, even if her parents disagreed. She owed it to her dead brother to offer help to his wife and child. By now it could be two children.

How was Isha providing for them? She had no money of her own. Every bit of her late father's estate had gone toward her terminally ill mother's expensive medical care. For Isha it had been one major tragedy after another since her father's death six years ago. How much more could the poor woman take?

Sheila started the car and began driving in the direction of the convent. But there were a couple of important stops she had to make before she got there.

Chapter 11

A knock on the door made Isha look at the clock. It was not even close to lunchtime, so it couldn't be Priya. Besides, Priya generally yelled *"Mummy."*

Putting aside Priya's uniform that she'd been mending, she rose from her chair to open the door. Her jaw fell. "Sheila!"

"Isha!" For some reason Sheila seemed equally astonished. "I—I hope you don't mind my coming here?"

At a loss for words, Isha stared at her for a moment. "No . . . no. Please come in." She noticed Mother Regina standing right behind Sheila, a censorious frown on her pale face. "Praised be Jesus and Mary, Mother," she said quickly, silently reprimanding herself for not saying it sooner.

"Forever. I hope you don't mind my allowing your sister-in-law to visit. I know you told me you did not want to have anything to do with your family." The nun inclined her head toward Sheila. "She was persistent, you know. She refused to leave until she saw you."

Isha smiled at the clearly incensed nun. "That's all right, Mother. Sheila and I have a good relationship."

Seemingly satisfied, Mother Regina took her leave, but not before she threw Sheila a disapproving glare generally reserved for recalcitrant children. "I shall leave you two alone, then."

Closing the door behind the old woman, Isha turned to Sheila. "I'm sorry about Mother Regina's attitude. She's only trying to protect me."

"I know. Don't forget I used to be a student of hers, too. When she clapped her hands to get our attention, it sounded like a cannon exploding in the corridors. Scared me to death in those days!"

"Me, too," Isha said with a shudder.

"She's still the old battleaxe, but she doesn't scare me anymore," said Sheila. "I even managed to break down her defenses."

"I never thought you'd be called persistent. You're usually so agreeable."

"I can be just as tenacious as Mother Regina when I need to be," Sheila admitted with a mischievous gleam in her eyes. They were so like Nikhil's eyes that Isha felt a sharp stab of pain. Then Sheila dropped her purse and a large plastic bag she'd been carrying and opened her arms wide to give Isha a hug.

Isha fell into her sister-in-law's arms. "Oh, Sheila!" The tears were already building up. "It's so nice to see you." She was probably ruining Sheila's cool and perfect chiffon sari in a warm shade of peach, but she didn't care. Her sister-in-law was such a welcome sight after the past few months of seclusion.

"Shh . . . it's okay." Sheila caught her close. She was taller and bigger-boned than Isha and held her like a child. "It's wonderful to see you, too." She abruptly stepped back and stared. "Your tummy's gone! You had the baby?"

Isha nodded and pointed to the bundle sleeping on the cot. "Three days ago."

Sheila turned to the baby and peered at the little face. "Oh my God!" She gazed at the baby for a long time, her eyes filling up. "She looks so much like Niku," she whispered, reminding Isha that Sheila was the only one in the family who referred to Nikhil as Niku. She sniffed and pulled out a handkerchief from her purse. "The same chin and cheekbones. Does she have his eyes, too?"

Isha wiped away her own tears with her fingers. "Yes. Those beautiful trademark *ghaaré dolé*—gray-green eyes—that you and Nikhil inherited from your mother seem to be very dominant. I'm glad both my children look like Nikhil. They're his only legacy I have left."

"What did you name her?"

"Diya."

"Lovely name," said Sheila. "And it suits her."

"I think so." Isha smiled as she recalled something. "Remember, right after Nikhil passed away, when I used to leave Priya with Sundari and go for those long walks to avoid facing your parents? I often went to the Ganesh temple."

"I remember."

"You know that *sadhu* who sits outside the temple, the one they say is a prophet?"

"Uh-huh. He seems to be meditating all the time."

"He surprised me one day by starting a conversation with me."

Sheila lifted a single eyebrow. "Interesting."

"All of a sudden he said some things that astounded me. He seemed to know I was newly widowed and that my in-laws were adamant about my aborting my child."

"How do you suppose he knew? The servants told him?"

Isha shrugged. "God knows. But he said my daughter would be born at full moon, *Kojagari Purnima* to be precise, and that she would bring light to the people around her."

"He even knew you were going to have a daughter?" Sheila was silent for a moment. "That's amazing." She turned to Isha, her eyes wide. "She was born three days ago. So that's . . . the exact day!"

"And the name Nikhil and I had been thinking about fits her perfectly." Realizing they were still standing, Isha gestured to Sheila to sit down.

"Maybe that old man really is an oracle." Sheila sat down on the cot next to the baby and looked around, wondering how her sister-in-law, who was used to living in a large and luxurious home, could live in this dark, musty hole with barely enough room to walk four steps in any direction. "Isha, I had no idea you were still in Palgaum. I wish you'd contacted me."

"I didn't want anyone to know. You know why, don't you?"

Nodding slowly, Sheila once again gazed at the baby. "I know. Ayee and Baba would have forced you to get rid of the baby, even if it was too late in the pregnancy."

"That's only *one* of the reasons for my decision to leave them." Isha settled herself in the chair, wondering if she should tell Sheila everything. She hadn't told this to a soul other than Mother Regina. After a second of deliberating, she decided to open up. Sheila had to know how rotten her parents were, even if it hurt her deeply. "They kept blaming Diya and me for Nikhil's death."

"I know that," Sheila admitted. "And I could never understand why."

"Don't forget, I was the daughter-in-law who produced girls, so my reputation went bad years ago. But Ayee kept saying Diya, too, was a symbol of *abshakoon*. Bad luck. First of all, she was a girl, and that in itself was a curse. Ayee felt that God was trying to warn us that this child would bring the family a lot of grief. She believes that if I'd had an abortion, Nikhil would be alive today."

"Oh, dear Lord!" Sheila bowed her head and put her face in her hands.

The simple gesture seemed so hopeless and dejected that it broke Isha's heart to be the one to give her sister-in-law the news.

Sheila looked up, her face a picture of misery. "If they weren't my parents, I think I'd have them arrested."

Isha couldn't help smiling. "Arrested for what? For believing in something hopelessly primitive and entirely illogical?"

The baby woke up just then and interrupted them. Sheila held up a hand. "Don't get up," she said to Isha. "I want to hold her." Very gently she picked up the baby and studied her face. "Hey, baby, you recognize me? I'm your Sheila-tayi," she said, using the same term Priya used to address her. Although *tayi* was the word for big sister, in their Maharashtrian culture one's father's sister was also called *tayi*. She glanced at Isha. "She's beautiful. I'm so glad you let her come into this world."

"I wouldn't have had it any other way. I don't care what Ayee and Baba have to say, but to Nikhil and me she'd always been our child."

The baby went quiet for a moment from being picked up, but started to fuss again, letting them know she was hungry. Sheila rose to her feet and placed her in Isha's arms. "She's not going to calm down till she's fed. Why don't we talk while you nurse her?"

So the two women chatted while the baby happily nursed at Isha's breast. "Sheila, can I ask you something personal?"

"Sure. We're sisters-in-law, aren't we?" asked Sheila quietly.

"Did your parents treat you the way they did Priya because you were a girl?"

Sheila took a deep breath and stared at the crucifix on the wall for a minute. She looked like she was gathering her thoughts. "What do you think?" she asked finally.

"I wouldn't know, because you were already married and gone when I became a part of your family. The only time I saw your parents interact with you was when we got together. And by then you had married a successful man and given them two beautiful grandsons, so you seemed to be just about a perfect daughter."

"They were stricter with me," said Sheila, "and I was scolded for the things Nikhil was never reprimanded for. Back then, I thought it was because he was younger, the baby. And double standards are the norm in our culture, so most girls like you and I never think of questioning them."

"True."

"As I grew older, I realized there were other reasons for the way they behaved, but I didn't pay much attention. Besides, I loved Niku. I wasn't jealous of him. And in my own way, I spoiled him too."

Isha adjusted the baby in her lap. "I know they doted on Nikhil. He was perfect, according to them. But he wasn't. He was a good man, but he could be impatient and arrogant, often short-tempered. Nonetheless Ayee and Baba still thought he was flawless. I didn't mind that because I, too, thought Nikhil was a great husband and father. I only wish he'd told his parents off more often, instead of pretending they had no faults."

Sheila shook her head. "I can't blame him for that, Isha. I was the same way . . . still am. I have no guts to stand before them and say they're bigots, and that their way of thinking is ridiculously flawed. Maybe Niku was a coward like me."

"No, he wasn't," retorted Isha, immediately springing to his defense. "He was only being a good son who never talked back to his parents. He was trying to do his duty. That's all it was."

"Whatever it was that made him do the things he did, it died with him, I suppose," said Sheila in a resigned tone of voice. "God knows what other secrets he took with him." She threw a wary glance at Isha. "I don't care what the police say, but I'm convinced his death was not connected to a robbery. Other than the cash in the office safe, practically nothing of value was taken. How could it be a robbery? I'm not entirely sure, but I suspect someone wanted him dead."

Isha felt her skin prickle. "So you feel the same way I do!"

"I've felt that way since the day it happened."

"Why didn't you say something to me?" All this time, Isha had tortured herself thinking about the strange way her husband had died.

"Isha, you were so torn and depressed, why would I add to your misery by telling you that someone may have killed Niku deliberately?" Sheila blew out a long breath. "Besides, it was only a suspicion. I have no proof."

It was such a relief to know she wasn't crazy that Isha couldn't help smiling. "When I voiced my suspicions to your parents about the possibility of Nikhil's death being premeditated, Ayee merely brushed it off saying I was trying to invent excuses to cover up for my own and my baby's *paaygoon,*" she said, referring to a term that, loosely translated, meant footprint or characteristic of the foot, but metaphorically a person's fate, good or bad.

"Ayee needs to have her head examined," said Sheila. "After Niku's death I think she's lost her mind completely." She let her eyes rove around the room once again, taking in every inch of it.

"Why are you here, Isha?" she asked, changing the subject. "Why St. Mary's of all places?"

"Why *not* St. Mary's? I get room and board and a safe place for my children in return for working at the orphanage."

Sheila gaped at her. "The orphanage! Those kids are filthy. Why would you want to work there?"

"It's not that bad. Besides, those poor children need a little mothering, and—"

"But you were born and raised in affluence," interrupted Sheila. "And then you married into a wealthy family."

Isha's temper stirred. "What was I supposed to do, Sheila? Let Ayee and Baba keep needling me about Diya? As it is, poor Priya was treated like a stepchild. Instead of comforting a little girl who was crying because her Papa wasn't around anymore, she got thoroughly spanked by your father."

"No! Baba struck Priya?"

"Oh yes. I couldn't imagine what Diya's plight would have been." She shuddered at the thought. "I had to leave before the situation worsened."

"I'm sorry; I wasn't thinking," murmured Sheila. "But didn't you take any money with you when you left? I know Niku and Baba kept a large amount of cash at home for emergencies."

Isha's chin came up instinctively. "I didn't want any of their money. I only took the small amount Nikhil kept in our room and my jewelry out of the safe deposit box."

"But Niku's hard-earned money is yours and his children's!"

Isha shook her head and lifted the baby to her shoulder, patting her back to help her stomach settle. "I didn't want them to feel I took anything that belonged to them. Even my clothes," she said, pointing to the suitcases stacked up in the corner. "I took the bare minimum with me—half a suitcase for myself. The rest are Priya's things." Unfortunately there was a pile of unwashed clothes sitting on the floor and Sheila was looking at them.

"What are you going to do for the future, Isha?" Sheila's expression was filled with concern.

"The nuns have allowed me to take four weeks off to recover. After that I go back to work, and I'll be allowed to keep Diya with me at all times."

Sheila stared out the window for a long time. "I have a suggestion," she said, finally breaking the uncomfortable silence.

"I refuse to go back to Ayee and Baba. That's not an option." Isha rose from the chair, laid Diya down on the cot, and unwound the sheet she was swaddled in to change her wet nappy.

"I'm not talking about that. Why don't you stay with Kumar and me and the boys? Our house is large enough for you and the girls."

Isha shook her head. "No. That's going to cause problems between you and your parents, and it's the last thing I want."

"But you can't stay here forever!" Sheila's eyes were pleading. "Look at this place. I'm not condemning it, but it's not a healthy environment for you or the children. Do you know how many diseases those orphans have? What if your girls catch something awful? You don't even have money for a doctor."

"I'll manage somehow." Isha threw the soaked nappy in a plastic bag, then cleaned the baby and pinned a fresh one in place. She glanced at Sheila. "I've done it for the last few months and I'll do it in the future."

"But how? How will you buy clothes for the children, medicines . . . all the necessities?" Sheila held out her arms, meaning she wanted to hold the baby again.

"I'm doing this only until I get the insurance money." Isha handed Sheila the child and went back to the chair. It was a warm feeling to observe Sheila cradling the baby with no inhibitions. She had to admit that her sister-in-law was a kind woman. How could such heartless parents produce two such nice and decent individuals like Nikhil and Sheila?

"What insurance money?" Despite her preoccupation with the baby, Sheila was obviously paying attention to Isha's words.

"Nikhil had taken out an insurance policy that Ayee and Baba didn't know about. I'm the only beneficiary. It's a fairly large amount and enough for me to invest in something and hopefully get some sort of regular income from it."

"There is some hope, then."

"I'm thinking about buying two flats in that new high-rise building not too far from your house. I can keep one for my use and rent the other. With the rent money and my job here, maybe the girls and I can survive." She rose from the chair and started to bag the clothes heaped on the floor. "But all that is only a dream until the insurance money comes through."

Sheila looked across at her and frowned. "So many months after Niku's death and they still haven't settled the claim?"

Isha shook her head. "I keep writing letters to the agent every two weeks, but he writes back saying he's working on it." She placed the bulging bag on top of the suitcases. "Something about the unusual nature of Nikhil's death making it harder to release the money or some such nonsense."

"Who's your agent?"

"Manoj Munshi."

"Kumar and I know him very well. I could talk to Manoj."

"You could?" Isha wondered why she hadn't thought of it herself. In the next instant she knew why. She hadn't thought about Sheila and her connections until now. In fact, she'd tried hard to put all the Tilaks out of her mind.

"Of course. I'll call him as soon as I get home."

"You're sure it's good to do that? He may think of it as inter-ference on your part and deliberately slow down the process, just to spite us."

"No. He's a laid-back kind of chap, but he's not spiteful. Besides, Kumar gives him so much business that he owes us a few favors."

"Thank you, Sheila." Until then Isha hadn't paid attention to the rather large bag Sheila had brought with her. Now that she was thanking her sister-in-law, she eyed it suspiciously.

Noticing Isha's eyes on the bag, Sheila smiled. "That's for you. Go ahead and open it. I brought something for Priya, too."

"You shouldn't have."

"It's not much. I was in a hurry, so I did the best I could as soon as I found out you might still be in Palgaum."

That's when it struck Isha. "How did you know I was in Pal-gaum? I haven't stirred out of this compound in months."

Sheila rocked the baby a little when she started to fuss. "You know my friend Anita Yalgi?"

"Of course."

"When she was dropping her daughter at school last week, she happened to see you. She said she recognized you. She didn't think it was important. In fact, she thought you were here to drop Priya off to school."

"Oh . . . she doesn't know about my situation, I guess."

"She didn't until I informed her. Hope you don't mind, but I had to explain my shocked reaction to what she told me."

Isha thought about it for a second. Sooner or later everyone would know she had left her in-law's home. "That's all right," she assured Sheila. "It's been several months since I disappeared and I bet the servants spread the news to most of the town's folks a while ago."

"No. That's the strange part. Anita is very good at sniffing out gossip, and she had no idea."

"That's odd." How could that be? Had Baba, in his attempts to protect his reputation, used some severe measures to keep his servants' mouths shut? Her gaze shifted to Sheila. The baby was now asleep in her arms. "But how did you know I was staying at the convent?"

"I didn't. I went to Mother Regina to ask if she knew your whereabouts. But she was very secretive and wouldn't tell me. When I convinced her that I meant well and I wanted to help you, she confessed you were here."

"I see." Isha opened the bag and pulled out three pairs of jeans and T-shirts in varied colors for Priya. There were also three sets of girls' underwear and pajamas. What a godsend! "Thank you," she said to Sheila. "I was just thinking that Priya's outgrowing all her clothes. In fact," she said, pointing to the uniform sitting on the arm of her chair, "I'm taking the hem down because it's getting too short. You know how the nuns are about short hemlines."

Sheila rolled her eyes, bringing an amused smile to Isha's lips. "Do I! If your kneecaps as much as peek out from below the hem, the nuns label you a loose woman."

Isha couldn't help laughing. It reminded her once again that Sheila and she, no matter what, had always shared some laughs. Sheila was nothing like the stereotypical sister-in-law portrayed in Hindi movies and books. She was a bit passive. Even now Isha couldn't believe Sheila had railroaded the iron-handed Mother Regina into spilling the truth. It only proved the old saying about still waters running deep.

Underneath the clothes for Priya, Isha found two saris with matching petticoats. "Oh, dear! Why did you bring gifts for me? I don't need them."

"Of course you need saris," scolded Sheila.

"Hardly." Isha grinned at her. "White cotton habits are the fashion trend around here."

Sheila chuckled. Noticing the baby sleeping soundly, she laid Diya down on the cot and covered her with a sheet. "She's so cute and cuddly, Isha. I wish I had a little girl to dress in frilly dresses and ribbons."

"A girl! You'd give Ayee and Baba a stroke by saying something inauspicious like that."

"I know." Sheila looked longingly at the sleeping infant. "Can I come and see her often?"

"Sure. She's your niece."

"I'll come by again in a couple of days. I'll bring something for Diya. If I'd known about her, I'd have brought something today."

"No more presents, please. This is too much already."

Sheila rose to her feet and approached Isha. "I have something else for you." She opened her purse and pulled out a wad of cash. "It's not much . . . only five thousand rupees."

"Five thousand!" It really wasn't a whole lot, but in her present circumstances it sounded like a king's ransom to Isha.

She stared at it for a moment. It was tempting.

Chapter 12

In the end, Isha backed off from her sister-in-law. "It's very kind of you, Sheila, but I can't take your money."

"Consider it Niku's money, then."

"But it's not Nikhil's money. It's yours and Kumar's." She put her hands behind her back. "Imagine what your parents will say."

"Ayee and Baba don't know about this. I'm not going to tell them and neither are you." Sheila stepped closer, forced Isha's hand to the front and pressed the money into her palm. "Nikhil's not here to take care of you and the children, but I'm here as his older sister. Nikhil would want me to look out for his daughters. Don't let your pride get in the way of your children's welfare."

Isha gazed for a second at the stack of bills tied with a rubber band. Sheila was right. There were so many things the children needed and she had to go shopping one of these days. Priya hadn't had any vitamins in several days and Diya was going to need some clothes soon. She couldn't stay swaddled in a nappy and a sheet forever.

She closed her hand over the bills. "Okay, for the children."

"Speaking of children, how's Priya holding up?"

"At first she cried a lot and constantly asked for her Papa and Sundari, but now she's used to their absence. She talks about you, the boys, and Kumar all the time, especially the boys, since they played with each other almost every day."

"And they miss her, too. They've been asking about Priya's absence for weeks. I told them she was visiting her cousins in Mumbai."

"I'm sorry." Isha knew it had been wrong to separate the cousins so abruptly, especially because they were more like siblings. But what choice did she have? "Priya mentions Ayee and Baba sometimes, but she doesn't seem to miss them much."

"I don't blame her. They never held her or spoiled her like most grandparents do." Sheila gave Isha's arm a squeeze. "I better get going. I'll talk to Manoj Munshi as soon as I can."

Isha got up from the chair, put the money on the nightstand and hugged her sister-in-law. Until that second she hadn't realized how truly heartwarming it was to see her. For a brief moment, it was like coming home.

She looked at the clock and realized they had been talking for more than an hour. "It's almost noon. Priya should be here any moment. Do you want to stay a little longer and see her?"

"Oh yes!" Sheila glanced at her wristwatch. "I didn't realize I'd stayed this long. I hope Mother Regina isn't standing at the gate with her ruler."

The two of them laughed and reminisced about Mother Regina's callous methods of disciplining kids. It felt wonderful to laugh again.

Minutes later they heard footsteps. The knock sounded. "Mummy!"

Sheila's eyes lit up. "Priya!"

"Yes, but unfortunately she has only a short break to go to the dining hall and have her lunch with the other boarders before running back to class." Isha opened the door and let Priya in.

Priya's mouth flew wide open the instant her eyes fell on her aunt. The next moment she took a joyful leap toward her. "Sheila-tayi!"

"Hello, sweetie pie," said Sheila and threw her arms around Priya, lifting the child off the ground. "How is my favorite girl?"

"You came to take us back home, Sheila-tayi?" Priya's innocent eyes were so full of hope as she clung to her aunt that Isha had to blink back tears. Home? Where in the world was that? Certainly not in that mansion her in-laws owned, where her children and she were considered a curse?

"No, baby . . . not just yet," Sheila replied, her voice sounding hoarse. "I came to see you and your mummy." She cleared her throat.

"Did you bring Sundari? And Milind and Arvind?"

"No. They were all busy. Maybe next time, all right?" Sheila let her niece slide down to the floor.

With her emotions now somewhat under control, Isha noticed Priya eyeing the bag.

"What's that?" asked Priya, a suspicious look on her face.

"A present for you," replied Sheila.

"Present!" Priya fell on the bag with all the enthusiasm of a healthy five-year-old. The next couple of minutes were spent in holding the jeans and T-shirts against herself and asking to be admired by the grownups.

"Time to go to lunch, pumpkin," Isha reminded her daughter, and put away the gift bag. "Sheila-tayi was just getting ready to leave, so say bye-bye to her and go down to the dining hall."

"Can Sheila-tayi stay and have lunch with us?"

"No. She has to go home to her family."

Sheila snapped her fingers. "I know what we can do. Why don't *you* go have lunch with her, Isha? I'll stay with Diya until you return."

"Are you sure?"

"Absolutely! I'm Diya's only aunt and I'd love to stay with her."

Priya tugged on Isha's arm. "Come on, then. Let's go."

Isha threw an apologetic look at Sheila. "I'll be back as soon as possible. I'm sorry."

Sheila shooed them away. "Don't be sorry. I'm looking forward to spending some time alone with my new niece."

Sheila watched Priya and her sister-in-law walk down the long passageway, then shut the door after they disappeared around the corner. She went to the cot to gaze on her infant niece.

This was her only brother's child—her beloved brother's lasting legacy.

All at once the memories of her dead brother came crowding into her mind. Niku had been such a handsome man and so full of life. How could anyone kill someone like that? How could they butcher any human being for no reason whatsoever?

She picked up the sleeping child, a miniature image of Niku. Sitting in the chair by the window, she ran her fingers over the baby's cheek and silky hair. She realized she'd done the right thing by coming here. Her brother's family needed her. What Ayee and Baba had to say didn't matter any longer.

She made a silent vow to her brother's soul: *Niku, I'll make sure your babies and your wife are okay. I'm sorry I didn't help them earlier. But now that I've found them, I swear I'll do everything I can to keep them safe.*

When a phone buzzed somewhere nearby, Sheila nearly jumped. She hadn't seen a phone in the room, so where were the odd vibrations coming from? Did the nuns even have phones in this place? She quickly rose from the chair and put the baby back on the cot. Looking around, she finally realized it was coming from under a pile of clothes beside the chair. She stuck her hand underneath and managed to locate a mobile phone. Flicking it open, she said, "Hello."

"Mrs. Tilak," said a male voice. "I'm glad you're there. I was just about to hang up."

"Who's calling please?" Sheila tried to guess. It wasn't Manoj Munshi's raspy smoker's voice. She would have recognized that at once. This one was smooth and refined, and she was fairly sure she hadn't heard it before.

"I'm sorry. Have I reached a wrong number?"

"No, this is Mrs. Tilak's phone." Entirely puzzled, Sheila racked her brain, trying to come up with a name. "I'm her sister-in-law."

"Oh . . . Is Mrs. Tilak all right?"

"Yes. Why wouldn't she be?" This was getting more mysterious by the second.

The man hesitated for a moment. "I just thought . . . well . . . if you're her sister-in-law, there might be an emergency with Diya or Priya."

Strange, but he seemed to know about the new baby and Priya. "No emergency," she assured him. "I just came to visit them. What is your name, sir?"

"I'm sorry. I should have introduced myself. I'm Diya's pediatrician, Dr. Salvi. I was calling to ask if I could stop by this evening to administer Diya's vaccine."

Despite his explanation, Sheila's confusion remained. "But Dr. Bajaj is the children's pediatrician."

There was a long moment of silence. "Uh, maybe you should talk to Mrs. Tilak. I'm not sure how much you know about her and the children, and their situation."

"I know the whole story, Dr. Salvi," she retorted. Who was this man who seemed to know everything about Isha and the kids and presumed to think Sheila knew nothing? "I'll tell Isha you rang."

"That'll be sufficient, thank you." His voice had turned a little cool, too. "Please tell her I'll stop by around seven o'clock. I've already cleared it with Mother Regina."

"I'll tell her that." She shut off the phone and put it on the nightstand. Well, well, he even happened to know Mother Regina. How about that?

So who was this mystery man who'd tried to reach her sister-in-law? On her mobile phone, no less. Isha hadn't given her mobile number to anyone in the past, not even Sheila. That made him even more mysterious. Well, at least he was a pediatrician. That was somewhat comforting.

Some twenty minutes later, Isha and Priya returned to the room. "Did Diya give you any trouble?" asked Isha.

"No trouble at all. She's been sleeping like an angel." Sheila smiled at Priya. "And what did you eat today for lunch?"

"Something yucky with beans and bread. I didn't like it." Priya stuck out her tongue in disgust. "I don't like anything in the dining hall."

"Beans and bread?" Sheila glanced at Isha, her heart aching.

What were her niece and sister-in-law eating? Priya was always slim, but now she looked skinny. And Isha had lost most of the weight she'd gained in pregnancy. There were purplish circles around her eyes that indicated lack of sleep and nutrition. Sheila made a mental note to bring some nutritious snacks and fruit for them the next time she visited. Her resolution to get them out of the convent as quickly as possible strengthened right there and then.

As expected, Priya was reluctant to go back to class. "Can't I stay?" she pleaded.

When Isha's attempts at coaxing her to go back failed, Sheila took the little girl by the hand. "How about if I walk you back to your class? That way you can show me your classroom."

"Okay."

"And I'll come back tomorrow with a present for Diya. Since you got a present and she didn't, I'll have to buy her something, won't I?"

That was all the incentive Priya needed to run and use the bathroom, then return and pick up her schoolbag. Sheila gave Isha's arm a quick squeeze on her way out. "By the way, someone named Dr. Salvi called for you. He said he'll stop by around seven to give Diya her vaccine."

"Oh!" Isha's brow creased.

"I thought your pediatrician was Dr. Bajaj."

Isha glanced at her sister-in-law and then looked away. "Dr. Bajaj is the most expensive pediatrician in town. Dr. Salvi does charity work for the orphanage and Mother Regina asked him to check on Diya."

The puzzled look on Sheila's face cleared up. "I see. Why don't you let me take Diya and Priya to Dr. Bajaj for a thorough checkup?"

"No. I won't allow you to pay Dr. Bajaj's fee on top of what you've already done for me." She glanced at the money sitting atop the nightstand. "Frankly, I like Dr. Salvi much better. He has a way with children. Mother Regina tells me the orphans love him."

"I like Dr. Salvi, too," chimed in Priya.

"Is that right?" Sheila ushered Priya out the door. "In that case, maybe one of these days I should check out this wonderful doctor myself." She looked back over her shoulder at Isha. "I'll stop by tomorrow. And I'll be sure to call Manoj Munshi for you."

Seeing her sister-in-law standing on the threshold of the pathetic little room she called home, Sheila sighed. *Niku, why did you have to die and leave your wife and children to rot in this?*

Chapter 13

Harish nearly smiled with relief when the rather shy Sister Rose informed him, "Mother Regina is busy this evening, Doctor, so I'll be escorting you to Mrs. Tilak's room."

He'd rather deal with Sister Rose any day than with the old Amazon. "Thank you, Sister. Please give Mother Regina my regards," he told the small, quiet woman as he picked up his medical bag and a plastic bag from the passenger seat of his car.

With a silent nod she led him into the boardinghouse. The nuns spoke as little as possible, especially with men. They both went down the long, now-familiar passage that reminded him of a prison scene from a movie he'd seen years ago.

In some ways this was a semiprison. The boarders were pretty isolated here. And that was probably the precise reason their parents had enrolled them in this school—the guarantee that their girls would be watched over night and day and receive a good education at the same time.

The food and living conditions were not much better than those in a prison, either, from what he'd learned so far. The nuns were about as formidable as prison wardens, too.

The strong odor of meat cooking hung in the air, telling him the dining hall was getting ready to serve the evening meal. Today, many of the doors on either side of the hallway stood open. He couldn't help venturing a quick glance into the rooms. Like Isha Tilak's room, they were tiny, and crammed with narrow cots and desks, with two girls to each room.

The young boarders appeared to be busy with their home-work. Hearing footsteps, they looked up. The shocked expressions on some of the faces spoke volumes. A man! He doubted if they'd ever seen a male anywhere within a hundred feet of this building.

Getting to the end of the corridor, Sister Rose knocked on Isha Tilak's door. Hearing an invitation to enter, she went in and Harish followed her.

Priya, who was sitting on the floor with a coloring book in her lap, looked up and smiled at him, her expression so sunny and welcoming, the drabness in that long passageway was all but forgotten. "*Namaste,* Dr. Salvi," she said, putting the book down to join her small hands.

"How are you, Priya?" he asked, returning her cheerful greeting. He put his bags on the floor and turned his attention to Isha, who was sitting on the bed beside the sleeping baby. "Hello, Mrs. Tilak."

"Hello, Doctor. And hello to you, Sister Rose," she replied, getting to her feet. "Thank you for coming all the way out here just for this, Dr. Salvi."

"It's not a problem." He moved his medical bag to the chair by the window and offered the plastic one to Isha.

After a moment's hesitation she took the bag. "What is it?"

He winked at her. "Just a few samples."

"Oh . . . okay." Her brow was still furrowed when she put the bag in a corner.

He breathed a quiet sigh of relief. She'd taken his hint. He started pulling out his paraphernalia.

Sister Rose moved forward. "Do you need help, Doctor?"

He shook his head. "Thanks, but this is quite simple."

A minute later, while Isha held the baby's arm in place, and Priya looked on with big, curious eyes, he administered the vaccine. Other than a sharp cry that lasted no more than a second or two, Diya took it quite well. Harish noticed the baby's face had lost its crepe-paper look. It looked smoother now and her features were more pronounced.

She no longer looked like a newborn. She was a very pretty

baby, too, with fair skin, delicately arched eyebrows, and a tiny pink mouth. She strongly resembled her sister. Both the girls had large green eyes with flecks of gray and gold, fringed by long brown lashes. They'd inherited those from their late father. He once again recalled Nikhil Tilak, the handsome athlete with the macho swagger from his college days.

"A small bump or scar might develop on Diya's arm," he advised Isha. "But don't apply any cream or bandage on it. It should be left open to dry and heal."

She nodded. "I remember it from when Priya got her BCG shot."

Now that his task was complete, it was time to go, but Harish was reluctant to leave. Sister Rose had clasped and unclasped her hands several times, making it clear that the two of them should make their exit. She must have a dozen chores to complete before she could go to dinner. The nuns probably kept the novices busy every minute of the day. Idleness was sinful.

Once again he scribbled something on the back of a calling card and handed it to Isha. "Please contact me if there are any complications or if you have questions."

"Thank you so much, Doctor." Her expression was the same as the last time—so full of gratitude that it embarrassed him. He noticed the tired look about her eyes. Did she get any sleep at all? She was probably exhausted from taking care of two small children. Babies could cause a lot of work and deprive the mother of sleep, not to mention the fatigue from all the feeding, bathing, cleaning up, and everything else that came with them—which Isha probably wasn't used to doing.

Sister Rose and he stepped outside after saying good night to the Tilaks. This time, when they walked down the hallway, a few of the bolder girls were at their doors, openly staring at him.

Sister Rose shooed them away. "Back to your homework, girls! Go on now."

Outside, she locked the gates the moment his car passed through them. Now that she was rid of him, the prison was once again secured for the night.

*   *   *

As he drove to his brother's house, Harish wondered if Isha would bother to read his message on the back of his card. He didn't know how else to alert her that there was food in the bag. He had carefully wrapped plastic bags around the containers to keep the strong aroma of his mother's leftover chicken curry from escaping. He must have been successful, because neither Priya nor the two women had sniffed suspiciously.

Unsure of how the nuns would react to food being delivered to someone in the convent, he'd had to resort to silly tricks. He hoped Isha wouldn't consider his offer an insult—something like charity.

He also wondered if he should mention Isha Tilak to his family. His parents definitely knew who she was and who her parents and in-laws were. Everyone in Palgaum had to know the prominent Ketkars and Tilaks. But did his parents know about Isha's separation from her in-laws?

Would Isha mind if he shared the information with his family? She seemed like a very private woman, and she was clearly hiding from society by staying in the convent.

As his thoughts shifted to Priya, an affable child with no television or games or other children to play with, an idea came to him. His niece was close in age to Priya. On Sundays, his family sometimes took the little girl to the park and for ice cream. Harish wondered if he could offer to take Priya along. Would Isha Tilak trust him with her precious child? He didn't think so. She hardly knew him. How could she entrust a five-year-old to his care?

How could anyone trust a child with an unknown man?

As soon as the door closed behind Sister Rose and Dr. Salvi, Isha opened the mystery bag. It was all very secretive, the way he'd silently requested her to keep her mouth shut. What could be so questionable that Sister Rose would disapprove? More chocolates for Priya?

She peeled off the multiple layers of packing and discovered the disposable plastic container with something that smelled delightfully spicy. There were also clear resealable bags with *chapatis* and rice. There was a note taped to the container.

> *"Hope you don't mind this. My mother's chicken curry is excellent and I'm only guessing you and Priya are nonvegetarians. If you're not, feel free to throw it out. Otherwise, I hope you enjoy it."*

The aroma made Isha's stomach growl. Priya looked up from her book and raised her nose like a puppy sniffing the air. "I smell something good. Is it . . . um . . . is it curry?"

"You guessed right." Isha opened the lid and took an appreciative sniff. How long had it been since Priya and she had had anything like this? They had survived on bread and boiled vegetables with little or no seasoning. No wonder they'd both lost weight. This was pure luxury.

But then the guilt started to scratch at her. How could she and Priya eat the curry when dozens of children, including the boarders and orphans, were forced to eat the slop they served in the dining hall?

Nonetheless her decision was made for her when Priya shot to her feet. "Chicken curry! Yum! And *chapatis!*" Priya's sudden interest in food in recent weeks was a source of both surprise as well as regret for Isha. Deprivation was forcing the previously picky eater to crave tasty foods, but sadly Isha couldn't give her much.

Priya must have been starving, because she could hardly wait for Isha to unwrap the *chapatis* and rice. In the next instant they were eating the best meal they'd had in months, even though it was cold. With each bite, Isha's guilt escalated, but she couldn't stop gorging herself. She watched Priya devour more food than she'd ever seen the child eat in one sitting.

She also prayed the odors wouldn't escape into the hall. If the nuns discovered the contraband, she and her girls would be out on the streets. She could only picture Mother Regina's eyes turning to blue ice, mutely questioning Isha's behavior. *How can you and your daughter eat like queens when you are surrounded by other children and starving orphans?*

Later, after Priya fell asleep, Isha read the message on the back of Dr. Salvi's card: *"My home phone number, in case you need to call."* So now he'd given her not only his office and mobile numbers but also the land-line to his home—his private number.

Why? What was she to him, other than someone he knew slightly years ago in college? Whatever it was that prompted him to do this for her, she was grateful. Her well-stuffed tummy was more than grateful.

She studied Priya's face in sleep and knew that she, too, slept better with a good, nutritious meal in her belly. Poor baby, she looked so thin.

Lord, she'd never imagined feeling overwhelming gratitude for one decent meal. She had taken good food for granted. She had assumed everything in life was her birthright. Until now.

She fished out her mobile phone, powered it up, and called his number. He picked it up on the second ring and she asked hesitantly, "Dr. Salvi?"

"Speaking," he said, sounding a little preoccupied.

"This is Isha Tilak." She heard what sounded like a television or radio in the background. Was she intruding on his personal time? But then he had given her his home phone number.

"Oh! How are you?" His tone changed to one of friendly interest.

"I wanted to thank you for the dinner. It was delicious."

"My pleasure," he said. "My mother packs so many leftovers for me that I thought I'd share some with you."

"Your mother lives with you, then?" Isha regretted her question the instant it flew out of her mouth. His personal life was none of her business. And he was likely to resent her nosiness.

"No. My parents live with my older brother, Satish. He's married and has a larger house, a young daughter who needs to be cared for, et cetera. I'm only a poor bachelor, so they insist that I have my meals with them. My family is close and they wouldn't have it any other way."

"How lucky for you!" A pang of envy skittered through her. He had a close-knit and caring family. She'd always wanted one like that.

"Do you . . . would you mind if I mentioned you and the children to my parents?"

She sighed. "I'm sure they know all about me by now."

"I don't think so. At least, I haven't heard them talk about it. And please don't be so formal. Call me Harish."

"All right, I'll call you Harish if you call me Isha."

"Fine."

An awkward silence followed. It was time to end the call. "I'll be in touch if Diya develops a strong reaction to the vaccine," Isha said.

"All right. And please don't hesitate to ring if you need help."

"Thank you. I appreciate that, but my husband's sister discovered I was still in Palgaum and she has offered help."

"That must be the lady I spoke to over the phone?"

"Yes. She's a good person and we're friends."

"Glad to hear you have someone you can depend on." He sounded genuinely relieved.

She wished him a polite good night and hung up.

Just so no one would guess what had occurred in their room, Isha rewrapped the empty container and tiptoed late at night to the rubbish bin located outside the dining hall to dispose of the bag. Buried under a lot of other smelly garbage-filled bags, she hoped nobody would discover it.

Returning to the room, Isha settled herself on the cot. The baby was already stirring.

Chapter 14

"So we were right! Nikhil's murder was premeditated!" Although Isha had believed that all along, the shock of hearing Sheila confirm it was too sharp to ignore. All of a sudden her knees felt weak.

"Are you all right?" Sheila looked at her with worried eyes, but Isha could do no more than nod at her sister-in-law. She was shaking all over.

Sheila quickly grabbed her arm. "Sit down." As Isha lowered herself to the cot, Sheila sat down beside her. "I'm sorry; I shouldn't have told you so bluntly about Niku's murder. You've gone through childbirth only days ago. You're still fragile."

"Don't be sorry." It was the old-fashioned Indian custom to pamper women in postpartum, but Isha had no illusions about such luxuries anymore. "I'm glad you told me. I don't know why I'm so shocked when I always knew something didn't add up. I guess I was hoping I was wrong."

Believing it would have been admitting that Nikhil had enemies, that someone had hated her husband with such passion that they'd be willing to kill him. Even the word *murder* was sometimes hard for Isha to use to describe her husband's death. It conjured up gruesome images that were too painful.

"I was hoping *I* was wrong, too."

Isha took a long, steadying breath. "So exactly why and how did you end up questioning the police superintendent about

Nikhil's death?" Now that the shock was beginning to wear off, Isha wanted to know the whole truth.

"When I called Manoj Munshi he started to dance around the issue, so I told Kumar about it. When Kumar forced Manoj's hand, he was told to talk to Patil, the police superintendent, about it. Apparently when there's a criminal investigation, the insurance company waits for the outcome before deciding whether to settle a claim. I guess they have to make sure it wasn't . . . um . . . you know . . . especially since the policy was so recent."

Isha stared at her stuttering sister-in-law. "What are you saying? They think I might have arranged to have him murdered, so I could grab his insurance money?"

"You know how the police—"

"I know," Isha cut in. "The spouse is always the main suspect."

"It seems to be standard procedure in murder cases, and the amount of insurance money in this case is substantial." Probably because Isha was still shaking, Sheila squeezed her hand. "Kumar and I don't think you had anything to do with it. We would never, ever think that way."

"Thank you." At least someone was on her side. "Since I had nothing to do with it, then who did?"

Sheila shrugged. "Who knows? But I think Manoj is frightened of opening his mouth because of what happened to Niku."

"Why?"

It took Sheila a moment to reply. "Maybe because he's afraid of meeting the same fate as Niku?" She raised a brow at Isha. "Did Niku say anything to you about going to the police?"

Isha shook her head. "He was terribly upset that a seemingly decent man like Karnik would even allude to something that's clearly illegal."

Sheila shook her head. "Knowing Niku and his strict principles, I'm not surprised at his reaction. But did he *specifically* say anything about going to the police about Karnik?"

"I remember a conversation when he said something to that effect in Ayee and Baba's presence and Baba reprimanding Nikhil."

"What did Baba say?"

"He ordered Nikhil to leave the doctor alone, because Dr. Karnik was only doing what his patients asked of him and that he was a good man and longtime customer."

Sheila rose to her feet and started to pace the tiny room. "From what Kumar gathered from Mr. Patil, Nikhil did file a report with him."

"He never mentioned it to me." Isha wondered what other secrets her husband had kept from her.

"Maybe he knew you'd try to stop him . . . or perhaps he didn't want you involved in anything dangerous. Based on Patil's limited explanation, Nikhil had no evidence on Karnik of any kind. And without any solid proof, they couldn't even touch Karnik. So they did nothing."

"Typical small-town police attitude!"

"They may be right, because they wouldn't have found anything, anyway. I'm sure Karnik makes a load of money, paid strictly in cash by grateful customers. But I bet there are no records kept of any shady activities. Karnik's no fool."

"I know that." Her obstetrician was an intelligent man and good at his craft. Wasn't that the main reason he was so popular with the upper class?

"Slightly before his death, Niku had apparently informed Patil that he had received anonymous death threats."

Isha drew in a sharp breath. "He didn't tell me that, either! I wish he had, Sheila! I would have prevented him from getting involved in any of this. As long as we didn't want the abortion and we had changed doctors, why did Nikhil have to pursue it?"

Sheila returned to sit beside her once again. "Because Niku was a man of principles. If he felt it was merely illegal, he would have turned a blind eye to it, but when it came to something highly immoral, you know he wouldn't rest until he did something about it."

"I know." Isha had tortured herself all these months, agonizing over whether Nikhil had suffered horribly while dying. Had he fought the killer, or was he taken by surprise? Had the killer at least finished the job quickly, or had he played with his prey like a cat with a mouse? What were her husband's last moments like? An endless list of questions burned a hole in her brain.

Now the scab on the slowly healing wound was reopened. And with it came rage. "Why couldn't Nikhil leave this particular issue alone? How could he be so careless?"

With a rueful smile Sheila turned to her. "He was like that even when he was a child. In school, if a boy attacked another, he'd go to the principal and make sure the offender was punished."

"But this wasn't a schoolyard fight! Didn't he stop to think about the consequences of going to the police? Weren't death threats serious enough for Nikhil?" How could an intelligent and practical man not consider the consequences of his actions?

"In Niku's mind, he was doing the right thing. He probably thought the threats were bogus. Anyone would, given the kinds of people we've always known in our town. Who would think anyone capable of murder?"

A sense of hopelessness came over Isha. "What a waste of a precious life." She sat with her face cupped in her hands for a while. Sheila brooded beside her in silence. They both had their own doubts and questions. At the moment, there were no answers.

Moments later, Isha asked her sister-in-law a troubled question. "So if the police never catch the murderer, does it mean the insurance claim will never be settled?"

"It will be settled within a day or two. Besides, I understand the police are thinking about closing the case because they can't find a single clue. As you know, they never found any fingerprints or weapons or even signs of a break-in."

"I find that hard to believe. But I guess I have to accept it." It was entirely possible the investigation was hushed up by Karnik. He was a wealthy doctor. All he had to do was hand over some cash to the right people and the matter would be closed. In fact, she was sure that was exactly what had happened. Her bitterness went up another notch.

"Kumar spoke to Manoj's boss. He even went all the way up

to the general manager, explained the situation, and vouched for your character. They've promised to settle your claim as quickly as possible."

Isha enclosed Sheila in a grateful hug. "Thank you so much, both you and Kumar. I don't know what else to say."

"Don't be silly," said Sheila. "We're family."

"Do Ayee and Baba know about any of this?"

Sheila shook her head. "No. In fact, I haven't told them I've found you and visited you. They have no idea their new granddaughter is here."

"I'm glad. If they found out the murder was premeditated, they might even believe what the police suspect: that *I'm* the one who might have arranged for Nikhil's death, or worse, that Diya is responsible for it somehow."

"That's ridiculous! Diya is an innocent infant."

"Not so ridiculous if you look at it from your parent's point of view. In their opinion, *she* is responsible for Niku's death, remember?"

"In that case, I'll keep my mouth shut. Patil and the insurance folks are keeping mum, anyway. They have to, since it's an official investigation."

"Thank God for that!"

"So, when do you want to go look at the flats you had in mind?" Sheila asked after a couple of moments.

Clearly Sheila was trying her best to cheer Isha up. "I don't know. I'll have to wait until the insurance check arrives."

"Kumar and I can lend you the money for now."

Isha mulled over that and realized it was probably the best thing to do. Now that she was assured she'd have some money to call her own, why not start moving forward with her plans? And Sheila was so eager to help. "I don't have a car, so I can't even get out of here."

"That's what *I'm* here for." Sheila did indeed look efficient and eager in her sunny lemon-yellow sari. "I can drive you in my car. Do you feel strong enough to go out?"

"I feel fine. But we can't just leave. What about Diya and Priya?" Isha looked about her helplessly. She hadn't left the room in several days, and the convent in months. Suddenly the prospect of venturing outside the steel gates was daunting.

"We'll take them with us," replied Sheila with a confident grin. "Between the two of us we can handle the kids."

Sheila's enthusiasm was infectious. Isha studied her generally subdued sister-in-law with narrowed eyes. Something was different. This was a Sheila unlike the one she'd known in the past. Isha had almost always seen her when Ayee and Baba were present. She realized that Sheila, too, was intimidated and inhibited by her parents. No wonder Sheila had always played the sweet, submissive daughter. Outside their stifling influence she was a different woman, vivacious and full of spirit.

Isha felt a sudden burst of optimism shoot through her veins as she observed the grin on Sheila's face. Her eyes gleamed with promise. "Okay. Can we do it this afternoon when Priya returns from school?"

"Why not?"

"There's something else I need to do—go to the District Registrar's office and apply for Diya's birth certificate."

"So we'll do that, too," assured Sheila. "I know a woman there who can get it done right away. We can go directly to her and bypass the red tape and all those clerks looking for bribes."

"Good. I don't have money for bribes."

The flats in the new building were smaller than Isha had anticipated, but the price was within her budget. In fact, like she'd been hoping, if she lived as frugally as she could for a while, she could afford to buy two. The dream of renting one and living in the other seemed viable.

She was ready to just about cry with relief, especially because she'd be within walking distance from food stores, the rickshaw stand, and the bus stop. Best of all, she could leave the convent. Since Diya's birth, it had begun to depress her more and more.

While Sheila held the baby, Isha settled Priya beside her on the sofa and talked to the owner of the building, Mr. Saraf. He was a short, rotund man with a pudgy face that glowed with

self-indulgence. He wore overpowering cologne. A pack of ciga-
rettes and a fancy gold lighter sat on the coffee table separating
the sofa from the chairs, one of which he occupied and the other
was taken by Sheila. His expensive clothes and the showy décor
in his office weren't exactly subtle reminders of his rags-to-
riches story.

Most everyone in town knew Saraf, the real estate baron. He
was a sharp businessman, and well known for his projects. His
high-rise buildings were scattered all over Palgaum's suburbs.
He was the king of ownership flats, or condominiums, as the
Americans called them.

Mr. Saraf raised an eyebrow at Isha. "Madam, are you thinking of buying the flats as an investment?"

"Not entirely, Saraf-saheb. I'm planning to live in one and
rent out the other."

"Oh . . . I see!" The man's eyes went wide with astonishment.

Isha wondered how much he knew about her circumstances,
other than the fact that Nikhil had passed on. This was the first
time she'd shown her face in public since his death.

"As you know, I'm a widow now," she explained to him.

"I am so sorry about your husband, Mrs. Tilak. I was shocked
and saddened by the news about his . . . his . . ." Saraf was clearly
at a loss for words.

"Thank you."

"I buy all my tires from your shop, madam," he said, recov-
ering quickly. "It is an honor to do business with you." He
smiled and offered her the official papers for the purchase.

"Likewise, Mr. Saraf." Isha glanced at the unsigned contracts
for a brief moment and put them back in the envelope. Sheila
had warned her not to sign anything until Kumar's solicitor had
studied and approved them. She rose to her feet and motioned
Priya to do the same. "I'll have our solicitor look at them. If
everything is satisfactory, then I'll bring the bank draft for the
advance."

"Very good, madam." He stood up and joined his palms in a
respectful good-bye.

"We'll give you a ring and set up an appointment," said Isha. "*Namaste.*"

They returned to the convent, listening to Priya's chatter in the backseat while Diya slept in her mother's lap. Perhaps sensing Isha's need for quiet contemplation, Sheila was the one who conversed with Priya as she drove them back.

Isha had too much on her mind to pay attention to anything around her. She was going to become a homeowner. Despite her upbringing, she'd never really owned anything by herself.

Was she making a mistake? Would she be able to handle life on her own? The convent, in spite of its gloom, was a sheltered place, and with the nuns forming a protective circle around her, it was the perfect place to hide.

Now she'd be out in the open. People would notice and recognize her. What was she going to tell them? There was no question that she'd end up embarrassing her in-laws once people started to converse with her, pry into her circumstances—just like Saraf had tried a little while ago.

Ayee and Baba would find out soon that she was not only still in Palgaum but was about to start living not too far from them.

Would they try to drive her out of town? Or would they pretend she didn't exist?

Chapter 15

December 2006

Isha looked around her new flat and inhaled. Who would have thought the mingled odors of fresh paint, varnish, and floor polish could be such a delight? And all this was *hers!*

She couldn't believe that the elusive insurance check had finally arrived two weeks ago. After fretting for months, she'd wept with relief at seeing the check, mainly because she could reimburse Sheila and Kumar for the huge amount of money they had loaned her.

The flat now belonged to her in the real sense. She and the children were gradually settling into their new home. Despite the odds against it happening, they had somehow managed to make it so far. New Year's Eve was right around the corner. They could celebrate it in their *new* home.

Nikhil would have been proud.

The maroon- and beige-striped curtains she'd hung over the drawing room windows were parted at the moment. They fluttered in the afternoon breeze, bringing in the sunshine and Palgaum's humid air, along with the toots and bellows of traffic sounds. She had missed that familiar clatter during her five-month stay at the convent.

She tore open the envelope that had just arrived from the District Registrar's office. It contained Diya's birth certificate.

Her mouth curved into a smile as she checked the information for accuracy. *Diya Nikhil Tilak*. The child that wasn't meant to be was very much here. And now it was official. Diya was an individual with her own unique personality. She had a right to live a decent life, gain an education, pursue a career, vote for the political candidate of her choice someday, and carve out whatever kind of life she wanted.

Isha opened the *almirah* to store the certificate along with the other papers that were in the thick brown envelope she'd pulled out of the safe deposit box. She settled herself on the bed to examine its contents. Nikhil had usually dealt with the safe deposit box, so she wasn't aware of exactly what was in the envelope. But it was time she learned.

Inside it she found three smaller white envelopes. The first one contained Priya's birth certificate, their marriage certificate, and two passports—Nikhil's and hers. They had needed those when they had taken trips to Nepal, Singapore, and Dubai when they were newlyweds. Before the memories of those happy trips could come barreling into her mind and bring on the tears, she quickly added Diya's birth record to the envelope and closed the flap. She was slowly learning to shut off those upsetting memories at will.

Now *that* could undeniably be termed *progress*.

The second envelope was filled with receipts going back a few years, most of them for jewelry Nikhil had bought for her.

The third envelope was bulky, and looked crisp and new. What could Nikhil have stowed in the safe deposit recently? Opening it, she pulled out a computer disk and three folded sheets of paper. Curious, she unfolded and smoothed them out on the bed.

They looked like tables of some kind, statistical information. Frowning, she studied them. Why would Nikhil keep accounting information in a bank vault when their accountant handled everything?

The tables had been done on a computer. Since she'd often observed Nikhil work on his home computer, she knew what a spreadsheet looked like. It took her several moments to recognize what she was looking at: numbers, dates, names, and amounts in rupees.

All at once it registered. Oh God! Oh God! She went very still.

They appeared to be printouts of records from Dr. Karnik's office. Or were they from his home? They contained data going back to the past three years. She studied the names, dates, times, fees collected. She knew some of the names—a few very well.

The money column added up to astronomical sums. The word *abortion* didn't appear anywhere, but anyone with half a brain would know what they were: a record of abortions performed, and meticulously maintained by someone—most likely Karnik himself.

So, the man had established some sort of database. More than likely it wasn't stored with his other paperwork—the legal kind. This probably came from a private computer.

And Nikhil had somehow managed to obtain copies! Karnik wouldn't be stupid enough to leave it in some obvious place. So, exactly how had Nikhil come by all this? Had he confronted Karnik with these records? Is that why a desperate Karnik had stabbed him to death? Had Nikhil even had a chance to show them to the police?

She turned that over in her mind for a moment. Her heart was racing. This was vital information about something sinister. She read some of the more familiar names once again. Shocking! Some of her close acquaintances had had abortions. Was there no end to this obsession with producing male children? Didn't all these bright and educated individuals recognize the folly in going against God's will and upsetting the balance of nature?

As she digested the information, slowly a few other pieces of the puzzle began to fall into place. Nikhil had probably realized that starting an investigation into a dangerous matter could end his life, especially since he'd received death threats, and that's why he had gone out and bought a large life insurance policy. Somehow he'd known that his parents would abandon Isha and his children if he died, and he had done his best to take care of them before that happened.

So, when he was attacked so brutally, was it still a shock or had he been expecting it?

Something else started to claw at her brain. What if the killer knew that Nikhil had copies of the spreadsheets? What if he presumed Isha may be holding on to them? The killer could come after her! The thought made her shudder. She couldn't afford to die, not when she was the only source of support for her children. She couldn't let them become orphans.

But now that she'd discovered the evidence, should she hand it over to the police? Should she mention it to Sheila and Kumar and let them handle it? In the next instant she abandoned both the ideas. Nikhil had died because of this. She couldn't place his sister and brother-in-law in danger. Whoever had killed Nikhil was a cold-blooded monster, and wouldn't hesitate to kill again.

Maybe she should just ignore the whole thing and let it go? It had brought her and the family so much misery. She didn't need any more of it.

In the end, she decided she couldn't ignore the significance of what she held in her hands. She had to do something. But not right now, not while she needed to concentrate on putting her life back together. It was barely two weeks since they'd moved into the flat. There was still so much for her to do.

One thing at a time, she told herself. Once she'd established herself and her girls in their new home, she'd give serious thought to what she'd do with this crucial piece of evidence against Karnik.

Carefully folding the sheets of paper, she put them and the disk back in their envelope. Then she locked it up in the *almirah*. But her hands wouldn't stop shaking.

Chapter 16

April 2007

Harish lifted the baby off the scale and laid her gently on the examination table. She had gained a fair amount of weight. Diya Tilak was an unusually amiable baby, too.

There was no doubt she'd grow up to be a beauty someday. He tapped her chin with his finger. "You want to smile for me, Diya?" It came instantly, a dazzling, toothless smile that settled like a soft, warm fist around his heart. She was delightful! Too bad her father wasn't around to see her and enjoy her presence.

Priya, who was standing on the other side of the table, staring at him while he performed his tasks, was no less a beauty in her own right. There was a marked resemblance between the siblings.

Today Priya was wearing a dainty white dress with a sprinkling of tiny red flowers and puffy sleeves. Her small feet were encased in white sandals. She, too, looked like she had gained a little weight, much needed in her case, since she was too thin for her height. From his estimate the girls were going to grow quite tall, much taller than their mother.

The two sisters were lucky to have inherited such superior genes in the appearance department. From what he'd gathered during his brief encounters with Priya, she was very sharp, too. Beauty and brains. Oh, to be able to father such magnificent children! With his looks, his potential kids had no more chance of being born beautiful than did a baby ostrich.

Now that Diya was more alert and learning new things, she was developing a distinct personality of her own. He peered inside her tiny ears and found nothing unusual. She was a healthy six-month-old.

Isha Tilak stood nearby and looked on anxiously, her arms folded across her middle. "How is she doing, Harish?"

He turned to face her. "Very well. You should be proud. Everything's right on schedule—height, weight, reflexes, color. She's beautiful."

"You're very kind." Isha gave a pleased smile, sending a mild tingle through his blood. "And a very caring doctor."

Lord, but the woman was attractive! She'd added a sparkle to his day the moment she'd walked into his office with her children—a breath of fresh air and sunshine.

It was good to see her smile for a change. He hadn't seen her since the day he'd stopped at the convent to give Diya her second round of shots. Isha had later called to inform him that she was finally able to move out of the convent and into a flat of her own. He'd been tempted to ask her where, but since she hadn't volunteered the information he'd left the matter alone.

There hadn't been a single day when he hadn't thought about her, wondered if she'd gone back to Dr. Bajaj for her children's care. A number of times he had nearly dialed her mobile number, then stopped himself. But now that she was here, he was glad that she hadn't switched doctors. In fact, she'd told him she wanted him to be Priya's pediatrician as well.

"I don't know about that," he said, secretly feeling ridiculously pleased with her compliment. He couldn't help staring at her a moment longer than necessary.

Today she looked so much more like the teenager he used to admire in college. The last couple of times he'd seen her, it had been under depressing circumstances and in a poorly lit room. She had looked exhausted and despondent on both occasions.

But now she appeared more content, and the smile on her face just now was clearly spontaneous, not something she'd pasted on for the world to see.

Noticing the flush blooming over her neck and face, he realized he'd embarrassed her by gawking too long. Quickly turning his attention back to the baby, he put the stethoscope to her chest. The heartbeat he heard was strong and vibrant. Since Priya's inquisitive eyes were on him, he asked her, "Do you want to listen to your sister's heartbeat?"

Priya's face lit up. "Yesss!" It was obvious the child was thrilled to be asked to participate. Dr. Bajaj probably never allowed any such playfulness around his office.

He looked at Isha to see if she had any objections, and when she nodded, indicating she had none, he invited Priya to come around the table. He placed the eartips inside her ears. For a while he let her listen, her eyes round with awe and her mouth open. She seemed enthralled. "What do you hear?" he asked her.

Priya grinned at him in delight. *"Thud, thud!"*

"It's called a heartbeat." In brief and simple terms he explained to her how the human heart worked.

Fascinated by the experience, Priya refused to part with the stethoscope. Isha had to pry it away with a mild rebuke. "Sorry, she can be a little stubborn at times," she explained to Harish and handed the piece of equipment back to him.

"Don't worry; that's how most kids are." He put the stethoscope out of Priya's reach and motioned Isha to approach the table and dress the baby. "Are you still nursing Diya?" He wondered if she'd run out of the formula he'd given her several weeks ago and if she needed any more samples.

As she pinned the baby's nappy into place, Isha nodded. "But I'm slowly weaning her by supplementing with some formula in the last few weeks."

"In that case Diya's going to need vitamin supplements. I'll give you some samples." He went to the cabinet that housed his many samples and threw various containers of vitamins, formula, and baby cereals into a plastic bag and handed them to her. "These should be good for a few months."

"Thank you," she said, looking hesitant about accepting the bag. But she didn't entirely resist taking it.

He wanted to ask Isha about so many other things. Did she like living on her own? How was she managing financially? Was she getting enough sleep? A dozen other questions came to mind, including whether he could help her in some way, but he refrained from asking them. Isha Tilak's personal life was none of his business, he reminded himself.

But she provided a few answers of her own accord. "I should give your nurse my address and phone number. I have a regular line in addition to my mobile phone now."

"So you've moved somewhere close by?" he asked cautiously as he watched Isha slide the baby's arms into the sleeves of her dress and button it up.

"It's the new Saraf building next to State Bank. I bought a flat for us and another one that I'm renting out to an officer of the bank."

"I'm glad you're out of the convent. So are you still working at the orphanage?"

"Yes."

Harish felt a pang of sympathy. "How do you manage all that *and* the kids?"

"Well, Priya's in class all day, and the nuns let me bring Diya to school. So both my children are nearby. At the moment school is closed for the summer holidays, so I have a few weeks' break."

"That's something, I suppose. But then it reopens in early June." He still wasn't happy about a woman like Isha working in such a depressing place. "Do you really need to stretch yourself that thin? I mean, can't you pull on with the rent alone?"

She shook her head. "Not if Priya keeps outgrowing her clothes and shoes so quickly and soon Diya will be getting there, too." Probably because his eyes fell on the kids' new-looking clothes, she added, "At the moment I'm managing by sewing their clothes myself."

He turned to her with raised brows. "You *made* the children's clothes?"

"Yes. My neighbor has kindly donated her sewing machine to me because she's getting too old to be able to see very well."

"But the clothes are beautiful!"

"Oh, well . . ."

"They look like store-bought. You're very talented."

She flushed at the compliment. "If there's *one* thing the nuns taught me well, it's sewing. I also happen to like it."

On hearing her mother mention clothes, Priya proudly pointed to the outfit she had on. "Look, Doctor-kaka, I have a new dress."

Priya had started calling him Doctor-kaka since the time she'd arrived, and it pleased him immensely. It meant the child had accepted him as family, or pseudofamily, because the official generic term for paternal uncle was *kaka*. He guessed that since her mother now called him by his first name, she had instructed her daughter to address him as such.

He made a production of studying the dress. "What a nice outfit!"

Suddenly Priya said something that caught him by surprise. "Mummy is making another new dress for my birthday."

He checked her chart to verify the date of birth. "That's right. You have your sixth birthday coming up soon."

"Will you come to my birthday party, Doctor-kaka? Sheila-tayi is bringing ice-cream cake and presents."

"Cake and presents, huh? Sounds great!"

"Will you come?" Priya tugged on his sleeve.

"I—I'm not sure . . ." He glanced at Isha, not knowing what her reaction would be. He was hoping for an invitation, but she didn't look too thrilled about her daughter's outburst.

Instead she bent down to pick up her purse. "How much do I owe you for today's visit, Harish?"

"Nothing."

She became very still. "What do you mean by nothing?"

"Exactly that. You don't owe me anything." He patted Priya's head. "It's a pleasure to treat such cute and friendly patients."

"But that's not fair to you, Harish. This is your livelihood. You can't give away your professional services for free."

He chuckled. She looked so earnest arguing her point. "I didn't spend more than twenty minutes of my time on Diya."

She bit her lower lip. "Are we . . . part of your charity case-load, then?"

"Of course not! I'm doing this as a friend. We were college

contemporaries at one time, and I'm hoping you'd consider me a friend of the family."

"Okay . . . then."

Had he put his foot in his mouth again? She was clearly strapped for money and he wanted to help the only way he could. "Look, I'm sorry if you think I have ulterior motives, but I don't. I just . . ."

He removed his glasses, wiped them with a handkerchief, and put them back on. It was an annoying nervous mannerism he'd cultivated over the years. Whenever he felt ill at ease or angry or nervous, he cleaned his glasses, giving himself a moment or two to adjust to the situation and compose himself. But now, he just couldn't shed the habit, no matter how hard he tried. "I don't know what to say other than to apologize if I've upset you in some way. That wasn't my intent."

She tenderly lifted the baby into her arms. "I believe you. But I'm so used to paying for everything. And Bajaj's fee wasn't cheap. His nurse always asked for the payment up front."

"We operate a little differently here. I like to help my friends in whatever small way I can. So please don't take it the wrong way."

"All right then, I'm very grateful for your help. I don't know what I'd do without it." She seemed to be deep in thought for a moment. "Would you . . . um . . . mind coming for Priya's birthday next week?" She inclined her head toward Priya, whose expression was still eager. "She obviously wants you to come."

"Mind? Are you kidding? I'd be honored."

"It's not really a party as such. It's just family—my sister-in-law, Sheila, her husband, Kumar Sathe, and their two sons, Milind and Arvind. It's next Sunday at six o'clock."

"I'll be there." Never in his whole life had a child's birthday filled him with such curious anticipation. He couldn't wait, although the thought of meeting all those relatives of the Tilaks was a bit unnerving. But he could handle it. He knew who Kumar and Sheila Sathe were and he'd seen them around town often enough. They were very influential in local social circles and active on the club scene.

If nothing else, the party would at least expand his network. Socializing with the pillars of the community was a big part of being a doctor, and he didn't do enough of it. This would be a good opportunity to start. Unfortunately, a medical practice these days had to be run like a business.

Isha started to move toward the door, so he stepped ahead of her and held open the door. "See you next week." He waved at them.

He watched her walk through the reception area and out the main door, an oversized bag slung over one shoulder, Diya held firmly against her chest, and her free hand holding Priya's hand. She carried such a large burden on such slender shoulders.

He felt something stir inside him. He wasn't sure what it was, but he preferred to think of it as admiration for a remarkable woman. How had she managed to step down from a pampered princess existence and adjust to the austere lifestyle of the convent and still keep her spirits intact?

Had she been happy in her marriage to Nikhil Tilak? he wondered.

He nodded at Saroj-bayi's curious lift of the brow, confirming his earlier instruction that she was not to bill Isha Tilak for the visit. As expected, she had argued with him about his over-generous attitude, but he'd convinced her that the Tilaks were old family friends and that all the kids' visits would be free.

"If you keep giving free treatment to every family friend, you'll be the poorest doctor in Palgaum," she'd warned him.

He'd laughed at her comment. "I haven't won that title yet, so let's not worry about it."

Noticing the number of people seated in his waiting room, he glanced at his watch. Back to work! He didn't have the luxury of being able to put his feet up and fantasize about a pretty woman called Isha Ketkar . . . or rather Isha Tilak.

Besides, Saroj-bayi was giving him the *look,* so he motioned her to send in his next patient.

Chapter 17

Isha checked on Diya slumbering in the pretty wooden cradle. She seemed to like sleeping in that elaborate contraption. It was an interesting piece made in the *Sankheda* fashion of the northwestern region of India. Its construction allowed Diya to stare at the bright colors of the multicolored painted spindles whenever she was awake.

Sheila had brought over the cradle, since she and Kumar had no intention of having any more children. Isha was grateful for the timely donation. She wondered what Ayee and Baba would have to say about that, if they only knew.

Her in-laws now knew about her presence in town. In fact, Sheila had informed them the very day Isha had purchased the flats. There was no way to keep it a secret any longer.

Apparently Ayee and Baba were furious about their daughter-in-law and grandchildren being in town. They were an embarrassment to the older Tilaks, especially if they were living in poverty.

"What the hell is Isha trying to do to us? Is she deliberately trying to ruin our reputation by making it look like we kicked her and our grandchild out, or what?" was what Baba had said, according to Sheila. "I will not tolerate such nonsense. Tell her to take the children and get out of this town."

Sheila had tried to calm him down by explaining that Isha had not said one negative word about her in-laws to anyone, nor did she socialize with their upper-class crowd anymore. But

Baba was allegedly on a rampage. Isha hoped he wouldn't start a campaign to hound her out of town just to protect his precious image. Unfortunately, he had enough clout in Palgaum to make her life uncomfortable enough to drive her out.

Since they'd moved into the flat, Priya went to Sheila's house to play with the boys at least twice a week. Isha often worried about the likelihood of her child running into her hostile grandparents. In a small town it was inevitable that their paths would cross at some point. But Isha wanted to avoid that possibility as much as she could.

If the old folks came face-to-face with Priya, God knew how they'd react. Another spanking? Humiliate and traumatize her by some other means? Isha shuddered to think of the ways Baba could express his wrath.

She went into Priya's bedroom and picked up the birthday dress that needed hemming. Although the second bedroom was Priya's, and it was furnished, the little girl chose to sleep with Isha in the large master bed. Isha indulged her because Priya had become used to sleeping in the same room as her at the convent. Besides, the child was still adjusting to her new surroundings and circumstances, and Isha didn't have the heart to inflict more stress on her.

At the moment, Priya was at Sheila's house, eating dinner and playing with her cousins, so Isha settled on the couch in the drawing room to finish the birthday dress. She held up the pastel-pink outfit and studied it critically for a minute. It looked rather nice.

She really did have a flair for sewing children's clothes. It was an unexpected blessing when Mrs. Shintre next door had asked Isha if she could use an old sewing machine and a bag full of fabrics, threads, and sewing notions that had been sitting around untouched for years.

Overnight, Isha was making clothes for the children and enjoying it, too. It was becoming her savior in other ways as well. Instead of brooding over things after the girls were tucked in bed each night, she sewed like a maniac. The result was a number of much-needed new outfits for the children, and the best thing was, she hadn't had to spend a single rupee on them.

What was it Harish had said about the dresses? They looked like store-bought clothes. She'd felt immensely pleased with his compliment.

Thinking of Harish, she recalled the way he'd looked at her the other day—or rather stared. She was woman enough to recognize frank admiration in a man's eyes. She'd experienced enough of it during her college years, when boys had stared at her, sent her silly little love notes, even tried to ring her at home. (Her parents had intercepted those calls and quickly put an end to them.)

But Harish was a grown man and the expression on his face was not that of a boy with a crush.

His gaze had left her all hot and embarrassed, but she had to admit she'd also enjoyed it. Her pulse turning erratic at his attention wasn't an accident. She'd felt something . . . slightly disturbing.

Was he interested in her as a woman? That may well be, but she couldn't really have any interest in him, now, could she? It wasn't even a year since Nikhil's demise. How could a woman totally in love with her husband have any feelings for another man? And so soon after her husband's death?

It was merely a reflex, a physical reaction to the opposite sex. She'd taken enough psychology courses to know that was quite normal.

Granted, Harish now looked rather distinguished in an academic sort of way. The crisp clothes, glossy shoes, and the professionally confident yet socially shy personality had a certain quaint charm. He was a genuinely nice man, too. Besides, she had loads of admiration for his superior intellect.

However, she had no interest in him other than as a friend, she told herself firmly. She couldn't!

Halfway through the hemming, a knock sounded on the door and she let Sheila and Priya in. "Mummy!" Priya gave her an exuberant hug. The child had stars in her eyes and her face looked flushed.

"Looks like you had a wonderful time at Sheila-tayi's place," Isha said.

"Guess what!" Priya looked up at her. "Milind and Arvind got a new puppy!"

"Isn't that nice!" Isha glanced at Sheila, who pulled a disgusted face. So the puppy wasn't Sheila's idea.

"Mummy, can we get a puppy, too?"

This was what Isha had feared. The moment Priya had mentioned the puppy she knew exactly what her little girl was leading up to.

Sheila held up a cautionary hand. "Say no, Isha. You'll save yourself a lot of headaches. That puppy is a menace." She rolled her eyes. "We've had that horrible dog for one day and already he's chewed up two pairs of my sandals and an expensive handbag. Plus he's stolen food from the kitchen. Our cook is ready to strangle the beast."

"That bad, huh?" Isha tried to sympathize, but her lips twitched. Poor Sheila looked like she was ready to choke the puppy, too. She turned to Priya. "You see how much trouble a puppy is? That's why we can't have one."

"Please, Mummy." She put her skinny hands around Isha's face to get her undivided attention. "I promise I'll make sure our puppy doesn't eat your shoes."

Isha put on her most forbidding expression. "No! We can't leave a puppy here by itself all day while you and Diya and I are at school." Besides, she barely had enough money to feed and clothe the kids, let alone a pet.

"Oh . . ." Priya's brow creased for a moment. "I can stay at home and take care of him. You and Diya can go to school."

Sheila started to chuckle. "Now *there's* a novel excuse for cutting school. I hadn't heard that one before."

Isha winked at Sheila across the room. "She can be very inventive in that department."

Taking Priya by the arm, Sheila pulled her over to the sofa. "Come here, darling. Your mummy is right. This flat is too small for a puppy, and all of you are too busy to take care of it." Seeing Priya's small face wilt, she added, "You know you can come to our house and play with Rambo any time you want to."

"Promise?"

"Promise. That way you get to play with Rambo *and* your cousins."

"Okay." Priya's smile returned with some of its former radiance.

Isha observed the interaction between her daughter and Sheila, and her heart warmed. Sheila was so different from her parents. Isha had always thought fondly of her, but in the last few months she'd become Isha's private savior, her best friend, the sister she'd never had.

Isha looked at the clock and then at Priya. "Time for bed, pumpkin. Go brush your teeth and put on your pajamas while I talk to Sheila-tayi."

Now that the small matter about puppies was resolved, Priya took off for the bathroom.

Meanwhile Sheila's gaze fell on the dress Isha was hemming and the other two that needed buttons sewn on. She stared at them in astonishment. "Are you actually *making* those dresses?"

"Yes." Isha looked at the expression on Sheila's face. "Are they that *bad?*"

"They're that *good.*" She picked up one and held it up to the light. "This looks so professionally made. I had no idea you could sew this well."

"I've always liked sewing, but I never bothered doing it." She didn't have to, until now.

Sheila put the dress down. "These are superbly tailored, like you'd see in a dress shop."

"I'm just trying to skimp on buying the girls' clothes. When Mrs. Shintre gave me her old machine and some fabrics, I went a little crazy."

Sheila became thoughtful for a moment, then snapped her fingers. "You know what? I have an idea."

"What?"

"If you can create dresses like these for some of Palgaum's rich kids, maybe you could start a business of your own."

Isha gave a hoot of laughter. It was the first time in months she'd laughed out loud, surprising herself and Sheila. "You must be crazy. Making a couple of frocks for my daughters is not the same as being a professional."

"But these *are* professional. All this lace edging and frills are hard to do. You already know how the women you and I socialize with go to Mumbai or some other big city to buy clothes for their daughters. If they could buy them right here in town, and have them custom-fitted instead of buying them off a rack in some expensive boutique, I'll bet they'd prefer coming to you."

A tingle of excitement crept through Isha. Could Sheila be right? Did she have it in her to do something independent like dressmaking? "I don't think I'm cut out to be a business-woman," she said nevertheless.

Sheila chuckled. "*Cut out* is a clever pun for a dressmaker. If you ask me, you never give yourself enough credit for being an intelligent and capable woman. In fact, we Indian women rarely expect anything from ourselves beyond playing adoring wives and mothers."

"But that's the way we're brought up, Sheila. We never think 'outside the box,' as they say."

"So you agree with me?"

"I agree with your reasoning."

"Then this is your chance to prove to yourself that you can do something with your life."

"But what if no one buys my homemade dresses? Then what?"

Sheila made a casual gesture with her perfectly manicured hand. "Then there's always the orphanage job, isn't there?"

"True, but how am I going to advertise? How will I know if I can meet customers' deadlines? I can only do so much with my regular job, the housework, and my kids."

Glancing at her wristwatch, Sheila rose to her feet. "Leave that to me. Just give me a couple of sample dresses. At my mahjong party next week, I'll show them to some of our friends. We'll see what they have to say."

Reluctantly Isha went into her bedroom and brought out two of her best creations: a white cotton one with eyelet edging in Diya's infant size and the other a full-skirted pale blue with a darker blue embroidered collar and matching sash made for Priya.

"I'm telling you," she warned Sheila, "Baba and Ayee will probably explode when they find out their rebellious embarrassment of a daughter-in-law is up to further tricks, like taking up tailoring, to further discredit them."

Sheila was quiet for a moment, making Isha wonder if she'd said something wrong. But Sheila picked up her purse, folded the dresses, and tucked them under her arm. "Ayee and Baba have other things on their mind lately to worry about such things."

Isha stilled. "Is something wrong, Sheila?"

"I didn't want to tell you this, but I suppose you'll find out soon enough. Ayee's been ill for the last few weeks."

"I'm sorry to hear that." Guilt crept up on Isha in an instant. Was it her own actions that had caused Nikhil's mother to fall sick? "I guess I was selfish in thinking only of myself and my children when I decided to leave. But Ayee didn't seem all that concerned when I told her I was leaving for good."

Sheila shook her head. "I don't think your leaving has anything to do with this. She was complaining of chest pains and breathlessness, so her doctor ran some tests."

"How serious?" Despite her bitterness about her in-laws, she felt a twinge of regret. These were people she'd lived with for several years, and she'd considered them surrogate parents all that time.

"They found two of her arteries were partially blocked, so they inserted stents in them."

"She looked okay when I left home that morning," said Isha. "I know losing Nikhil was hard on her, but . . ." Was the heart blockage something that could be caused by trauma and heartbreak? Had Isha inadvertently been the cause of her mother-in-law's problems? If so, she'd never be able to forgive herself.

"The doctor says this started years ago, well before Niku's death. Her cholesterol levels have always been high, and she's overweight. These conditions run in her family. My grandfather died of a heart attack when he was quite young, and so did Ayee's older brother. Besides, you know how Ayee and Baba hate going to the doctor unless they're really sick. Anyway, when the chest pains started, Baba forced her to see the doctor. That's how they found out she had a blockage."

"How is she doing now?"

Sheila looked up at the ceiling, biting her trembling lower lip. "She's seems okay at the moment. The pain's gone and she has eased back into her old social life, but she has to watch her diet and take better care of herself." The tears abruptly started to pool in her eyes. "I know she's not a warm, caring woman, but . . . She's still my mother."

"Of course she is." Isha tried to think of something appropriate to say, but she couldn't. What could she say? She wasn't even a part of that family anymore, but technically she was still a Tilak, and they were still her in-laws. "Is there anything I can do to help?"

Sheila shook her head, looking so miserable that Isha instinctively put her arms around her. She couldn't help the tears of sympathy that stung her own eyes. Sheila was hurting and so was she. The woman who was her children's grandmother was ailing, and that hurt, too.

Sheila extricated herself from Isha's arms and sniffed. "I better leave before Priya comes out and finds both of us crying. She'll start asking questions."

"All right." Isha quickly dried her eyes and opened the door for Sheila. "I wish you'd told me earlier."

"You have enough to worry about. The last thing you need is more worry and guilt." Sheila stepped outside the door, hesitated for a beat, and stopped again. "Maybe it's best that I tell you this. Ayee's now convinced that Diya is responsible for everything, including her heart condition."

Isha took a fortifying breath. "Is she still in that 'blame the baby' mode?"

"I'm afraid so. I just thought I'd warn you before you heard it from someone else. Ayee was telling that to all her friends who came to visit her during her illness."

"I see." Isha tried to summon a smile despite the tightness in her chest. "And do you believe that, too?"

"Never! I've never subscribed to that nonsense at any time in my life. I think we all come with our fates sealed and delivered the day we're born. Someone else can't change what's going to happen. I love Diya like my own."

"Thank you, Sheila. And I'm glad you warned me. Just keep me informed of everything, will you?"

"All right."

Isha waited till her sister-in-law walked away, then closed the door and heaved a deep sigh. If Ayee's condition worsened, how was Baba going to survive losing his son and possibly his wife, too? And why was her Diya, her innocent little baby, being held responsible for all the unfortunate things that were happening? If only her in-laws would see their beautiful granddaughter and find out for themselves what a sweet fountain of joy she was.

But that would never happen. Ayee would never want to lay eyes on her imagined nemesis.

For the first time since Nikhil's death Isha felt sorry for her father-in-law. Despite his rigid ways and complete lack of warmth, and although she couldn't forgive him for spanking Priya so mercilessly, Isha felt something akin to pity for him.

On the one hand she thoroughly resented the man and on the other she sympathized with him. Was it possible to have such polarized feelings about someone?

In the next instant she realized her softer sentiments were because of Nikhil and Sheila. He was their father and now anything she did that hurt him would hurt Sheila. But if she did feel sorry for Baba for some convoluted reason, what could she do to help? He'd only spurn her offer.

She decided it was best not to tell Priya about her grandmother just yet. In any case, the child had almost forgotten her grandparents by now. Priya rarely talked about them anymore.

That night, as Isha lay in bed, mulling over Ayee's illness, she made a decision to talk to Harish about it. He'd be able to explain it in layman's terms. Modern medical science had supposedly made heart conditions more treatable these days.

Ayee would be fine. She *had* to be fine.

Chapter 18

Isha sprinkled the finely chopped coriander to garnish the chicken curry, and then set it and the salad on the dining table. It was a simple meal with an accompanying vegetable dish, rice, and *chapatis*.

After much debate over whether to cancel Priya's birthday party because of the news about Ayee's illness, Sheila had convinced Isha that they should go ahead with the plans. Besides, Priya was looking forward to it so much, Isha didn't want to break her heart. The previous year, she'd had no party at all. And there was such little joy in her children's lives to begin with.

Priya was in her element, dressed in her new dress, her pigtails secured with matching pink satin ribbons. Her little girl looked like an angel. And she became six years old today. Nikhil would have been ecstatic to see Priya reading and writing and learning so many new things in school.

At least he'd had an opportunity to enjoy the first five years of Priya's life. But he'd never see his younger child, the baby he'd fought so hard to save when she was no more than a tadpole swimming in Isha's womb.

The doorbell rang and Isha brushed aside her thoughts to get the door. Sheila stood outside with a cardboard box in her arms—the ice-cream cake. As always, she looked perfect, complete with shoulder-length hair fashionably styled, electric blue crepe-silk sari, and matching sapphire and pearl jewelry at her neck, ears, and wrists. Isha never stopped marveling at her sister-in-law's skill at looking so poised and attractive at all times.

Arvind and Milind stood on either side of their mother, each one holding two presents. They were typical boys and Sheila had a hard time keeping their clothes clean. But today the boys looked well scrubbed in their clean pants and T-shirts. Their dark hair was brushed back neatly and their cherubic faces with the gorgeous hazel eyes were a quite a sight. Isha knew they had been told to be on their best behavior for their little cousin's party.

"Wow! What a striking threesome!" Isha exclaimed with a grin. "Come right in. The birthday girl's been waiting for you."

Priya greeted her cousins and aunt with a gleeful whoop. "Yeah, presents!"

With an indulgent "Happy Birthday" for the animated Priya, Sheila put the ice-cream cake in the small refrigerator in the kitchen. Then she bent down to lift Diya off the floor and into her arms.

"What time should I serve dinner?" asked Isha.

"Kumar is coming directly from work," replied Sheila, glancing at the clock. "He should be here soon. We can have an early dinner and then cake later."

"Doctor-kaka is coming to my party, too," announced Priya, while her impatient hands were already tearing into the gifts.

Sheila's brows flew up. "Doctor-kaka?"

Isha busied herself with picking up the scraps of wrapping paper Priya and the boys were strewing around. "Priya asked Harish Salvi and I seconded the invitation. It just sort of . . . happened."

"I see." Sheila gave her a veiled look. "Looks like Priya is becoming rather fond of this Dr. Salvi. She's mentioned how nice and how clever he is several times recently."

"He seems to have a way with children. Priya and Diya like him a lot."

"And he's coming here today, huh?" Sheila threw Isha that oblique look again. "I'll tell you what I think after I meet him. If he's that good, I might switch my boys from Dr. Bajaj to him."

"But you're addicted to Bajaj," reminded Isha, tossing the scraps into the dustbin.

"He's getting a bit cranky in his old age. The boys are beginning to grumble about him."

"Then you might seriously consider Harish Salvi. He's not a rich, established old chap like Bajaj." Isha went into the kitchen to get the plates and spoons, with Sheila close on her heels. "He's quite young, and has started practicing recently. But he's thorough and he's patient. He explains things well when I ask questions."

"We'll see," said Sheila.

The doorbell rang again. One of the boys ran to get the door. Isha looked up to find Harish standing on the threshold, looking a little awkward. He was dressed in elegant black pants and a steel-gray shirt. He held a package in his hands. With his straight bearing, glasses, and old-fashioned haircut, he could have passed for a young college professor.

A surge of warmth crept up on her the moment their eyes met. Despite knowing he was coming, the joy of seeing him was unexpected. "Hello, Harish. Come on in."

She introduced him to Sheila and the boys. When all the formal *namastes* were over, he handed the gift-wrapped package to Priya. "Many Happy Returns, Priya. I hope you like what I got you."

Priya took the gift and beamed at him. "Thank you. What is it?"

"If you're allowed to open it now, you can see for yourself."

Isha laughed at the remark. "Look at the mess here. You can see all the other gifts have already been opened."

Priya tore open the wrapping in an instant and looked at the flat cardboard box with a mild frown. She turned it upside down. "What is this?"

"It's a chess set."

"What is a *chess* set?"

"It's a game. It has a board with squares and various pieces that have to be placed in a certain fashion inside the squares."

Milind, the bright ten-year-old and know-it-all, mocked his young cousin. "Don't you know that? I know what chess is."

Arvind, his cheeks still chubby from the last of the lingering baby fat, gave his brother a disdainful look. "No, you don't! You can't even play chess."

"Yes, I do!" Milind stood with his hands on his hips, clearly ready to take on his brother. Tussles often broke out between the two brothers at the slightest provocation.

Sheila handed the baby over to Isha and put an end to the bickering before it got serious. "That's enough! Dr. Salvi is a guest and doesn't need to watch you kids fight like hooligans." She gave the boys a forbidding look. "Papa will be here any minute, so you better behave yourselves."

The boys had a healthy fear of their father, so Milind moved to examine the chess set while his brother and Priya went back to talking to Harish.

Isha excused herself. "I'll be right back after I feed Diya and get her dressed." She looked at Sheila and Harish. "Why don't you two get acquainted in the meantime?"

While she fed the baby, Isha kept her ears tuned to the conversation between Sheila and Harish in the drawing room. At first it sounded a little stilted, but it seemed to get smoother after a while.

The kids kept interrupting them by asking Harish all sorts of questions. He answered them with his usual patience. Isha was amazed at how well he handled them—not condescending, like some adults. What was interesting was that the kids were listening attentively, or at least it seemed that way from what she could hear.

Several minutes later, she had Diya dressed in her own pink dress that more or less matched her big sister's. If only her father could see her now, lamented Isha—all rosy-cheeked smiles and soft hair beginning to curl just like Priya's. She was such a beautiful baby.

As she stepped outside the bedroom, the doorbell rang again. Arvind let Kumar in. "It's Papa."

Kumar was a large man with a belly that was steadily grow-ing in size. Unlike his wife, who kept up her figure with exercise and a strict diet, he indulged himself when it came to eating. But he was still good-looking, with his sharp nose, hard jaw, dark mustache, and thick, straight hair with the first streaks of silver creeping in. Being a tall man, he looked imposing.

He rubbed his hands together. "So, are we ready for some cake?" His eyes fell on Harish and he stopped in his tracks.

Sheila jumped in to introduce Harish to her husband. They shook hands. Kumar's sharp eyes assessed the younger and smaller man. "Dr. Salvi, hmm . . . I've heard your name."

Harish looked surprised. "You have?"

Kumar laughed, looking a bit more relaxed, perhaps because he had heard the name Salvi somewhere. "Oh yes. Pediatrician, correct?"

"Yes."

"Some of the doctors I play badminton with at the club hap-pen to know you."

"Oh . . . through the Palgaum Medical Association, I sup-pose."

"Must be," said Kumar before he gave his full attention to Priya, who had her arms wound around his waist. "Happy Birthday, big girl," he said, returning her hug and tugging on one pigtail. "So, did you get a lot of presents?"

Isha watched the scene fondly as Priya proudly displayed all her gifts to her uncle.

She felt immense gratitude to Kumar for being a surrogate fa-ther to her girls. He'd always been affectionate with Priya, just like Sheila was. There seemed to be no bias against girls in his attitude. In fact, Priya always seemed to get that little extra, sweet-angel treatment from them. And Diya was the spoiled lit-tle darling who was always being cuddled.

The party proceeded, with the kids eating very little dinner but digging into the ice-cream cake with gusto. Harish seemed to get along well with everyone. And Kumar seemed to warm up to him considerably through dinner.

By the end of the evening, the men were deep in discussion

over what they both seemed to be interested in—politics—specifically India's foreign policy.

Isha was glad to note Harish had lost his uneasy look and settled into the rhythm of the evening. He had wiped his glasses with his handkerchief only once so far. She had come to notice that quaint habit of his.

Priya couldn't have looked happier, surrounded by people who adored her and brought her presents.

Harish got up to leave a little after nine o'clock. "Thank you for inviting me, Priya and Isha," he said.

Priya looked up at him. "Can you teach me how to play chess?"

"I certainly can. I bet you're going to be the cleverest six-year-old when you master the game," he promised her.

"I'm eight, and I'm cleverer than her," said Arvind, looking very important.

"Ten-year-olds are more clever than eight- and six-year-olds," chimed in Milind, not to be outdone by the two younger kids.

Harish handled them with remarkable tact. "A young person's IQ increases with every year until they reach a certain age, so all three of you can be the smartest in your own age group." He glanced at the boys. "Do you two also want to learn chess?"

He got enthusiastic nods from them.

Sheila looked a little skeptical. "Aren't Arvind and Priya a little young for chess?"

Harish shook his head. "My brother was seven and I was four when our father started to teach us the game. Both Satish and I were champion players by the time we hit eleven and eight."

"Really!" Sheila stared at him. "That young?"

Isha wasn't one bit surprised. The boy she'd known in college was considered a genius. She could very well believe he could beat adults at chess when he was eight.

With a promise to start the first chess lesson the following week at Isha's flat, Harish left. When the Sathe family departed half an hour later amidst a lot of hugs and kisses and thanks, Diya was thankfully fast asleep.

An exhausted Isha tidied and cleaned up the flat while Priya reluctantly got out of her dress and into her pajamas. The child's cheeks were flushed. She was still riding high from all the attention she'd received. It would be a while before she'd wind down and get some sleep.

Later, as she tucked Priya into bed, Isha felt a sense of peace for the first time in a long while. They'd been in the flat for a few months now and it felt like home. Slowly, even her fear about that secret disk and papers she'd hidden in her *almirah* was beginning to ease off. Maybe nothing would come of it.

Everything seemed to have fallen into a comfortable pattern. Ever since they had moved in, they'd been offered convenient transportation by Sheila and Kumar. Isha and the girls were picked up and dropped off by Kumar's chauffeur each day since the boys attended St. John's School across the street from St. Mary's. And their schedules coincided well.

Besides, several orders for her custom-made dresses had come in, leaving her surprised and pleased. But they also left her with very little time to do anything else. She'd been working late almost every night. Sheila had done such an efficient job of showcasing her handiwork that all the society women who had girls had apparently fallen in love with it.

Isha had been tempted during the last week or so to quit her job at the orphanage and take up dressmaking full time. But giving up a steady job was risky.

She'd have to give the dress designing and sewing idea some serious thought, though. Until recently she hadn't even known that she had a talent for such things. She'd done it from instinct, mostly out of necessity.

However, could she make it on her own? Would she be able to start a small business all by herself and run it effectively?

She'd never had to work for a living before, let alone run a business. But now, the challenge of doing something different beckoned as much as it frightened. After all, hadn't she managed to survive, and feed and clothe her kids?

She remembered her father-in-law's contemptuous remark that she'd never be able to make it on her own.

If she could make it this far, then surely she could do other things. Riskier things. Exciting things. In fact, she was enjoying the sense of independence and accomplishment. She could see why Nikhil had liked the challenge of running a business. Kumar clearly thrived on his, and Harish seemed to take great pride in his medical practice.

But then Harish would excel at most anything. He was an exceptional man with an exceptional mind—and a heart of gold.

So, what was his personal life like? She'd been thinking about it a bit lately—in fact, too much since she'd become aware of him as more than just a doctor and acquaintance. What did he do after he ate dinner with his family and went home? Did he read, or watch TV, or was he so exhausted that he went straight to bed? What kind of a house did he live in? What were his tastes in food, movies, books, television?

Mainly, why wasn't he married like most men his age?

As she slid into bed a little later, she forced her mind back to more mundane things and made a mental list of all the tasks she had to complete the next day. Running a business had its share of headaches.

Priya, nearly asleep now, stirred beside her and mumbled something.

Isha kissed the little girl's head. "I'll take care of you, baby," she whispered to her daughter. "You and your sister won't starve. I promise you that."

Chapter 19

July 2007

Isha observed the foursome sitting on the floor. Milind and Arvind had their brows furrowed in thought while Priya sat cross-legged, her hands cupping her face, equally contemplative. The fourth person was Harish. He sat with his legs crossed like Priya while he explained something to the three children.

In the midst of the four individuals sat the chessboard, with its handsome polished finish and each piece a finely crafted specimen made of teakwood. The set had to have cost a lot of money. Isha had no idea what those things sold for, but she felt a little guilty each time she looked at it. Harish shouldn't have bought such an expensive gift for a little girl.

Every Thursday evening, since Priya's birthday some months ago, the boys and Priya got a lesson in chess from Harish. All three kids had latched on to the game. Harish had explained it so well that even Priya—especially Priya—had been riveted.

They'd started to play for about two hours each week, and from what Harish had told Isha, the children were picking up the game much faster than he'd anticipated. "Priya is an extremely bright girl," he had said. "I don't want to say this in front of the boys, but she'll be ready to beat them in a few months."

Isha had smiled indulgently. "Oh come on, you're just trying to make a mother feel good."

"No, honestly," he'd assured her. "She's very good. The boys are bright but their attention span is short. It's typical male behavior at that age. Priya, on the other hand, concentrates on the game, so she has a deeper understanding of the logic."

At the moment, the children played as a team of three against Harish.

Diya had been fed earlier and put to bed, leaving Harish and the other kids to pursue their game in peace.

Since the little one had started to crawl recently, it was hard to keep her away from the chess game. She enjoyed scattering the pieces and putting them in her mouth, driving the older children crazy. Harish always laughed about it and managed to save the game.

"Time for dinner," announced Isha, knowing full well the youngsters were having too much fun to think about eating.

The kids had only a half day at school, so they could finish their homework in the afternoons and devote their evenings to learning the intriguing game of chess. But Harish usually came directly from his clinic on Thursdays. The poor man needed a break.

"Already?" asked Priya, not bothering to look up from the chessboard. "But we just started."

"You started over two hours ago, pumpkin. It's getting late and Doctor-kaka has given up his entire evening for you kids. It's time to stop," Isha said, her hands on her hips. Sternness was not one of her strong points, but she had to try her best. Priya was not beyond taking advantage of Harish's kindness.

The boys rolled their eyes and groaned dramatically.

"Do we *have* to stop? Mummy's not picking us up for at least an hour," protested Milind.

Harish was the one who rose to his feet and put an end to the complaints. "Yes. We all need to eat." He patted the crew-cut hair that stood at attention on Arvind's head. "Chess needs a lot of brain power. If you don't get proper nutrition, then you can't play well. So let's all feed our brains to make them work efficiently."

The kids moaned some more and reluctantly went to the

bathroom to wash their hands, then gathered around the table. Isha glanced at Harish. "Why don't you stay and eat with us?"

"Thanks, but my family's expecting me."

"Why don't you ring them and say you're invited to eat here?" She wasn't sure if it was a good idea, but Harish had started to become a part of their household. He had gradually gone from being pediatrician to grown-up friend, as well, for her children and Sheila's.

Kumar and Sheila seemed to like him a lot, too. In fact, they had recently switched from Bajaj to Harish for their children's health care, which seemed to please the boys immensely. So it looked like Doctor-kaka had somehow wound up becoming an uncle of sorts—a true *kaka*. He was *almost* family.

He looked hesitant about her invitation, like he wanted to accept, but didn't quite know how. He took off his glasses and wiped them with his handkerchief before replacing them. "I'm not sure it's a good idea."

"Oh, come on, Harish, you've been so good with the children. The least I can do is offer you a simple meal." So far, all he'd accepted from her was an occasional cup of tea and a snack to tide him over until dinner.

The kids joined in with their pleas for him to stay, so he pulled out his mobile phone and called his mother.

Isha put an extra *thali* on the table, and they all ate together.

The children chatted steadily with Harish. He looked completely at ease conversing with them. Isha was happy to remain mostly silent, especially since the boys were behaving so well. There hadn't been a single food fight or argument between them.

As she finished her meal, Isha realized she'd thoroughly enjoyed the evening. It felt like a family meal, just like sitting around the dinner table when Nikhil was alive.

Then another thing struck her. She hadn't been thinking of Nikhil much, at least not with the kind of heartache she used to suffer when images of him flitted through her mind. Her body didn't yearn for him as much, either.

It looked like her brain and heart had finally begun to accept Nikhil's death and the fact that she had to move on—what was often referred to as *closure*. It was up to her to carry on his legacy, to make sure their children were well taken care of.

Nikhil would have wanted his girls to have the very best they could afford, and she was determined to do exactly that.

But what bothered her were her mixed sentiments about Harish. He fitted so well into their lives. In some ways it was a blessing, but in others it was disturbing. Was she being disloyal to Nikhil by enjoying the company of another man? And that strange sense of euphoria when she was in Harish's presence—it wasn't right for her to experience anything like that, was it? According to tradition she was still the grieving widow.

She studied the three angelic faces with their matching hazel eyes focused on Harish's face. She hadn't been able to use the word *enjoy* in a long while. Simple *chapatis, dal,* rice, and *palak-batata bhaaji*—potato with spinach curry—hadn't tasted this delicious in some time.

When the boys were ready to go home, it was their chauffeur that showed up because Sheila and Kumar were attending a party. The house suddenly turned quiet after Milind and Arvind left.

When it came time for Priya to go to bed, she looked pleadingly at Harish. "Doctor-*kaka*, will you read *Harry Potter* to me?"

"I'd love to read *Harry Potter*," he replied, gazing longingly at the books on the table. "I haven't had a chance to read a single one in the series yet."

Isha gave him a grateful smile. He was giving her a precious half hour to catch up on her work.

He sat on the sofa while Priya settled herself nearby and listened to him bring to life the adventures of Harry Potter.

Isha occupied the chair across the room and picked up her sewing, but she stole frequent glances at those two. She observed Priya looking at Harish's face with the same rapt adoration she used to reserve for Nikhil. At the same time, Priya's thirsty mind absorbed the story like a sponge. The child rarely missed a single detail in any story. Harish was right. Priya paid close attention to the things that captured her imagination.

With a sudden heavy heart Isha realized what Priya was doing. Her little girl was subconsciously looking to replace her father, the man who'd read to her, hugged her, and kissed her good night. It brought back a flood of memories of past happy times, and Isha quickly averted her eyes and went back to her sewing, lest her emotions get out of hand.

Harish had chosen to read to Priya in the drawing room instead of the bedroom, implicitly letting Isha know that he had no intention of encroaching on their privacy. And for that she was grateful. He was a gentleman.

After reading a few pages, he sent Priya off to bed, assuring her that he'd see her again the following Thursday for their weekly chess game. Isha and he watched with some amusement the child reluctantly drag her feet toward the bedroom.

"She's a bundle of curious energy. I'm sorry she's made you the target of that," Isha said to Harish.

"Please don't ever apologize for Priya or Diya," he chided. "I happen to like your children very much. And I like Milind and Arvind, too."

"You really mean that, or are you being polite? Every mother likes to think her children are special, you know."

"But your children *are* special. They're both delightful."

"I'm afraid I *have* to agree." Isha gave him a pleased grin.

"Priya seems very interested in science, especially medicine. The other day, she asked me some really interesting questions about heartbeats that wouldn't normally captivate a child her age. She's fascinated by hearts and stethoscopes."

"I noticed that when you let her borrow yours in your office. She talked about it for several days after that visit—something about how the chest makes interesting sounds."

"Maybe she'll pursue a medical career when she grows up."

Startled, Isha stared at him across the room, her needle and thread poised in midair. Wasn't that what the *sadhu* had hinted at? Something about Priya being a healer?

He looked wistful. "I wish I had kids like yours."

"So why don't you get married and have some of your own?"

"Maybe I should." He held her gaze with a contemplative expression. "I hadn't given it much thought until I started to spend time with your children and Kumar and Sheila's. I'm beginning to realize I'm missing a lot in life."

"Then do it, Harish. Do it soon. God gave Nikhil very little time with his child. He never even got to see Diya, let alone hold her and enjoy her. One never knows what lies ahead in life. Live yours to the max while you have a chance." She shut her eyes for an instant. "I wish I'd spent more time with Nikhil, taken some interest in his business, traveled, laughed more with him, and even just talked. If I only knew then . . ."

"I'm really sorry about Nikhil. I'm sure it's hard to lose someone you cared so deeply about."

"I'm slowly learning to accept it as my *naseeb*." Destiny.

"It's all part of the long grieving process," he said wisely. "Acceptance takes time."

"I'm realizing that. But the hard part is coming to terms with the fact that someone deliberately set out to kill him. If it were an accident or illness, one can accept it as God's will . . . But premeditated murder is difficult to live with."

His brows rose high. "Good Lord! It was deliberate?"

"Yes."

"How do you know that?"

"I'd suspected all along that Nikhil's murder was intentional, and it was later confirmed by the police. Nikhil must have gone to the superintendent about Dr. Karnik's illegal abortions and—"

At once realizing what she'd said, Isha skidded to a stop. She had no business bad-mouthing one doctor to another, especially in a close-knit community. She couldn't risk tarnishing Karnik's reputation, even though she had some sort of proof sitting in her home at that moment. If Karnik ever found out about it, she'd be in grave danger.

"Abortions?" Harish's eyebrows snapped together.

"It's nothing. Please forget I said anything." Oh dear! He looked like he was determined to find out more.

"No, I want to hear this," he insisted. "My family and I have had our suspicions about Karnik and a few other ob-gyns in this town, but this is the first time I'm hearing about it from someone else."

"Why do you have suspicions?" She had never thought of Harish as a suspicious sort.

"It's a little beyond coincidence that some obstetricians seem to have mostly male births amongst their patients. Nature isn't that selective, unless it's given a helping hand." He leaned forward in his chair, his gaze firmly fixed on her face. "Tell me . . . please." When she shook her head, he said, "I promise not to tell another soul."

She turned it over in her mind for a second. She knew his sister-in-law was an ob-gyn, and she didn't want to point fingers at anyone in his family. Also, although there was no doubt that the man who sat across from her was trustworthy, she didn't know if it was safe for him to know such things. Knowing dirty and dangerous secrets about his fellow doctors could be both uncomfortable and risky for him.

In the end she decided to tell him all. She'd come to know him well. He was the persistent type and would find out the truth one way or the other. "You have to swear you won't say or do anything that might end up hurting you."

"Why would it hurt me? I'm a pediatrician."

"You seem to be a man of principles, just like Nikhil. I'm afraid you'll inadvertently get involved in this because of what I'm telling you. It could mean trouble for you. I don't want that to happen." God, she most certainly didn't want another man dead because of Karnik, especially a man who'd become an ally, a trusted friend of the family.

He mulled over that for a bit. "Tell me this: How did your husband get caught up with something like abortion in the first place? I don't see the connection between a tire dealer and a medical ethics issue."

"There is a direct connection in our case." She proceeded to tell him everything from the start, including her in-laws' obsession with wanting grandsons and not granddaughters.

"They blatantly asked you to have an abortion?" Harish's expression showed total dismay.

"Yes. And Karnik was more than willing to perform it. In fact, the way he suggested it, I had a feeling it was very commonplace for him."

"Did your in-laws ask you to do the same thing when you were expecting Priya?"

"Back then we didn't know it was going to be a girl. We didn't have a sonogram done. Thank goodness, because if we did, I'm sure they'd have forbidden me to have Priya, too."

"My God! Is there no sense of morality whatsoever in your in-laws?"

"That's the ironic part," she said with a wry laugh. "They consider themselves the personification of high-caste morality. Even their justification for an abortion is what they claim the scriptures prescribe—that only a son can bring his parents *moksha*." Salvation.

Upon a parent's death, a son was supposed to pour *Gangajal*—holy water from the Ganga River—into his parents' mouths and thereby guarantee their souls' direct entry into *swarg*. Heaven. It would ensure liberation from the tedious karmic cycle of birth and death.

Harish shook his head. "I can't believe people still use that silly notion to justify their actions. I suspect the real reason is their ego—having a boy to carry on their precious name and all that."

"I think that's what got Nikhil so riled, that the parents he loved and respected so much could be two-faced, so full of righteous bluster on the one hand and so ruthless and amoral on the other."

"Why would he hide it from all of you?" Harish looked genuinely puzzled.

"His father had warned him not to make waves in a small town like ours, where the Karniks are respected members of the community. And Nikhil didn't like to upset his father. I'm sure he didn't confide in me because I would have told him the same thing—to stay out of Karnik's dirty dealings, mainly because it could lead to ugly repercussions."

She glanced at the framed photograph of a radiant Nikhil and herself, which she placed on the end table. They'd been on their honeymoon in Mount Abu. "But even my worst fears could never have foreseen murder." She pressed a hand over her mouth to keep the emotions at bay. "I believe someone killed Nikhil for triggering an investigation into Karnik's business affairs."

It took Harish a minute to absorb that. "I can see how Karnik would consider Nikhil a threat to his livelihood and his reputation."

"I know your sister-in-law is an ob-gyn and I don't want you to think I'm including her with the likes of Karnik."

"Don't worry. Prachi has strong opinions on women's rights. She'd never dream of performing abortions just to get rid of girls, especially when she has a little girl of her own."

Isha took a short breath of relief. "Thank goodness for a few good doctors."

"Hopefully more than a few," he said dryly. "I know every one of them through the local medical association and they seem so dedicated, so humane, including Karnik. I can't imagine the mild-mannered old man could be capable of murder."

"Neither could I, until I found out it wasn't a robbery gone bad but a foul murder that was probably planned and executed by someone whom Nikhil and I knew so well. I still can't believe such a gentlemanly individual could possibly be involved with such primitive violence. I guess he hired some killer to do his dirty work for him."

"Of course. Karnik wouldn't soil his own hands with something gruesome like that. Did Nikhil seem different just before he passed away? Did you notice anything strange?"

She attempted to recall those difficult, stressful days prior to Nikhil's death. "There was a lot of tension around the house with my pregnancy progressing and Baba and Ayee gradually increasing the pressure on us. There were arguments, and naturally it led to problems between Nikhil and his parents, and as a result between him and me."

"Did he even hint at anything?"

She shrugged. "The whole stupid affair was a strain on our nerves and Nikhil was in a surly mood. The stress left him brooding a lot, which wasn't his usual nature. He had a short fuse, but he also got over it quickly, and he always laughed a lot. He was a charming, likeable man."

"And your in-laws don't see their son's death as a direct result of this illegal abortion business?" Harish still looked dubious.

"I'm not sure if they *don't* see it or *choose* not to see it, because if they do, then the blame shifts to them. I can't say for sure, but maybe if they hadn't pressured us, Nikhil wouldn't have been so rebellious and so adamant about exposing Karnik."

"You mean if his parents had never suggested abortion, Nikhil would have left the matter alone despite knowing that Karnik was performing illegal abortions?"

"I really don't know, Harish. Maybe I'm just deluding myself, dreaming up every excuse to blame my in-laws for what happened." She folded the dress she was working on and laid it aside. "Perhaps Nikhil would have done it anyway. I'll never know."

"But your in-laws were wrong in pressuring you to do something that went against your conscience. And it's insane for them to blame *you* for producing girls."

"No more insane than blaming a baby for being the cause of her father's death and her grandmother's heart problems."

His frown deepened. "They blame *Diya* for Nikhil's death?"

She nodded. "According to my mother-in-law, Diya is a bad omen. That she's bringing doom upon the family. First her father dies, and now this health issue. As the baby's mother, I'm evil, too."

He gave her a long, thoughtful look. "Is that why you left them, Isha, because they made life impossible for you?"

She nodded reluctantly. "If it were only me, it wouldn't matter so much, but I wasn't going to let them crucify my daughters."

"I now understand why you stayed in the convent and why you want to raise your children on your own. At first I wondered why you had given up the comforts the Tilaks could afford to give you and their granddaughters." He studied the happy young couple in the photo for a moment. "I'm really sorry about everything."

"No sorrier than I am," she said. "I keep praying that Ayee will be healthy again and that she'll stop laying the blame at Diya's door. If Ayee dies of a heart attack she'll go with a curse on her lips." Isha shuddered at the notion of a dying woman's curse falling upon her child.

He looked at his watch and rose to his feet. "I better get going. Thanks for the delicious dinner."

"It was nothing." She stood up and followed him to the door. "I'm sorry I burdened you with my problems."

"I'm glad you told me, Isha. It's all beginning to make a lot of sense." He took her hand in both of his. "You were forced to take a bold step and you did."

"I . . . did what I . . . had to." The unexpected physical contact was disturbing. Her pulse shot up. Oh no! It couldn't be. This was crazy. He was only being sympathetic.

"I enjoyed the evening very much," he said, the sincerity in his eyes telling her he was being totally honest. His hands seemed a bit unsteady, too.

"Y-you're welcome." Was his pulse as erratic as hers?

"Perhaps you'll let me reciprocate? You can bring the girls and have dinner with my family sometime?"

He held on to her hand. Her heart was hammering against her ribs. But it felt good, so she didn't attempt to reclaim it. Instead she smiled at the thought of meeting his family. They sounded like nice, uncomplicated people, just like him.

"I'd like that . . . if it's okay with them," she said. She wasn't sure they'd approve of their precious son socializing with a widow and her two small children. They were likely to misconstrue what was only a friendship—if it could even be called that.

Abruptly he dropped her hand and wished her good night. Then, picking up his umbrella, he was gone.

The house suddenly seemed very quiet. Empty. It surprised her that she should feel that way. Her children were sleeping in the other room. There was no cause to feel lonely and blue. And yet it was there, that void in her heart that never seemed to heal.

This was silly thinking. *I'm losing my mind.* It had to be the constant drizzle outside that was dampening her mood, she told herself. The monsoon season would forever be associated with Nikhil's death and the choking grief that had come afterward. Thank goodness, by the end of the month the rains would be gone.

What she needed right now was something constructive to keep her mind occupied. So she went into the second bedroom, switched on the light, and pulled off the cover from the vintage sewing machine. She started working on another one of the many dresses she had begun during the week.

It took a while for the tingling in her right hand to go away.

Chapter 20

After reading the same paragraph for the third time and not absorbing a word of it, Harish knew his attempts were hopeless. He flung the medical journal on the nightstand and shut off the bedside lamp. Lying on his back, he stared into the darkness.

Generally he fell asleep the moment his head settled onto his pillow, but tonight sleep was a long way off. His mind seemed to be in overdrive at the moment.

It was far too occupied with other things—Isha Tilak for one.

He couldn't help recalling the evening's events. It was one of the most momentous evenings of his life, if not the most. He had driven Isha and her girls to Sunday dinner at his brother's house earlier. It had been a couple of weeks since he'd asked Isha if she would like to meet his family, and it had taken him nearly that whole time to introduce the subject to them.

Explaining to them her rare circumstances hadn't been easy, especially since they knew who Isha's late parents and her in-laws were—well-known families with deep roots in Palgaum.

At first they were shocked to learn that she had walked out on her in-laws—something unheard of, even in this day and age, especially when a woman had children. They looked at him with surprise and wariness, probably contemplating his relationship to Isha. But then their curiosity to meet the mystery woman overcame everything else.

"Of course," Satish said. "Please invite her and her children."

"I'd love to meet her," was Prachi's eager response. No surprise there, since Prachi was a warm and gregarious soul.

His father remained silent, while his mother's first question after a moment's hesitation was, "Is she vegetarian or nonvegetarian?"

"What difference does *that* make?" Harish asked.

"*Arré*, she is a *pukka* Brahmin." Purebred Brahmin. "They are usually strict vegetarians, and I have to know what kind of dishes to cook, no?"

"She eats chicken, I know," Harish replied with a shrug. He'd never understood why women made such a big deal over something as basic and simple as food.

So after that little introductory discussion, they had all agreed to entertain Isha and the girls a few days later. That had happened only hours ago.

During the evening, his father had on his schoolmaster face. He threw occasional glances at Isha. Harish could tell Dada was doing his usual study-and-assess thing before saying too much—always the cautious observer and researcher. He was a hard man to please, but once he took a liking to or disliked someone or something, it was hard to change his opinion. Harish could only hope Dada had put Isha on his "likeable" list.

Mamma was smiling a lot, trying hard not to stare at Isha. She was the one Harish was most concerned about. When he'd mentioned Isha a couple of times, she had given him that watchful and penetrating look that told him she was trying to gauge whether the woman called Isha Tilak was a bad influence on her precious son. After all, every eligible girl she'd brought to his attention had been rejected by him because he'd claimed he had no time for marriage. So why was he suddenly making all this time for some upper-class widow with children in tow?

He could sympathize with his mother's concerns. She had only his best interests at heart.

Prachi, as expected, carried on a friendly conversation with Isha, asking curious but not prying questions. Her dark eyes were alight with interest. "Oh, your Priya is only a few months older than my Reshma? How nice! We should see if we can get the girls together on Sundays if possible."

His brother played the genial host by trying to join in the conversation and passing around a plate of potato wafers and glasses of soft drinks. "So, I hear you recently moved into that new high-rise building. Looks like Saraf is making a killing on that venture." Satish was a typical accountant. Everything was judged in terms of profit and loss.

The two older girls got along like the proverbial house on fire. Reshma, being an extrovert, had discovered an instant friend in the equally outgoing Priya. Baby Diya had crawled all over the area rug in the center of the drawing room, surrounded by some of Reshma's old toys, and had been on her best behavior.

But most of Harish's attention had been focused on Isha. She looked pretty in her white sari with some kind of subdued yellow and blue print on it. All she wore as accessories were a gold chain and earrings. Perhaps in deference to his mother's sensibilities, she had no *bindi*—the red dot—on her forehead. Hindu widows weren't supposed to wear the traditional symbol of marriage, but most modern widows sported a *bindi* anyway, just as a fashion statement. He'd seen Isha both with and without a *bindi* at various times.

She sat a little stiffly next to Prachi on the sofa, answering her questions with a polite smile. He had noticed Isha hadn't volunteered too much information about her personal life.

His family, no matter how much of an upper-crust veneer they had acquired in recent years, were still lower-middle-class in their ways. They had to try hard to entertain someone like Isha, the club-going, card-playing, wine-sipping type of woman— or at least that's what they would consider her. Little did they know that she was a very down-to-earth, caring woman with no affectations. Harish had come to learn that about her nature.

Dinner was a little less stilted than the drinks-and-appetizers portion of the evening, since Priya and Reshma kept up a continuous stream of chatter, making plans to get together again. Diya had been fed her baby food and bottle earlier and was left sleeping on a blanket spread on the area rug in the drawing room.

The adults tried to carry on a conversation above the kids' voices. Harish was glad to have the children at the table; they made it less awkward for everyone around. His father had started to talk a little, too, and it was a relief. It meant he was beginning to thaw and feel comfortable around Isha.

By the time dinner ended, it seemed like everyone was feeling more at ease in Isha's presence. She was a warm and amiable woman despite her guardedness, and she'd been trying hard to be a good guest, complimenting her hosts on their home, on the food—and on Reshma, the center of their universe. Harish could find no fault in Isha's behavior. In spite of her nervousness, he knew she was making a sincere effort to enjoy the visit.

Later, when it came time to leave, Isha joined her palms in a cordial *namaste* to her hosts. "It was nice meeting all of you. Thank you so much for inviting us, and for the lovely dinner."

Prachi had responded with something equally polite, while Satish and his parents had smiled and returned her *namaste*.

As Harish drove them back to their home, it turned out to be a quiet ride. The kids were asleep, and he noticed Isha was in a pensive mood.

But his mind was swirling with questions. Had she hated the evening? She had smiled and said the right things, but that came from her good breeding. Courtesy and proper social etiquette were likely to be in her blood. But who knew what she'd been going through on the inside? He'd never seen her socialize with anyone outside Sheila's family. With them she was openly affectionate.

For a woman who'd probably had an active social life, Isha seemed to have become a recluse. Where were all her friends? Had they abandoned her or had she deliberately cut herself off from them? Never having had any sisters, Harish knew very little about women's friendships.

Once they reached Isha's building, he offered to carry the

sleeping Priya upstairs and lay her on her bed. Then he left quickly, afraid he might be tempted to grab Isha's hand again and drive himself insane. He'd fiercely fought the need to linger.

Oh, he was itching to linger, all right. He wanted to run his fingers along that soft-looking skin of hers, wanted to read what was buried within the depths of those honey-colored eyes. He wanted to do a whole lot more: undress her, one fold of her sari at a time, watch the color slowly rise in her cheeks, caress her full breasts till they turned to hot satin in his hands, and hear her moan and beg him to make love to her.

Sex! It all boiled down to basic sex. For a workaholic who wasn't obsessed with sex like most men, he'd been thinking about it a lot lately—way more than a lot. With no woman but Isha.

But it was out of the question. She had never encouraged him, and he couldn't cross that boundary of friendship they had mutually created around their relationship. What he had with her was infinitely precious to him and he wasn't about to ruin it. If it was friendship she wanted, it was friendship he'd give her.

In the recent past, he'd had dinner at Isha's a couple of times, each occasion feeling more and more like he belonged there. He was getting addicted to Isha and her little ones. Was he trying to play surrogate husband and father to fill the emptiness in his personal life? Perhaps. All he knew for certain was that being around Isha and her children felt right, and what felt right couldn't be all bad, could it?

What he was experiencing wasn't illegal, immoral, or un-healthy, either, he assured himself.

As he shifted to set the alarm on the bedside clock, he finally came to the conclusion that somewhere between his first meeting with Isha at the convent and this evening, he'd fallen in love with her.

In all honesty, it wasn't all about sex. There was so much more he felt for her. It had to be *love*. He couldn't think of any other word to describe his emotions.

It seemed inevitable, too—almost like it was meant to be. Had fate cast her in his path at a time when he was starting to be affected by his family's ramblings about him getting married? Had her destiny thrust him onto her doorstep when she desperately needed a man, especially a doctor, to help her in her time of need? Or was he being foolish and sentimental by reading too much into a situation that was no more than a coincidence?

Was he trying to justify his feelings by applying reason to them? But then, wasn't he always the scientist and analyst who had to see logic in everything? This was no different.

Whichever way he looked at it, there was no doubt he had come to love Isha. In college she was like no other girl—and she was like no other woman now. For the first time in his life he was sure he wanted marriage and family. Needed them. He wanted Isha and her children to fill that need.

So what was he going to offer them? Back then, he'd had nothing to give a girl like Isha. But his circumstances had changed since their college days. Now he could give her a comfortable home, security, respectability, and a lot more.

Before he fell into a fitful sleep, he made a resolution to have a talk with his brother and sister-in-law about Isha and his feelings for her. Maybe they had a better idea as to how he should proceed. He hoped they did, since he had no clue whatsoever. That's what came from being a reclusive nerd all his life.

Chapter 21

As Isha stared at the folded stack of gorgeous silks, organzas, satins, and taffetas, and the spools of lace and ribbon, she wondered how she was going to finish all those dresses. What in heaven's name had prompted her to make promises to so many people? Or should she call them *clients* now?

She had become a bit too optimistic since she'd quit her job with the convent and taken up tailoring full time. It was madness to take on so much when she was alone in this enterprise. To top that, all she had was a beat-up sewing machine that threatened to break down any minute. She badly needed some state-of-the-art equipment if she wanted to be a seamstress.

While she worked on an organza dress in a shade of pistachio, she recalled the previous week, her last week at the orphanage. She had finally come to the conclusion that she couldn't handle the dressmaking and keep her job, too. Each evening she'd been sewing well past midnight, and then waking up at dawn to get the girls and herself to school on time. It had left her feeling exhausted and irritable, constantly craving sleep.

There wasn't enough time to devote to the children, and Isha missed them. Sheila was kindly taking them to her place often and she kept them happily occupied. But that wasn't fair to Sheila—after all, she wasn't a babysitter.

Every other day Sheila would bring in more work orders from

her friends and acquaintances. With dancing eyes she had brought Isha an armful of lovely fabrics. "Looks like you're in business, my dear. Maybe you should make it a full-time thing and quit your job with the nuns."

"I'm not sure if I can do that," was Isha's response. The convent and the orphanage had become a part of her life. The nuns had come to depend on her and she relied on them for not just a living but the security they provided her, the feeling of solidness that came from inside those stalwart walls.

But that was some time ago, before her dressmaking was turning into a bona fide business. She'd approached Mother Regina and explained her predicament and her regrets at having to leave her job. However, Mother Regina had wished her well and blessed her with an unexpected hug.

So Isha had reluctantly tendered her resignation. She hated leaving the orphans, every one of them. They had depended on her to fulfill certain needs. And she had come to love them. Children, no matter where they came from, had a way of creeping unawares into one's heart.

It was heartbreaking to leave all of them, but she had to look at the practical side of her life. She had an obligation to her own children and herself.

At least she was making a fair income from the dressmaking. The women who placed orders were willing to pay her the same amount they paid those exclusive tailors and boutiques in Mumbai and Delhi.

The income from the second flat was helping, too, but the renters had told her they were being forced to leave in two months. The man was going to be transferred to a State Bank branch in another town. That meant Isha would have to find a new renter right away.

Despite all the stress, she was content at the moment. After those frightening months of impoverishment, she was finally on stable ground. She was able to pay her bills, and feed and clothe her children. She didn't need to sell any more of her jewelry, or accept handouts from Sheila, either.

Nevertheless her workload was a killer. That's when she'd

started rolling an idea around in her mind and mentioned it to Sheila. "I'm thinking of asking Sundari if she'd consider leaving your parents and come work for me. Do you think she'd be willing?"

Sheila's eyes had lit up. "She'll jump at the chance! Sundari adores you and Priya. She misses both of you."

"Will you ask Sundari on my behalf? I can't ring her there for obvious reasons."

"I'll contact her immediately," Sheila had promised.

But Isha wasn't sure Sundari would leave her employers. She'd spent most of her life with them, and she was a very loyal woman.

Not long after, the doorbell rang. Diya—who had just woken up from her afternoon nap and was playing with her favorite toy, a stuffed monkey—gave an excited screech. Tossing the toy aside, she started crawling toward the drawing room. She had a built-in alarm clock. Every afternoon, after her nap, she eagerly waited for Priya to return home from school.

When Isha hurried past the crawling baby and opened the door, she gasped. Time seemed to stand still for a few seconds. "Sundari!"

The old woman stood on the doorstep, a hesitant smile on her face. She hadn't changed one bit, except for perhaps losing a little weight. The beloved face with its innumerable wrinkles, and every gray hair that was neatly tucked into her bun, were the most welcome sights Isha had seen in ages. It was almost like seeing her mother again. But then, Sundari had always been her surrogate mother.

Isha threw her arms around the old woman with an exultant cry. "You're here! I can't believe it!"

"*Namaste,* Isha-bayi." The old woman started weeping.

"It's so wonderful to see you, Sundari."

The two women clung to each other and cried with abandon. Isha had hoped Sundari would respond positively to her request, but it was wishful thinking on her part to assume the old woman would give up her contented life and come to her aid.

Even now, maybe she had come just for a brief visit. But what mattered was that she was here. And it was still wonderful to see her.

Sundari was the first one to recover from the cry-fest. Drying her eyes and nose with the edge of her sari, she studied Isha for a second. "Isha-bayi, you have become so thin."

Isha gave her a watery smile. "That's because I'm not pregnant anymore."

"Sheila-bayi told me that you are very busy and needed my help."

That's when Isha noticed the small metal trunk and the bedroll tied with a sturdy nylon cord sitting on the floor. "You mean you'll really come to work for me?"

Sundari nodded. "Of course! I would never say no to you. Sheila-bayi said you are working too hard and not getting any rest."

Realizing that amidst all the excitement she was being a terrible hostess, Isha invited Sundari inside. "Please bring your things in and sit down."

Sundari dragged in her trunk and bedroll, then noticed Diya staring at her with curious eyes from behind the coffee table. After realizing it wasn't Priya but a stranger at the door, Diya had instinctively crawled away to a safe distance. The old woman studied the child for a moment and started to cry once again. "*Ayyah!* This is your new baby!"

Isha dried her own eyes and hoisted Diya into her arms. "Yes, this is Diya, my new little pumpkin."

"She looks just like Priya-baby and Nikhil-saheb." Sundari brushed her hands down the baby's face then fisted and placed them against her own temples, gently cracking the knuckles. It was an old-fashioned gesture to ward off the evil eye. When she opened her arms, inviting the child, Diya turned away and buried her face in Isha's shoulder.

"She's a little shy with strangers," explained Isha and sat on the sofa with Diya in her lap. "Sit down, Sundari, and tell me everything that's happened since I left you."

Sundari, as appropriate to her station in life, sat on the floor.

Servants, no matter how close to the family and how valued, never shared the furniture with their employers. She gave Isha a detailed account of how much she had worried over Isha and her children. Then she told her how Ayee-saheb, Isha's mother-in-law, got sick. She painted a very dramatic scenario of Ayee's heart problems and the convalescence.

A fresh pang of regret went through Isha.

After Sundari had finished talking, Isha offered to make her tea. As expected, Sundari got to her feet and strode straight into the kitchen. For a woman approaching seventy, she was amazingly agile. All those years of hard work kept her in excellent shape. "I will make the tea, Isha-bayi; you sit down. I am here to work for you, am I not?"

"You don't know how much I appreciate that, but I can't afford to pay you much right now." Isha put the restless, wriggling Diya down and followed Sundari into the kitchen. "I could never match what Baba and Ayee gave you."

Sundari tucked her loose *pallu* around her waist to prepare herself for work. "Who says you have to pay me a lot? I will be eating with you and staying with you, so what expenses do I have? I am happy to work for you for whatever you can afford to pay me."

Isha watched the old woman as she quickly located the right-sized pan, filled it with water, and put it on the gas burner—the picture of efficiency.

"Are you sure Ayee and Baba won't mind you leaving them?"

"I took care of Ayee-saheb when she was sick, no? Now she is okay and I am not doing anything special for her. But you and the children need me." Sundari threw a fond glance at the baby, who had crawled into the kitchen on Isha's heels and was raising herself to her feet by holding on to a dining chair.

Being more like family than a servant, the devotion Sundari had shown to Isha and Nikhil, and especially to Priya, was beyond the call of duty. Now the strong, selfless woman was standing here, offering to work for a pittance.

Sundari had been abandoned by her alcoholic brute of a husband while she was still young. He had left her because she had failed to produce children. But from what Sundari had told Isha years ago, she was grateful for the man's departure. He had abused her so much that he'd sapped all her spirit. She was glad to be rid of him. Disgusted with her experience, she'd never looked for another man.

She had been content working for the Tilaks, happy when Isha had married into the family and later given birth to Priya. Sundari had given up her other duties and dedicated herself to Isha and Priya. "After I hire a seamstress to help me, perhaps you can go back to Ayee and Baba," suggested Isha.

"Please do not send me back to them, Isha-bayi. I want to work for you only. After Nikhil-saheb died, and you and Priya-baby left," explained Sundari, "that house has been hell for me. Nobody smiles. Tilak-saheb and Ayee-saheb hardly talk to me."

Isha patted the old woman's shoulder. "I'm glad to have you. But do Ayee and Baba know you're here? I don't want them accusing me of stealing you from them." It would be both a luxury and a pleasure to have Sundari around. She was a good cook and housekeeper and she was marvelous with children. Isha couldn't have dreamt of a better solution to her problems.

"I told them I was going to go to your house." Sundari handed Isha her cup, then took her own and proceeded to sit on the floor, while Isha occupied a chair at the table.

"And they didn't mind?"

"They didn't stop me from leaving." Sundari's expression spoke volumes.

"So they still resent me." Isha took a sip of the scalding tea. It tasted delicious, so much better than her own brew.

Sundari waved away Isha's concerns. "They can say whatever they want, but the servants are all very sad that you left. They respected you and Nikhil-saheb very much." She drank the last of her tea and rose to her feet. "Now, I better start making dinner."

"Wait a minute," Isha protested. "You just got here. Rest a little."

"Rest?" Sundari looked at her like she'd lost her mind. "I don't like to rest. I like to work."

"I know that, but since you want me to treat you like family, I'm telling you to take it easy. If you really want to do something useful, maybe when Priya returns from school, you can take both the girls to the park. It'll give me a couple of uninterrupted hours to do some serious sewing."

Sundari's eyes brightened visibly. "Okay. Where is the park?"

Isha motioned toward the window and pointed outside. "When you step out of the building, cross the street and make a right turn. Priya knows where it is. It's only a five-minute walk."

"All right." Sundari looked immensely pleased, like she'd finally found something worthwhile to do.

A little while later Priya came home and, as expected, went hysterical with joy when she saw Sundari. "You really, really came here to stay?" Priya asked her, her eyes alight with hope.

"Yes, Priya-baby, I really, really came here to stay and take care of you and your sister," assured Sundari, the tears trailing down her cheeks once again.

After feeding Priya and Diya biscuits and milk, Isha put Diya in the baby buggy that had once belonged to Milind and Arvind, and the girls headed out to the park with their new nanny.

Isha observed the trio from the window as they crossed the street, Sundari carefully watching for traffic and holding on to Priya's hand, while her other hand remained firmly on the handle of Diya's buggy.

The children were in capable hands.

She breathed out a relieved sigh. Who would have dreamt that the old woman would respond to her query almost instantly, and at the precise moment Isha had been fretting about how she was going to handle so much work and the house and the girls? Fate was a strange thing.

While she steadily cut and sewed and hemmed for two solid hours, a spark of an idea flared in her mind. In two months, her renters were leaving. If her orders for dresses continued to grow at the present pace, she'd need more room very soon.

She had already decided that she was going to have Priya sleep in the spare room from now on, since Sundari could sleep on her bedroll on the floor to provide the child a sense of security.

But the plan would entail moving Isha's sewing from that room to someplace else. And that place could be her other flat. Of course, she'd be losing rent on it, but it could be offset by her having the time to do more sewing and earn more. It could become a full-fledged business with its own space. Then she could keep it separate from her private life, while at the same time Sundari and the kids could have complete access to her at all times.

The more she thought about it, the more appealing the idea became. She'd have to get advice from Kumar about setting up the business. Like everything else in India, the red tape would probably take years. She'd also have to learn the dreadfully boring facets like maintaining accurate accounts, paying business taxes, and heaven knew what else.

Nevertheless the designing and sewing portions were both stimulating and challenging. She was beginning to feel more and more confident about becoming a dressmaker to the children of Palgaum's elite.

Chapter 22

The phone started to ring and Sundari answered it since Isha was feeding Diya her dinner. A second later Sundari called Isha to the phone, her voice sounding urgent. "Isha-bayi, come quick! Sheila-bayi wants to talk to you."

Isha handed the baby over to Sundari and grabbed the phone. "Sheila, what's wrong?"

"I have some bad news." Sheila sounded like she'd either seen a ghost or just emerged stunned and battered through a wind tunnel.

"Has something happened to Priya?" Isha inhaled a sharp breath and tried to brace herself for the worst. Priya was at Sheila's house, as she was more and more these days. The little girl tried hard to keep up with her bigger and bolder cousins, and as a result, got into trouble sometimes. But it usually meant grazed knees, scratches, or minor bruises. Had something serious happened this time?

"No. It's Ayee. She had a heart attack."

"Oh Lord! She's not . . . I mean . . . how is she?" *Let her not be dead, God.*

"I'm calling from the hospital."

Isha's hand tightened around the receiver. "How bad?"

"They're trying to stabilize her. They found a third artery with major blockage."

"She's alive, then! Thank God!"

"Yes, thanks to Priya."

"What!" So far, Sheila had succeeded in keeping Priya from running into either of her grandparents. It hadn't been that difficult because the elders hardly ever visited Sheila and Kumar. It was the Sathes that visited the elderly couple. It had always been like that—the old-fashioned custom of the younger generation visiting the ancestral home in deference to the elders. Isha remembered very few occasions when Ayee and Baba had gone over to Sheila's house, and that was only when there was a party or special occasion. "What does Priya have to do with this?"

"Ayee stopped by unexpectedly to drop off a sari she bought for me at the silk exhibition. Rambo ran to greet her and knocked her over. You know how Ayee is terrified of animals."

"I'm sorry to hear that." Isha was aware of Ayee's phobia with animals, insects, and most anything that moved.

"Priya and the boys were playing some video game upstairs. They heard Ayee screaming in the drawing room when Rambo attacked her."

"I thought Rambo's always tied up because he's so destructive."

"The children must have let him loose or something. Unfortunately I was at the beauty salon, getting a haircut. The front door was unlocked, so Ayee let herself in and Rambo probably sprang at her."

"I see." Finally Isha was beginning to get the picture.

"The kids, the servants, and Ayee's chauffeur heard her scream and ran to her rescue, but they didn't know what to do when she fell on her back and couldn't breathe. They all panicked."

"So what exactly did Priya do?"

"Priya was the only one with the presence of mind to grab the phone and ring Harish Salvi. He arranged to have an ambulance come to the house immediately."

Isha frowned. "I didn't realize Priya knew Harish's phone number."

"She obviously did. Not only did she call the doctor, but she kept Ayee calm and comfortable until the ambulance and medics arrived. With Harish's instructions she made sure Ayee was positioned correctly and all that."

"But Priya's only six years old! She knows nothing about heart attacks."

"The youngest of the bunch, but obviously the most resourceful. I asked her how she knew what to do. She said Doctor-kaka gave her precise instructions over the phone."

Amazing! "Where's Priya now?"

"On her way home. The chauffeur is driving her and the boys to your place."

Thank goodness, thought Isha. She didn't want Priya anywhere near Ayee in her present condition. The poor child had gone out of her way to help her grandmother, but even that was likely to be misconstrued. It could always be said that Priya's presence had turned a minor heart attack into total heart failure. But that didn't mean Isha wasn't worried about Ayee's condition. "Anything I can do to help?" she asked Sheila.

"Can you keep the boys with you for the evening? I don't know how long Kumar and I will be here."

"Sure." She wondered how her excitable father-in-law was handling the catastrophe. "Where's Baba?"

Sheila's voice sounded taut with anxiety. "Baba's here now and he's naturally very upset. I'm worried about him, too."

"Of course you are. He's had more than his share of grief lately." Isha thought about it for a moment. "I'll pray for Ayee's recovery, Sheila."

Sheila was silent for a long time, making Isha wonder if she'd hung up. Then she broke the silence by saying, "It's generous of you to do that after the way they've treated you."

"They're still Nikhil's parents, and still my in-laws and the children's grandparents."

Sheila left it at that. "The kids should be arriving in a few minutes. I'll ring you back when I have more information."

"Okay. And, Sheila, everything will be all right. Don't worry too much." She hung up the phone.

Isha wasn't sure if her words had sounded hollow. They sounded insincere to her own ears. If circumstances were different, she would have been there with the rest of the family, fretting with them, praying with them, offering and taking comfort. Surrounded entirely by men, Sheila could probably have used a woman's touch to comfort her. But all Isha could do was offer her words of kindness over the phone, and nothing more.

When Isha had left the Tilaks in a fit of rage that monsoon morning the previous year, she would have gladly watched Ayee or Baba keel over and die a painful death. In fact, in her heart she had maliciously wished them every kind of pestilence she could think of. Vengeance had been burning her insides.

But now, after all these months, her emotions had mellowed to a simmering resentment. It was odd how even the people one supposedly loathed with a passion suddenly became worthy of more charitable thoughts and prayers when they arrived at death's door. It looked like Ayee had landed at precisely that spot.

She turned to Sundari, who was staring at her with an anxious look on her face, Diya perched on her hip. Isha explained everything to her.

"Poor Ayee-saheb," rued Sundari. "Since Nikhil-saheb's death she is getting sick all the time. I don't think she will ever recover from the loss."

Isha slumped in the chair. "You're right. Losing a child has to be the most devastating thing in the world." If something happened to either Priya or Diya, would she ever be the same again?

A minute later there was a loud knock on the door. The moment Sundari opened it the three children rushed in, excited and flushed, all of them talking at once about their grandmother, and cutting each other off.

After several minutes Isha managed to get the story straight. It was a highly dramatized version of what Sheila had told her, with various colorful details thrown in.

It took Sundari and Isha a while to get the children to wind down and sit at the table to eat dinner. All through the meal they kept recalling details about the incident, making Isha realize that they were affected deeply by what had happened. The excitement seemed to linger.

Sometime later, Isha called Harish to thank him for his role in the evening's events. "I don't even know how to begin to thank you," she said to him.

"Don't be silly," he scolded. "You can save the praise for Priya. Instead of panicking she listened for a heartbeat and then made sure her grandmother was made comfortable. All I did was guide her along. For a child her age, she did brilliantly, with no sign of fear or hesitation."

"We're still very grateful for your help, Harish."

"By the way, I called the hospital a little while ago and got a status report on your mother-in-law. She's stable at the moment. I know her cardiologist quite well. He's the best there is, so she's in excellent hands."

"But I'm still worried about her. Can you tell me in simple terms what's wrong with her?"

He did, as clearly as always, easing Isha's concerns to some extent. "Tell Priya I'm proud of her," he added.

She smiled at that. "I will."

Around ten o'clock, Sheila called again. "Ayee's condition is much better . . . more stable, but Kumar and I plan to stay with Baba for a while," she explained. "Can you keep the children for the night?"

"Of course. What are the doctors going to do for Ayee?" asked Isha.

"At the moment, they can't do much. If she remains stable, within a week they want to perform bypass surgery. They feel the stents are proving to be only a temporary measure at this time."

"I hope everything goes off okay." Isha still couldn't get over the fact that her thoughts about Ayee genuinely bordered on sympathetic. How could that be when she still resented the older woman so much?

Milind and Arvind had never spent a night at Isha's flat, so the children were treating it like a pajama party. They wanted to stay up and chat, play games. Combined with the earlier excitement, it was hard to get them to go to bed.

It was quite late by the time the boys settled into bed in the second bedroom, with Sundari sleeping on the floor. Isha put Priya in her own bed in the master bedroom.

Finally, when the lights were shut off and Priya snuggled against her in the dark, Isha said to the little girl, "I'm proud of you, pumpkin. I hear you took good care of your grandmother."

"Doctor-kaka told me to what to do and I did exactly like he told me. He said I was very brave."

Isha smiled in the dark. "He said to tell you he's proud of you, too. You may have saved Ayee's life, you know." She stroked the head lying beside hers on the pillow. "Now, get some sleep."

"Can we go to the hospital to visit Ayee?" Priya asked.

"We'll see. They may not allow her any visitors in the intensive care unit." Isha didn't know how else she could curb Priya's desire to visit her grandmother. She couldn't very well tell her she was unwelcome. The child had all but forgotten the way she'd been mistreated by her grandmother. Besides, children were so forgiving—such an enviable trait.

A few minutes later, Priya was fast asleep, her breath warm on Isha's neck. There were no whispers coming from the room next door, either, which meant Milind and Arvind were asleep, too. Sundari's gentle snoring was unmistakable.

Lying awake for a long time, Isha wondered about her mother-in-law's future. Would Ayee recover from this latest setback? What if she didn't? Baba would be a lonely old man, living by himself in that big house with no one but the servants to keep him company.

But then, if he had no granddaughters to comfort him in his old age, it was his own fault.

Chapter 23

Taken aback, Sheila stared at her mother. Had those words come out of Ayee's mouth? Ayee lay in her hospital bed, dressed in a soft blue dressing gown. Her hair dye had faded and all that silver hair seemed to blend into the white of her pillowcase.

She had seemed to age by some ten years in the weeks immediately following Niku's death. Now she looked like the lifeblood had been sucked out of her. It was frightening.

How long would she survive at the rate she was deteriorating?

The walls of the private room were a dull shade of brown. The place smelled, not awful, but it had a typical clinical odor that Sheila disliked. It reminded her of being in the hospital after the two Caesarian sections she'd had when she'd given birth to Milind and Arvind. It brought back memories of waking up in a room just like this, with a burning pain in her midsection.

She forced her attention back to Ayee. Sheila hadn't imagined the words after all, because her mother repeated the question, "If it weren't for Priya, I would have been dead, *nah?*"

Sheila nodded. "Priya had enough presence of mind to call her pediatrician and he in turn called the ambulance. You made it to the hospital with mere minutes to spare—literally."

Ayee had undergone open-heart surgery three days ago. Afterward, for the first couple of days she had been groggy and incoherent from the drugs. But now she was conscious and alert, talking a little. Despite the lingering pain, the doctor had pronounced the surgery a success. She would be going home soon. A full-time nurse had been lined up to stay at the house and take care of Ayee for the next couple of weeks.

The convalescence would be long and Ayee would have to make a complete lifestyle change. No more sweet-as-syrup tea with loads of thick milk, no more deep-fried *pakodas*—vegetable fritters—dipped in ketchup at the ladies' afternoon meets, and no more late-night mahjong and bridge parties. She would have to start exercising a little, too, something she'd never done before.

Ayee winced. "It was very brave of Priya," she said, breaking her gaze away from Sheila's, clearly ashamed of admitting it.

"For a six-year-old child, it was incredibly brave—and thoughtful, considering how you and Baba treated her." Sheila noticed the flush that came over her mother's face, and wondered if perhaps this kind of emotional talk was suitable for a woman in her condition. Notwithstanding the doctor's optimistic pronouncement, she still looked ill.

Ayee closed her eyes and lay in that state for several minutes, making Sheila think she was resting. But then she opened her eyes and stared at Sheila, the hazel gaze so much clearer and more focused than it was only hours ago. "I want to see Priya."

"Why?"

Ayee let out a soft breath. Her breathing was still shallow. "I want to thank her."

In spite of her mother's weakened condition, Sheila's temper sparked. "You haven't seen her in over a year. Why now?"

A ghost of a smile appeared over the older woman's face, making the dry, chapped lips look like they were fashioned out of parchment paper. "I might die. I don't want to go without talking to her."

Instead of replying, Sheila rose from the bedside chair and went to stand by the window. Her temper continued to simmer. Priya and Diya had been treated like lepers by her parents and now that her mother had made it to the other side and back, she suddenly wanted to atone for her sins.

A moment ago Sheila had thought it was genuine regret that had prompted her mother's request, but then Ayee had said something about not wanting to die before talking to Priya. So Ayee wanted absolution before she could face her God. Never mind about Priya and what she'd done to save her callous grandmother's life.

She turned around to face Ayee once again. "So this is all about you, not about her."

"I want to tell her I'm sorry." Ayee's eyelids were drooping.

"A little late for that, isn't it?" Sheila shot back. "You had six years to show her your affection and you never gave her any. You never once held her or bought her a present. You didn't even stop Baba from spanking her. And yet the child did everything she could to save you."

"I know." Shutting her eyes, Ayee seemed to meditate on the thought. "It was stupid of me . . . thoughtless." Tears gathered in her eyes. "It was wrong."

"Ah, so you recognize that you and Baba were mean and petty toward your own grandchildren."

"Yes. I want to apologize before it is too late." Ayee's voice had shrunk to a whisper, indicating that she was rapidly getting tired. The tears were trickling down her temples and soaking into the white pillow, making wet circles on either side of her head.

As Sheila watched her mother cry, her heart began to constrict. And her temper vanished. Ayee rarely cried—or rather, that used to be the case before Niku's death.

After Niku's passing her mother had wept and wept, making Sheila aware for the first time in her life exactly how much Niku had meant to Ayee. She'd always known it, of course, but witnessing her relatively detached mother fall apart emotionally in mere seconds, crumble to pieces, had brought home the stark reality of it.

It was as if producing a son was the only reason Ayee had been put into this world. So when he was gone, there was nothing left for her to live for. Sheila had wondered several times since Niku's death if Ayee would have reacted the same way if it was she who'd died and not her brother. She knew the answer: After a brief period of mourning, Ayee would have moved on. Sheila was only a daughter, a product of her and Baba's marriage, but not the light of her parents' lives.

The knowledge hurt like hell. But she had to live with it.

She started pacing the length of the room. What was she going to do about this latest development? Should she ask Isha if Priya could visit her grandmother? Isha was likely to balk at the idea. And who could blame her?

But on the other hand, Ayee was in genuine pain, scared that she might die and would never have a chance to apologize to her granddaughter, never be able to make up for a lifetime of mistakes.

Sheila had heard about near-death experiences and how they changed a person completely. Ayee was turning into living proof of that phenomenon. Sheila had never dreamt that her mother, with her obstinate streak, would regret mistreating her granddaughter.

She went back to sit in the chair. "I'll have to ask Isha about it." She gave Ayee a candid look. "She has every right to turn down your request. You know that."

Her mother nodded.

"I'll try my best, Ayee, but I can't promise." She thought of something else. "You know you have another granddaughter, don't you? Her name is Diya."

Another brief nod.

"Diya is just as beautiful as Priya, maybe even more so. She's a happy, friendly baby . . . delightful. Kumar and I would have loved to have a baby girl like her."

Ayee sniffled. "I know."

"Both the girls have taken after Niku. They have your eyes, Ayee—the exact shade, too." She shook her head sadly at her mother. "You don't know what you've missed by keeping them out of your life. By rejecting them you've rebuffed Niku's spirit."

"I want to see Diya also," her mother murmured.

One of Sheila's eyebrows flew up. "Are you sure? Don't forget you never wanted that child to be born in the first place. You called her a curse."

"Another mistake." A minute later Ayee seemed to be asleep, her breathing becoming more regular and the lines of strain in her brow easing out.

Sheila watched her mother sleep the uneasy sleep of a woman who'd made a lot of mistakes in her life. Once again she felt a twinge of anguish. Getting caught between a mother she loved deeply and a sister-in-law and her children who were equally dear was exhausting. And painful.

With a sigh Sheila dabbed the moisture around Ayee's eyes with a handkerchief. "If you really mean it, I'll try my best," she whispered. "Who knows? This may be the best thing that's happened to our family. Good things can come out of bad ones sometimes."

As she tiptoed out of her mother's room she noticed her father walking down the corridor toward her, his long, purposeful strides unmistakable. He looked tired and his clothes were uncharacteristically disheveled. Even his hair was a little longer than his usual neat, conservative style. He obviously hadn't visited his barber in several weeks.

Baba hadn't reacted well to Ayee's breakdown in health. He hadn't looked this weary since the days immediately following Niku's death. Between going back to managing the business full time and worrying over his wife, his life was more stressful than ever.

"She's sleeping," Sheila warned him as he came to a stop in front of her.

"Is she still in a lot of pain?" he asked, inclining his head toward the partly closed door.

"She's much better today than the last couple of days. By the way, she talked quite a bit."

"About what?" Baba gave her a suspicious look.

Better to tell him the truth, concluded Sheila, before he heard it from Ayee and yelled at her. Ayee couldn't handle his kind of temper tantrums at the moment. "She wants to see the children."

"But Milind and Arvind already visited her this afternoon, didn't they?"

She glanced at him for an instant, then looked away. "She wants to see Niku's children."

"Oh, that!" Baba's cheeks turned a dull red. "She mentioned that to me last night."

"So you know about this? Why didn't you tell me?"

"Because it is insanity! What is done is done. Isha left home on her own. We didn't force her to go."

"Maybe not in words, but certainly by your behavior. You beat up Priya and made her life and Isha's miserable after Niku passed away." Even before that by putting pressure on Isha to have an abortion. But Sheila decided to leave that out. Her father looked beleaguered enough without her punishing comments.

"Priya was being disobedient and Isha was being insolent. She was talking back to me." Baba folded his arms across his chest and scowled. "What else was I supposed to do?"

"If you ever spanked either of my children, I would do the same thing Isha did." Sheila was amazed at her own temerity. She had never, ever spoken disrespectfully to her father. He had been a strict disciplinarian while she was growing up and she'd obeyed his every command.

But now she couldn't stop herself. The emotional dialogue with her mother a little while ago had touched a dormant nerve. She felt the need to set him straight. "A mother has to protect her children by any means she can, and Isha did just that."

"If that's what you call her arrogant behavior," he retorted. "She is on her own now." Baba grasped the doorknob, getting ready to enter Ayee's room. "I want nothing to do with her."

"She may be on her own, but she still cares about Ayee and you," Sheila countered. "She's even praying for Ayee's recovery."

Baba snorted like an incensed bull. "*Cares?* She has brought shame on the Tilak name by running away and staying in a convent like a homeless woman. By deliberately living in poverty she has made your mother and me look like fools. She has made all our friends and the entire town label us as abusers. People are either laughing at us or calling us heartless because of her. Why would we want to have anything to do with her?"

"You better ask Ayee that question. *She* wants to see both her granddaughters."

Baba dismissed her in his usual, haughty fashion. "I will talk her out of it. All those strong medicines are affecting her mind. When she goes home and feels better, she will come to her senses."

With a frustrated groan Sheila took off down the corridor. There was no arguing with her headstrong father. She was convinced he'd bully Ayee out of seeing her grandchildren. Such a shame! She only hoped he would come to recognize his mistakes just like her mother seemed to have done in recent days.

And she sincerely hoped it would happen before it was too late.

"You want to *marry* Isha Tilak?" Satish Salvi gave his brother a wide-eyed look.

"Yes," Harish replied.

"Bad idea, Harish."

"Why? Just because she's a widow or because she has children?" Harish picked up the remote and began flicking channels on the television in his brother's drawing room. It was a little after dinner. Their parents and Reshma had gone to bed some time ago. Prachi was out on a medical call, delivering a baby. Harish had seized the opportunity to catch his brother alone and broach the topic that had preyed on his mind for so long.

"Both," said Satish, settling back in the easy chair and crossing his ankles. "You know Dada and Mamma have high hopes for you. They want you to marry a doctor, or at least some type of professional."

"What does marrying a professional have to do with being happy?"

Satish linked his hands over his middle and eased his head back onto the headrest. "A lot. Our parents have always wanted us to have a better life than they did."

"And we do. Look at the two of us. Our incomes are astronomical compared to what Dada's salary used to be."

Satish groaned. "I didn't mean just economically. I meant in every other way. Dada married a woman with limited education. No doubt Mamma is a bright woman, but she's not an intellectual. Dada and she could never connect on that level despite having a satisfactory marriage. But you and I can have better by marrying someone that we can relate to on every wavelength."

"Oh, come on! There's no such thing as a perfect marriage."

"True, but Prachi and I have a closer relationship than Dada and Mamma—a more equal partnership. You know what I mean."

Harish shut off the TV and threw the remote back on the coffee table. "Are you trying to say Isha is not good enough for me?"

"I didn't say that. All I'm saying is marrying a widow with children is not the wisest thing to do."

"That's what I had thought, too . . . when I first met her. But the more I get to know her and her kids, the more I like them. I want to offer them a home and the security of having a husband and father." He glanced at his brother across the room. "Is that so wrong?"

Satish's response was a sardonic grunt. "Are you trying to convince *me* or yourself that your intentions are entirely altruistic? I noticed the way you kept staring at Isha Tilak when she was here. You've fallen hard for her, man."

Instead of protesting, Harish threw him a sheepish look. "That obvious, huh?"

"As obvious as my nose. I've noticed you're not working on Saturdays and late evenings anymore. You used to claim you had no time for marriage. Now all of a sudden you're making plenty of time to visit her frequently."

Harish sighed. "Do you think Mamma noticed?"

"Mamma notices *everything*. I saw her looking at you and Isha with that speculative expression the other evening. She knows, but she hasn't said anything to me—yet."

"I used to know Isha in college. Well, not really know, but I used to see her on campus. A lot of boys were interested in her."

"I don't doubt that. She was the pretty, rich girl who came in a chauffeured car and stuck to her own circle of friends." Satish snickered. "And you were definitely not part of that circle."

Harish glanced at his brother with raised eyebrows. "*You* knew her in college, too?"

"No," said Satish, still looking amused. "She's too young to be my contemporary. But I know the type. There are girls like Isha in any given year."

"What do you mean?" Harish demanded with a scowl.

"What I mean is they're typically upper-class girls. Their lives are simple and predetermined: get a bachelor's degree in some easy, low-pressure subject, acquire a rich husband, have two perfect children, and live in luxury. The most stressful thing in their daily lives is probably deciding what to wear to a party or what kind of appetizer to serve their guests."

"I'd say that's a fairly accurate description," admitted Harish grudgingly.

"Poor boys like us look at those girls from afar, fantasize for a bit, then go about our business of studying hard and trying to make a decent living someday."

"Exactly."

"So, Isha was your fantasy in those days, I guess?" Satish winked at Harish. "I can't blame you. She's an attractive woman."

Harish chuckled. "Don't let Prachi hear you say that."

"Don't let Prachi hear what?" Prachi chose to walk into the room at that very moment. She looked tired. "Are you boys discussing me behind my back?"

"So, what did you deliver tonight? Girl or boy?" asked Satish.

"Beautiful baby girl. Both mum and child are doing fine, thank you," she replied, then switched her gaze from one man to the other. "Well?"

"Satish thinks Isha Tilak is an attractive woman," said Harish, with a sly look aimed at his brother.

Prachi sank wearily into the nearest chair and kicked off her *chappals*. "I happen to agree."

It was Satish's turn to smirk at his brother. "See, she agrees. And you thought you'd stir up trouble for me just because *you* happen to be in trouble."

Prachi stretched forward and helped herself to a handful of grapes from the bowl sitting on the coffee table. "Why is Harish in trouble?"

"Should I tell her?" Satish glanced at Harish, clearly serious this time.

"Go ahead. She might be more objective than either of us."

"Objective about what?" Prachi popped a juicy green grape into her mouth.

"Our confirmed bachelor is finally considering marriage," said Satish, lazily eyeing his wife consume grapes.

"That's great!" Prachi sat up, her eyes alight. "So have you asked Isha yet?"

Satish turned to her, his brows arched. "*You* guessed this, too?"

"Of course," she answered with supreme confidence. "Women have a sixth sense about these things."

"They do?" both the men asked in unison.

"Sure." She glanced at her husband. "I'm surprised *you* figured it out."

Satish shrugged. "Even a moron like me couldn't help but notice Harish drooling over a woman."

"Every night Harish managed to drop her name into the conversation," said Prachi, wiping her damp hands on a handkerchief. "That's when I got suspicious. But the day she came over for dinner, I knew for sure."

Harish shut his eyes and groaned. "Can't a man have *any* secrets in this house?"

Prachi smiled. "Not while Mamma and I are around. She knows, too."

"Did she tell you that?"

"Not in so many words, but I heard her discussing it with Dada the other day."

"You were eavesdropping!" Satish feigned shock.

She rolled her eyes. "They knew I was in the next room while they were talking."

"Dada knows?" Harish slapped a palm over his forehead. "I'm in deep trouble!"

"I don't think so," said Prachi. "I heard him say something like, 'Better a widow than no marriage at all.' I was very surprised myself."

"You're not kidding?" Satish gave his wife a dubious look. "I would have expected Dada to have serious objections to a woman like Isha Tilak. You know Dada is adamant that we marry professionals."

"That probably would have been the case if he hadn't met Isha. But after her visit the other day, I think he rather liked her." She chewed her lip thoughtfully. "He did have some choice things to say about her father-in-law, though. He called him an unscrupulous black marketer and *pukka badmaash*—an utter scoundrel."

"Exactly what did you hear him say about Isha?" Harish asked.

"Mamma asked Dada if he'd noticed how you were gawking at Isha all evening."

Harish slumped against the cushions. This was getting worse and worse. It seemed like everyone in the world knew about his feelings for Isha. Was he that transparent? "What did Dada say to that?"

"He said you looked like a starving dog staring at a piece of raw meat."

"No! Tell me he didn't say that!"

Prachi grinned. "He didn't. But he said you were a fool to think someone like Isha Tilak would fit into your life."

"He may be right," confessed Harish. "I may be aiming for something entirely beyond my reach."

"Dada also said a pampered, high-class Brahmin woman like her would never marry a schoolmaster's son, especially a non-Brahmin."

"But Isha's not like that," Harish protested. He'd come to know her well. She was unspoiled and guileless. In fact, she was a caring woman with a big heart. Despite her circumstances, she was not bitter, either. Most women in her shoes would have been complaining and pouting about their lot, but Isha did neither. And she was coping well.

"I realize that," admitted Prachi. "I liked her a lot, too. I don't think she's spoiled or pretentious or condescending."

"I know that for a fact. That's what attracted me to her in the first place." He looked at his brother and sister-in-law. "What do you think I should do? Talk to Mamma and Dada before I summon the courage to ask Isha?" He looked at the wall clock, realized it was time to leave, and rose to his feet. "She may turn me down flat, of course."

"She'd be a fool if she did." Prachi stood up and stretched, looking even more exhausted than she'd looked a few minutes ago. An ob-gyn's work entailed long, grueling hours.

"You're biased because you're my brother's wife," Harish said to her.

"Maybe, but I still think you're a good man and Isha should recognize it. You even adore her daughters. Who could ask for a better man than that?"

Satish reluctantly rose from his comfortable chair. "You want me to talk to Dada and Mamma about this?"

Harish looked at him. "You'd do that for me?"

Satish smiled and put an arm around his wife's shoulders. "By that I mean I'll get my wife to talk to them."

Harish walked toward the door. "Whichever one of you is the more daring of the two, go ahead and talk to the elders. I'll go say a few prayers."

"So when exactly are you going to ask Isha?" asked Prachi.

"I'm not sure. One of these days."

"Good luck," said Satish with an amused chuckle.

"I could use some luck." Harish closed the door behind him and headed home.

Chapter 24

Isha paced the length of the hospital corridor and glanced at her wristwatch once again. It was late evening and the kids had yet to be taken home, fed dinner, and put to bed. She had to add the finishing touches to some dresses that were promised to customers within the next couple of days. There was so much to do—too much.

The children had been in Ayee's room for the past seven minutes. The door was closed. What the heck was happening in there? What was keeping them so long? The longer she stayed, the tighter the knots in her stomach became. Her efforts at making herself relax weren't working.

She wanted to be inside that room, and yet, she didn't want to be. She felt smug satisfaction that Ayee was suffering (paying for her sins), but she also felt sorry for her on some level. Isha's emotions were so mixed up she didn't know what she wanted.

Sheila was in the room, so she wasn't worried about her daughters' safety. But Priya was old enough to get her feelings hurt, and Isha didn't want that for her daughter. The kids had suffered enough without being subjected to their grandmother's ugly remarks.

If Sheila hadn't begged Isha to let the girls visit Ayee, Isha would never have allowed them anywhere near their grandmother. Besides, Priya had asked several times if they could visit Ayee, and Isha was running out of excuses.

In the end, there was nothing Isha could do but agree to let Sheila take the girls to visit the ailing Ayee. Nonetheless Isha had insisted on accompanying them to the hospital and then planted herself right outside the room—just in case.

Sheila had dropped her bombshell on Isha the previous evening when she'd said, "I know this is going to come as a shock, but I have to ask a favor of you . . . for Ayee's sake."

"Ask me what?" Isha had responded, wondering where it was leading.

"She wants to see the girls."

"No!" Isha had stared at Sheila for a long second. Was her sister-in-law insane?

"Please, Isha."

"Why?"

"She says she wants to apologize to Priya."

"Apologize for what?" When had her mother-in-law ever apologized for anything? Did she even know the word?

"For having treated her badly all these years."

Isha hadn't been able to suppress the snicker. "A little late for that, isn't it?"

Sheila had nodded sadly. "I think Ayee has finally come to terms with her own mortality and wants to make amends for her sins before she dies."

"These are the children Ayee couldn't stand. She didn't even want Diya to be born. She wanted the fetus flushed down the sewer pipe."

"A near-death experience apparently changes a person's out-look," Sheila had argued. "Ayee sounds like she wants them in her life now."

"I'm not sure if *I* want Ayee in *their* life." Seeing Sheila's disappointed expression, she'd added, "You know I have every reason to refuse."

"Yes. But please think about it, Isha. I gave it a lot of thought before coming to you with my request. I almost decided not to ask at all, but then, what if, despite the alleged success of the surgery, Ayee doesn't make it? Then I'd feel guilty for not allow-

ing her to make peace with her grandchildren and Niku's soul."
She'd thrown Isha a hopeful look. "You may come to regret it,
too. Think about what Niku would want."

"That's the *only* reason I'm even having this conversation,"
Isha had replied.

"I'm sure you won't regret it."

So Isha had slept on it, conferred with Sundari at length and
even with Harish. They were both wise people who cared about
the girls' welfare as well as Isha's. They were also more objective
than she.

"Isha-bayi, I know Ayee-saheb never wanted girls," said Sundari. "But I think she has come to regret it. You know what a
proud lady she is. For her to admit that she is wrong means that
she is feeling very, very bad about it. Why punish her at the end
of her life? I think Nikhil-saheb would want his mother and his
children to make peace with each other, no?"

Harish had more or less expressed the same sentiments.
"Look at it from the point of view of the kids, Isha. Carrying
around a negative image of their grandparents is not healthy for
them, especially when they're in the same town. Let them have
some contact with her. Maybe the time has come to repair the
scars left by Nikhil's death and all that happened before and
after. Who knows, maybe your father-in-law will also come
around."

"But the kids may be hurt even more than before," Isha had
countered. "Poor Diya hasn't known them at all. Imagine finding out that she has grandparents not two miles away from her
house and they didn't want her; they rejected her even before
she was born."

"But that's exactly why Diya may need to know that her
grandmother has reversed her thinking," said Harish. "When
Ayee is gone, at least your children will be left with pleasant
memories instead of bitter ones."

Finally, after taking into consideration every angle she could
think of, Isha had consented. But she had set her own parame-
ters. "If Ayee says one offensive thing to my children, I'll never
let her see them again," she'd warned Sheila. "One more thing:

I don't want Baba anywhere nearby, unless he feels the same way as she does. And if he raises his hand to either one of them, I'll break my silence. I'll tell everyone about his abusive ways and the nasty abortion story with all its shocking details."

Sheila had agreed to all of Isha's demands. And so here they were, Isha waiting outside in the corridor, vibrating with tension, while Sheila and the kids were in that room, behind the closed door.

As she paced she observed other people enter the small, exclusive private hospital, walk up to the front desk, get directions, and go on their way. Some of them looked familiar.

The three other private rooms in this wing were occupied, and family and friends of the patients were going in and out. She heard conversations, some whispered, some loud enough to eavesdrop on.

There was a little awkwardness when one of the women visiting a patient next door recognized Isha, hesitated a bit, and then stopped to chat. Very few acquaintances had come face-to-face with Isha in the past year because she'd rarely been out in public. With Sundari now able to do the grocery shopping, Isha practically never went out.

She briefly explained to the curious woman that her mother-in-law was a patient there, letting her draw her own conclusions. After a moment of polite conversation the woman said good-bye and left, looking somewhat relieved.

A minute later, Isha was surprised to see Harish walk in the front door, talk to the receptionist at the desk, and start heading toward her. Merely seeing him was enough to bring on a sigh of relief. Despite the fact that her heart had started to do some strange things whenever he appeared, he still had a calming effect on her. What was it about the man that both excited and soothed at the same time?

She waited until he got close enough for them to talk. "Hi. What brings you here?"

"I knew you were very nervous about this visit," he answered. "I stopped by to see how things were going. I was worried about you."

She raised a brow. "Why were you worried about me?"

"Well, all this . . . uh . . . stress is not good for your health, you know." He took off his glasses and wiped them with a handkerchief, then put them back on.

"Hmm." Isha didn't quite know how to respond to that except to be grateful that he cared so much. Maybe too much? He had gradually become one of her best friends. But lately there had been a thread of awareness between them. It went beyond friendship and bordered on tension. It hadn't been there in the beginning, but it seemed to buzz around them almost all the time now.

Tired from her restless pacing, Isha sat down in one of the four chairs in the waiting area. Harish took the one across from hers.

She inclined her head at the closed door nearby. "They've been in there for several minutes."

"I'm sure Sheila has it under control," he said. "She's a very capable woman."

"That she is. If it weren't for her, I wouldn't have allowed my girls to see Ayee."

He gave her an approving look. "You made the right decision. I knew you'd eventually do what's in your children's best interests."

"How did you figure that?"

"Because you're a devoted mother. Even if you're angry you'll ultimately do what's best for your daughters."

"I'm still not sure it was a good idea to let them see Ayee, but Sheila begged me to reconsider and I couldn't say no."

Harish's attention suddenly shifted to something behind her. "Uh-oh!"

"What?" Isha had her back to the entry foyer and she couldn't see whatever had captured his attention. But from the expression on his face she could tell it was bad news. Assuming it was Baba showing up when he wasn't supposed to, she braced herself for the confrontation. She had to face the old man sooner or later.

She turned around, and the breath was knocked out of her. Karnik! Or was he a figment of her imagination? But as the man kept walking at a brisk pace down the passageway, coming closer, the characteristic skimpy gray hair, the slight build, and the grandfather glasses were hard to mistake. It was Karnik all right.

This was Nikhil's killer! What was *he* doing here?

In a split second she was on her feet. Her legs quivered but she managed to face him. She opened her mouth but no words came out. Her tongue was paralyzed. She had so much to say to this loathsome creature but didn't know where to start, how to start.

He had no right to be alive when Nikhil was dead!

Karnik noticed her and looked taken aback for a moment but then recovered instantly. He approached her with a smile, his hands joined in greeting. "*Namaste,* Mrs. Tilak. What a pleasant surprise."

She continued to stare at him, her body taut and still. How could the swine behave like nothing had happened? He had struck her husband down brutally, ruined her life and her children's, and now he stood before her looking like a gentleman and making small talk.

His faux smile remained. "You don't recognize me? I'm Karnik, your doctor."

"You're no longer my doctor." There, she'd managed to say at least a few words.

Karnik's smile faded instantly. "I—I'm sorry about that . . . silly m-misunderstanding."

"It wasn't a misunderstanding." She savored the sweet satisfaction of hearing him stutter and look uncomfortable. So much for the façade of a confident and amiable old man.

"Oh, I'm sure it was. Your father-in-law and I see each other at the club. We chat all the time."

"My father-in-law, perhaps, but not me." How could Baba pretend to be friends with his son's killer? How shallow was that?

Karnik gave her a look filled with sympathy. "I'm very sorry about Nikhil. I hope things are getting better now, and we'll see more of you at the club."

Isha shook her head. "That's not likely to happen." She narrowed her eyes at him in speculation. "You know why, don't you, Doctor?"

Panic flashed across his face for a brief moment before he reverted to his formerly benign expression. "What are you talking about, Mrs. Tilak?"

She sensed Harish come up behind her. He touched her hand lightly. "Isha, isn't it time you checked on your children?"

She ignored Harish and maintained her steely focus on Karnik. "You know what I'm talking about."

"Isha, please . . ." whispered Harish in her ear.

"Let's not pretend anymore, Doctor," she said to Karnik. "You and I both know precisely what happened to Nikhil and who was behind it." From the corner of her eye she noticed a couple of men emerge from the neighboring room. They stopped to stare. But she didn't pay attention to them.

Karnik glanced at Harish, finally dropping the pretense and acknowledging this wasn't a friendly encounter. "I don't understand." Although his expression remained the same, his voice now sounded like chipped ice. "What in heaven's name is she implying?"

"It's time to get the children and go home, Isha," reminded Harish and put a warning hand on her arm.

Once again she ignored the plea in Harish's voice. "I'm referring to certain documents, Doctor."

Harish's fingers dug into the skin of her forearm. "Isha . . . please!"

But she couldn't stop talking. Seeing Karnik had triggered an eruption of the volcano that had been churning and heating up inside her for a long time. "I'm tired of pretending nothing's wrong when there's enough material to prove certain things."

"That's enough!" Harish's voice cracked like a whip. It silenced her instantly. He motioned to Karnik to go away. "I'm sorry, sir. She's . . . not feeling very well."

"Obviously!" Karnik turned visibly pale before throwing her one last look of disdain and turning around. "I think she needs some intensive psychiatric treatment."

Isha watched Karnik glance at the two men before striding away. She collapsed onto the nearest chair, trembling all over. "How dare he pretend to be a caring healer and family friend! How dare he!"

A second later the door to Ayee's room opened and Sheila stepped out, Diya in her arms and Priya close on her heels. She threw a suspicious look at Isha's face, then at Harish. "Is something wrong?"

"Just . . . uh . . . a minor problem," replied Harish.

Sheila's voice gentled when her eyes switched again to Isha. "What's the matter?" With Diya still in her arms, Sheila crouched on the floor in front of Isha when she didn't get a response. "What happened, Isha? You're shaking."

Gradually becoming aware again of her surroundings, Isha's gaze came to rest on Sheila's face. "Karnik was here."

"Oh, no!" Sheila's eyebrows plunged. "What was *he* doing here?"

"I don't know. Maybe he was here to visit Ayee. But he had the audacity to behave like nothing had changed between us."

"What did he say?"

"Pretended to be all friendly and sympathetic."

"Of all the nerve!" exclaimed Sheila, trying to keep Diya's inquisitive fingers from pulling her earring.

"I gave him a piece of my mind," Isha informed her. That's when reality started to sink in. Oh God! What had she said to him? She recalled her bitter tirade—every word of it. Had she completely lost her mind? How could she?

Suddenly realizing the enormity of her actions, she burst into tears.

Sheila bit her lip. "You didn't threaten him or anything, did you?"

Priya, noticing her mother crying, threw her arms around her neck and buried her face in her shoulder. Then she began to wail. Isha's arms instinctively went around her child.

Sheila, noticing Diya's lower lip trembling in response, rose to her feet. "Isha, you have to stop this! You're upsetting the kids."

Isha continued to shed tears. "I can't help it. I saw Karnik and . . . I went berserk."

The two men were still standing in the same spot, still staring curiously.

Harish looked pointedly at Sheila. "Can you take the children home to Sundari? I'll take care of Isha."

"But . . ." Sheila looked in helpless misery at Isha and the children for a second before she nodded. "All right, I'll take the girls home. What should I tell Sundari?"

"Tell her to feed them and put them to bed. And she shouldn't worry if Isha's late in getting home." He eyed the sniffling Isha. "It might take her a while to calm down."

"What exactly happened here?" Sheila asked him.

"I'll explain later. I think it's a case of stress building up over an extended period of time. Karnik's unexpected arrival was merely the trigger."

"You may be right," Sheila said. "Call me later, all right?"

Harish nodded, and Sheila pried a reluctant Priya away from Isha and went, taking the tearful children down the corridor and out the building.

Chapter 25

Harish pressed a steaming cup of tea in Isha's hand. "Drink this." He had driven her to his house and made her sit on the sofa in his drawing room while he brewed the tea. He had brought her to his home because he didn't know where else to take her. She obviously needed some privacy to recover from the episode.

He watched her hold the cup in both hands. They shook as she took a few careful sips. "Thank you," she said and put the cup on the table beside her.

Her eyes were bloodshot and swollen from crying. Her hair was mussed, and even though the tears had stopped, her sniffling continued. She kept her arms folded, hugging herself. She looked so hopeless, so lost, so young.

He was tempted to go to her, hold her close, and comfort her. But he stifled the urge. She was likely to take it the wrong way. Besides, at the moment, verging on hysteria like she was, there was no knowing how she'd react. He knew enough about psychiatry to recognize a woman teetering on the edge of an emotional breakdown.

A single wrong word or move could send her over the edge.

The moment he had spied Karnik approaching, he'd known there was trouble ahead, but he had never expected Isha to react quite like that. It had stunned him to the point of immobilizing him for a minute. Isha wasn't the type to lose her self-control easily. One minute she was sitting down, with her small, elegant hands in her lap, talking to him, and in the next she was saying the most bizarre things to Karnik.

Watching Karnik lose his composure a little, Harish had experienced a moment of perverse satisfaction. But that had vanished the second Isha had started to allude to certain odd things. That's when Harish had realized she was doing something very self-destructive. If indeed it was Karnik who had arranged to have Nikhil killed (and Harish was sure it was), then Isha could be setting herself up for a similar fate as her late husband.

Letting Karnik know she had knowledge about the murder, and even evidence, was foolish. She could have been bluffing, but it was still risky, considering someone had killed her husband in cold blood.

But then again, more than a year's worth of strain, combined with the tension surrounding the children's visit with their grandmother, had stretched her nerves to the limit.

Now it was time for some damage control. So he went to sit beside her on the sofa. "Feeling a little better?" He noticed most of her tea was still in the cup.

She nodded. "I'm sorry I embarrassed you. I don't know what got into me."

"That's okay."

"I just sort of . . . snapped. I couldn't help myself."

He nodded. "I understand. You've had a lot to deal with."

"But still, it was stupid to explode like that." She turned to face him. "I'm usually not an impulsive type."

"I realize that." He patted her hand. "But you had good reason this time."

"No matter how good the excuse, I had no business saying nasty things to someone in a public place and upsetting my children and embarrassing you and Sheila on top of that."

"Children are resilient. They'll forget it by tomorrow. Besides, they didn't witness it, so don't worry."

"But I *am* worried," she insisted, blowing her nose into a handkerchief. "I've just realized that I'm not as docile as I thought I was. I have a temper, just like Nikhil's, and almost as fiery as Baba's."

"Every human being has one," he said with infinite patience. "It's perfectly normal."

"But I've never seen *you* losing your cool."

"I have my moments. I'm no saint." He cracked an amused laugh. "Besides, Karnik deserved it. You should have seen his stunned expression when you started talking."

"I noticed that look on his face," she said. "I must admit I got some kind of odd satisfaction from that."

"Now that it's out of your system, you'll feel better. Would you like something to eat?"

"I guess so." She leaned her head back and shut her eyes, looking like she had no strength left to do anything but brood over the evening's debacle. "Thank you."

"I have some leftovers in my fridge. I'll heat them up." He headed toward the kitchen.

Thanks to Mamma's leftovers, inside ten minutes he had *chapatis,* sprouted *moong*-bean—mung-bean—curry, *dal,* and rice on the dining table.

He noticed Isha ate very little. She seemed preoccupied. When she offered to help him wash the dishes, he accepted, just to keep her busy.

After they cleaned up the kitchen, they once again settled on the sofa. "Now that you've calmed down a little," he said, "I want to make you aware of the negative part of what happened at the hospital."

"You mean there was a *positive* part?" she asked with cutting sarcasm.

He kept his mouth shut. She needed to vent.

"I realize I did something entirely stupid," she conceded a moment later. "Everyone around me will be humiliated again, including you. I'm sorry."

He shook his head. "That's minor. What worries me is what you said to Karnik about some sort of documents."

"Oh my God!" Isha's eyes went wide with comprehension. "I did say that, didn't I? I told him everything!"

Harish drew in a tight breath. "You mean you *really* have proof?"

"I had it all along, but I didn't know it. I discovered it recently, when I was going through some papers Nikhil had put into our safe deposit box. I took them out of the vault the day I moved into the convent."

"But you didn't say anything to anyone?"

She shook her head. "I decided to leave it alone, unless I *needed* to do something with it."

"I see." The situation was a lot worse than Harish had imagined.

The despair was clear in her voice. "Now I've gone and ruined it. What am I going to do?"

Harish winced inwardly. "What exactly did you find, Isha?" He was almost afraid to ask.

She turned to face him. "You'll never believe it."

Isha didn't know how much she should tell Harish. Just by knowing what she knew, his life could be in jeopardy. It was bad enough that she'd probably placed herself in peril, but she had no business endangering other people's lives.

Now that the earlier shock had worn off, she rubbed her cold arms and looked about her for the first time since she'd stepped into Harish's house.

It was simple—a small, basic one-story bungalow. The drawing room had a black leather sofa, which they were occupying at the moment, and two matching chairs. A plain teakwood coffee table and two end tables along with a couple of lamps completed the seating arrangement. There were no paintings, rugs, decorator pillows, or photographs anywhere. It was a bachelor's house—a busy bachelor with not much time for a personal life.

But the very simplicity of the room spelled security. It was a reflection of the man—genuine, honest, solid, and reliable. No fussy trimmings, but a comfort to have around.

Despite the day's heat and humidity, she was surprised to find herself chilled. "I don't want to put you in danger," she told him.

"I'm not in any danger." He must have recognized she was

cold, because he took her hands in his and massaged them. "Now tell me everything."

He looked so earnest, and his hands—slightly rough from all the handwashing and preop scrubbing—felt warm and soothing as they stroked hers. She felt the need to confide in him despite her misgivings. "I found a computer disk and three printouts in an envelope."

"What do they contain?"

"The printed spreadsheets have names, dates, and monies paid."

"And the disk?"

She shrugged. "I don't have a computer."

"I forgot about that. We could insert it into my computer and see what it is. Does it have a label?"

"The label's blank, but I'm guessing the disk has similar information as the printouts." An involuntary shiver ran through her and he noticed it.

"You're cold." He got up, disappeared for a minute, and returned with a thick gray cardigan. "Here, put this on."

"I don't know why I'm freezing. The temperature is downright hot today."

"Your chill comes from shock. It happens when a person experiences a trauma of any kind. This is a delayed reaction."

"Oh." She gratefully slipped into the cardigan. It was soft and hand-knitted in a complicated cable design. Someone, maybe his mother, had lovingly made it for him. She glanced at him as he came to sit beside her again. "What do you think I should do? Go to the police?"

"That's probably best . . . but not before we make a few copies and store them in different locations."

"Why?"

"Because this may be the only evidence that exists. Do you know if they found anything similar when Nikhil's body was discovered?"

She had to think about it, recall what the police had said back then. "If they did, they didn't tell me." She mulled over it some more. "Besides, if they had, they would have acted on it. I'm sure the killer found what he was looking for and disappeared with it. Otherwise, he'd have come after me or Nikhil's parents, wouldn't he?"

"Maybe. But what if the killer didn't find it because Nikhil had already hidden all the evidence in the safe deposit box? What you're hiding may be the only copy Nikhil had."

"Oh, Lord!" The chill zipped through her once again. She pulled the cardigan tighter around herself. "So Nikhil died for nothing?" All at once Isha was overcome by hopelessness. "I can't believe Nikhil kept so many secrets from me. It's been fifteen months since he died and I'm still discovering things he kept from me." Tears welled up in her eyes. "I wonder what other nasty surprises await me."

"Don't cry, Isha. I hate seeing you cry. Come here." He shifted and put an arm around her, drawing her closer. "Hopefully there won't be any more unpleasant surprises."

She leaned into him, grateful for the strength and solace he offered. He smelled clean and wholesome—nothing but soap and man—a wonderful male scent she'd almost forgotten. "You don't really believe that, do you?"

"We'll never know. What we need to do now is to go forward with what we have and hope for the best."

"There's no *we* in this," she said. "This is my problem, not yours."

"Don't be silly," he chided. "I *want* to be part of it."

"Why?"

He took a deep breath. She could feel his chest expand and contract, hear his heart thumping. "Because I'm your friend, and I care about you and the children."

"That's very generous of you. But does friendship extend to putting your life in danger?"

He took her hand and rubbed his thumb over the knuckles. "Maybe not an ordinary friendship, but my . . . feelings for you go beyond that."

At last, there it was—an admission of his feelings. She'd known it in her heart, seen it in his face, and felt it in her bones, that he cared about her, but now he was expressing his sentiments—in a certain fashion.

Lifting her head, she studied his face for a long minute. At one time she had thought of it as a plain, homely sort of face. But she'd come to appreciate the mouth that so easily curved into a smile, the slightly blunt nose, the scholarly glasses, the thick brows that nearly met in the center to form a single line, the dark, intelligent eyes that seemed to see way beyond what most people saw.

And the heart that beat under that sensible blue-and-white striped shirt? Surely it was much too generous and much too large to fit into that average-sized chest?

She had yet to come across a more selfless, more caring man. He was extraordinarily brave, too, from what he'd done for her so far, and was offering to do for her in the future.

Right now, he was practically devouring her with his warm, reverent expression. The familiar tingle was traveling through her veins, making her aware of him as more than just a friend.

"I'm not sure if I want to know what those feelings are, Harish," she replied, feeling the regret settle inside her chest. Most women would give anything to have a man like him interested in them. If only things weren't so complicated . . .

He brought her hand to his lips. "You have no idea why I want to be involved in your life, do you?"

Oh, yes, she did! She'd have to be blind, deaf, and denser than a brick not to notice the adoration on his face whenever he looked at her, the amount of time he took out of his hectic schedule to devote to her and the children, the thoughtful things he did for her. He did far more than Nikhil had ever done for Priya and her.

But while she'd gladly welcomed Harish into her life as doctor, advisor, friend, and confidant, she'd deliberately ignored his obvious interest in her as a woman. She'd disregarded her own awakening emotions for him as well, and shut herself off from the possibilities surrounding a young single man. A widow wasn't even supposed to *think* about such things, let alone act on them.

However, despite her attempts at insulating herself from emotional attachment, her feelings for him had undergone a vast change in the past few weeks. She wasn't sure exactly what they were at this point. They were far too complex. And she had deliberately not taken the time to examine them under a microscope.

Besides, in the traditional sense she was still Nikhil's wife. Her official name was Isha Nikhil Tilak. And at the moment she was a threat to Harish's safety. Two excellent reasons not to get involved with him. She turned her gaze away from his. "I think I do."

"I realize you don't return my feelings, but I'm willing to wait." He tightened his arm around her shoulders. "However long it takes."

"Don't punish yourself so, Harish. I know you want a family, so go marry a nice girl your parents pick for you. Someday you'll have children. And you'll make a fabulous husband and father." It tore her up to say that. But she had to do it—for his sake.

He gave a chuckle. "How did you come to *that* conclusion?"

"As if you haven't devoted every hour of your free time to me and my girls! You'd make a great family man. My kids and Sheila's boys think you can walk on water." She looked down at the square brown hand that held hers. There was so much skill and strength in it. "I have lots of fond regard for you, Harish. But I'm afraid I can't give you more. I think a part of me died when Nikhil died, and it's not likely to be resurrected anytime soon."

"Fond regard is a good start," he said. "Most arranged marriages start with no emotions on the part of either partner. A majority of them still work out well."

She turned to him with a gasp. "Marriage!"

"Why do you look so stunned? I'd never offer you anything less than marriage, Isha. Just because you're a widow it doesn't mean all you're fit to be is someone's mistress. You deserve better than that. Besides, I don't believe in pointless love affairs—and I don't do things piecemeal, either."

"No. You wouldn't." She should have known that an honorable man with high moral standards would never proposition a woman—widow or not. He'd offer only the complete package—the sanctity and security of marriage with a lifetime's commitment.

"I know I can't give you a big house and luxuries like Nikhil did."

"It's not that. Material things are not high on my list of priorities," she said. "You know me well enough by now to know it."

"I'm certainly not a good-looking chap like your late husband, either," he continued. "But I can promise you a decent living, a home of your own, and a father for Priya and Diya—even grandparents."

"Harish, please—"

"And," he interrupted, "my parents happen to love girls just as much as boys." He dropped her hand to cup her chin and tilt her face upward, forcing her to meet his eyes. "I've come to not only love you very much, but your children, too."

Oh God! Why was he doing this to her? She managed to hold his gaze. "I'm honored, but I'm sure your parents have some special young lady in mind for you."

He rolled his eyes.

So, she thought, his parents had probably been pressuring him to get married. What old-fashioned Hindu parents wouldn't?

"Face it, Isha! I want to marry *you*. Can't you see that? I want to provide for you and the girls, protect all three of you."

"I don't need protection. I've proved that so far, haven't I?"

"You have, and very admirably," he allowed. "But a woman still needs a man to take care of her. In our society, a married woman commands the respect a widow never could. Children with two parents grow up a lot more secure, too."

"Not in this day and age," she argued. "Nobody cares about marital status anymore. And there are lots of children raised by single parents all over the world."

"Palgaum isn't the whole world. Just look around you. Does

anyone from your previous social circle bother with you any-more? Do your coffee-club friends stop by to see you like they used to?"

"It's not their fault. In spite of our busy social life, I was never a party lover, and I never had any close friends, much to Ayee's disappointment."

"But still, you had close acquaintants, didn't you?"

"Yes."

"Now you're single, while they have husbands. I want to give you the status and security afforded by marriage."

"I can see that, but . . ." He wasn't making this easy for her. "I still think of Nikhil as my husband."

"Of course you do! You were a devoted wife. But Nikhil's been gone some fifteen months and you're still alive and well."

"But that's just it! I'm still here and he's dead."

"So you feel guilty that *you* were spared and *he* was taken?" he asked, his tone incredulous.

Isha blinked. "I . . . I guess so." Harish had managed to ana-lyze her in a second when she had failed to recognize her own hang-ups.

Guilt was precisely what it was. She was just as responsible as Nikhil for rebelling against the elders' dictates. They had both been in it together, and yet he had fought the battle alone, and paid the ultimate price. And why had she been so blind to what Nikhil had been doing in the days prior to his death? She had al-ways prided herself on being able to read her husband like a book, detect his every mood.

She'd failed miserably at both.

"How long are you going to play the martyr?" Harish asked after a lengthy silence.

"Is that what you think I'm doing?" Was he correct in his as-sessment?

He nodded. "Denying yourself a normal life because of your guilt isn't going to do either you or the children any good, or even Nikhil's departed soul, for that matter."

"There's a lot more than guilt involved in all this. You wouldn't understand."

"Were you happy in your marriage to Nikhil?"

She was taken aback for a moment. What a strange and unexpected question! No one had ever asked her that, not even her parents. "Our horoscopes were matched by two different astrologers, and our families did a lot of research and careful deliberating before Nikhil and I were considered suitable for each other."

"That's not what I meant. I asked if you were *happy* with Nikhil."

"Very happy, despite his parents' constant interference in our lives. I was in love with my husband."

"Right from the start?"

"Yes. He was also my best friend." She sighed, long and deep. "In fact, Nikhil was everything to me. That's why it's taking me so long to put my life back together."

"I understand."

"It'll be a long time before I consider replacing him with someone else—if I *ever* consider it. And that's not fair to you."

"I realize you loved your husband very much. It's not easy to forget one's spouse just because he or she is gone from one's life."

"How would *you* know that?" she shot back.

"You're right," he said softly. "What the heck would I know about losing a spouse?"

Dear God, she'd hurt his feelings. "I'm sorry. That was uncalled for." How could she lash out at *this* man of all people? "I'm really sorry."

He remained silent for a long minute. "That's okay," he said finally. "You're under a lot of stress."

She stared at him, startled. "You're willing to forgive me that easily?"

He nodded. "And I'm also willing to wait."

"It may be a very long wait."

"I'll give you all the time you need." He caressed the side of her face with his knuckles, a gesture so tender that Isha's heart did a painful somersault.

The jolt took her by surprise. Despite what she'd been experiencing lately in his presence, she hadn't expected such a powerful reaction to being touched by him.

"Meanwhile, please don't push me away," he said. Abruptly peeling off his glasses, he tossed them on the coffee table and put his hands on her shoulders. "Don't shut me out of your life, Isha."

The unexpectedness of his move made her go still. "I . . . won't," she mumbled. She couldn't shut him out, even if she tried.

Her pulse skyrocketed. The warm, urgent pressure of his hands on her was like a balm and an aphrodisiac combined—a promise of sustenance for her starved heart and body. His eyes, without the glasses, were burning laser beams. She was willing to bet he could see all the way into her soul.

Warmth spread through her like hot water poured into her blood vessels.

"You're a very attractive woman, Isha Ketkar," he whispered, using her maiden name for the second time since they'd met. "I'm in love with you . . . crazy about you." Maybe to prove his point, he shifted, pulled her into the circle of his arms and gazed at her intensely for a second, the black of his irises turning to gleaming onyx.

She drew in an astonished breath, held it there for an instant. *My, oh my!* This was even more unexpected than the embrace.

Perhaps expecting her to withdraw, he said, "Relax. There's no cause for guilt. Let me show you what I mean. I promise I won't hurt you."

She tried to relax, without much success. Every nerve in her body was on high alert. He waited one more beat. When she didn't flinch or resist, he tightened his hold and brought his lips down on hers. It was a slow, calculated motion, perhaps to give her and himself time to adjust to each other. Most men in his place would have roughly grabbed what they desired. But he was so careful, so gentle, so thoughtful, as always.

And he was right. Despite the light touch, the kiss was . . . delicious! How long had it been since she'd experienced anything like this—the thrill of a man's hard chest pressing against her soft, sensitive breasts? She had all but shut herself off from such sensations the night Nikhil had died—or so she'd assumed.

But her body obviously hadn't forgotten the instant surge of excitement that came with an unanticipated kiss, the breathlessness, the tingling energy zipping through every nerve, all the way from the top of her head down to her tiniest toe.

As his mouth moved across hers and grew bolder and more insistent, she sighed and gave in to the myriad sensations, surrendered to his firm hands stroking her back. He was right. There was no need to feel guilty. She was a single woman. He was an unattached man. She wasn't betraying Nikhil.

Little by little she allowed herself to thaw, come to life, and experience the electricity building up, until it gradually suffused her entire mind and body.

How could she resist him when his mouth was so hot and alluring? So demanding? So filled with unspoken promises? How could any woman who'd been kissed often and loved well forget the enchantment of being held in a man's strong arms and kissed with such desperate hunger? The coarse evening stubble on his face felt wonderful even as it abraded her skin. His unabashedly bold hand searching out and then cupping her breast was even more delightful.

Who would have thought Harish Salvi capable of making a woman reach fever pitch? There was no doubt he was succeeding in seducing her. And she was welcoming it!

Setting aside the last of her misgivings for the moment, she placed her arms around his neck and pressed against him. She returned his kiss with equal parts need and desire, for heaven knew how long, and with how much ardor . . . until . . . somewhere in the vicinity a clock chimed the hour.

With a gasp she realized it was indeed a clock and not a warning bell clanging in her brain. But it very well could have been, for the harsh wake-up call it gave her.

She pulled back. And saw Harish close his eyes and groan in frustration. She knew the feeling. He let go of her with obvious reluctance and raked shaky fingers through his hair. His breath sounded ragged. This was the first time Isha had seen him like this. And she realized it was she who'd done this to him, rattled his confidence, and made those eminently capable hands quiver. There was satisfaction in knowing she still had the capacity to arouse and disturb a man to this degree.

Thank goodness the clock had saved them just in time! A few more minutes of that frenzied kissing and groping and she'd probably have ended up in his bed, trembling and needier than ever. How could she have overestimated her own willpower and underestimated the human need for warmth and physical love? She was a woman first, with all the weaknesses of the flesh. She'd have to remember that in the future.

She'd never have forgiven herself if she'd gone to bed with a man who was offering her his heart while she used him for fulfilling no more than a primitive need for release.

Now she was convinced that all that excitement that had her sparking and smoking whenever he was around was nothing more than pent-up physical need—the natural reaction of a body that had gone through a very long dry spell.

But the magic of the moment had vanished in an instant. "Take all the time you want," he said after a minute of awkward silence. "There's no rush." He put his glasses back on and smoothed his hair with steadier hands. He seemed to have regained most of his composure.

Good thing he hadn't offered her an apology. He didn't owe her one. She'd enjoyed the thrill of it just as much as he had—maybe more. And it had certainly made her forget the horrible episode earlier at the hospital, at least for a while. She let her gaze drop, tried to steady her unstable heartbeat. She couldn't look into his eyes and promise him anything she wasn't able to deliver. Not at this time, anyway.

Right now she had more pressing problems to worry about, like Karnik.

"Do you want any tea or coffee . . . anything?" he asked.

She knew he was trying to help both of them recover from an embarrassing *after* moment. "No, thank you."

He chuckled. "My tea was that awful, huh?"

She smiled. "It wasn't all that bad."

"You're not a good liar, Isha." He laughed out loud. "Your expression just now said it was worse than awful."

"It wasn't the tea, honest. I was trying to think of a way to address my problem with Karnik."

"It's *our* problem now," he said, turning serious again, "whether you like it or not. First of all, let's take my laptop computer to your house and check out the disk. If we find something useful, we'll make copies."

"But you could end up like Nikhil." The very idea of it gave her the chills. She couldn't let this gem of a man die because of her.

"Don't worry about me. I can take care of myself." He placed a quick kiss on her cheek and shot to his feet. "Come on, let's get started."

"Now?" The peck on the cheek was a sweet, subtle affirmation of his intentions.

"Yes, now. If Nikhil's killer was either Karnik or his hired assassin, don't you think Karnik is going to panic after what you said to him and act on it right away?"

"That's true." The stark reality of her stupidly impulsive behavior came back to her with full force a second time. What had possessed her to poke a sharp stick at a potentially deadly man? As a result she'd roused the sleeping beast and brought danger right to her doorstep.

Maybe Karnik had already put his evil plans into action. At the very least he could take her to court for defamation of character. There was no choice but to let Harish help her and hope for the best. She took off the borrowed cardigan, folded it, and placed it on the sofa.

Meanwhile, Harish disappeared for a minute into one of the rooms leading off the drawing room and returned with a black leather computer case slung over his shoulder. Pulling his car keys out of his pocket, he nodded. "Let's go."

She picked up her purse and allowed him to usher her out the door. Once settled inside the car, she prayed she wasn't too late. The killer could be waiting for her right now.

Chapter 26

Isha and Harish let themselves into the flat. The place was quiet, which meant the kids were asleep. Isha found Sundari in the kitchen, obviously waiting up for her.

"Isha-bayi, are you all right?" Sundari rose to her feet, casting an anxious look at Isha. Sheila must have told her about the scene at the hospital.

"I'm okay, Sundari. I'm sorry I had you worried."

She seemed a bit startled to see Harish at this time of night but quickly joined her hands to greet him. "*Namaste,* Doctor-saheb."

"Doctor-saheb is helping me with something on his computer," Isha explained to Sundari.

Sundari said nothing in response and showed no emotion whatsoever. It wasn't Sundari's place to question Isha about what she did or the fact that a man was in her home late at night. In their world, servants couldn't presume to judge their employers' conduct. Instead she politely offered to make them tea, which Harish and Isha refused.

Isha glanced at her. "Why aren't you in bed? You've been up since dawn."

"I waited to tell you that Sheila-bayi wants you to ring her as soon as you get home."

"It's rather late to disturb her," said Isha, looking at the clock.

Sundari shook her head. "She said whatever time you come, you must ring her. It is not urgent, but it is important."

"All right, then." Isha turned to Harish. "Why don't you go ahead and power up your computer while I ring Sheila?"

As Isha picked up the phone, she watched Sundari quietly slip into Priya's bedroom and close the door behind her. Meanwhile Harish set up his computer on the kitchen table, plugged it into the nearest outlet and started working the keyboard.

Within a single ring Sheila answered the phone. "Isha?"

"I hope I didn't disturb you."

"No. I was waiting for your call. I couldn't sleep until I heard from you." She was silent for a second. "So . . . what's going on? Are you feeling better now?"

"A lot better, thanks to Harish. But I've realized what an idiot I've been, shooting my mouth off like that."

"It's all that accumulating stress, Isha," said Sheila on a quiet note.

But Isha could hear the note of worry in her voice.

"Harish is a good man. I'm glad he was there when it all happened. He took charge right away."

Yes, he had the commonsense and presence of mind to defuse a potentially volatile situation and make sure it didn't turn into a major crisis, thought Isha with a bitter sigh. She didn't want to tell Sheila that Harish was in her home at the moment. That would mean telling Sheila everything about the information she'd been hiding in her *almirah*. It would also mean putting one more person in danger.

So she stuck to a safer topic. "How did the children's visit with Ayee go? I never got a chance to ask you."

"Better than I'd anticipated. Ayee can't talk a lot at the moment, but she touched the girls and thanked Priya for saving her life. Then she asked her about school and other activities. Priya, of course, chatted a lot." Sheila chuckled. "The chatterbox was a godsend in an awkward moment. She told Ayee all about her stay at the convent, her new flat, her new sister, your dressmaking, Doctor-kaka, and her chess games—just about everything."

"What was Ayee's reaction?"

"Ayee seemed shocked and dismayed. This was the first time she was hearing the details of what your life and the girls' has been for the past fifteen months. I had given Ayee only the bare facts and no more."

"I see."

"I noticed the sadness and regret in Ayee's expression. I think she's feeling badly about what her granddaughters and you had to endure."

"So, what happens now?" Isha hoped Ayee had her fill of her grandchildren and wouldn't ask for more. She'd made peace with God and her conscience. Now things could go back to the way they were.

But Sheila stunned her by saying, "I think she felt guiltier than ever, subjecting her own flesh and blood to such difficult circumstances. She wants to continue to see them."

"You're not serious!"

"Isha, there were tears in Ayee's eyes when she saw Diya. She kept staring at her all the while and asking to hold her. I think the baby's strong resemblance to Niku is what affected Ayee so sharply."

"Really? I thought she'd detest Diya more than Priya because . . . well, you know why."

"You're wrong. Diya resembles Niku even more than Priya does, even down to the expression. Ayee recognized that right away. I think her need to see the kids again grew stronger after she met Diya."

"That means you'll be stuck chauffeuring the girls back and forth to visit Ayee. I don't want to burden you with that."

"Don't be silly!" said Sheila. "The boys and I go there frequently. I'll just take the girls at the same time, if it's okay with you, that is."

"I'll think about it. At the moment I have other things to worry about. My confrontation with Karnik may have caused more trouble than I thought. Harish pointed it out to me, so now I have to see what I can do to patch things up."

"Exactly what are you going to do? Ring Karnik and apologize?"

Isha bit her lip. "I might have to."

"Let me know whatever you decide."

"Okay." Isha said a hasty good night and put down the phone. From Harish's expression she could tell he had the computer up and running, and was waiting for her. "I'll get the disk," she told him and went into the bedroom. A minute later she returned with the envelope.

Harish inserted the disk into the appropriate drive and clicked the mouse a couple of times. He frowned at the screen when something popped up. "Interesting! Pull up your chair," he instructed her. "I want you to take a look at the date the information was saved to the disk."

She moved her chair closer and studied what he pointed out. "June 23rd!" She turned to Harish. "It was the night Nikhil died! That means he obtained the information the same day he was killed."

"Look at the time—12:21 AM. That's a little after midnight of June 22nd." Harish leaned back in his chair and stared at the screen for several seconds. "I don't mean to offend you, but do you think Nikhil stole the file from Karnik's computer?"

"Nikhil wasn't a thief! He'd never break into someone's place and steal something."

"He may have been enraged and desperate enough to do it. Or he could have hired someone to do it for him."

"I'm not sure about that." She didn't know what to think. There were so many secrets and so many unanswered questions. Did she really know Nikhil at all? Could he have been a thief? Again she wondered, what else had her late husband been doing behind her back? The thought made her cringe. It was tantamount to being betrayed by a dead man.

Harish's voice brought her back to the present. "I'm sorry. I didn't mean to upset you." He had the file opened and displayed on the screen. "Do the spreadsheets contain this?"

Despite knowing more or less what to expect, Isha still drew in a sharp breath when she saw the same data that she had on the paper copies. "I think so." She spread out the papers on the kitchen table for him to see.

He took a couple of minutes to examine and compare the information, then let out a low whistle. "Wow! The old man's been busy, and becoming very wealthy with his ugly side business. Besides, all these are probably cash transactions, so the income-tax folks have no clue. The money is all his, free and clear." He shook his head. "Incredible!"

"Exactly my sentiments when I first saw this. Despite what I already knew, when I saw how extensive the list was, I was stunned." She pointed to a few names on the list. "These are people I know well. At least I thought I did. I never imagined these women would resort to selective abortion." She pondered it for a second. "No wonder they're all giving birth to boys while I've had two girls."

"And some of those precious boys are my patients," he said. The sarcasm in his voice wasn't lost on Isha.

"How eerie is that? Aldous Huxley's *Brave New World* in motion?"

"If not that, then it's close," he said dryly. "Did you know that a conservative estimate puts anywhere between eight and ten million girls as either aborted or killed in infancy in the last two decades?"

"That many!" She'd been under the impression it was a few hundred thousand. "Are you sure?"

He nodded. "I started reading up on the subject after we discussed it the other day. I was shocked. And, remember, it's only a conservative estimate, meaning a certain percentage of the cases are never recorded."

"So there could be lots more that never come to light . . . like Karnik's cases." She gave herself a moment to absorb the fact. "It could even be twice that number. My God!" It was sickening.

Harish gave her a searching look. "I don't mean to pry, but do you think Sheila and Kumar may have gone through this?"

"No way! Sheila was shocked when I told her Ayee and Baba

wanted me to have an abortion. Her distress was genuine. I've known Sheila and Kumar for many years and I know they'd never resort to something like this. You've seen how much they love both my children."

"I'm glad," murmured Harish. "I've come to like and respect them."

"Besides, I think they were hoping for a girl the second time around. They got Arvind instead."

Harish saved the data from the disk onto his hard drive and pulled out three blank disks from a storage pocket in the computer case. A few minutes later he had the information copied on the new disks. "Tomorrow I'll print up a set for my office safe and one for the safety deposit box."

"What's the third one for?"

"For the police," he said, looking at her across the table. "Don't look so alarmed. I'll take them directly to the superintendent. I know him."

"You mean Patil?" When he nodded, she gave a contemptuous sniff. "I know him, too. Fat lot of good he did when Nikhil took the evidence to him! And just look at his investigation of Nikhil's death. More than a year and a quarter later, what does Patil have to show for it?"

"But that could be because Nikhil never had a chance to get this evidence to Patil. We now know he was killed only hours after he got the disk."

"Hmm." He had a point. She hadn't thought of that.

"Assuming Nikhil never had a chance to turn this over to Patil, it's up to us. We need to share with him what we have." He shut down the computer. "Besides, with no clues whatsoever, what could Patil do? Karnik must have hired a pro to do such a thorough job." He stopped what he was doing and shifted his gaze to her. "All the more reason why I'm concerned about *your* safety."

A shiver went through her. "Should we tell Patil that we have copies of everything?"

"He'll know that anyway. He's a seasoned police officer." Putting the three disks in his shirt pocket, Harish packed up the computer. "I'll take care of storing the copies in the appropriate places. Make sure you keep yours locked, too."

"All right." The icy feeling still lingered. "I'm sorry," she said.

"For what?"

"For turning your nice, uncomplicated life upside down. You're probably wondering why in the world your path crossed mine."

He gave her a slow, heartwarming smile. "I'm wondering why our paths didn't cross when we were both young and single."

"They did in college."

"But they didn't cross in the real sense. We were kids then— students."

"*You* are still young and single, and the world is yours to take, Harish. Go grab it with both hands before it's too late."

"I *am* trying to grab the world with both hands. I'm hoping you'll be part of it."

She patted his hand. "Give me some time."

"All right." He gently brushed his thumb across her lips, making them quiver. "Be very, very careful, Isha. Don't go out alone or let any strangers into the flat. Let Sundari screen your phone calls. If she doesn't recognize the voice, tell her to say you're busy."

"You better take care, too," she cautioned him. "Karnik knows we're friends." She waited while he picked up his computer bag and headed for the door.

"Get some rest now," he advised, and then took off.

Chapter 27

Harish wasn't quite sure if it was his imagination, but a vehicle had been behind his car for a while and seemed to be folllowing him. As he'd left his office after working very late, started his car, and merged into the traffic, he had noticed a Jeep pull out of a parked spot and get in behind him. This late in the evening, when it was pitch-dark, it was impossible to tell its color.

There was plenty of distance between the two vehicles, so at first he hadn't paid any attention, but as he snaked his way through the traffic inside town and then out into the suburban section where his brother's house was located, he noticed the vehicle still trailing behind him.

Very few people took the route he traveled, from one end of the town to the other—a shortcut via small side streets. It was a convoluted route, but he had figured it out by trial and error as the quickest and most convenient one at this time of the evening. Who else would use the exact same pattern?

Odd, he thought, looking at the headlights in his rearview mirror once again. Could it be the police following him? If so, why? Had he broken any traffic laws?

Then something clicked in his mind. And a spark of fear ignited with it. That morning he had called Patil's office and had been told that Patil was out of town for a couple of days. Since Harish didn't trust anyone else in the department, he had left only his name and phone number with a message for Patil to call him back. He had asked that his request be marked urgent.

And now someone was following him home? He believed in coincidence up to a point. This didn't seem like one. Besides, in Palgaum, this type of utility vehicle was almost exclusive to police, the armed forces, the public works department, and a couple of other government entities. Could this be someone in Patil's office? Someone who had access to Patil's messages? It could even be the very man who'd taken Harish's message.

That's when Harish wondered if it had been wise to leave a message for Patil. Once he'd learned Patil was out of town, he should have hung up and tried again in a couple of days. But it was too late to change that now.

So instead of leading his tail to his brother's house and possibly putting his family in danger, he made an abrupt turn and drove toward a popular restaurant in town. On the way he called his mother and told her not to hold dinner for him because he was meeting a friend.

He parked in a well-lit area outside the eatery and went in. Even this late, the place was crowded. When he asked for a table that faced the door, the waiter informed him he'd have to wait. While he waited he stood by the entrance, watching the parking lot. Despite keeping his eyes peeled, he didn't see the vehicle anywhere. Ten minutes later, he was seated at a small table that had a clear view of the entry door.

With his stomach in knots and his gaze fixed on the entrance, he ate very little of the meal he ordered. But he took his time over it, hoping the person who'd followed him would get tired and go away.

Customers walked in periodically, but no one seemed particularly interested in him. In fact, nobody even bothered to look his way except one young couple whose child was his patient. They stopped by his table to exchange a few friendly words. While he deliberately lingered over his dinner, the restaurant crowd thinned out to only a handful of patrons.

Much later, after paying for his dinner and returning to the parking lot, he took a careful look around, and even at the backseat of his car, before he climbed in and drove home. There was no one following him.

But he knew it was a false sense of security. He could feel the disquiet in his bones. Besides, everyone in town knew where he lived, where his family lived, and by now perhaps even where Isha and her children had taken up residence. She'd been there for some months. The post office and all the utility companies had her address.

And that brought on a renewed surge of fear. What if his tail had abandoned him to go after Isha? He'd never considered that possibility until this minute.

The instant he entered his house he dialed her mobile number. There was no point in calling the land line and disturbing the children. They'd be in bed by now.

When she answered the phone in her usual manner he took a deep, relieved breath. He heard music in the background, which meant she was sewing. And that was reassuring. She always had the radio on for company when she worked. "Is everything okay, Isha?" he asked her, trying to sound casual.

"Sure. Why do you ask?" Her voice took on a wary note in spite of his attempts at nonchalance. It seemed like she was jittery, too.

"No particular reason. Since last night I've been a little on edge. I tried calling Patil, by the way. But he's out of town attending a conference, so I couldn't meet him."

"I guess we'll have to wait until he returns." She must have guessed something was bothering him. "Harish, what's wrong?"

"Well . . ." In the end he decided it was best to err on the side of caution. "Look, when I called Patil's office, I left a message with someone to have him call me back . . . and . . . it may not have been a wise thing to do."

"What else could you do but leave a message?" In spite of her supportive words he could hear the undercurrent of disquiet in her voice.

"But one never knows who's listening in or who's reading the messages. So please be careful, understand?"

"I'm trying my best. I've cautioned Sundari against taking the children out to the park, or anywhere, for that matter. And we're keeping the doors to both flats locked at all times. In any case, I'm the one Karnik might come after, not the children or Sundari. They have nothing to do with this."

"I know you're being vigilant, but I still worry about you. All four of you."

"It's nice to know we have someone strong and dependable watching over us."

"Are you mocking me, Isha Tilak?" he jested.

"No."

"You make me sound like that senile old knight, the fellow who fought imaginary windmills. We read that book in our high school English class."

"You mean Don Quixote?"

"That's the one." Harish was having a hard time keeping the smile out of his feigned indignation. She had a way of making him smile.

But she was serious. "Of course not! I meant every word. It's nice to be able to depend on someone like you when I could be headed for trouble."

"Good. Now make sure the locks are secure and keep your mobile phone close by."

"At the moment, I'm working, and since I'm talking to you I obviously have my mobile with me, Doctor," she informed him with a chuckle. "And before you ask me the next question, let me assure you that your number and Sheila's are programmed into my speed dial."

"Excellent. Are the children asleep yet?"

"A while ago, and so is Sundari. I checked on them before I came to the shop. I'm trying to meet a deadline for a birthday party dress."

"I'll let you get back to it, then. I'll talk to you tomorrow," he said and rang off, hoping he hadn't scared her too much. But putting her on her guard was better than letting her become complacent and hence careless.

To practice what he'd preached to Isha, he made sure all his windows and his front and back doors were locked. He'd have to depend on the ceiling fan in his bedroom to keep the air circulating. To add a little extra security, on each doorknob he placed a small battery-operated device. Any movement on the door was supposed to set off a shrill alarm.

They were a gift from a college classmate and close friend, Phillip D'Souza, who was a police inspector in a neighboring district. Harish had never used the fancy gadgets before. He hadn't seen any use for them. But tonight he felt insecure enough to take them out of their boxes, read the instructions, and install them. They were probably not much of a deterrent to a seasoned criminal, but they'd let Harish sleep a little better.

He made a mental note to go to a store the next day and look for a similar device for Isha's flat.

After changing into pajamas and turning off all the lights, he parted the thick curtains on his bedroom window a crack and made a quick visual survey of the street. It was dead, the only movement being the giant moths flitting around the vapor lamp of the streetlight. There wasn't a single vehicle. Maybe that Jeep *had* been a figment of his imagination?

But that little voice in his brain said it wasn't. His instincts were usually right on target. Someone had been tailing him for a reason.

And then he saw it, the vehicle from earlier, making a slow pass on the street in front of his house. There was no way he could read the license plate.

And his fear for Isha's safety went up another notch.

He picked up the phone and rang his friend the police officer. "Phillip, sorry to disturb you at this hour, but I need your help urgently. How soon can you get here?" He figured if Phillip started right away and drove fast, he could arrive in an hour or so.

Phillip must have been asleep. He sounded irritable and groggy. "You want me to drive to Palgaum *now?*"

"*Now!*"

It was past midnight by the time Isha finished the last of her sewing, ironed the dress, and put it on a hanger. Her back was stiff from sitting at the old machine for hours and then hand-finishing the necessary items.

Sheila had suggested that she buy a modern machine with the capacity to do a number of things like buttonholes, hems, seams, and simple embroidery, literally within minutes. To that end, Isha had saved up a little. Soon she was going to go out and buy herself one of those sleek machines that would save her time, effort, and, in the long run, money.

She was also planning on hiring some help. She'd never be able to keep up with the work at the current rate. At the moment, she was so swamped she could barely meet her obligations. Although, she had to admit the income was excellent. She was planning on increasing Sundari's salary.

Her mind reverted to Harish's phone call earlier. To hear a calm, rational man like him sound so worried was more frightening than what she'd felt the previous night. It wasn't like him to caution her again and again about something.

It had been more than twenty-four hours since her strange altercation with Karnik. She had this eerie feeling that something was going to happen soon as a consequence of that. But what? The thought of dying a gruesome death like Nikhil's was terrifying.

All of a sudden she realized it wasn't a good idea to be alone in the shop so late. Nikhil had apparently been caught when he was by himself, finishing up his work for the day and closing the office. That's exactly what she was doing now.

Thank goodness her home was barely fifteen feet from the shop's threshold. There was no long drive or walk in the dark.

Shutting off the radio and turning out the lights, she stepped out into the hallway. It was deserted. She did this practically every night, and yet, tonight the silence, which she generally considered blissful, was almost eerie. During waking hours there were often voices coming from the other flats in the building, music and sounds from someone's radio or television, and traffic noises from the street.

Quickly securing the lock, she crossed the aisle, her home key held ready.

She froze in her tracks when she noticed the door to her home. It was slightly ajar. Sundari had strict instructions to keep the door locked, and never open it without first looking through the peephole. Besides, it was way too late at night to leave any doors unlocked.

Her immediate reaction was annoyance. What was Sundari thinking, leaving the flat wide-open to intruders? But then again, Sundari never ignored instructions. That's when Isha recalled Harish's call and his advice about keeping her doors locked. She felt an icy thread of fear slither down her spine. Instinctively she flipped open her phone and pressed the speed dial button for Harish's mobile.

He picked up on the first ring. "Isha!"

"Harish, the front door to my flat . . . is open," she whispered, "and . . ." She didn't even know what to say beyond that. She was afraid someone would hear her.

"And what?" When she remained silent, her gaze fixed on the door, he asked, "Exactly where are you, Isha?" There was a note of alarm in his voice she hadn't heard before.

She took a deep breath, telling herself to calm down, spell it out to Harish, one word at a time. "I'm . . . uh . . . standing in the corridor between the two flats. I just finished working and was heading back home when I noticed the door was open . . . so I called you."

"Then turn around immediately and go back into the shop. I'm on my way. I have a police officer with me, so stay right there behind locked doors. Don't move!"

"But the children . . . and Sundari—"

"Do as I tell you," he ordered. "Now go! I'll keep the phone line open."

But in the next instant a shrill beep sounded in her ear, making her jump. The phone went dead. It took a moment to realize the battery had just died. Oh no! Of all times to run out of power!

She stared at the door, torn between barging in and turning around to run for her life. Should she go in and see for herself? Maybe it was just a matter of Sundari dozing off without locking the door. After all, the woman was getting old and a bit forgetful. How foolish would it look if Harish and some police officer arrived with guns blazing, only to find an old woman fast asleep on the drawing room floor and Isha standing over her, hyperventilating like an idiot?

But her heart was pounding madly. Her instincts were on full alert. It was much too quiet inside. Her babies were in there. Anything could have happened to them. She *had* to go in.

No matter what Harish said, she couldn't very well abandon her children and Sundari to God knows what and hide in her safe little dress shop. She'd never forgive herself if she could have done something to prevent a catastrophe but was too afraid to open a door.

Drawing in a single, fortifying breath, she grasped the doorknob, gently nudged the door open, and stuck her head inside. The drawing room was in total darkness, except for a single, thin shaft of light from the streetlight coming in through the gap in the curtains. All she could hear was her own harsh breath, the blood pounding in her head. She let her eyes adjust to the dimness before taking a visual inventory.

She reeled backward in alarm. The place had been ransacked! The furniture was upside down, the children's toys were tossed on the floor, and all kinds of papers were strewn around.

What in heaven's name had happened here?

In spite of the fact that every nerve in her body sensed danger, she stepped inside, stood still for a moment, her damp right palm curled around her keys. With the hair on her arms prickling, she waited for someone or something to pounce on her. When nothing happened, she forced her rubbery legs to move, to tiptoe and pick her way through the clutter into her bedroom to check on Diya. The baby was her first concern.

The bedroom was in worse shape than the drawing room. In the glow of the nightlight she stood gaping at the destruction. Her *almirah* and dresser stood open and all the contents were spilled on the floor. The bedsheets were also on the floor; the pillows and mattress had deep gashes, with their cotton ticking pulled out and tossed in every direction.

It looked like something from a horror movie—the work of a sick monster on a rampage.

Despite the sense of utter loss, her mind was still on Diya, so she stepped over the debris, eased up to the cradle and looked in. Empty! The tiny mattress was slashed all over. Her stomach plunged. Had the baby been hacked to pieces, too?

Oh God! No. Not Diya, please!

But there was no blood anywhere. *Calm down,* she ordered herself. *Don't assume the worst. Maybe the baby's asleep beside her big sister in the other room, or in Sundari's lap.*

Making a mad rush to the other room with no thought for her own safety, Isha stumbled on something large—and squealed. Blindly reaching for the wall with one hand, she barely caught herself from falling on her face. Then fumbling for the light switch, she turned on the light and looked at the floor. Sundari lay on her stomach on the bedroll.

"Sundari!" she squeaked, forgetting the children for the moment. "I—I'm sorry I stepped on you." But Sundari didn't budge. She was lying dead!

Sinking to her knees beside the prostrate woman, Isha touched her arm. It felt warm. Reassured a little, she gingerly touched the side of her neck. That's what they did in television shows and the movies. There was a pulse! It was slow, but it was there. She patted the old woman's back. "Sundari, wake up."

But Sundari lay still. It wasn't like her. She was a light sleeper and woke up at the slightest noise. Isha put her hands on her shoulders and shook her hard, but Sundari's deep breathing continued on. What was wrong with Sundari? Had she suffered a stroke? Had she slipped into a coma? "Sundari! Please tell me you're not unconscious!"

Was she totally paralyzed? Well, at least she was still breathing. That was worth something, wasn't it? The good thing was Harish was on his way. He'd know what was wrong with Sundari.

"Please, wake up," Isha cried to the old woman, despite knowing Sundari couldn't hear her. "Are you in pain?" No response. "Don't die, Sundari, please," she whispered and took one rough, wrinkled hand in hers. "Help is coming. We'll take care of you."

Guilt settled in as Isha looked at the disheveled coil of gray hair and the rumpled and faded pink sari that had ridden up to her calves, exposing dark, dry-skinned legs, and heels with deep cracks caused from walking barefoot for years and years. Dear, sweet Sundari. How could Isha have thought of her as careless? Sundari was never remiss in her duties. In fact, where the children and their well-being were concerned, she bordered on obsessive. The poor woman had suffered a stroke, perhaps a seizure, or a heart attack.

But the children? That's when the alarm exploded in Isha's brain once again. Where were they?

She shot to her feet and ran to Priya's bed and found her asleep and breathing. The mattress beside her was slashed like everything else. Peeling back the sheet to examine the sleeping child, she ran her hands over Priya from head to toes to make sure everything was okay. Disturbed by the probing, Priya stirred and changed positions.

Priya seemed fine. She had obviously slept right through whatever had occurred to hurt Sundari and turn the room upside down. Priya was always a deep sleeper. An incredible *whoosh* of relief left Isha's lungs to see her daughter unharmed.

She looked about the room. Every drawer in the dresser was open and the contents tossed, just like the *almirah*. Nothing had been left untouched by the robber. He had invaded her home and everything private and precious.

There was a sickly sweet odor in the room. But she didn't recognize it.

Never mind the odor, she told herself. It wasn't important. Priya was fine and Sundari was obviously in serious condition. The minute Harish got here he'd have to examine Sundari. She probably needed to be moved to a hospital immediately.

But then . . . where was the baby? "Diya," she whispered and looked on the floor, feverishly picking up clothes and linens to see if she was sleeping, buried under them. Had the child slept on the bed with her sister and rolled off? Desperate for a sign of her baby, Isha looked under the bed, inside the ransacked *almi-rah,* every conceivable nook. But Diya was nowhere to be found.

Frantic with worry, Isha turned on all the lights in the flat and searched the drawing room, the kitchen, and the bathroom. Every room looked like a cyclone had passed through it, even the kitchen. Every container had been ransacked. Sugar, flour, cereal, rice, and *dal* lay scattered on the kitchen floor. The refrigerator door stood open.

What could have happened to the baby? Diya was a mischievous little imp and managed to get around very well. She was also a lighter sleeper than Priya. Had she woken up, found Sundari unconscious, her sister fast asleep, and crawled out of bed?

"Diya, where are you, sweetie?" she repeated several times, the pitch of her voice rising progressively and turning more frantic. She wondered whether the child could be underneath a piece of furniture, crushed by the weight of it. With some effort she set the sofa back on its feet.

When that yielded no sign of Diya, she tried something else. "Diya, Mummy has ice cream for you." The child loved ice cream and no matter where she was, the word *ice cream* enticed her to come crawling forward and clap her tiny hands with glee.

But all Isha got in response was silence. She cocked her ears, listening for the familiar sound of Diya's knees and hands shuffling along the floor. But there was nothing but emptiness and the ticking of the kitchen clock.

Had the child seen the open door and found her way out? Dear God, she could have crawled through the hallway and tumbled down the stairs. She could be badly hurt . . . even dead by now.

"Diya!"

Just as Isha moved to make a beeline for the door, her eyes fell on a piece of paper on the upturned coffee table. It had a single sentence written in bold red crayon, meant to grab attention.

DO YOU WANT YOUR CHILD BACK?

Priya's box of crayons lay open beside it.

Both the handwriting and the message were precise and neat— a grownup's note written with a child's crayon—mocking evidence of how easy it had been to break in and take her baby.

The terse simplicity of it was terrifying.

Clutching the piece of paper in her trembling hands, Isha collapsed onto the wrecked sofa. The same shade of ashy gray that had enveloped everything when she was informed of Nikhil's death now seemed to settle over the room. Even the vivid maroons and yellows in the throw pillows gradually turned gray. Every one of the spilled crayons acquired the same frozen tint.

Her brain lurched, then shifted into slow motion, and gradually shut down.

Only a single thought remained: Her baby was gone.

Chapter 28

Harish tried to take the shortest and quickest route to Isha's flat. In the process he ran his car through a couple of red lights, despite Phillip's wry comments about blatant disregard for the law. His big, muscular friend sat in the passenger seat, reminding him to use more caution.

But Harish had neither the time nor the inclination to take his wise friend's advice.

Isha and her children were in grave danger. That was all he could focus on. She had hung up the phone abruptly, or maybe she'd dropped it. That must mean something had happened to her. Maybe someone had grabbed her? She was so petite, so fragile. He could only pray she had enough strength to fight her attacker.

Phillip put a reproving hand on his arm. "Slow down, Harish! You want to get there in one piece or not?"

"Come on, Phillip! They could all be dead by now—stabbed, just like Isha's husband was. I'm telling you, that bastard Karnik has no conscience and no scruples whatsoever."

"Then why didn't you call the local police? This is not my jurisdiction."

"I told you why. I don't trust them! Right after I left a message for the superintendent, someone started to follow me home and now they're after Isha. Some blackguard in the police department is on Karnik's payroll. Who knows, maybe it's the same man who's Karnik's hired killer, too. There may be more than one."

"How did you come to that conclusion?"

"Karnik is over seventy years old and not at all big or fit. I know he couldn't take on a man of Nikhil Tilak's age and size. Karnik wouldn't be foolish enough to do it himself, either. Believe me, Phillip, there's a rat in that rotten-as-a-sewer police department."

"Okay, okay," said Phillip, attempting to placate his disturbed friend. "But you're going to get yourself and me killed if you don't slow down," he repeated, between clenched teeth. "This is not a Bollywood movie. The streets here are narrow and there are still some cars and pedestrians around. At least give some thought to *their* lives if not yours and mine."

Heeding Phillip's voice of prudence, Harish eased his foot off the pedal, but only a fraction of a millimeter. "I know Isha's in trouble, or she wouldn't have hung up on me."

Two minutes later he brought his car to a grinding stop in front of Isha's building.

In a heartbeat he was out the door and running toward the main entryway. Phillip ran after Harish, his gun drawn . . . just in case. Their shoes made a loud, clapping sound in the quiet of the night as they sprinted across the concrete footpath, through the short lobby and then up the stairs to the second floor, taking them two at a time.

Harish veered right at first, toward the dress shop, but seeing the door to her home wide-open, he abruptly swung left and barreled in. When he stopped dead in the next instant, Phillip bumped hard into his back, swearing under his breath.

The lights were on everywhere. The floor was littered with papers, pillows, and toys. Two chairs and the coffee table lay upside down. The photographs Isha had so lovingly placed in wooden frames were ruined, their glass shattered.

Harish sucked in a painful breath. What the hell had happened here?

His eyes went instantly to Isha. She sat on the battered sofa with a piece of paper clutched in one hand. Her eyes were fixed on a spot on the floor.

"Isha!" His immediate reaction was to reprimand her for entering the flat when he'd specifically ordered her to go back to the dress shop and lock herself in. But something stopped him from tearing into her: that dazed look on her face. Going closer to her, he asked gently, "Why did you hang up the phone, Isha?"

It took her a moment to come out of the trance. "I didn't. The battery ran out."

"Oh." Why hadn't he thought of a simple explanation like a dead battery? "Are you all right?"

She held out the piece of paper. "They took Diya."

"What!" He grabbed the paper and read the note—a couple of times. There was no mistake. Someone had kidnapped Diya and left behind this: a not-so-subtle threat.

He passed the note to Phillip, knelt on the floor beside Isha, and put a hand on her knee. "We'll find her. I promise you, we'll find Diya." He knew he was making empty promises, but he'd do anything to get her to snap out of this frozen, expressionless state. He would have preferred to see her sobbing, hysterical, livid—anything but this.

"Sundari . . ." she murmured.

"What about Sundari?" He looked around, his eyes once again measuring the destruction wreaked over the room, wondering what kind of demon could have done this. "Where is she, anyway?" Wasn't she supposed to be watching the children?

"I—I think she's had a stroke." Something seemed to be lodged in Isha's throat, because she kept swallowing. "She won't wake up. I tried to wake her . . . I tried so hard."

"A stroke? What makes you think it's . . . ? Never mind." How was she supposed to know the symptoms? "What about Priya?"

The look on Isha's face was still not entirely focused. "She's sleeping in her room."

"I'll take a look at Sundari." Leaving Isha in Phillip's capable hands, Harish rose to his feet and turned toward the bedroom he knew was Priya's and Sundari's. That room, too, was a scene of devastation.

And, sure enough, Sundari lay on the floor with her face down. Her body looked unnaturally still.

He knelt down and checked her pulse. It was a little sluggish, but it wasn't life-threatening. He checked for possible broken bones and injuries. Finding none, he carefully rolled her onto her back. She moaned a little. Her eyelids fluttered a bit and then closed again. "Sundari," he said, but another whispery moan is all he got from her. He forced open her eyelids to check her pupils and found them slightly dilated.

From what he could see, he suspected she may have been anesthetized, most likely with something like chloroform or ether. There was a vaguely familiar, sweet odor in the room, further confirming his suspicions.

If it was indeed an anesthetic type of substance, thank God she hadn't been administered a dangerous dose, because her vital signs were near normal. She'd wake up soon, most likely with a headache, exhaustion, or nausea—or all three. He hoped that was all it was.

He sat back on his heels amidst the litter and attempted to visualize what may have happened before his arrival. The kidnapper had obviously broken into the flat while Isha was working in the other one.

It was a little after ten o'clock when Harish had seen the Jeep pass by his house. The kidnapper probably had driven directly to Isha's place. It was Harish's call to Patil that must have assured Karnik and his informant that Isha's threats had substance. If only he hadn't left that stupid message!

Even later on, after he'd realized the man in the Jeep was probably headed for Isha's place, he could have come to her immediately, kept her and the family safe. Instead, he'd panicked and waited for Phillip to arrive. Even more stupid! But it was too late to lament that now.

Most likely the goon hadn't found what he was looking for, so he'd started to slash and tear apart everything, looking for it. When he still couldn't find it, what did he do? He took Diya!

The bastard must have been awfully quiet or Isha would have heard something. But on second thought, she had the hallway separating the two flats and both doors were closed. She also had the radio on. Her ceiling fan must have been running, and possibly her noisy sewing machine. All those things combined would have prevented her from hearing anything going on in the house.

Rising to his feet, he went to check on Priya. Her pulse and eyes were perfectly normal and her color looked healthy. Thank God! She was sleeping peacefully on her ruined mattress, an innocent little girl who had no idea about the evil destruction that had occurred all around her. It was a miracle she'd been left untouched.

He felt the most powerful urge to pick up the child and hug her from sheer relief, but quashed it in the next second. Let her sleep.

But where had the kidnapper taken the baby? Harish had come to love the little tyke. Could she be hurt or even killed by now? The thought was too horrifying to dwell on. And Isha? Dear God, if it bothered him to see her cry, it was downright heartbreaking to see her shed no tears at all, and instead stare at the floor like all her emotions had drained through a sieve.

He checked on Sundari once again. She was stirring. It was a promising sign. In a little while she'd wake up and stay groggy for an hour or two. So he went back to the drawing room. Phillip had returned one of the chairs back to its upright position and was sitting in it. "I checked the door," he said to Harish. "The lock was picked. Clean job, though. It's hard to detect. He's clearly an expert."

Harish stopped in his tracks. "Hmm." Palgaum wasn't exactly a town filled with expert thieves. All his suspicions about the perpetrator possibly being a policeman were becoming stronger by the minute. Who was he? Or was there more than one?

Probably reading Harish's thoughts, Phillip nodded at him in acknowledgment.

"I checked on Sundari, Isha." Harish went to sit beside her. "It's not a stroke. She was probably given an anesthetic by the intruder. She'll be all right once she wakes up."

"You're sure?" Isha asked, her expression still a little unfocused.

"I'm positive. She'll be fine."

Phillip started questioning Isha. "Tell me exactly what happened when you entered the flat."

She haltingly told them everything she'd seen and done. The kidnapper had obviously had plenty of time to do whatever he wanted to do and take off. He'd even had the luxury of being able to find a blank sheet of paper and crayons to write his menacing note. It seemed like he'd gone on a sick demolition spree, delighting in all the devastation, and then gloating over it.

Phillip tapped his steepled fingers together. "Since he took the baby I'm assuming he didn't find what he was looking for even after a thorough search—in this case the evidence against Karnik." He leaned forward to face Isha, his gaze intense. "So, exactly where is this *evidence?*"

"In my shop, locked up in the *almirah*. I don't think the killer knows about my other flat, otherwise he would have come there looking for it, wouldn't he?" She frowned at Phillip.

Phillip nodded. "Most likely." He looked about the wrecked room. His silence spoke volumes. *If the thief had easily found what he was looking for, he'd have taken it and left the rest of the house alone. And he wouldn't have taken a hostage, either.*

Isha must have read his mind, too. "I should have left it in the *almirah* right here, where I'd always kept it. But for some insane reason, this morning I decided to move it far away from the children and Sundari." She pressed her fingers to her eyes, a gesture of extreme frustration. "In my attempt to protect my children, I did the exact opposite: I gave him the perfect reason to abduct one of them."

"It's never easy to foresee how a decision will affect the future, Isha," consoled Harish.

"But it all started with my conversation with Karnik. It's all *my* fault."

The look of pure anguish on her face stabbed at Harish. He pressed her hand in both of his. "You can't keep blaming yourself for something you did on impulse. Let's hope Patil returns soon and Diya will be found."

"Do you really trust this Patil?" Phillip asked, looking skeptical. "I know of him, but I don't know him personally."

Harish nodded. "I'm acquainted with him. His grandchildren are my patients. He loves playing politician, and he's hungry for publicity, but I don't think he's all that corrupt."

"Are you sure?"

"I can't be one hundred percent positive, but I know he's not the type to condone murder and kidnapping. I'd be willing to bet he lines his pockets at every opportunity, but nothing more than that."

"Then see if you can contact him," said Phillip. "Call his wife, or do whatever you have to, and explain it's urgent. Every minute is precious in cases like this. It gives the kidnapper that much more time to get away." When he saw Harish reaching for the phone directory, he added, "And *don't* call Patil's office!"

"I won't. That was my biggest mistake. It won't happen again."

"And if you talk to his wife, make sure she tells no one at his office. And emphasize that point."

"All right." Harish inclined his head toward the land line phone in the kitchen. "Meanwhile, why don't you call Isha's sister-in-law, Sheila Sathe, and inform her about this? Sheila and Isha are close and Sheila will want to help. I'm sure the number is by the phone." When Phillip hesitated and kept looking around the room, Harish raised an eyebrow. "What?"

"I'm wondering if the man left any fingerprints." He let out a sigh. "If he did, they're mostly contaminated now with Isha having touched some of the things."

She glanced at Phillip. "I doubt there would be fingerprints."

"Why not?"

She shrugged. "The same man or men who killed Nikhil may have taken Diya. The police didn't find any unaccounted fingerprints or a weapon at the murder scene. They found nothing, not even a hair or fiber."

"Which is why I'm convinced this fellow's a policeman," Harish said. "He knows how to cover his tracks and he probably knows what goes on at police headquarters. That Jeep following me and this break-in can't be coincidence."

"I agree," said Phillip, turning toward the kitchen.

Harish watched his friend go before turning his gaze back to Isha. Although she was answering all of his and Phillip's questions coherently, she was still not herself. There was something detached and mechanical about her speech. She continued to sit very still and stare at nothing in particular. Seeing her like that doubled his resolve to find the man who'd done this to her and Diya, then see him punished—given the death penalty.

It surprised him that his thoughts had turned violent. He'd taken a sacred oath to save people. He'd never wanted to see anyone dead—until now.

But then, he'd never been in love before, either. He'd do anything for Isha and the girls.

"You did what!" Karnik gaped at Ishwar Gowda, trying hard to ignore the ringing in his ears. Maybe he hadn't heard it right. He'd just been given two terrifying pieces of information by Gowda: first, the alleged evidence was nowhere to be found in Isha Tilak's flat; second, Gowda had kidnapped the Tilak baby, with the missing evidence serving as ransom in exchange for the child.

Karnik pressed a hand to his perspiring forehead. This couldn't be happening! *Please, God, tell me this is not true. Tell me it's only a cruel nightmare.*

Gowda, a large, slightly potbellied man with a thin mustache and a face that could be considered handsome, stood with his feet apart and his arms crossed over his broad chest. "You told me she had the evidence and that I should get it. I looked everywhere; I couldn't find the damn thing."

"So you took her child instead! Are you insane or what?" Karnik was beginning to suspect the man standing before him truly was a madman, a psychopath.

A shrug was all Karnik got from Gowda. "If she values her

child, she will give you what you want. Women are soft-hearted when it comes to their children."

"But you were not supposed to do anything beyond getting the information quietly. Kidnapping was not part of the deal!" Karnik remembered the casual way Gowda had informed him about Nikhil Tilak's murder more than a year ago. The terrible news had led to weeks of sleeplessness and anxiety for Karnik. Until the whole episode had been put to rest, he had suffered from insomnia, indigestion, and angina attacks.

He still had nightmares about it occasionally, where a bloodied Tilak came at him with a knife, making Karnik thrash around and even scream in terror at times. He had woken up in a cold sweat, shaking all over, several times this past year. He had turned into Macbeth.

There was never going to be any real peace for him. Tilak's ghost would hover over him for the rest of his life—and most likely in all his future incarnations. The Hindu scriptures clearly stated that evil deeds haunted one's soul forever, or at least until the debt was fully repaid. He shuddered at the morbid thought. The killing was done by Gowda, but the blood tainted his own hands just as much.

Feeling his heartbeat turning dangerously erratic, Karnik took several deep breaths. "Where is the child now?"

"Don't worry about her. She's okay," Gowda assured him.

"Where is she?" Karnik demanded on what sounded like a choked sob. "Did you kill her? Please tell me you didn't kill her." A murdered child was something he couldn't stomach.

"No. She's being taken care of. She's with my wife." Gowda rolled his eyes in apparent frustration.

"And your wife is going along with this bloody scheme of yours?"

"I told her the mother was in an accident," replied Gowda, "and the police had to care for the child until the father returned from a business trip."

"My God! Is there no end to your wickedness? What are you planning to do with the child?"

"It's all in the plan. I told you, *nah,* don't worry."

"Of course I'm worried! This is a human life you're talking about, you idiot!" Karnik's hands were shaking uncontrollably. He knew his heart was starting to wobble.

Gowda laughed. The sound of it was like distant thunder—growling, ominous. "A man who performs abortions is lecturing me on the sanctity of human life?"

"That's different!" Karnik retorted. "A fetus is nothing more than a mass of cells. A living, flesh-and-blood child is another matter."

"Tell that to the government who passed the law banning gender-based abortion." Gowda fingered his mustache thoughtfully, then picked up the tiny silver figurine of the Statue of Liberty on the doctor's desk. It was a souvenir Karnik had bought while on a trip to the United States. "I see you're interested in *liberty,*" he added with a snicker. "Is this what gave you the idea?" he asked, twirling the statue in his hands. "Allowing your patients the *liberty* to abort girls?"

"Shut up! Just shut up!" Karnik pressed his hands over his ears. He didn't want to hear moralistic talk coming out of a deranged killer's mouth. "You were told to find whatever evidence she was holding and bring it to me. If it wasn't there, you were supposed to give up and go home. Maybe she was bluffing. Instead, you took it upon yourself to drug her servant with chloroform and snatch her sleeping child. What kind of animal are you?"

"Wait a minute! *You* gave me the chloroform."

"That was last year, for Nikhil Tilak, in case he failed to cooperate, not for the helpless old servant, and not for his widow."

"The widow wasn't even in the flat."

"Then where the hell was she?"

"I don't know. Maybe with her boyfriend, that doctor chap, Salvi." Gowda gave him a sly wink. "It looks like the widow is having a love affair. She is quite a woman, *nah?* First she needles you with insinuations in public, and then she goes off with her boyfriend for some *majah.*" Fun.

Karnik's jaw tightened at being reminded of his public humiliation by a slip of a woman, one less than half his age, too. Fortunately only a handful of people had overheard the conversation, and nothing incriminating had been said—only insinuations, like Gowda said. But it was embarrassing nevertheless, especially for a reputable doctor. Gossip in this town could spread faster than a dysentery epidemic during the monsoon season.

He'd never forgive the little bitch for talking to him like that. It was *her* pregnancy that had set in motion this bloody chain of events in the first place. And he'd never forgive that Salvi, either, the snotty young pediatrician, for being her champion. Maybe he *was* sleeping with her.

"I followed Salvi home after he left his office last evening," added Gowda. "I didn't think she was with him. But who knows? All I can tell you is she definitely wasn't in her flat when I broke in."

"Thank God, or you would have given her a dose of chloroform, too—or worse, killed her. If that servant woman dies of an overdose, it will be one more murder on my conscience." He blew out a shaky breath, thought about it for a moment. "So how are you planning to swap the child for the evidence without the police knowing about it?" Slanting an anxious look at Gowda, he asked, "You *are* planning to give the child *back,* I hope?"

"*Tsk-tsk,*" Gowda clucked, but said nothing.

"Promise me you won't hurt the child and you will return her to her mother," growled Karnik. A massive headache was beginning to set in and he rubbed his temples to keep it at bay. He felt sick.

"*Arré,* why are you having a fit? I'll give her back, okay?"

"When?"

"I will make them a little more anxious, make them wait." He scratched the back of his head, probably working it out in his demented brain. "Leave the details to me. You just have to pay me for my services."

Fear skittered down Karnik's spine when he heard Gowda talk so casually. Things were spinning out of control. The man standing in front of him was a perverted bastard. How had he not recognized that right from the beginning? Why hadn't he seen that maniacal gleam in his devilish eyes? As a doctor, he should have noticed the man wasn't quite normal, despite the good looks and personable demeanor.

A heartless, knife-happy kidnapper-killer, who laughed about his crimes, was positively *not* normal.

The first time, what had started out as a harmless way to get the evidence back from Nikhil Tilak had ended up in Tilak's murder. This time, what was meant to be a simple theft had turned into a kidnapping. Coming on the heels of the scene at the hospital, the police were bound to look at Karnik as the prime suspect.

It didn't take a genius to figure it out, even if Gowda had assured him that Salvi's message for Patil had been intercepted by him, therefore no one at the superintendent's office knew about a call coming in for their boss.

Isha Tilak had probably already called all her friends and started an ugly rumor about Karnik's alleged role in the kidnapping of her child. Before the sun came up, the police would be on top of it.

Then the media would go wild about the latest crime to hit the small, previously unsullied town of Palgaum: a beautiful, fatherless baby girl kidnapped from her bed and her devoted nursemaid rendered unconscious with drugs. And the baby just *happened* to be the posthumous child of a recent, high-profile murder victim—and that murder was still under question. It was so damned dramatic, exactly what the public loved, a made-for-Bollywood type of sob story.

And then Karnik would be ruined for life—if he wasn't already.

"I can't go on with this," he told Gowda after a minute of silent deliberation. He'd had enough. He was getting too old for this kind of excitement. Murder and kidnapping had no place in his ordinary life in this dull little town.

Gowda went still. "What do you mean?" His scowl was ferocious. His mustache twitched with barely concealed fury, making Karnik's head snap backward.

Nonetheless Karnik put on his bravest front. He couldn't show Gowda that he was scared stiff, terrified enough to piss in his pants. "Exactly that. I'm obviously dealing with a lunatic. You have landed me in more trouble than it is worth."

Gowda stepped forward and poked a long finger into Karnik's bony chest, his eyebrows joined together over the bridge of his nose in an enraged knot. "Don't blame this on me, old man! Nikhil Tilak attacked me like an angry bull when I asked him to hand over the stolen material."

"Likely story," Karnik shot back. His legs were shaking.

"I asked politely, but he turned on me. I only defended myself."

"By stabbing him again and again? That was not self-defense; that was unnecessary butchering. If you had to kill him, why couldn't you use your gun and put a quick bullet through the brain?"

"My gun is a registered firearm and the bullets are traceable." Gowda threw him a disdainful grunt. "You should know that simple fact. Don't you watch any crime shows on television?"

"How would I know anything about guns?"

"Well, I do!" Gowda fumed. "And stabbing was the best way to make it look like an armed robbery gone wrong. And after all the trouble I went to for you, I found nothing in his office."

"He was apparently not foolish enough to keep it in an obvious place," Karnik hissed. "He kept it at home. And now his wife has it."

"I'm telling you, it's nowhere in that flat. She has nothing."

"Then it could be in her father-in-law's house, or her safe deposit box. Maybe that's where Nikhil had always kept it." He should have known an astute man like Tilak wouldn't store incriminating data in an easily accessible place like his office.

"Aha! Then the only way she will give it to us is if she knows her child's life depends on it."

Karnik slumped in his chair and blew out a long, labored breath. "I don't know. I just don't know." The ringing in his ears had just gone up by several decibels. It was getting harder to breathe. What the hell was he going to do about Gowda, about the kidnapped child, about himself, his family?

Gowda leaned forward with his hands braced on Karnik's desk, his face barely inches above Karnik's. "You better get the money together." His voice was menacingly low. "*I'll* worry about the child. If losing her baby doesn't work, I have something else that will work on Isha Tilak. I have a hunch the evidence is hidden in Salvi's house. They were both in his house after she confronted you. They went to her flat late at night and he returned home with a bag on his shoulder. His house is probably where they're hiding the material."

Karnik shook his head. "Please, no more killing. I'll give you the money I owe you. But just go away and leave me alone." He shut his eyes and pressed his fingers over his temples. His mind was revolving in such tight circles that he couldn't think or concentrate on anything at the moment. He was too dizzy for rational thought.

Straightening up from the desk, Gowda headed for the door. "If the money is not in my hands by tomorrow, I'll never leave you alone. My own reputation and career are at risk, Karnik. I have a family to support. You may be a rich old man, but I'm not." He pointed a finger at Karnik, his hand emulating a gun. "Don't forget that, Doctor-saheb."

Watching the man leave, Karnik knew Gowda's threat wasn't an empty one. That evil man would stoop to anything. To make matters worse, the bastard was a police officer. He was not only trained to kill, but he was bright enough to rise from a mere constable to the rank of inspector, greedy enough to get rich on bribes and crimes, and clever enough to cover up his bloody tracks.

It was Karnik's bad luck that he had stumbled upon Gowda, or rather Gowda had found him, when he had unexpectedly come poking around to review Karnik's records some two years ago. Somehow Gowda had got wind of the abortions and secretly approached him, talking about an investigation. He had also dropped subtle hints that if Karnik paid him a certain amount, he would forget the whole thing. So Karnik had paid him the requested amount, and everything had been blissfully quiet after that point.

Of course, at the time, Karnik had been so scared and naive that he hadn't thought of questioning Gowda about the legitimacy of the so-called investigation. In a state of panic, he had assumed it was an official directive from the police department. It was only later, after he'd paid the man an exorbitant amount of cash, that he'd analyzed the whole episode, even wondered if Gowda had played the same trick on other doctors in town. The man was both conniving and convincing. He was evil.

Back then, Gowda had also hinted that he'd do most anything to make extra money on the side. That's the reason why Karnik had gone to him for help when Tilak had become a threat. But that was his first big mistake. That single error was now turning into a ghastly nightmare: one gruesome murder, one kidnapping, and heaven knew what else in the future.

Gowda had just mentioned something else—something perhaps deadly.

The media would cover every sordid detail, just like they had with Tilak's murder. This would turn into a sequel to that story. Palgaum had never seen so much excitement.

What other horrors were about to break out? Karnik cringed at the thought.

He absently massaged his shoulder. It had begun to throb. His throat felt dry and his stomach churned. He didn't know how much longer he could go on like this. His blood pressure problem had escalated recently. He was suffering from insomnia and heartburn once again, too.

His wife was worried about his deteriorating health. She had even called their son and daughter about her concerns, and those two had started asking him curious questions.

On a tired breath he leaned back in his chair and stared at his hands for a very long time—a killer's hands. And yet, they were trained to be healing hands.

The clock on his desk read 2:16 AM. There would be no sleep for him tonight.

He shut his eyes—and wondered if it was better to die than to lose face and end up in prison.

Chapter 29

There was a knock on the study door. "Vivek."

Karnik's eyes flew open. Oh no! Neela! "Yes?"

The door opened and he turned his head to see his wife standing on the threshold.

"Why aren't you in bed?" he asked her, wondering how long she'd been standing there. There was something about her stillness and expression that made him wonder how much she'd heard.

Her kaftan looked rumpled, and her graying, plaited hair was disheveled, which meant she'd probably just climbed out of bed.

"I couldn't sleep," she answered, studying him with that anxious look she had more and more lately, which seemed to cast a shadow over her pleasant face. "And you never came to bed."

"Try to sleep, Neela." He felt too ill to face an interrogation by his wife. "I'll be there in a minute."

"That's what you said two hours ago."

"I was busy!" he snapped.

"You don't look busy. And you don't look well," she murmured. "Is it the angina again?"

He nodded. "Don't worry. I just took my pills; I'll be all right."

"That *man* was here again—the computer repairman," she said, approaching him. It was the way she said it—wariness bordering on accusation—that told him she knew more than she was letting on.

His fists tightened. "How long were you standing outside the door, Neela?"

"Long enough." She pulled up a chair beside him and sat down. "Isn't it time you told me what is going on, Vivek?"

Her eyes continued to search his face. What was she looking for? Guilt? Shame? Regret? He was suffering plenty of all three, and then some. The physical pain in his upper body more than matched his emotional torment.

"It's nothing." He dismissed her question with a wave. "Just a complicated computer problem."

She placed a hand on his arm. "*You* know and *I* know he isn't a computer repairman." When he opened his mouth to deny it, she cut him off. "Show me a single repairman in Palgaum who works at this time of the night."

"I—" He didn't know what to say. His wife was too damn perceptive.

"I'm not stupid, Vivek!" Her grip on his arm tightened. "This has to do with the Tilaks, doesn't it? And please don't try to deny it."

He was silent for a minute. He'd never heard such angry reprimand in his wife's voice in the more than four decades he'd been married to her. "How much did you hear?"

"Most of it. But then I had suspected it long before tonight."

His labored breath came out in a hiss. "How?"

"I'm not blind, either," she said. "You have been stressed and restless for well over a year now. Your blood pressure and heart problems have escalated. What is *happening* to you?"

"I'm seventy years old, Neela. Hypertension, heart problems—these things come with old age," he said, rubbing his burning eyes.

"Does dishonesty and immorality come with old age, too?" When his eyes went wide at her cutting sarcasm, she added, "Oh yes, I know more than you think. I have been observing you very closely. You had something to do with Nikhil Tilak's death, didn't you?"

Dear God! She knew! She'd known all along. He scrubbed

his face with one shuddering hand. "Not directly. I didn't want it to happen, Neela. I swear!"

"How could you stoop to *this?*" Her eyes were ripe with enraged disappointment. "How could a doctor *kill* a man deliberately?"

"I didn't! That . . . that man, who just left, ended up killing him when he shouldn't have. I never wanted anyone dead." He knew his excuse sounded lame. And it *was* lame, even to his ears. He was just as guilty as Gowda.

"And you never told me about this?" The anger was gone from her eyes now. There was only pain there, and it broke his heart to see what he was doing to her.

"What could I tell you? That I hired someone to do something mildly illegal, but things didn't go as planned, and somehow it ended up in a man's death?"

"Then why *did* you hire someone?"

"Because I had to protect myself and you and our reputation."

"And what exactly is mildly illegal?" she demanded. When he hesitated, she groaned like she was in real, physical agony. Maybe she was, just like he. "All this has to do with killing unborn female babies, doesn't it?"

He sucked in a stunned breath, wondering how she had figured all this out. Always caring, always nurturing and supportive of his career, she had never once asked pointed questions about his work, nor indicated that she suspected anything—at least not in this fashion. "You know *that,* too?" he asked, frowning.

"I may not be highly educated like you, but like I said, I'm not without a brain. Don't you think I can figure out why your patients have so many baby boys and so few girls? Even my friends ask me how you can be so lucky as to have practically every patient of yours give birth to a boy." She sighed. "I have no logical answer to their curious questions."

He remained silent. While he'd gone about his tasks quietly and efficiently (or so he had assumed), his wife and everyone else had been drawing certain conclusions.

"And why is it that only in the last few years you have been working so often on Sunday afternoons and very late evenings? At a time in your life when you should be taking it easy and not doing additional work, you have been working harder than ever. What does that say?" She stopped to stare at him. "You have been secretly performing abortions, haven't you?"

In all his years of marriage to Neela, he'd never lied to her, nor hidden anything from her, except this matter of abortion—and all the nasty things that had come as a result of it. Because of how honest and religious she was, he had never worked up the nerve to confide in her. He couldn't lose the respect of the one person who loved him unconditionally. She had been a faithful, trusting, and adoring wife.

He nodded. "It was wrong on my part." And foolish.

"Why, Vivek?" she queried softly. "You are such a brilliant doctor and you have made more than enough money with a large and wonderful practice. When God has been so generous to us why did you need to do something unconscionable like this?" She put a hand to his face. "Does it not bother you to kill so many unborn babies?"

He leaned his head back and gazed at the rotating ceiling fan. She was right—so bloody right.

"Don't you think of our own daughter when you get rid of all those tiny infants?"

He mulled over her hurtful questions. At first he *had* thought of his own daughter and the joy she had brought into their lives. But just like a doctor gradually learns to accept blood and pain and disease and death as part and parcel of the medical profession, he'd become immune to the procedure.

That's all it was after the first few times—a sterile clinical *procedure*.

"What will you teach your grandchildren, my dear?" she asked, her voice a mere murmur. "And don't forget you have a young granddaughter who loves you very much. What if she had been eliminated when she was just a fetus?"

His precious little granddaughter! Dear God! Hearing those words from his wife's mouth was like a knife being thrust into him again and again. He felt his chest constrict. The angina was worse than ever. The pain was becoming unbearable.

Despite his iron control on his emotions the floodgates opened up. Everything he'd been holding inside for months erupted at once. He leaned forward, placed his arms on the desk, and rested his head over them. The sobs that came were loud and pitiful.

He felt Neela's hands gently stroke his back. "Shh. I'm sorry I said some hurtful things," she said, weeping with him. "But you needed to face this, Vivek. You need to resolve it. You cannot go on like this. All this internal turmoil is killing you little by little."

As a strong man, he had never wept before his wife. In fact, he couldn't remember crying since he was about twelve years old, when his bicycle had been damaged in an accident. Now he just couldn't stop sobbing. He lifted his head, turned around, and wrapped his arms around Neela. "I'm s-sorry. I'm so very sorry."

She cradled his head on her bosom. "Shh, it's okay. It will be all right. You can stop this abortion nonsense right now, and ask God for forgiveness. Then we'll pray together," she consoled. "We'll do a special *vrath*," she said, referring to an intensive religious cleansing ritual that included fasting and praying and making special offerings to the temple.

"No *vrath* in the world is going to absolve me, Neela," he sobbed. "You don't know the worst of it."

He felt her stiffen. "You mean there is more?"

Retrieving a handkerchief from his pocket, he pulled away from her and dried his eyes and nose. He *had* to confess to his wife, or he would explode. Now that the cathartic process had been put in motion, he couldn't seem to stop it from barreling ahead. He wanted to get the burden off his chest. If he died tonight for some reason, he would at least go with a clearer conscience. "Some time ago, my records of the abortions were stolen."

Neela's eyes went wide. "You actually kept records of those . . . horrible procedures? Where?"

"In my home computer," he said, inclining his head toward it. He tried to take a deep breath to ease the increasing tightness in his chest, but it didn't help much. His wife's expression was so full of contempt it made him squirm. "I had to, Neela! Don't you understand? It was a medical procedure. Somehow I had to keep an account of when and where and how much money was involved in each transaction."

Comprehension slowly descended over Neela's face. "But what does Nikhil Tilak have to do with all this?"

"Tilak was the one who stole my abortion data and threatened to take it to the police. So I paid Inspector Gowda to get it back from Tilak."

"Who is this Inspector Gowda? How do you know him?"

"It is a long story." He haltingly explained to her everything from the beginning, including his recent run-in with Isha Tilak. "So he ended up murdering Tilak. He claims it was self-defense."

"Dear God!" Pressing her hand to her mouth, Neela sat in silence for a minute.

Karnik could see the grief she was suffering—feel it. She had never had any part in his actions, and yet, he now realized, as his wife, she suffered just as much as he—perhaps far more.

She looked up. "Clearly the murder investigation was hushed up somehow. But what was Gowda doing here today, at this time of the night?" She searched his face with narrow-eyed suspicion. "Is he blackmailing you?"

"Not really. But the news is bad—worse than the murder."

"What could be worse than murder?"

"When he couldn't find the records in Isha Tilak's house, he kidnapped her infant and took her hostage."

"Kidnapped!" Neela drew in a stunned breath.

"I tried to tell him to return the child, but the man will not listen. He is a pervert, a lunatic."

"Has he ... killed the child, too?" Neela sounded like she was terrified to ask.

He shook his head. "He says the baby is with his wife and he will return her when Isha Tilak hands over the abortion data."

"What are *you* going to do about it?" she demanded.

"What *can* I do?" he asked with a helpless shrug. "He is a policeman—and a ruthless killer."

"Then ring his boss, that Patil chap, right now, and tell him everything!"

"Tell him what?" Karnik managed to work up a bitter laugh. "That I'm an abortionist and that I had Tilak killed and his child kidnapped? I will end up in prison for the rest of my life. Your life, my life, and our children's lives will be ruined."

She raised an eyebrow. "You didn't think of all this when you started performing those abortions?"

"I did . . . in the beginning. But as time went by—"

"You ignored your conscience," she interrupted. "Greed got the better of you," she said with a resigned sigh. "So what do we do now?"

He rubbed his chest and shoulder. Perspiration was gathering on his face. He knew he was in the first stages of a heart attack. "That's what I was trying to think about when you came in."

"What's there to *think*, Vivek? A man was brutally murdered because of you, and now his child is missing. Poor Isha Tilak must be beside herself."

"If I go to the police, I'm ruined, Neela." Breathing was becoming harder.

"You were ruined the day you performed your first abortion," she informed him matter-of-factly.

She was so right. Tears of regret gathered in Tilak's eyes once again. His soul was ruined a long time ago—if he had one left anymore. His reputation was going the same route. His heart was giving out. The pressure on his chest was increasing by the second.

How had he managed to sink to this level? What kind of monster had he turned into?

He took his wife's hand. "I should confess to the police."

She nodded. "At least you will have saved an innocent baby from a brutal death. It is your last chance to redeem yourself. And apologize to Isha Tilak and her family. The poor girl has suffered such hell because of you."

He rubbed his chest and struggled for breath. "I'm not . . . feeling well, Neela," he admitted.

She gazed at him for a moment. "Vivek, are you having a heart attack?"

"Y-yes," he whispered. "I may not be able to . . . rescue my soul after all."

She took his clammy hand. "Yes, you will! I won't let you die, Vivek." Then she picked up the phone and rang for an ambulance.

He tried to take a breath but managed to suck very little air. The agony was spreading like fire from his chest through his entire body. With some effort he whispered, "Death will be better . . . than prison."

"No! You will live! And if they send you to prison we'll find you a good lawyer." Tenderly she loosened the buttons on his shirt and wiped the sweat off his brow with the handkerchief he'd left on the desk. "Don't worry. I will ring Isha Tilak and apologize for both of us."

"But . . . this is . . . not your fault," he argued weakly. His vision was beginning to blur.

"As husband and wife, we're in this together."

"But . . ."

"Shh, don't talk. Save your breath." She took off his glasses and put them aside. "I hear the ambulance."

Two minutes later he was being lifted onto a stretcher and loaded into the ambulance. "Neela . . ." he called out, but couldn't complete his sentence.

She patted his hand, her eyes filling with tears. "I know. I will take care of everything."

Karnik's last conscious thought was of the kidnapped child. *Lord, please save that child.*

Chapter 30

Isha hugged the tiny yellow dress with the white dots against her chest. Diya had been wearing it the day before. It smelled like Diya. The baby had been changed out of the dress and into clean pajamas before being placed in her cradle.

And sometime after that she'd been abducted. Even now they didn't know exactly when she'd been taken. It was somewhere between the hours of ten and midnight, after Isha had checked on the sleeping kids and Sundari. She'd made sure all the windows were secured before she'd locked the door behind her and gone to work.

Bad decision. Shortly after that, the kidnapper had managed to break in, destroy the place, and snatch the baby.

Isha could deal with the invasion of her home, the ruined furniture, bedding, and personal belongings. But Diya's disappearance had left a gaping wound that wouldn't stop bleeding.

Isha sat in the semidarkness of her bedroom, all the life squeezed out of her. *It's all my fault,* she rued for the thousandth time, the tears rolling down her cheeks. The previous night's numbness had diminished, only to be replaced by tears and pain. And guilt. Despite knowing how dangerous the situation had become, and in spite of being warned by Harish again and again, she had still neglected her children and gone over to the other flat to sew her dresses, to conduct her business.

If only she'd done her work right here at home, Diya would

have been here now, crawling, making baby talk, and getting into all kinds of mischief.

Isha should have at least left that stupid disk and the spreadsheet in the *almirah*. The intruder would have taken that and left Diya alone. Maybe. Who knew how evil minds worked?

As she stared at the empty cradle with its ruined mattress in the glow of the nightlight, Isha could picture Diya's sparkling, long-lashed hazel eyes, and smell the baby powder on her neck. Isha could almost feel it now—the oh-so-soft skin, the warm weight of Diya in her lap, the steady thumping of the baby's little heart beating against her breast when she fell asleep in her arms.

Where was Diya? Was she crying now for her mother and sister and Sundari? Was she locked up somewhere, all alone? The poor darling didn't like the dark. Was she cowering in some filthy, smelly, godforsaken hole, suffering excruciating hunger pangs? Or was it too late for any of that? Had the breath been snuffed out of her tiny lungs already?

Don't even go there, Isha warned herself. She couldn't afford to think like that. Her baby couldn't be dead, not now, not when Isha had fought so hard to keep her alive in her womb against all odds, not when she'd made sure the baby had a decent home and a happy life, not when she was surrounded by love despite everything that was going on around her.

Diya's birthday was less than three weeks away. Would she see her first birthday at all?

Sheila abruptly walked into the bedroom and flipped on the light switch. She carried a cup and saucer in her hand. "Isha, you can't sit in the dark all day," she scolded.

The room was flooded with light and Isha blinked at Sheila, snapping out of her misery for a second. "I don't really care if there's light or not."

"Look, Sundari made you some refreshing *gavthee chah*." Lemon-grass tea.

Isha ignored the tea as well as Sheila's poor attempts at cheerfulness. Despite her usual impeccable appearance, Isha knew

Sheila was just as worried as she. Her eyes, too, were puffy from weeping.

"Where's Priya?" Isha asked. Since Diya had disappeared she had felt the need to keep a strict eye on her other child. She'd kept her close to herself and hadn't even sent her to school that morning. What if the kidnapper was out there, watching, waiting? What if he took Priya, too? It was inconceivable.

"Priya's fine," Sheila replied. "She's at our house, playing with the boys. She's being watched closely by the servants and Rambo."

"You're sure?"

"Positive. Rambo is turning into an excellent guard dog. He doesn't let any strangers within fifty feet of our property. Besides, Harish just called there and talked to Priya. He's worried about her safety, too, you know."

"But the kidnapper could be watching your house."

Sheila inhaled a deep breath, clearly summoning some patience. "We *had* to send her there, Isha, and you know why. It's not healthy for a child to be surrounded by so much tension. She needed to be with her cousins and Rambo."

"Okay. As long as she's safe . . ." Sheila was right, of course, but Isha was still worried about Priya. She was terrified of losing her, too. "Where's Harish?" He had become her solid, unshakeable source of support. He was not only the first to arrive with help, but he was holding her hand through this crisis more than anyone else. Somehow she'd come to depend on him much more than she'd expected to.

He was right. This was *their* problem now.

"Harish is in the drawing room." Sheila inclined her head toward the door. "He canceled his appointments and spent most of the day here, helping Sundari and me clean up the mess in the house. After that he's been on the phone, talking to all kinds of people, trying to get any information he can."

"He's been such a comfort." Isha glanced at Sheila. "And so have you . . . and Sundari."

"Phillip, his friend, has been working hard on our behalf,

too." Sheila offered her the cup. "Here, have some tea. You'll feel better."

Shaking her head, Isha hugged the dress even closer. "I'm not hungry."

Clucking like a mother hen, Sheila sat down beside her on the edge of the bed. "You didn't sleep at all last night after you found out Diya was missing, and you haven't eaten a thing all day. Come on, have a biscuit at least. You need to keep up your strength."

Isha laid her tired head on Sheila's shoulder. "How can I eat or drink when my baby could be dying of hunger? The last meal Diya ate was before she was put to bed last evening." Her voice wobbled.

Sheila laid the cup on the nightstand so she could put an arm around Isha's waist. "She'll be home soon. Patil should be getting back into town, and I'm sure he'll do everything he can to find her. Palgaum's entire police force will be looking for her."

"I wish we could hand over the evidence to someone now and have them arrest Karnik. I want this to be over."

"But we can't hand it over to anyone but Patil. We don't know who the rotten apple in the police department is. There could be more than one—a whole bunch. We can't risk it now."

"But the kidnapper hasn't called or anything." She noticed the time on the clock next to her bed. It read 6:55 PM. "It's been more than twenty hours since Diya disappeared and there's no communication whatsoever. He could have killed her by now. He killed Nikhil, didn't he?"

"Shh, don't say that! Don't even think that. He wants something you have, and as long as that's of value to him, he won't hurt her. She's his insurance policy."

"Then why hasn't he called yet? I hate that dreadful old man, Karnik. I know he's behind this. And yet the police won't do anything about it."

"Officially they can't do anything."

"It's so obvious that he's the villain. What more proof do they need? This thing occurred right after I confronted him. Nikhil's murder happened immediately after he lodged a complaint about Karnik with the police. The connection is so clear and still they won't as much as question him—not even when it's staring them in the face."

"You and I know it's Karnik. At this point, I bet the police are pretty sure about it, too. But he can claim he knows nothing about this, Isha. He could have hired any petty criminal to carry out his orders. What can the police do with no evidence of any kind?"

"But I *have* evidence—"

"A bunch of names and dates," interrupted Sheila. "What does that prove? Don't forget Karnik is a respected man in our town and has considerable influence in government circles. And so do all those people whose names appear on your list."

"But the police are law-enforcement officials, for God's sake! Can't they do *something?*"

"Not *can't,* but *won't,* if they're being bribed handsomely by Karnik."

"I'm willing to give every rupee I have if it'll bring my baby back." The waiting was so frustrating. Every minute felt like a lifetime.

Sheila handed her a clean handkerchief. "Look, I didn't want to say anything, but since you brought up the matter of money . . . I . . . um . . . think I should mention it. Baba and Ayee have offered to pay a ransom if the kidnapper demands it."

Isha pushed away from Sheila, her eyes wide. "I don't believe this!"

"I'm not making this up, Isha. Baba himself called me this morning. Last night when I rang them to tell them what happened, Ayee got very upset. She must have talked him into making the offer. They want Diya returned to you."

"I don't want their money! I don't care how upset Ayee is and I care even less about Baba's sentiments. This is the child they both loathe. Now all of a sudden they want to rescue her?"

"Both of them are beginning to recognize the mistakes they've made, Isha."

"Then let them stew in their regrets. It'll serve them right. I don't want their help or one single *paisa* of their precious money."

Sheila put a hand on Isha's arm. "Look, I know you're upset, but please try to look at it rationally."

"Do *they* have a single rational bone in their bodies? Tell me what's rational about carelessly aborting a baby because it happens to be a girl."

"Ayee's brush with death and Priya's valiant efforts to save her have changed Ayee's attitude completely, and consequently Baba's, too," argued Sheila. "If you see him now, you'll realize he's not quite the same man he used to be when Nikhil was alive."

Isha snorted in disdain. "Fine time to come to their senses, isn't it? Now that they know my child could be tortured or dead, they've decided they want her back? Is this some kind of sick joke?"

Harish must have heard her tirade because he appeared at the door. His troubled gaze settled on Isha for a second, then went to Sheila. "What's going on?"

Sheila sighed. "I just informed her about Baba's offer to pay a ransom if necessary."

Harish took a cautious step inside. "And?"

Isha's head immediately snapped up. "I don't want Ayee and Baba's help in any way, shape, or form." The tears were falling now, fast and furious.

Hands thrust inside his pockets, Harish stood for a moment, obviously turning her words over in his mind. "But you may be forced to accept their help, Isha."

"No! I've already done more than my share of compromising by letting my children visit Ayee during her illness. I want nothing more to do with those self-centered, heartless people."

Before Harish or Sheila could respond, his phone rang. He flipped it open and answered. Both women sat motionless, hoping to catch every bit of Harish's conversation. His face looked grim as he listened and responded in monosyllables. "All right." He sighed. "Just keep me informed."

The instant he hung up, Isha looked up at him. "Is Diya . . . ?" Her voice came out in a frantic whisper. "Is my baby dead?"

He pocketed the phone and shook his head. "No, Isha. Patil is on a flight back from Delhi. Unfortunately, he has to change flights in Mumbai and there's only one flight from Mumbai to Palgaum each day, and that doesn't arrive until early morning. Phillip took a taxi to the airport so he can wait for Patil to arrive and catch him before Patil has a chance to go to his office."

"What took the man so long to get out of Delhi? Doesn't he know this is a matter of life and death?"

"Patil was attending some police officers' conference and he was a special speaker. Unfortunately he's the only one I trust, so I asked Phillip to wait for him to come back before producing the records. The minute he arrives in Palgaum, Phillip will personally hand them over."

Isha buried her face in her hands. It was fifteen and a half months since Nikhil was gone. It had taken that long for this day to arrive. Was Karnik going to get what was coming to him? Was Nikhil's death finally going to be avenged?

But at the moment, that fact was secondary to finding her child. She dried her eyes and nose. "But what about Diya? Is Karnik holding her hostage?"

"Karnik is too clever to hold her hostage. He no doubt has someone else doing his dirty work." Harish glanced at the tea in the cup and the biscuits sitting in the saucer. "Isha, you should eat something."

"The thought of eating makes me sick." She looked up at him. "Would you be able to eat if it were *your* baby that had disappeared?"

Turning to Sheila, he asked, "Would you mind if I have a few minutes alone with Isha?"

"Not at all." Sheila rose to her feet, looking relieved. "Please see if you can talk some sense into her and get her to eat something." She not only left them alone but, after exchanging a meaningful glance with Harish, closed the door behind her, assuring them complete privacy.

Harish walked over to occupy the spot Sheila had vacated. "Isha, I know this is hard for you to believe, but I consider Diya my own. I've seen her and cared for her since she was a day-old infant. I've come to love her and Priya as much as any adoptive father can."

When he got no response from Isha, he wrapped his arms around her. "You already know I love you, too. I want what's best for you. And what you need now is some nourishment."

"I'm nauseated by the sight of food."

"That's because an empty stomach produces excess acid. If you eat a little, the nausea will go away. I promise." He pried the baby's dress away from her and laid it aside. Then he leaned forward and picked up the cup and saucer. "Do it for me if not for yourself."

Unable to resist his caring touch and his gentle plea, Isha took the cup and sipped the tea. She hated admitting it, but it tasted good. It had turned tepid, but the sweet, milky brew Sundari had made for her was astonishingly soothing as it trickled down her throat and into her stomach. Maybe she did need nourishment. All the while, she was conscious of Harish's strong arm holding her up.

"Now the biscuits," he said, and waited till she'd crunched on them and washed them down with the last of the tea. "Good girl." He smiled. "See, that wasn't so hard, was it?"

She nodded. "You were right. I feel better."

"Now, I want you to lie down and rest for a while. You haven't had a moment's sleep."

"But I can't sleep until I have Diya back." She tossed him an accusing look. "*You* haven't slept, either."

"I've become accustomed to that since I was an intern." He put her empty cup back on the table. "I'll give you something to help you sleep." As soon as her mouth opened to protest, he clamped a hand over her shoulder. "Doctor's orders! The minute I hear something, I'll wake you."

"Promise?"

"Absolutely."

She watched him open the door and leave. Exhaustion was gnawing at her brain, making it feel like a giant ball of wool. She'd had a throbbing ache around her temples for hours. It had set in the moment she'd realized Diya was gone. It had steadily become worse. But it was easing a bit now. As usual, he was right. Some food and rest were what she needed. They would make her function better. But the need for assurance of her baby's safety was vastly greater than the need for rest.

A few minutes later, Harish walked in with his medical bag, rummaged through it, and located a bottle of pills. Shaking a single tablet into his palm, he went to the kitchen for a glass of water and returned in seconds. "Take this and lie down."

She obeyed him and swallowed the tiny pill, albeit with some hesitation. What if it made her sleep for hours? What if there was news of the baby and she slept through it? But then he'd promised to wake her. And she trusted him—with her life and Diya's. He took the glass and motioned to her to lie down.

Again she followed his instructions with no protest. She was too exhausted to put up a fight, anyway. Besides, it felt good to be taken care of by a man. And something surprised her: Harish's firmness in dealing with her. She'd rarely seen the strict, no-nonsense Doctor-saheb demeanor before. But instead of resenting it, she realized she liked it. Side by side with his humane qualities, there was a tough-as-steel backbone in him.

The combination of gentleness and hard resolve was what made him a strong man—a very special man.

As her head settled on the pillow and Harish shut off the light and pulled a sheet to cover her with, she realized her eyelids were already heavy with weariness. Then he bent down and kissed her. It was just a whisper of a kiss, an unexpected brush of his lips against her mouth, but it was wonderful, like a warm security blanket tucked around her.

"Get some rest. I'll be in the drawing room if you need me," he whispered and closed the door behind him.

As she drifted into sleep she knew for sure he'd be there—right outside her room.

Chapter 31

Sheila decided to spend the night in Isha's flat. Although Sundari was now completely recovered from her harrowing experience of the previous night, she wasn't quite up to taking control of the household while Isha and Priya slept. Harish was still around but he could easily get called out on an emergency.

Besides, Sheila had made that promise to her deceased brother that she would take care of his family. And nothing would deter her from carrying out her duty toward Isha and her nieces.

Sundari had looked relieved when Sheila had informed her that she was going to spend the night with them. The attack had scared the old woman more than anyone had realized. She was still baffled about what exactly had occurred, and she'd been crying a lot, blaming herself for not protecting the baby, despite everyone's assurances that it wasn't her fault.

When questioned about her comatose state the night before, Sundari had looked puzzled. "I heard the front door opening, but I thought it was Isha-bayi coming home, so I went back to sleep. I cannot remember anything after that."

From his observations, Harish had explained to Sheila what may have happened to Sundari. The kidnapper had probably pressed a rag soaked in chloroform over Sundari's nose and mouth while she slept. She had no idea what had hit her. Whatever it was, Sheila was grateful it hadn't had any adverse effect on Sundari's health.

Changing into one of Isha's kaftans, Sheila settled in the bed next to the sleeping Priya. The poor child had been driven home earlier by Kumar. Before Priya could ask too many questions and become upset once again, Harish had read her a bedtime story, and Sundari had tucked the tired little girl into bed.

Sundari shut the bedroom door, unrolled her bedroll onto the floor, and lay down in her usual spot. Both the women were wide-awake, so they conversed in whispers.

"Sheila-bayi, do you think Diya-baby will be . . . okay?" Sundari's voice was filled with dread.

"I hope so. I'm praying hard for Diya's return, Sundari. All of us are." Sheila tried to keep her own voice steady. She couldn't afford to let the old woman see how scared she was. Sleep was going to be impossible to come by. If it wasn't for the sleeping medicine Harish had forced on Isha, she would have been awake and obsessing, too.

"Poor Doctor-saheb," said Sundari after a minute of silence, referring to Harish resting in the drawing room. "He is trying so hard to help. And he looks so uncomfortable sleeping on the sofa."

"He is a very gallant man. He wouldn't let anyone else take the sofa and give him the bed."

"Very good man he is—so patient and such a good doctor. He is doing so much for our Isha-bayi and the babies, no?"

"You're right." Sheila stifled a tired yawn, but she was still too wound up to close her eyes. "I'm glad he takes such an active interest in Isha's life." She wondered exactly how far things had progressed between him and Isha.

She had observed the evolving relationship between those two. It was clear that Harish was in love with her sister-in-law. He spent almost all his free time with Isha. His expression often bordered on worship when he gazed at her. But Isha's attitude toward him was more that of a close friend than as a potential lover or wife.

"Nobody would do so much for someone who is not a family member, no?" remarked Sundari, interrupting Sheila's thoughts.

"Hmm," agreed Sheila. Sundari's observation only convinced

her further that Harish was serious about Isha. Maybe he even wanted to marry her. A twinge of resentment stabbed at Sheila. Isha was still very much Nikhil's wife and her children were Nikhil's. They were Tilaks by birth.

Sheila wasn't sure she liked the idea of another man taking Nikhil's place. If Harish did end up marrying Isha, then Sheila would no longer command the same status in their lives. She'd be an outsider to her own nieces, and to her sister-in-law, too.

Probably guessing where Sheila's thoughts were going, Sundari said, "Nikhil-saheb is not here anymore to provide for his wife and children. But God is taking care of that problem by sending Doctor-saheb to them, no?"

Sheila shut her eyes and mulled over the comment. "The girls need to remember who their real father was."

"And they will. Isha-bayi will never allow them to forget their father. You see the photos of Nikhil-saheb in the drawing room? She is always showing those to the children and mentioning their father. And Doctor-saheb will not allow them to forget, either. He is an honorable man."

"You may be right," admitted Sheila grudgingly. "But they're *my* family."

"Of course they are. But Isha-bayi is so young and beautiful—and lonely. How long can she be alone, huh? She needs a man."

Sheila sighed. "I suppose I have to stop being selfish and look at what's best for the girls and Isha." She thought about it for another second. "They do need a man in their lives. And you know what else, Sundari?"

"Hmm?"

"I honestly can't think of anyone more reliable or decent than Harish Salvi to take my brother's place. He's a good man."

"I am thinking the same thing, no?" Sundari said. "So, you are not worried that he is not a Brahmin?"

Sheila nearly laughed. "That's the last thing I'm concerned about. All I want is for my nieces to have a caring father and Isha to be happy once again."

Sundari's sigh was long and audible. "But I am not sure that Isha-bayi will agree to marry him."

"Has he asked her to marry him?"

"I don't know. She does not tell me these things. But I know her well and I am thinking maybe she has decided not to get married—to anyone."

"Why do you say that?"

"I think she worries about losing another man. And she still remembers Nikhil-saheb and is not ready to forget him."

"It's hard to forget one's husband, you know." Sheila thought about her feelings for Kumar. She couldn't imagine anyone else taking his place. That was the way Isha and she were raised, in a culture that groomed individuals, especially women, for monogamy, unconditional acceptance, and lifelong commitment. Men sometimes betrayed their wives, but women rarely strayed away from the straight and narrow path carved out by their mothers and grandmothers. Total devotion was the norm. Anything else was unthinkable.

"I know, I know," said Sundari quietly.

Her answer reminded Sheila that the old woman had been abandoned by an evil husband when she was barely out of her teens. But she'd never remarried. Maybe she, too, had worried about losing another man.

"That's right. If anyone should know, it's you."

"But my time was different. In the olden days, if our husbands died or left us, we stayed alone for the rest of our lives; we were no more than *kachra*. Garbage. But now it is modern times and everything has changed. Widows and divorced women can marry again now, and Isha-bayi should think about it."

Sheila was silent for a long time before she suggested, "Maybe you and I could persuade Isha to accept Harish's proposal if he decides to offer her marriage."

Sundari snorted, a sardonic sound Sheila didn't hear very often from her. "Isha-bayi may be gentle and kind, but she makes up her own mind. No one can force her to do anything she does not want to do."

"Right again," concurred Sheila. For a mild and relatively pliable woman, Isha could be surprisingly stubborn when it came to certain things. Hadn't she proved that by standing up to Baba and Ayee and refusing to have an abortion despite their efforts to coerce her? Later, when the oppression had become unbearable, she'd walked out on them, once again proving that she was a strong woman who did what she thought was right.

Within the next minute Sheila heard Sundari's breathing turn deep and even, then gradually transition into snoring. So she turned onto her side and shut her eyes, wondering if Diya would ever be found alive. Tears burned her eyelids. *God, please bring her home.*

The doorbell rang. Harish woke up with a start and sat upright from his sleeping position on Isha's sofa. He pushed his glasses over his nose and was on his feet in an instant, despite the stiffness that had set in from lying on the cramped piece of furniture with its slashed cushions. Years of responding to emergencies any hour of the day or night had made him immune to such minor inconveniences. The brain snapped into action at a split-second's notice.

Barefoot he strode to open the door and was puzzled to find no one there. He stuck his head outside and looked in both directions in the hallway. There was nobody. Then his eyes fell on the envelope lying on the floor.

Harish's chest quivered and tightened. It had to be from the kidnapper! Bending down to retrieve it, he noticed it was addressed to Isha. Someone had just delivered it in person mere seconds ago. The deliverer had to still be in the vicinity.

He instantly raced down the hallway and down the stairs, all the way through the foyer and out the building. Outside, there was not a soul to be seen. No sound of running feet, no soft rustle of clothing. Nothing. Not a single vehicle was in sight, either. The neighborhood looked dead.

Keeping his eyes and ears wide-open for any kind of movement or sound, he stood on the footpath a long time. Several minutes later, there was still nothing. Whoever it was had been quick as lightning—and stealthy.

Frustrated, he returned to the second floor. If he'd gone to the door two seconds earlier he could have nabbed the bastard—at least caught a glimpse of him. If only he'd been wide-awake instead of fast asleep, he would have heard something and opened the door before the bell was rung.

But it was too late for any of that now.

Studying the envelope once again, he noted there was no address, just Isha's name. He entered the flat to find Sheila and Sundari standing in the drawing room, staring at him, their eyes wide with the same kind of ominous anticipation he felt.

"What is it?" Sheila demanded.

"It's an envelope for Isha," he said, fighting the urge to tear it open.

"Who delivered it?"

"No idea. Someone rang the bell and disappeared by the time I got to the door. I ran and looked outside on the street, but there's no one. I found this on the doorstep."

"Open it!" she commanded.

"But it's addressed to Isha."

"Then wake her up, for heaven's sake!" She plopped into the nearest chair and blew out a sigh. "I'm sorry. I shouldn't snap at you." She tucked her disheveled hair behind her ears. "It's all this stress . . ." She put her hand forward. "Give it to me; I'll open it."

Harish handed it to her and watched her tear it open with little ceremony. Her eyes grew wide.

"Oh my God!" She put a hand to her chest.

"What is it?" Panic leapt into his throat. Had they killed Diya? Unable to keep himself from peeking, he noticed it was a typewritten letter, or rather something printed off a computer. Naturally the kidnapper didn't want to reveal his handwriting. And he'd probably worn gloves to handle the letter and the envelope.

"He's asking for ten lakhs in cash," Sheila murmured, "along with the information Isha's holding, to be left in a designated spot."

One million rupees!

"Good Lord!" Harish started to pace the floor. Ten lakhs was more than his gross earnings in a six-month period. But if the kidnapper was looking for cash, then there was a good chance Diya was still alive. But was she well or was she scared and hungry, possibly dehydrated?

He drove a tight fist into his other hand, flinching at the self-inflicted pain. It was so infuriating! He'd never experienced this kind of desperation to reach a resolution with his hands tied behind his back.

Who was this evil son of a bitch who obviously worked for Karnik? How did he know Isha lived separately from her in-laws? How had he found her new address in the first place? It only served to confirm his suspicions, once again, that the man was connected to the police.

"He's probably taking money from Karnik on the one hand and trying to extort more from Isha on the other," he said. "Double-dipping, as the Americans call it." He turned his attention back to Sheila and the note lying in her lap. "What else does the note say? It looks like there's more."

Sheila read further. "He's giving Isha until eleven o'clock in the morning to come up with the cash."

Harish looked at the clock. It was a little past midnight. Daybreak wasn't too far off. "He knows the banks open at ten in the morning. The lunatic is giving us precisely one hour to get together an enormous amount of cash."

"He says if there are any copies of the evidence anywhere, and he finds out about them later, he'll resort to other means. If his demands are not met by eleven tomorrow . . . Oh Lord!"

"What?" Fear was like an octopus that spread a million tentacles through Harish's body. He'd never known anything like it in his whole life. It left him petrified.

"He . . . uh . . . he threatens to blow up your house."

"*My* house!" It took Harish a moment to digest that. The bastard was going to use every bit of leverage he could find.

Sheila's fair complexion turned even paler. "Wait. There's more. He threatens to turn to Priya and my boys if he ever finds out you and Isha have copies of the incriminating information." Her hands were shaking as she held up the note. "Shouldn't this be enough evidence to prove Karnik's culpability in this affair, that he's the mastermind?"

"Not necessarily. What if he claims he knows nothing about this, that he has never performed an abortion in his life? He's clever, so he will have erased all traces of his records by now. There are ways to completely deprogram a computer's hard drive." Harish took off his glasses, wiped them with a handkerchief, and put them back on. "I'm quite sure what we're holding is the only evidence there'll ever be about Karnik's illegal activities."

Sheila arched her brows at him. "Exactly how many copies do you have?"

He hesitated. "It's best that I don't tell you." He noticed Sheila's piqued look at being shut out. "I'm sorry, but it's safer for you that way."

"I don't care about what's safe for *me*. He's threatening to hurt my children and Priya!"

"All right." Harish came to a standstill. "I made three copies, but I can't tell you where they are. Phillip knows and so does Isha . . . in case something happens to me."

Sheila glared at him for a second, then slumped in the chair, grudgingly accepting defeat.

The nightmare was becoming more terrifying by the second. Harish's pacing became more frantic. When was Patil arriving? Patil was the only one who could shake down Karnik and find out who the evil enforcer was. And all that had to be done immediately.

He checked his phone and found there was no message from Phillip. That meant Phillip was still waiting for Patil to get in. It also meant Harish couldn't call someone else at the police headquarters and have them provide security to Sheila and Kumar's home, or his own home and clinic. The spy in the police department could be anyone, and he or she could have any number of accomplices. Plus, news traveled fast in police circles. Calling the police would do more harm than good—could be lethal, in fact.

No matter which way Harish looked at it, his hands were tied. It was impotence of the worst kind.

Meanwhile, even if Patil could do something tangible, the situation was still treacherous, hopeless, even. First of all, Isha didn't have the kind of money the kidnapper wanted. But her father-in-law had offered to raise the ransom money. And he could do so easily as soon as the banks opened in the morning. For that matter, both Srikant Tilak and Kumar Sathe were men of such great influence in this town that they could probably wake up a bank manager from his sleep and request a favor.

Money wasn't so much an issue as the concern that, after grabbing it, the kidnapper could still go ahead and kill the baby, still blow up Harish's home, even his clinic. The man seemed remorseless.

That was a nightmare Harish didn't even want to think about. His home, despite his strong sentiments about it, was mainly a place to relax and sleep. But his clinic was his life— everything he'd worked toward since he was a little boy. Becoming a doctor was more than a lifelong dream. It was a calling. It was a passion. It defined the individual he was. He couldn't afford to lose it—that vital part of himself.

Sundari, who'd stood in silence so far, was the one who brought their attention to the fact that Isha needed to be told about the note. "We should wake Isha-bayi and tell her, no?"

"I'll do it," offered Harish. "She's likely to be a little disoriented from the medicine."

He noticed the two women defer to him without hesitation. Was it because they trusted him enough to leave him alone with Isha? Or was it because he was the sole male amongst them in Kumar's absence and they automatically let him take the lead? He would have taken the lead anyway. Consciously or unconsciously he had put himself in the role of protector and male authority figure in Isha's life and her children's.

They were his responsibility now.

Gingerly turning the knob, he opened the door to Isha's bedroom and stuck his head in. All was quiet except for the steady hum of the ceiling fan. He stepped inside and stood for a second to acclimate his eyes to the room, lit only by the nightlight.

Then he saw the huddled figure on the bed. She lay on her side, with her face to the door and both hands fisted under her chin, asleep in the fetal position. It broke his heart to see her like that—curled up like a frightened little girl reaching inside herself for strength.

Although she seemed to trust him with most things, he sensed a small part of her still remained private, something she didn't share, not even with Sheila or Sundari. It was almost as if she was afraid of trusting anyone but herself. Fiercely independent Isha—she hadn't yet recognized the fact that even the strongest of individuals had to let down their guard once in a while and put their trust in others. But she was learning.

"Isha," he said softly, reluctant to disturb her badly needed rest. The pill was working, because she slept on. So he called her name again and touched her shoulder.

This time she came awake with a start and squinted at him in the dark, her body taut with alarm. He must have scared her, coming into her darkened room unannounced. "It's only me, Harish," he said.

Recognizing his voice, she visibly relaxed, then opened her eyes fully. "There's news?"

"Yes." He saw her struggling to shed the drug-induced bleariness and sit up, so he offered a helping hand. "A note from the kidnapper." He could see the last traces of sleep vanish from her eyes. She was on full alert now.

"So he didn't use the phone."

"Someone left the note outside the door." When she looked confused, he added, "Whoever delivered it dropped it on the floor and disappeared before I could answer the doorbell."

She sat still and stared at the floor for a moment, probably trying to absorb the news and make sense out of it.

"I'm sorry, Isha."

In the next instant she was on her feet. "What does the note say?"

"You might want to read it yourself. Sheila read it to Sundari and me a minute ago." Before he could say another word, she was out the door and in the drawing room, snatching the sheet of paper from Sheila's hand.

A wave of helplessness seized Harish as he watched Isha read the message once, twice, then crumple onto the sofa and shatter to pieces.

Chapter 32

Nearly five hours after reading the note, Isha still felt the shock waves rolling through her. Until the ransom note had arrived she'd managed to convince herself to some degree that it just might work itself out, somehow, and that Diya would be back, sooner or later. She hadn't been willing to give up that diminutive ray of hope.

But the note staring at her from the coffee table had managed to erode much of her confidence.

She glanced at the clock. She couldn't help looking at it every few minutes. It was a little after five o'clock. Diya had been missing for slightly more than a day and a half now. It was still dark outside. The rest of the building slept while her flat was a hive of activity. It had been like that all night, ever since the ransom note had arrived.

According to Harish, Patil's flight was due to arrive soon and Phillip was waiting at the airport. But Isha wasn't sure what good Patil's involvement would do at this point. He was clueless about what had been going on in his absence. If no one knew who the kidnapper was or where he was holed up with Diya, then what was the use? Did even Karnik know?

With every passing minute, her sense of hopelessness was rising.

Sheila had phoned Kumar and he had come over immediately, the dark shadow of a beard on his face and his untidy hair an indication that he'd hopped out of bed and rushed there in an instant. It was a testimony to how much he cared about Isha and the girls.

At the moment, Sheila and Kumar were whispering in the kitchen, trying to come up with a way to raise at least some of the ransom money in the incredibly brief window of time the kidnapper had given them. No one, not even rich folks like Kumar and Sheila Sathe, had that kind of hard cash on hand.

Sundari sat on the floor near Isha's feet, wiping away her tears with the edge of her *pallu*. She was still convinced it was all her fault. *Arré Deva, what have I done?*

Despite her resolve not to borrow money from anyone, Isha knew it was futile. How could she turn down cash that could possibly bring Diya back? Did she have any choice in the matter?

But then, how was she ever going to repay a debt that size? If she worked her hands to the bone for the rest of her life she still wouldn't be able do it. All she had in savings was the small amount set aside for a new sewing machine. It was a mere drop in the bucket.

Ten lakhs! Where had the kidnapper come up with that precise figure? Did it have special significance for him?

Just when she'd thought the worst was over, this thing had come to haunt her. What next?

But she couldn't blame this latest catastrophe on anyone but herself—not even fate. Instead of controlling her tongue, she'd revealed her secret to a dangerous man like Karnik. It had ricocheted back and then surrounded her like wildfire. It was consuming not only her but everyone around her.

The sound of the doorbell interrupted her thoughts. She stiffened. Another note from the kidnapper?

Harish was at the door in an instant. But this time he was talking to someone in whispers, and Isha could tell it was a man's voice. Then Harish stepped aside and said, "Please come in." The man entered.

Isha went still. "Baba!" She stared at him for a second, unable to move or say another word. She couldn't help but notice he'd lost a bit of weight. His hair was longer than usual and

brushed the collar of his gray bush shirt. He looked old now—
looked his age. His clothes, too, weren't quite as well fitted as
she remembered.

She hadn't come face-to-face with her father-in-law since that
day she'd left his home. Once the shock of seeing him began to
recede, the pent-up rage and abhorrence sprang to the surface.
"What are you doing here?" she demanded.

Srikant Tilak remained silent. Kumar and Sheila, having heard
the doorbell, were already in the drawing room.

Sheila stepped forward to greet her father. "Baba, I'm glad
you're here."

Isha turned accusing eyes on Sheila. "*You* invited him here?"
How could Sheila betray her like this? Why?

Sheila bit her lip. "I . . . uh . . . he offered his help, Isha."

"I don't want his help!" Isha was on her feet now, her swollen
eyes shooting sparks at him. "You're here to gloat, aren't you?"

"No, that is not true," Tilak murmured.

"Diya is the child you and Ayee wanted aborted."

"A lot has changed since then, Isha."

"Oh, it's changed all right! Diya may even be dead by now.
So go home and rejoice with Ayee." The bitterness in her voice
was hard to quell. She made a dismissive gesture with her hands.
"Go celebrate your success."

"How can you say such horrible things to Baba, Isha?" Sheila
protested.

Isha ignored Sheila's outrage as something clicked in her mind.
Could it be? She narrowed her eyes at the old man. "Did . . . did
you have something to do with this? Are you and Karnik working together to destroy my children and me?"

"No. I would never do something like that." Tilak looked at
Sheila with what bordered on a plea for support.

Sheila instinctively moved closer to her father. "Isha, please,
you know Baba wouldn't do something unconscionable like that.
Please understand he wants to help. He has the *means* to help."

"I'd rather die than accept his charity."

"Be reasonable, will you?" begged Sheila.

"You want me to be reasonable with a man who struck his

little granddaughter because she was crying for her dead father and refused to go to school? You want me to be reasonable with a baby-killer?" It gave her immense satisfaction to see her father-in-law flinch.

Harish, who had been a silent observer until then, stepped forward. "Isha, Sheila's right. Now is not the time to hold grudges. We have very little time to put together a huge sum of money. I think you should accept Mr. Tilak's help."

"No, I—"

"You have no choice!" bellowed Kumar, silencing everyone instantly. He was the most pragmatic of them all and a hard-nosed businessman. "Just *forget* the past and think of what you have to do to get Diya back. Your child should be your main concern." He aimed a forbidding scowl at Isha, reminding her of Mother Regina's expression when thoroughly irked. "You do want her back in one piece, don't you?"

"Yes." Isha plopped back onto the sofa and hugged one of the mutilated pillows. It was humiliating to be scolded like a wayward child—but Kumar was right. This was not the time for airing petty resentments. Only Diya mattered.

"Good! Now let's sit down and discuss how to get ten lakhs together in the least amount of time." Kumar lowered his substantial bulk into the nearest chair and barked at Sundari, "Make some tea for everyone!" A clearly rattled Sundari ran to the kitchen to do his bidding.

The niggling doubt remained in Isha's mind. All of a sudden, why did her father-in-law want to rescue a child he detested?

The shrill ringing of the phone made everyone go quiet once again. Kumar answered it while every eye on the room fixed itself on him. His brows snapped together. "What!" He listened for a minute. "Pardon me, but exactly *what* do you need to discuss with Isha Tilak?"

Isha sprang to her feet. "Is it . . . is it him?" She was afraid to even say the word *kidnapper*. It reminded her that Diya was at his mercy.

When Kumar handed her the phone with his hand pressed over

the mouthpiece, he still had the puzzled frown. "It's Karnik's wife. She says it's urgent that she talk to you. She sounds upset."

The loathsome name of Karnik set Isha's blood simmering. "What does she want—*her* portion of her husband's ransom?"

"I don't know."

"Isha Tilak speaking," she murmured into the phone, every nerve inside her itching to lambaste the woman, but she reigned in the need to lash out. She'd done enough damage with that uncontrollable urge to vent. Besides, Mrs. Karnik was a social acquaintance, even if theirs was an occasional nod-and-smile type of relationship.

"Mrs. Tilak," said the woman, her voice quivering.

"What do you want, Mrs. Karnik?"

There was a moment of silence. "My husband had a serious heart attack a little while ago."

"Really!"

"He's had heart problems for several years."

"I see." What else could she say under the circumstances? The woman was obviously distraught. "So what exactly do you expect *me* to do?"

"Vivek is in no condition to talk to you, so I'm doing it on his behalf."

Isha swallowed hard, the rage returning. "About what, Mrs. Karnik? About the ransom your husband wants to extort in return for my child?" Until now it seemed that the wily old man had been doing his dirty work himself. But to have his wife involved in it? That was hard to believe!

"No! You don't understand."

"I understand very well! Since he's too sick, you're doing it for him."

"Please! Listen to me," the woman pleaded on what sounded like a sob. "I don't want your money! I want to help get your baby back. I'm calling to confess and apologize on Vivek's behalf," she said.

Isha took a long, deep breath and forced herself to listen. "What do you want to tell me?"

Neela Karnik cleared her throat and proceeded to tell Isha everything she had learned the night before.

Despite the woman's pauses and sniffles, Isha heard the message clearly. The room was silent, except for the hum of the fan. The tension emanating from the tightly held breaths of the people surrounding her was so dense, so palpable, that Isha could almost reach out and touch it.

Shock and confusion warred in her mind. Was it really a heart attack? Or could Karnik have attempted suicide because he'd suffered a sudden attack of conscience?

In the end, she had very little to say to the older woman. "I'm sorry. I know it's not your fault." Despite her own grief, she pitied Mrs. Karnik. That poor woman probably had no idea what her rotten husband had been up to all these years. Or did she?

Hanging up the phone, Isha turned around to face the five pairs of eyes staring at her. They were waiting for her to speak. "Karnik has suffered a major heart attack."

"Good Lord!" said Baba.

"His wife called on his behalf to confess the truth about his illegal abortion business, about hiring someone to go after Nikhil . . . everything." She noticed the color drain from Baba's face. His gaze shifted away from her. He started staring at his hands like he'd never seen them before. Isha wondered if he was finally beginning to recognize that he and Ayee may have inadvertently caused the death of their son. "In the end she apologized for causing us so much grief."

"Any *other* information?" asked Harish.

Isha nodded, knowing what he meant. "Nikhil's killer and the kidnapper are one and the same. His name is Ishwar Gowda. He's a police inspector and has been on Karnik's payroll for some time."

"I was right!" said Harish. "He *is* a policeman!"

"He . . . um . . ." The mixed emotions were making Isha tremble. "He killed Nikhil supposedly in self-defense."

"How could it be self-defense when he broke into our store

and stabbed my son to death?" demanded Baba, his mouth quivering.

"Apparently Gowda couldn't find the evidence, so he and Karnik left the matter alone, assuming that since Nikhil was dead Karnik would be safe."

"So what is happening now?" asked Baba, abruptly and unexpectedly subsiding into resigned calm. His color was beginning to improve but he was unusually subdued, very unlike the arrogant, demanding man Isha had known. She knew for sure then that he blamed himself, at least partly, for Nikhil's death.

"Because of my actions, Karnik hired him again," she admitted. "But Mrs. Karnik told me Gowda is a deranged and dangerous man who's been extorting money from Karnik. And the killing and kidnapping were Gowda's ideas, not Karnik's. All Karnik supposedly wanted was to recover what belonged to him."

"Did she mention where the baby is?" Sheila asked, putting a comforting arm around Isha's shoulders.

"Gowda supposedly has her in his house. His wife is taking care of her." Overwhelmed, Isha put her face in her hands. "If he's unstable I'm afraid he may have . . . killed her by now."

"Don't say that!" Sheila wrapped her arms around Isha. "Don't even *think* that. If Gowda's wife is keeping an eye on her, I'm sure Diya's safe."

"Sheila's right," concurred Harish. "I know Mrs. Gowda. The Gowda's children are my patients. She seems like a pleasant, normal woman."

Harish's phone started to peal and he flipped it open. "Phillip?" He listened for a second. "Oh, Patil *has* landed? Excellent!"

"Tell him about Neela Karnik's call," prompted Sheila.

Nodding at her, Harish quickly described the situation to Phillip.

There was a long pause while he was put on hold, so Harish explained to the rest of them that Phillip was discussing the latest developments with Patil. Then Phillip came back on the line with information, and Harish asked him, "Right now? Very good! And ring me as soon as you know the address. I'll meet you there."

Harish ended the call and thrust the phone back into his pocket. "Patil is gathering his best armed policemen and they'll head to Gowda's house as soon as they can. It will take a while for him to make some phone calls, pick up his Jeep from the airport parking lot, and then drive to Gowda's house. Phillip's going to let me know when they're ready to leave the airport."

In spite of the new information the word *deranged* still disturbed Isha. If Gowda was indeed a psychopath, Diya could be dead by now, or perhaps badly hurt. God, she couldn't bear to think that. A quick and painless death would be better than being tortured. *Why, Lord? Why did you give her to me as a gift after that long struggle, only to take her away now?*

They all sat in taut silence, sipping cups of Sundari's tea and willing the phone to ring.

Exactly thirty-eight minutes later, Phillip called Harish to inform him that he and Patil were getting ready to leave the airport. He also gave Harish Gowda's address.

Harish was striding toward the door in the next instant. "I'm going there to meet them."

"I will go with you," announced Baba, rising to his feet.

"The police don't want any civilians around, sir," said Harish, trying to keep his voice respectful despite his contempt for Srikant Tilak.

"Then how come *you* are going?" Tilak demanded.

Harish sighed. "I'm a doctor. I can help in ways you can't."

Kumar nodded in assent. "He's right, Baba. It's best that we leave this to the police."

"Harish." Isha went to him. "Can I please go with you?"

He shook his head. "Phillip and Patil said no. It's risky."

"Is it safe for you to go, then?"

"I'll take care of myself. Don't worry."

"I can't help worrying." When she saw the determined light in his eyes, she knew he would go, no matter how dangerous it was.

Then she thought of something. "Wait one second." She ran to the bedroom and returned with a fuzzy stuffed toy—a chocolate-colored monkey with a silly grin on its face. It had miraculously missed the kidnapper's wrath. "Take this. It's her favorite toy. She stops crying when she sees it, no matter how upset she is."

Harish tucked the toy under his arm. In spite of the riveted audience, he put a hand to Isha's face. "I'll do my best to bring Diya back. Meanwhile just keep praying."

She nodded. "Thank you, Harish. I'll never forget your kindness."

Chapter 33

As Harish raced to the address Phillip had given him, his heart was hammering wildly against his ribs. Despite his outward calm, put on mostly for Isha's sake, he was thoroughly scared. He had handled a variety of medical emergencies, but this was an entirely different type of crisis for him—so much more personal—with so much more at stake.

Nonetheless, he had to keep his faith in the fact that Diya was in a woman's care. With some luck the baby would come out of this alive and well.

It was still very early in the morning, not quite seven o'clock, and the sun was barely out when he turned onto Temple Road, a community of middle-class individual homes, most of them built some twenty-five to thirty years ago. The streetlights were still on, and he could see that on many homes the paint was mottled with mold in places that didn't see the sun. Lights were on in some windows.

Deep pink and purple streaks painted the dawn sky. Flocks of crows were already perched on rooftops, foraging for insects and tidbits. It was a cool, dewy, typical Palgaum morning, with puffs of fog still lingering in places. If he wasn't in such a heightened state of dread, he'd have driven at a more leisurely pace, savored the scene.

On the street, there were three police vehicles parked at odd angles amidst the civilian ones. Obviously the police had rushed there and done a haphazard parking job.

He left his own car several houses down so as to remain inconspicuous. Phillip had warned him that the only way Patil would allow the presence of a civilian during a police raid would be if Harish stayed a good distance away and didn't interfere in the operation. Even Phillip was allowed to be there as a professional courtesy and because of his crucial role in the evolving crisis.

Taller and wider than the other officers, Phillip was clearly visible. Also, he was the only one not wearing a uniform besides Patil, who had probably driven there straight from the airport. The two men stood a little distance away from the others, who were huddled behind a Jeep. They stood in a tight circle surrounding one man who was talking and gesturing.

They were obviously working out a strategy to approach Gowda.

Despite the clandestine nature of the police activity and the early hour of the morning, there were a few curious people already emerging from their homes and standing on their verandas, staring at the men. One bald old man stood bare-chested in white pajamas, speaking into a mobile phone. He had probably jumped out of bed and immediately started calling his neighbors and friends, inviting them over for a front-row view of whatever was about to happen.

Noticing Harish's arrival, Phillip signaled him over. It surprised Harish, who'd planned on standing at a safe distance because of Patil's instructions. But Phillip motioned to him again, so he approached the two men.

"Got here rather fast, I see," said Phillip, slapping Harish's shoulder in a gesture of friendly support. His expression said: *you were speeding again, weren't you, you devil?*

Patil offered his hand to Harish. "Dr. Salvi. I'm sorry about the Tilak child." He raised one thick brow. "The baby is your patient?"

"Yes." But Diya was much more than a patient. She was his baby, as much *his* as she was Nikhil's. His fear about the possibility of losing her was proof of that. "The Tilaks are close family friends," he added in response to Patil's speculative eyes summing up Harish's role in the nasty business.

Harish surveyed the modest, single-story house that looked similar to his own bungalow. Not a curtain stirred in the two windows facing the street as the first rays of the sun began to penetrate the fog and cast a dull glow on the panes. Were Gowda and his family still asleep? Or was the lunatic awake and pacing? And where was Diya?

"The inspector is getting his troops ready to surround Gowda's house," Patil explained, indicating the huddled circle of men.

"Is it safe to do that? What if Gowda panics and does something rash?" *Like kill the baby.*

"It's our last resort," answered Patil with a resigned shrug. "We know he is in there, but he refuses to answer his phone, and it's too dangerous to go knock on the door. He could start shooting." He narrowed his eyes on the house. "But he knows we're here."

"How do you know that he knows?"

"He's aware of our presence, Harish," said Phillip. "I bet he hasn't slept a wink all night, since he's been writing ransom notes and planning a means of escape."

"You think he may have expected this?"

Patil shook his head. "I don't think so. But it is no longer a surprise. He is able to see what's happening outside his house and must realize that we're here to apprehend him."

"And yet he hasn't tried to make contact with you?"

"He is overconfident, and he has some psychiatric issues. We have had problems with him ever since he joined the department. Over the years, he has been getting bolder and more . . . uh . . . difficult."

Harish frowned at him. "Then why is he still on the force? Why wasn't a renegade police officer with *psychiatric issues* fired?"

"Lack of solid proof, Doctor!" snapped Patil, his tone both defensive and condescending. "Government does not function like the private sector, you know." He obviously considered Harish's question ridiculously naive.

"But there must have been *something* to make you aware of his activities?"

"Minor infractions here and there, which we tried to address."

Harish noticed that Patil didn't elaborate on them. The police fraternity was a tight-knit group and very defensive. They preferred to keep their dirty secrets hidden from the harsh, censorious glare of the civilian world.

"Temporary suspension and other disciplinary measures have not worked with him," admitted Patil. "He thinks he is invincible." He let out a tired sigh. He was unshaven and tousled from his long overnight journey. "Gowda is too clever to leave any evidence of his crimes around."

"He probably never expected Karnik to confess—or rather, confess through his wife. He certainly wouldn't have thought Karnik would have a heart attack and ruin his plans."

"This must be a shock to Gowda," granted Patil. "Like I said, he probably had everything planned—taking the money and escaping from the country, most likely to some place like Nepal. I understand it is quite easy to disappear into those mountains."

Some movement from behind the Jeep caught their eye and all three men glanced in that direction. "Looks like they're ready," said Phillip.

Harish's back stiffened. He returned his gaze to the house. As if on cue, a curtain stirred in one of the windows. He couldn't see beyond it inside the darkened room, but the eerie prickle on his arms was enough to signal that Patil and Phillip were right. Gowda was watching them, and he, too, knew something serious was about to happen. He had to be at least a little concerned—the sick, arrogant bastard.

The armed policemen moved quickly and stealthily, like ghosts flitting about in the first light of dawn. Within seconds they surrounded the bungalow, crouching behind bushes and any other reasonably safe place they could find. Harish watched them position themselves out of direct range of the windows and doors.

Looking around the area, he noticed there were more neighbors spilling out now, some of them getting rather close. News was spreading fast. Patil at once rushed to shoo the closer ones away. They reluctantly moved back a step or two. He returned and motioned to Phillip and Harish to crouch beside him behind one of the Jeeps, the one farthest from Gowda's house.

With a mixture of dread and fascination Harish followed Patil's orders. If it weren't for the fact that there was a child very precious to him facing grave danger inside that house, he'd have considered it an adventure, straight out of a thriller movie.

How much more Bollywood-ish could it get than this? A kidnapped child, an outrageously large ransom demand, and an elite police team deployed in the predawn hours to apprehend a psychopathic criminal—a policeman himself. No wonder all those spectators stood riveted. They were Gowda's neighbors. They had to know Gowda personally.

As for Harish, his heart was pounding with terror. Despite the coolness of a typical Palgaum morning, perspiration was gathering on his back and chest, making his shirt damp. A bloody shootout could start any second. People could be killed. Diya could be killed.

But he couldn't afford to indulge in such dark thoughts. He had to focus on getting her back in one piece.

As he observed the inspector bring out a mobile phone from his pocket and start to dial, Harish knew the showdown was about to begin. He had always imagined a tense, dramatic scenario like this would mean the use of a bullhorn. But in the next instant he realized a device like that would attract the entire neighborhood and beyond. A mobile phone and a quiet conversation with the hostage-taker were more practical.

But Gowda supposedly wasn't answering his phone. So *then* what?

Harish glanced at the other two men and realized it wasn't just he who was vibrating with anxiety. The tension emanating from Patil and Phillip matched his own. Perspiration beads were glistening on Phillip's forehead and patches of sweat were forming around the underarms of his dark blue T-shirt. Patil's troubled eyes were fixed on the house.

Even the spectators, who so far had been whispering amongst themselves, now stood in tense anticipation. Harish held his breath as he heard the deep bass voice of the inspector speak into the phone. From that distance it was hard to hear every word, but Harish managed to catch some of it. He was informing Gowda that he was surrounded and requesting him to come out unarmed and with his hands held up.

His call probably went to voice mail, because he dialed again a minute later and repeated his words, very slowly this time, enunciating every syllable so there was no room for misunderstanding.

Although Harish didn't move an inch from his crouched position, from the corners of his eyes he could see more people pouring out into the street. The sun was rising higher and getting brighter by the minute, too.

He noticed Phillip and Patil making a quick survey of the burgeoning crowd around them. "Bloody hell!" whispered Patil. "Why are they all crowding here? We don't need more casualties. That idiot could start shooting any sec—"

Boom! A muffled crack split the air, cutting him off in midsentence.

A gunshot!

Chapter 34

The sound of the gunshot sent a jolt through Harish. Instinctively he ducked, shuddered. He'd never heard shots fired from a gun in real life before, only in movies and TV shows. A few shocked sounds emerged from the crowd nearby.

Turning around, he saw a man with a large, professional-looking camera furiously taking photographs. The media had arrived!

He wasn't sure whom the shot had come from—Gowda or one of the policemen. He was itching to rise and take a peek, to find out for himself. But Patil and Phillip had warned him about such behavior, so he remained in place, his sense of doom mounting.

Phillip's gaze met his. He must have read the question in Harish's eyes. "It's Gowda's gun."

"How do you know?" Harish's mind was conjuring up the most horrifying images of Diya blown to bits. Now that Gowda knew he wasn't going to get his ransom, and that his defeat was near, killing Diya could be his final act of frustration and rage.

"I can tell from the sound," replied Phillip. "It came from inside the house. It could be a foolish attempt at bravado in the face of adversity. I hope he hasn't harmed the child."

Harish's mouth went dry. "What happens now?"

Patil answered his question. "We continue until we get him—dead or alive."

A fresh wave of panic washed over Harish. Dead or alive?

Gowda could end up butchering everyone in that house along with a few of those brave policemen before he gave himself up or died. Either way he had nothing to lose. The man didn't seem to have a conscience or a care for his own family. What kind of man would put his wife and children in jeopardy?

Only a psychopath. What Patil had chosen to call *psychiatric issues* could very well be serious flaws in the brain.

Harish braced himself for another shot. When nothing happened for several minutes, he glanced at Phillip, whose brow was creased in speculation. "Everything's too quiet."

"He may be a nut, but he's a clever one. He's biding his time, waiting for the police to lose patience and make a move. Then he'll pounce on them. Cat-and-mouse game."

A strange buzzing sound made Harish startle and look around for its source. Then he saw Patil produce his mobile phone out of his pocket and flip it open.

"Patil speaking." The man frowned as he listened to the caller, only grunting out monosyllabic responses, looking more and more befuddled as the caller continued to speak. "Are you sure? Did she leave a number?" Tucking the phone between his ear and shoulder, he pulled out a pen from his pocket and wrote the number on his palm. Then he shut the phone and shoved it back into his pocket.

"Problem, sir?" Phillip asked Patil.

"That was my assistant. Apparently Gowda's wife just called the station, asking to talk to me. She's very upset."

"She actually managed to make a phone call with her husband listening in?" asked Harish, his eyes wide.

Patil blew out a shaky breath. "He was not listening . . . because he . . . shot himself."

"What the hell!" swore Phillip and pointed to the house. "That shot we just heard . . ."

"I believe that's what we heard," said Patil with a nod. "He supposedly shot himself in the mouth."

Harish flinched. "Good God!" Despite his medical training there were certain things that still made his stomach turn.

"I think he finally realized he was finished."

"The gunshot could be bogus, a plan to trick us, sir," Phillip cautioned. "His wife could be in this as deep as he is. Her call might be a ploy to create a diversion and help him escape."

Patil stroked his chin, the stubble making a raspy sound as he turned over Phillip's words in his mind. "That's doubtful. I've met the lady once or twice at social gatherings." He rubbed his chin again. "But then, it's hard to judge someone after a few superficial contacts."

Harish shook his head. "Mrs. Gowda is a nice woman, decent and very devoted to her children."

"You know her?" Patil tossed him an astounded look.

"Both their boys are my patients," he explained to Patil. "I've never met their father, but their mother doesn't seem like the kind of woman who'd be involved in anything like this. That's why when I heard Gowda was the man involved I was shocked. His wife is such a normal, sociable person."

Phillip frowned at him. "Are you sure about her? The team could walk into a trap if they think they're going in there to find a dead man and instead he's very much alive and shooting away like a maniac."

Harish pondered Phillip's words for a long minute. What if his friend was right? After all, his own acquaintance with Mrs. Gowda was superficial, as Patil described it. He met her briefly three or four times a year when she brought the children in for their checkups and sick visits.

The Gowda boys, about nine and five years old now, had been coming to him for the past three years. How much did he really know about their mother? Very little, other than the fact that she seemed friendly, educated, and concerned about her children's welfare.

"I can't be a hundred percent sure," allowed Harish. "But I honestly feel she's not the type to be engaged in anything illegal, especially if it means endangering her children." He felt sorry for the poor woman. Had she watched her husband shoot himself? And if those innocent children had witnessed it, they could end up disturbed for life.

Patil did his chin-stroking and pondering routine one more

time and rose to his feet. "I guess I better speak to the inspector, then."

Harish and Phillip observed while Patil spoke to his man in whispers. Then he dialed the number written on his palm, waited for a reply, and started to talk. The conversation was brief, with Patil nodding several times. Then the two men started to converse quietly again.

After what seemed like ages, Patil motioned Phillip and Harish to approach him. "I think the lady is telling the truth. She is sobbing, and the baby is crying in the background, so it was hard to hear everything, but it looks like he may be dead or seriously injured." Patil threw a distressed glance at Harish. "Dr. Salvi, would you be able to examine him and see if he's . . ."

"Of course," replied Harish, trying hard to keep his mind off the nausea in his stomach. This was not the time to feel squeamish about examining a man with half or all of his face and brain missing. *Salvi, you're a doctor, for heaven's sake! So deal with it,* he ordered himself and raced to his car to retrieve his medical bag.

The one thing that kept him moving was Patil's comment about the crying baby. That had to be Diya. She had to be alive. There was hope.

From the trunk of his car, Harish grabbed his bag and the toy monkey. By the time he started running back toward the scene, the front door to Gowda's house was open, with two policemen guarding it against the curious onlookers. As Harish jostled through the crowd, various people bombarded him with questions, in three different languages.

He managed to ignore them and quickly made it to the house. Patil pulled him inside and immediately shut the door. It took Harish's eyes a moment to adjust to the dimness and gloom in the house after the bright sunshine outside. A maroon sofa and two matching chairs sat around a small oval coffee table. It was a modest drawing room.

The familiar metallic smell of blood reached his nostrils. A doctor could recognize that odor anywhere.

His attention immediately went to the man lying on the floor beside the window. A handgun lay on his chest. Harish figured Gowda must have been standing at the window, looking outside on the grim scene that spelled his doom. A little later, having given up all hope, he must have sunk to the floor and put the gun in his mouth.

The bile crept up into Harish's throat, hot and bitter, the acid burning his chest. True to his expectation, a portion of the man's head and face were missing, the bloody pieces strewn across the room. It was a revolting sight, with the nearest wall, the curtains, the furniture, and the floor splattered with blood, bits of flesh, and bone. Harish didn't even have to look twice to know the man was long dead. More than a third of his brain was gone. His face was worse.

God, poor Mrs. Gowda had to witness *this?*

Setting aside his private thoughts for the moment, and suppressing the need to throw up, he crouched down and went through the dispassionate motions of pronouncing the man officially dead.

Somewhere in the house he heard a woman weeping. Mrs. Gowda. A little boy's desperate sobs mingled with hers. One of her sons—most likely the little one. He was only five years old. The mournful sounds made Harish wince. He looked again at the dead man. *How could you do this to your family? What kind of insanity made you do this?* It *had* to be insanity.

A baby started crying. He knew that cry. Diya! Everything else flew out of his mind. She sounded hoarse, which meant she'd been howling a lot.

He wanted to run to her and grab her in his arms, soothe away the fear. But first things first. He slowly rose to his feet and nodded at Patil. "No question. He's dead. If you want me to sign any official papers to that effect, I'll do it."

Patil remained silent, his expression turning odd. The blood seemed to drain out of his face. Was he going to pass out? A second later he pressed a hand to his mouth, ran to the front door and out onto the stoop.

Harish clearly heard the retching sounds. Despite his police background, Patil probably hadn't seen anything as disturbing as this. Fortunately, his own stomach was beginning to settle a little.

He glanced at Phillip, who stood in stoical silence, staring at the gruesome sight on the floor. It looked like good old Phillip had a stronger stomach than most people. "Enough to make anyone sick," Phillip murmured. "God, what a waste of life—and all that for money."

"With this man it was beyond money," Harish said, thinking out loud. "I think he was insane. He should have been in therapy years ago." He shook his head. "And don't forget, this all started with Karnik's illegal abortions. That, too, had its roots in money."

Phillip blew out a deep, regretful breath. "I feel sorry for the poor widow. She's so young. And the children are cute little boys. I just got a glimpse of them. They're all devastated."

"I'm sure they are. But in the long run they may be better off without a lunatic for a husband and father, don't you think?"

"Patil said he's going to contact her relatives so someone can come over and help her cope with all this."

Harish thought of something else as he looked at the bloodshed around them. "From a medical point of view, I think the police department should offer her some sort of psychiatric counseling as well. An episode like this is hard to recover from."

Isha should have received counseling, too, he thought, after what she'd been through. Instead of getting help she'd suffered more agony. No wonder it was taking her so long to bounce back from Nikhil's death and everything else.

"I'll mention it to Patil. He could probably arrange for medical help." Phillip inclined his head toward the room where all the weeping was coming from. "So, you want to get that baby or what?"

Harish hesitated. "Would you do me a favor? I'm just not up to facing Mrs. Gowda and her children right now. Could you go inside and bring Diya to me? Since you're a stranger to the lady, it might be . . . you know . . . easier." He was being a coward by avoiding Mrs. Gowda, but neither his stomach nor his brain was being cooperative at the moment.

Phillip headed in the direction of the bedrooms. Moments later he emerged with Diya in his arms. The instant she saw Harish, a face she knew well, she sent up a pitiful wail.

Very few things in life had made Harish's eyes fill with tears. This was one of those occasions. He blinked back the moisture. Seeing the baby was like nothing he'd ever experienced before— a rush of mixed emotions: relief at seeing her alive and well; sadness at seeing her beautiful eyes swollen from crying; rage at Karnik and the man lying dead not five feet away from him; frustration at his own inability to prevent any of this devastation from happening.

Despite his best efforts to rein them in, a couple of errant tears spilled out. Quickly he brushed them with his fingers, replaced his glasses, and stepped forward. "Thank you, Phillip."

Diya literally jumped into his welcoming arms. He hugged her close to his chest and started to rock her gently. "Shh, baby. You'll be all right." He never wanted to let her out of his sight. He pulled out a handkerchief from his pocket and dabbed at her eyes and nose. Her fair skin was flushed pink. Her hair hung in damp curls around her face.

He wondered how long she'd been crying so hard. He could feel her frantic heartbeat against his chest. To add to her misery, her nappy was soaked, and some of the dampness had leaked out of the plastic panty and onto her pajamas. The acrid odor of urine was strong on her clothes.

Phillip stood with his hands in his pockets, looking on helplessly. "Is she okay?"

Harish nodded. "As far as I can see. She's scared, that's all. Getting kidnapped and then thrust into the midst of strangers is very traumatic for a baby." He patted her behind. "And she's wet—maybe hungry, too."

"Hell, all this would be traumatic for a grown man," replied Phillip.

The gruffness in his voice told Harish that his friend was genuinely touched by the reunion.

That's when Harish remembered the monkey. Retrieving it

from the chair where he'd tossed it earlier, he handed it to the baby. "Look, Diya. Look who came to find you."

The transformation was almost like magic. Just like Isha had said, Diya clutched at the grinning object like a lifeline. After a while her crying subsided, although the tiny hiccups continued. "Good girl," he said and kissed the top of her head.

Phillip watched the scene with interest. "Harish, I've never seen you like this with any of your other patients."

"That's because this baby's special."

"You mean you love this one like your own?"

Harish smiled down at Diya, who had buried her face and the monkey into his shoulder. "Her father was Nikhil Tilak, but she feels like mine," he said, stroking the baby's back. "I saw her when she was less than twenty-four hours old, and I fell in love."

"I can see why. She's a beautiful child. But what about her mother?"

"What about Isha?" Harish recognized that incisive look in his friend's eye. Phillip had guessed about his feelings for Isha. There wasn't much he could hide from Phillip. They'd been close friends since elementary school and had very few secrets between them.

An amused smile flashed across Phillip's broad face. "So, that's how it is, huh?"

"That's how it is," Harish confessed. "I want to marry Isha— whenever she's ready—if she'll *ever* be ready."

Just then Patil returned, looking much better. His stomach was obviously on the mend. He looked at the baby. "Found the child, I see. Is she all right?"

"Yes. And thank God for that," said Harish. "I'm very grateful to you, Mr. Patil. The baby's mother will be very relieved."

Patil shrugged and shifted his gaze to the body on the floor. "I wish it had happened differently. Two men are dead . . . and one is in the hospital, and we may never have the answers to many of our questions."

"Why not? All this started with Karnik and he can provide

you the details, can't he?" said Harish. "I hope the old man rots in prison for what he's done to so many innocent people—not to mention a few hundred female fetuses."

Patil seemed to mull it over. "Karnik may not be in any condition to stand trial for several months. Perhaps never. Apparently his condition is very serious." His looked at Diya's tiny back, still convulsing with hiccups. "But I'm glad the child is okay. Otherwise her grandfather, Mr. Tilak, would never forgive me."

"If you don't need me here, I'll take Diya back to her mother," said Harish.

"Our forensic staff is on the way to pick up the body and transport it to the mortuary, so you are free to leave," said Patil, and then rubbed his belly, as if the nausea was still bothering him.

Meanwhile Phillip closed the flap on Harish's bag and picked it up. "I'll walk you to your car."

"Thanks." Harish raised his free hand in a casual salute to Patil and headed out. The chattering spectators still lingered on the periphery, despite the policemen keeping an eye on them. They went silent the instant they saw the two men emerge from the house. They stared at the baby in awe for a second. Then they barraged him and Phillip with questions.

Once again the two men ignored the crowd and kept walking. Phillip waved away a pesky news reporter.

Diya's hiccups began to diminish and her heartbeat became softer, steadier, as Harish walked back to the car. She was going limp as she lay with her head on his shoulder. She was obviously falling asleep. A good thing, too. A little rest would go a long way in washing away the trauma of the last several hours.

Inside the car, he seated the slumbering child upright in the front passenger seat and buckled her in tight, with the monkey pressed snugly against her, while Phillip stowed his bag in the trunk.

Harish turned to his friend to shake his hand. "I can't tell you how grateful I am for all your help, Phillip."

Phillip shrugged. "What are friends for? But next time, try and give me some advance notice—at least enough to get out of my pajamas," he said with a wry smile.

"I'll try," Harish promised with equal dryness. "Get in the backseat. I'll drop you off at my house so you can take a bath and grab some sleep."

"No need." Phillip put his hands in his pockets. "I have my car here. Patil took me by your house so I could pick up my vehicle before he and I got here."

"That was thoughtful of him."

"Actually, I asked for the favor. So I think I'll just drive back home right away."

"Are you crazy? You haven't had a wink of sleep all night, and no food, either." Seeing the bleary-eyed look of exhaustion on Phillip's face, Harish pulled his house keys out of his pocket and pressed them into Phillip's hand. "Doctor's orders! You're going to my place. I'll deliver Diya to her mother and meet you there. If I'm late, help yourself to whatever is in the fridge and then sleep in my guestroom."

"I suppose you're right," conceded Phillip, suppressing a yawn." Pocketing the keys, he pulled out a mobile phone from his other pocket. "I'll ring Cece and tell her." Cecelia was Phillip's wife of two years.

"Will your boss get upset with you for taking an unexplained day off? I can have Patil give him a ring."

Phillip shook his head. "I'll tell him I was involved with a case in Palgaum. He'll find out from the radio and newspapers anyway."

"Hmm." Harish recalled the photographer and reporter at the scene. The news flash would reach the public within hours. The crowd around Gowda's house was gradually thinning out.

When he'd arrived here, it was with the certainty of seeing a bloody shootout and the fear of discovering that Diya was killed. He was prepared for injury to himself as well. Neither of those things had happened. He was immensely grateful on both counts.

Flipping open his own mobile, he dialed Isha's number. She answered on the first ring. The desperate note in her voice nearly choked him with emotion once again.

"Is she . . . is Diya . . . ?"

"She's all right," he said.

"She's alive!" There was a long pause.

Harish gave Isha plenty of time to digest the good news. "She's fine except for a wet nappy and a little exhaustion. Right now she's asleep in the passenger seat—with her monkey."

"She is?" Isha sniffled. "Thank you, Harish!" She made a throaty sound that could have been either a laugh or a stifled sob. "You don't know what . . . this means to me."

"I *do* know," he said quietly. Before pulling out from the parking spot he waved to Phillip and made sure Diya and her monkey were still buckled in.

Chapter 35

December 2007

Isha looked up when she heard Priya's high-pitched laughter. It was heartwarming to see her little girl happy. Priya was by nature an upbeat child. Nonetheless, lately she seemed really content, although actually it didn't take much for children to find contentment.

At the moment, Isha was sitting in a chair across the room, sewing tiny beads onto the collar of a dress while Priya was absorbed in the book Harish was reading to her. It had become quite a ritual with those two, the nightly story-reading.

Priya sat cross-legged on the sofa beside Harish, wearing a frilly nightgown, as he made a simple story of a talking camel come alive by changing his voice to suit the different characters and their personalities.

Diya was fast asleep in Harish's lap while he read. The little imp had been fighting to keep her eyes open, but fatigue had won the battle. She was walking these days, a typical fourteen-month-old with boundless energy.

Watching Diya now, peacefully slumbering with her head cradled in the crook of Harish's arm, Isha swallowed the lump that formed in her throat. She had nearly given up hope of seeing Diya alive after that kidnapping event. The memory of it was still fresh after two months. It still made her heartbeat quicken with anxiety. It still left her feeling powerless.

Meanwhile she empathized with the kidnapper's wife. That poor woman was now suffering a similar fate as Isha had suffered the previous year: unexpected and instant widowhood and the responsibility of raising two children.

In many ways Mrs. Gowda had it a lot worse. She had to live with the horror of watching her husband shoot himself, alongside the painful fact that he was a deranged killer.

Then there was Karnik, the other villain in her life. A few days after the onset of his heart attack, he had suffered a massive stroke. Paralyzed on one side, he was now confined to a wheelchair, speechless, nearly motionless, and more helpless than an infant. Naturally he was incapable of standing trial. God had obviously seen fit to punish him in his own way. Living like a vegetable, or barely living, in this case, was probably a lot worse than prison. Meanwhile, his innocent wife and children were suffering unnecessarily.

Another hoot from Priya drew Isha's attention. Harish looked very much at home with one child asleep in his arms and another demanding his attention. He was a remarkable man, a miracle that had come into her life almost like an answer to a prayer.

And she'd come to care for him deeply. She hadn't told him that yet because doubts continued to nip at her mind. If she indeed considered Harish's offer of marriage seriously, would his family accept her and her children? They'd been cautiously polite the one time she had met them, but that didn't mean they would want her for a daughter-in-law, especially when their older son's wife was such a brilliant and successful doctor.

What about Sheila and Kumar? Would they resent her if she married again—in essence betraying Nikhil's memory? In the future, would Harish want children of his own? There was no end to the speculation.

When Priya bounced over to kiss her good night and interrupted her wandering thoughts, Isha realized the reading session was over. She set aside her sewing and caught Priya in a hug. "Did you remember to thank Doctor-kaka?"

"Yes. I gave him a good night kiss, too."

"Good. Now go get ready for bed."

Priya raced to the bathroom, followed by Sundari, who'd no doubt carefully supervise the bedtime ritual.

Harish rose to his feet, holding Diya in his arms like a precious and fragile piece of glass. "I better put this one in her bed," he said and headed toward the bedroom that was now shared by both girls.

Diya had outgrown the cradle and so Isha had bought her a bed. Sundari slept on the floor between the two girls, their self-appointed nursemaid and guardian. Since the kidnapping she'd become paranoid about the children's safety.

Isha went in ahead of him and turned down the bedspread so he could lay Diya down. Then she tenderly tucked the baby in and sent Harish a grateful look. "You don't have to do all this babysitting, you know."

"I like doing it." His gaze remained on the sleeping baby. "Amazing how children forget bad experiences so easily, isn't it? Nobody would know she'd been traumatized only two months ago."

Isha watched Diya's sweet face in repose, oblivious to their whispered conversation. "Wish we could all be that way. I'd give anything to be able to forget the nightmares of the past six years."

"You could do it, Isha, if you gave yourself half a chance." He took both her hands. "My offer still stands."

"I know." His hands were warm and firm and reassuring. She loved the feel of his hands. She loved the timbre of his voice, the way he tilted his head when he listened to her or the children, the meticulous care he put into everything he did. She loved the whole package. Not a surprise! She'd never thought she'd ever care for any man the way she'd cared for Nikhil.

"I'd like to try and erase those nightmares from your memory if you'll let me. Forever, if possible."

His eyes behind the glasses were intense, sincere, unblinking. The message in them was as clear as the mirror hanging above the dressing table in the corner: he wanted her; he wanted marriage; he wanted permanence.

Sundari and Priya came into the room just then, prompting Isha to withdraw her hands and prevent her from responding to his remark.

Priya aimed a gap-toothed smile at Harish. New teeth had grown in, but others were now missing, leaving a wide space in the top row. "You won't forget my concert tomorrow?" She was taking piano lessons at school and there was a recital by all the children who were learning to play various musical instruments.

"I won't forget," he promised solemnly. "Five o'clock?"

"Uh-huh."

"Who else is invited besides me?"

Priya started counting on her fingers and reeled off a long list of names including family and friends—even Ayee and Baba.

"Wow," he said. "That's a lot of people. I'm impressed!" He patted the top of her head. "Now be good and get plenty of sleep, so you're fresh and ready for the concert."

"Okay." In her usual fashion she threw herself with abandon on the bed, giggling when the mattress bounced.

Isha glanced at him. "Notice how she obeys you instantly? Neither Sundari nor I can get *that* kind of cooperation."

"I noticed." His grin was unabashedly smug.

"So, what's your secret?"

The grin widened. "There's no secret. Priya just happens to like me."

A clearly amused Sundari chuckled and started tucking Priya into bed.

Harish closed the bedroom door, and Isha and he stepped out into the drawing room.

He arched a puzzled brow at Isha. "Is it true that her grandparents are attending the concert?"

She pulled a wry face. "Hard to believe, isn't it? As you know, since Ayee's surgery and Diya's kidnapping, they've been asking to become more involved in the children's lives."

"After Mr. Tilak showed up here with his offer to raise the ransom money, I had a feeling he and his wife wanted a reconciliation of some kind." He gave her a measured look. "How do *you* feel about it?"

She lifted a shoulder. The resentment from the past still rankled. "Sheila and Sundari and you have made me understand that the children are more important than my ego, and that they have Tilak blood in their veins. So I'm letting it happen, one day at a time."

He gave her an approving nod. "Wise decision."

"But if I find my in-laws going back to treating my children like second-class citizens just because they happen to be girls, then I'll put a stop to it."

He put a calming hand on hers. "Give it some time, Isha. The old folks obviously want to make amends. If you meet them halfway, I'm sure things will get better."

"I hope so, at least for the children's sake." She sat down in one of the chairs and motioned for him to sit in the other. There was new furniture in the room now, a replacement for the pieces destroyed by the abductor. This time she'd bought a brown vinyl-upholstered couch and matching chairs to withstand all the abuse the children dished out.

She proceeded to tell him in brief about her experience with the *sadhu* and his strange prophecies, words that came back to her more and more lately. "The holy man was right in so many ways, Harish. Diya has indeed turned out to be my good-luck charm."

"How so?"

"The insurance money was paid out despite months of delay before her birth, so I could buy my two flats. Then my dressmaking business took off unexpectedly, and it's doing really well."

"Hmm." He frowned a little, looking like a typical man of science, skeptical about prophecies, holy men, and what he probably thought was religious mumbo-jumbo. "What else did the *sadhu* tell you?"

"He said Diya, despite the pressure for abortion, was destined to be born and that she'd share her good karma with the people around her. You see, all of a sudden, you came into our lives when we badly needed you, within a day of her birth, and you've given us so much and so generously. Then Sheila and her family, and even Sundari came back when I asked her. All of you have proved to be my source of strength and good fortune."

"We all happen to care about the three of you. It's as simple as that."

"True, but it's not mere coincidence. It was all *meant* to be." Then she recalled the *sadhu*'s predictions for Priya. "And he said some good things about Priya, too—that she was a very bright girl and a healer."

"There's no doubt she's exceptionally bright and curious." His voice was filled with parental pride.

"You know what else? He said Priya would heal that which was broken. I didn't understand his words then, but now I'm beginning to decipher the deeper meaning. I think he meant the broken relationship with Ayee and Baba. It's Priya who's been instrumental in bringing them around. Ayee is convinced she'd be dead if it weren't for Priya."

"I'm glad things are finally looking up for you," he said.

"I wish my problems hadn't touched you, though." He'd been through hell because of her.

"Do I look like I have problems?" he asked with a chuckle.

"Not anymore, I guess." He did look happy lately. Maybe she and her children had something to do with it. He deserved to be happy.

"It's getting late." He fished his car keys out of his pocket. "I better get out of here." Before heading for the door he placed a gentle kiss on her cheek. "Now stop obsessing over problems and start thinking about some positive things for a change—like what I said earlier."

"I will. Soon," she promised.

"Perhaps you should consult your wise friend, the *sadhu*, about it. *He* should be able to dispel all those silly doubts in here," he said, tapping a finger over her temple, "and convince you that you and I and the children are *meant* to be together."

"Maybe I *will* consult him," she replied. Of course, she didn't need a sage to tell her that together with her daughters, Harish Salvi was the best thing in her life.

"Then do it soon, will you? The New Year is coming up in

less than two weeks and I'm not getting any younger. Saroj-bayi says if I wait too much longer I may not have any hair or teeth left."

"Oh dear! In that case I better make an appointment with him."

"Be sure to tell the holy man it's *extremely urgent*," he said with a mocking grin.

She couldn't help smiling. That grin of his was infectious. "I'll see if he can fit me into his tight schedule before the end of the year—before all your hair falls out."

Author's Note

Dear Reader,

The practice of selectively aborting female fetuses in India is the central theme of *The Forbidden Daughter*. While the plot is a product of my imagination, there is an element of truth in it. Truth can often be not only stranger but significantly more disturbing than fiction. In this case, it may very well be.

Some two decades ago, patriarchal cultures like India discovered that ultrasound or echogram technology could be used for purposes other than what it was designed for. Overnight, the sonogram went from being a way of detecting tumors, abnormalities, and life-threatening conditions in unborn children to an easy method of detecting the sex of a fetus.

Consequently, millions of couples in India have allegedly resorted to female feticide with the help of medical practitioners. In a culture where a daughter is viewed as a burden because of the dowry and other archaic but persistent customs, ultrasound has become a useful as well as dangerous tool in empowering families to rid themselves of female children before they come into the world.

The Lancet, a British medical journal, reported in January 2006 that, according to a study, nearly 10 million female fetuses may have been aborted in India over the past two decades. Besides the moral issues involved in gender-based abortion, the unbalanced female-to-male ratio could lead to severe social repercussions in the future: a disproportionate number of males with no hope of marriage or healthy long-term relationships. Just imagine how that could affect crimes against women!

Earlier, under pressure from activists, the Indian government had passed The Pre-Natal Diagnostic Techniques (PNDT) Act in 1994, banning the use of ultrasound machines to reveal fetus gender. Furthermore, a 2002 amendment stiffened the penalties.

And yet, the practice of selectively destroying female fetuses apparently continues.

When I wrote *The Forbidden Daughter,* it was not only to draw my readers' attention to an alarming social issue in the world's largest democracy, but also to tell a compelling story that brings to light the spirit of a woman, and a mother's strength and conviction in standing up to societal pressures when it comes to protecting her children.

And as a hopeless romantic, I love stories written in a positive vein with love at their center.

I sincerely hope you enjoy reading and sharing with others *The Forbidden Daughter* as much as I have enjoyed writing it.

Best Wishes,
Shobhan Bantwal

THE FORBIDDEN DAUGHTER

Shobhan Bantwal

ABOUT THIS GUIDE

The suggested questions are included
to enhance your group's
reading of this book.

DISCUSSION QUESTIONS

1. The protagonist, Isha Tilak, makes the decision to keep her baby and not abort it despite repeated attempts by her in-laws to coerce her into doing so. Do you think this is wise on her part, considering she will alienate them and may have to give up a comfortable lifestyle for her first child? What would her life be like if she decided to obey her in-laws instead?

2. In the opening of the book, I have quoted a folksong from northern India. How do you view the sentiment in that song? Does it portray the dilemma some women from certain cultures may have to face?

3. Are Isha's in-laws entirely wrong in thinking their would-be grandchild should be aborted because it will be the second female child when they want a boy? Or is this a valid concern for certain families?

4. Isha's opinion about arranged marriage is that it always comes as a package deal—the in-laws and extended family come hand-in-hand with a husband. Do you think this is a positive thing for a woman's emotional and mental growth, or is it a hindrance? Discuss the pros and cons.

5. Isha, although college educated, chooses to be a housewife and mother. Do you think this is a wise decision on a woman's part in the twenty-first century? What are some advantages and disadvantages for most women of choosing a career versus staying at home?

6. Is Palgaum, the fictitious and conservative Indian town in this story, reminiscent of any town that you know? Discuss whether contemporary small towns are essen-

tially the same, no matter where in the world they are located.

7. Do you think the kidnapping in the story perhaps helps Isha gain a better understanding of her in-laws and a more tolerant attitude to them and to life in general? What lessons does she gain from almost losing her daughter?

8. What role does Sheila, Isha's sister-in-law play in the story? Discuss how she becomes a catalyst in Isha's life as well as her children's.

9. Was it a good idea to add romantic elements to this story? Does the romance help the story become more interesting?

10. *The Lancet,* a British medical journal, reports that, according to a study, nearly 10 million female fetuses may have been aborted in India in the last two decades. How do you feel about this? Will selective abortions have a significant impact on the world?

11. Do you think ideas about producing male heirs are likely to change in the male-oriented cultures of the world? If not, what are some of the things that are likely to bring about change?

12. Isha feels guilty about developing a fondness for Harish because she is a recent widow. Is she justified in her feelings? How does widowhood affect women like Isha, who live in a society that still treats widows differently than other women?